CHILDREN OF THE DARK 2:

THE NIGHT FLYERS

CHILDREN OF THE DARK 2:

THE NIGHT FLYERS

JONATHAN JANZ

CEMETERY DANCE PUBLICATIONS

Baltimore

— 2024 —

Cemetery Dance Publications
132B Industry Lane, Unit #7
Forest Hill, MD 21050
www.cemeterydance.com

ACKNOWLEDGMENTS

So many folks to thank, but I'll try to mention a few: Kevin Lucia, Dan Franklin, and Richard Chizmar from Cemetery Dance for publishing these books; Matthew Revert for his exquisite covers; and my pre-readers Tim Slauter and Tod Clark for making all my stories better. Thank you also to my manager Ryan Lewis for his constant support.

Two people who make a profound difference in my life are Brian Keene and Josh Malerman. Josh is one of the best friends I've ever had. He inspires me and gives me constant support; he also makes me laugh almost every day. And Brian? He's the big brother I never had, the mentor I'll always need, and the kind of friend who'll be there in the best of circumstances or the worst. I love both Brian and Josh and am so thankful for them.

Thank you to my mom, who raised me in a tiny house on the edge of town, with a graveyard to the west and a forest to the north—the same house Will and Peach lived in during *Children of the Dark*. Will Burgess's life looked a lot like mine when I was a kid. Only instead of Will's mother, I had my mom, and she was extraordinary. She still is. She's the grand champion of single mothers and the person who always encouraged me to dream big.

Thank you most of all to my family: Monica (my wife), Jack/Bubba (my son), Juliet/Jewel (my older daughter), and Evana/Peach (my younger daughter). Good days and bad, celebrations and disappointments, all of it. You're here for me. You give me love, hope, purpose, warmth, laughter, inspiration, companionship, understanding, and unconditional support. I love you so much and am thankful for every moment I get to spend with you. As long as I have you four, I have everything I need.

Juliet, this one's for you: my daughter, my horror movie buddy, my confidante, my joy. You mean the world to me, Boo. I love you more than words can express, and I'm so thankful I get to be your dad.

"I understood then what courage is all about. It is loving someone else more than you love yourself."

—Robert McCammon, *Boy's Life*

"No good friends, no bad friends; only people you want, need to be with. People who build their houses in your heart."

—Stephen King, *It*

PART ONE

THE SUNNY WOODS REHABILITATION CENTER

BEFORE (1)

Transcript of Psychiatric Assessment Session
Subject ID: 05316
Session #: 57
Date: 16.July.20—

Therapist(s): Dr. Fleetwood (T1) and Dr. Klinger (T2)

T1: I'm here with subject 05316, and it is... (pause, shuffling sound)... eight-thirteen A.M.

P: Make sure you get the thirteen in there.

T1: You were late again, Will. The record should indicate that.

P: Why do you refer to me by a number, then call me by my name?

T1: That's just the way it's done.

P: Without thinking, you mean.

T1: That isn't — it's the established format.

P: Established by whom?

T1: Well… everyone.

P: Be your own person, Dr. Fleetwood.

T1: Yes, well. We were talking last week about your anger.

P: (no response)

T1: Maybe we could talk some more about your anger.

P: (no response)

T1: Can we talk about—

P: Oh for Christ's sakes.

T1: Okay… I suppose we could discuss something else. To begin the session, I mean.

P: Before you start ripping off emotional scabs?

T1: That's not what I… I hope you realize I only intend to—

P: What's your first name?

T1: I hardly think that's germane.

P: It would humanize you.

T1: (chuckling) Do I need humanizing? I'd have thought after all this time —

P: Trust is key, Dr. Fleetwood. You often say that.

T1: Yes, the patient must trust his appointed medical professional…

P: Appointed medical professional? You sound like you work for the government.

T1: I *do* work for the government. At least partially. We receive private grants, but the majority of our funding —

P: That's not what I'm talking about. Ordinarily, you seem like a decent enough guy. A bit unimaginative. Stodgy, even…

T1: I'm not—

P: But okay, overall. I don't think you're out to harm anyone. Not like that other douchebag.

T1: (quietly) Dr. Klinger.

(A pause)

P: Hey, I just realized something. You don't like him either.

T1: (sounds of papers scraping) I hardly believe my opinion of Dr. Klinger is relevant.

P: We both know I'm not getting out of here. Not any time soon. Maybe not until I'm older than you. How old are you, by the way?

T1: I'm thirty-seven.

P: No kidding? I thought you were closer to fifty. You know, the baldness…

T1: Thanks.

P: No offense. Like I said, you're not that bad. Not for someone who works in a place like this.

T1: This isn't a penitentiary, Will.

P: We both know what it is, Dr. Fleetwood.

T1: We care for those in need of—

P: Reprogramming.

T1: That isn't fair.

P: You know there's nothing wrong with me.

T1: Do you really believe there's nothing wrong with you?

P: (a sigh) Here we go.

T1: What am I supposed to do? Ignore the evidence? Nine physical altercations in thirteen months, three of them brutal enough to necessitate the infirmary.

P: So passive resistance is the key? I should be like Gandhi, let them smash my face like a cantaloupe?

T1: I'm not saying that.

P: You're judging me.

T1: You're not *helping* yourself. Can't you see that? If you'd only… you know…

P: Be a good boy and let them kick my ass?

T1: That's not what I'm suggesting. I'm merely urging cooperation. If you'd show me a glimmer of the young man I know is in there, the one who took care of his sister all those years —

P: Don't talk about Peach.

T1: I only mean —

P: Don't *talk* about her.

T1: If it makes you uncomfortable…

P: Uncomfortable? You think I'm *uncomfortable?*

T1: (swallows) My God.

P: What?

T1: Your eyes. They're…

P: They're *what?* Profound? Crossed? What the hell are you trying to say?

(A pause)

T1: Nothing. I was wondering if you'd be able to discuss —

(A door opens.)

P: Ah, hell.

T1: (quietly) Dr. Klinger.

T2: I see you've succeeded in disturbing the subject, Dr. Fleetwood. Thanks for that. There's nothing more pleasant than having one's work complicated beforehand.

T1: (resigned) We'll talk again next week, Will.

T2: That's doubtful, Steve.

P: Wait, your name is Steve Fleetwood?

T1: Why?

P: My mom used to listen to Fleetwood Mac. Their lead singer…

T1: …was Stevie Nicks, yes. How on earth could you know such a thing?

P: People always say I'm an old soul.

T1: (sadly) I would agree with that. I'll see you next week.

T2: I beg to differ.

T1: (bristling) You don't have the right to interfere with our progress.

T2: Is that what you call it? You've wasted over a year shying away from William's very real issues. You're relieved from this case.

P:Hey! You can't just fire Dr. Fleetwood—

T2: I just did. (sound of chair legs scraping). I'm your chief therapist now.

T1: I won't stand for this.

T2: The paperwork is signed. You're no longer needed.

T1: You conceited… *pompous*…

T2: Do you need assistance finding the door? My men are in the hallway.

T1: (with dignity) Yours isn't the final word, Klinger. I'll fight this with everything I have.

T2: (cheerfully) Good luck with that.

T1: We'll see each other again soon, Will.

T2: Bye now.

(Door creaks.)

P: Hey, Dr. Fleetwood?

T1: Yes?

P: (A hesitation) I'm sorry I was such a pain in the ass. You're not a bad guy.

T1: (A pause) Thank you, Will.

T2: Should I call Agent Castro?

T1: No need for that.

(Door closes.)

T2: Ah, peace. (shuffles papers). So... William. How have you been?

P: Hey, Dr. Klinger?

T2: (brightly) Yes, William?

P: Go fuck yourself.

BEFORE (II)

Transcript of Psychiatric Assessment Session
Subject ID: 05316
Session #: 57 (continued)
Date: 16.July.20—

Therapist: Dr. Klinger (referred to here as T2)

T2: Resumption of session with Subject 05316, interrupted earlier by threats of physical violence. This is in keeping with subject's tendency toward hostility…

P: What a load of crap.

T2: So where were we? Oh yes. You were spouting obscenities and embarrassing yourself.

P: You still pluck the legs off insects? Fry ants with a magnifying glass?

T2: Are your restraints comfortable, William?

P: Did the penis augmentation surgery allow you to function as a normal man, Dr. Klinger?

T2: (thinly) Witty, William. Crude, but witty. I'll be sure to have the library cancel the Stephen King novels they ordered.

P: (exploding) You can't! I've waited over a year, and Pierre says—

(Will falls silent.)

T2: Yes, William? Tell me about your special friend.

P: (swallows) He's not…

T2: We'll have to remind Pierre about following protocol. He's permitted you to read, what? *Under the Dome*? *The Tommy…* (shuffling papers)

P: *Tommyknockers*. It took me months to get those. You can't just—

T2: I can do whatever I deem necessary to procure your cooperation. That includes vetting your reading material.

P: Censoring it.

T2: Our library will be just fine without Stephen King. And another arrived today by… Richard Matheson? *Hell House*? I glanced at that one. So tawdry!

P: This is bullshit.

T2: Crassness is not becoming, especially from a precocious teenager.

P: You'd call any teenager who can form a coherent sentence precocious. It threatens your self-image to think that someone younger than you might have a brain.

T2: Why, William! I would never accuse you of being unintelligent. To the contrary, I credit you with an abundance of cunning. It's allowed you to shirk the blame for the murders you committed —

P: I didn't —

T2: — and the myriad other crimes in which you were complicit.

P: You know I'm not responsible —

T2: For the seventeen deaths that occurred in Shadeland last summer? Oh, I don't believe you killed *all* of them.

P: Why can't I have a lawyer?

T2: Because you've not been arrested. You were committed to a rehabilitation facility by qualified professionals.

P: This is a nightmare.

T2: And thus far, though I'm loathe to admit it, the treatment you've received at Sunny Woods has done little good. You still harbor the same delusions. You still—

P: They're not —

T2: — refuse to provide an unvarnished account of the events involving Carl Padgett —

P: Don't talk about him.

T2: — your biological father, or these fanciful creatures on whose doorstep you place the blame for the bloodshed so clearly authored by your dad —

P: HE'S NOT MY DAD!

T2: (scribbling) Subject shows lack of self-control when confronted with factual evidence.

P: You're such an asshole.

T2: You're the one wasting valuable government resources with this farcical horror story, which was no doubt fueled by your abysmal reading selection —

P: Come on. That was below the belt.

T2: You continually stonewall our attempts to gain clarity —

P: My story has never changed.

T2: — and you dishonor the dead with your taletelling.

P: (voice lower) Don't say that.

T2: Including your best friend, Chris Watkins.

P: Damn you…

T2: And Rebecca Ralston, your girlfriend's best friend.

P: (hoarsely) I can't believe you'd —

T2: Providing, of course, she's still your girlfriend. It *has* been a while.

P: (sound of chair clattering) You evil son of a bitch.

T2: Sit down. We don't want someone to intervene, do we? Agent Castro has been gnashing at the bit.

P: Chomping at the bit.

T2: And of course, there's the matter of your mother.

P: How… *could* you?

T2: This is where I grow baffled. Most of your… *yarn* portrays you as the hero, the stalwart defender of the meek.

P: Don't.

T2: Yet, in this one detail, you demonstrate a regrettable lack of feeling.

P: (no answer)

T2: I'm speaking of your mother's death.

P: (barely audible) Shut up.

T2: You don't have anything to share on the matter?

P: (unintelligible muttering)

T2: Excuse me? I couldn't hear that.

P: I'm not talking anymore. Not to you.

T2: Of course. Whenever you're faced with a truth that doesn't align with your delusion, you grow enraged. One could almost believe you care about your mother's senseless drowning.

P: Bring Fleetwood back.

T2: He's been relieved.

P: You're a monster.

T2: (soft laughter) You'd know, of course.

P: How can you live with yourself?

T2: Am I the one whose mother died because of my apathy?

P: (barely a whisper) Apathy?

T2: Am I the one who allowed my best friend to be murdered?

P: (through tears) *Stop it.*

T2: Am I the one who'd rather spend the rest of his teens hospitalized while his little sister grows older, until the memory of her older brother fades?

P: You sick —

T2: The *truth*, William. At some point, you must come around to —

(Commotion, followed by a door opening and the sounds of a scuffle)

T2: (discomfited) It's all right, Agent Castro. Will was only attempting to frighten me. He does love to posture. But I suppose now's a suitable time to terminate the interview. (Footsteps) I'm afraid I'll have to recommend that your medication be increased. And I see no reason for any alteration of your privileges... save the removal of pernicious reading material. Yes, clearly that's had an adverse effect on your impressionable psyche.

(Yelling)

(End of recording)

CHAPTER ONE

PRISON, PROTECTOR, ATTACKER

My name is Will Burgess, and if you don't believe what I'm about to tell you, congratulations, you're in the majority. In crappy coming-of-age books and even crappier coming-of-age films, no one understands the young hero, no one tries to help. The adults are jerkoffs with condescending grins, and the hero's peers are even worse: sneering, smarmy delinquents who get their kicks tormenting the main character, who by the way is the only person in the story who exhibits anything resembling healthy human behavior.

The problem is, the above description? It pretty much describes this place.

That sounds melodramatic, but if you'd endured what I have over the past thirteen months, you'd be jaded too. But since I've come this far, I might as well be honest and admit there's at least one good soul in this hellhole. And no, I'm not talking about myself. I don't know if I qualify as a good soul any longer. If I ever did.

And stop, okay? I'm not feeling sorry for myself. I'm simply saying that whatever I am, Pierre is better.

But Pierre is supremely pissed at me as he approaches my table in the recreation room. I can tell by the way his lips are drawn taut.

I dogear a page of the novel I'm reading—Cormac McCarthy's *The Road*—and take a moment to study Pierre as his eyes flick to me, his rangy limbs moving with a grace that belies his age, which I guess to be around fifty. His hair is a shade darker than his skin, with only the subtlest threading of white strands, not at the temples the way you'd expect, but near the back of the crown, like he's wearing a winged helmet.

Pierre can't possibly enjoy working here. Who could? They call it a psychiatric hospital, but what it really is, it's a maximum-security prison for individuals society wants to forget about.

Pierre nears my table and mutters one word in passing: "Alcove."

Oh man, I think. *Pierre really is pissed.*

I count to twenty to avoid suspicion, then stand up and scoot my chair in. I make my way over to the rear of the rec room and an architectural anomaly we call the alcove door. It's recessed enough that you can't see anyone exiting unless you stand in the far corner of the room, and the only thing back there is a shelf full of tattered paperbacks that no one besides me reads. That means Pierre can let me out with his swipe card without arousing suspicion, and we can make our way down to the courtyard, the one place where the cameras might have a hard time picking up what we're saying. I'm still not certain whether the cameras are wired for sound or if the authorities here are gifted lip readers.

I stash my paperback on the shelf, cross to the alcove door, and Pierre, not looking at me, lets me out with his swipe card. He doesn't put his hand on my shoulder the way he sometimes does, and that worries me too. No hand on the shoulder either means he's too preoccupied to play-act or too livid to touch me; either way, the tension sweat is beginning to bead on my forehead. Something is seriously wrong.

Pierre doesn't say a word to me until we're standing in the grassy courtyard, which at midmorning is just beginning to catch some daylight. It's July and already sweltering. In a couple hours, it'll be unbearable out here, a fact to which the sun-scorched grass can attest.

Pierre turns to me, stone-faced, then pivots and moves away.

Uh-oh, I think.

He passes a hand over his mouth, works his jaw a moment, then circles back to loom over me. He's every bit of six-three, and though I'm growing—six feet tall now, according to my last physical exam—he makes me feel like a toddler instead of a sixteen-year-old.

I brush away the thought. Whenever I remember my age, I think of how I marked my last birthday alone, how I'm old enough to drive but unable to even *ride* in a car, much less operate one. Sixteen is a big deal, dammit. I should have celebrated it with my sister and my friends.

Friend, a voice in my whispers. *You only have one friend left.*

I close my eyes, and the face of my best friend — my dead best friend — rises in my mind. My throat begins to close up, and that feeling of wanting to run away from it, that awful, strangling guilt, overwhelms me. I think of Chris Watkins's face and know he's dead, and I'll never get over it, never feel better about it. That old saying about time healing all wounds? It's bullshit. You miss the person. Full stop. If anything, you miss them more as time goes on. Every day you wish they were still alive. The ache spreads and grows and pulls you down into it, and you can never claw your way out because that ache is part of you, a pit that widens a little every time you remember they're gone.

Goddammit, I think. *Why did he have to die?*

Unable to bear the silence, I force myself to confront Pierre's flinty gaze.

"What?" I ask.

His face transforms into a look that's at once marveling and angry. "We really gonna play that game? You're gonna pull the innocent act with me?"

I can feel my composure cracking. "What was I supposed to do?"

"Oh, I don't know. Maybe *do what we talked about?* Give 'em something tantalizing. Throw 'em a bone. Provide some information that might help you get out of here before you're too old to move your bowels without prune juice."

"Hey!"

"*Listen*," he snaps, then throws a worried glance over his shoulder. There's a camera in the far corner of the courtyard, mounted on the brick façade. Newly installed a couple weeks ago. I tell myself this wasn't because of my talks with Pierre, but I can't make myself believe it.

He shuffles closer, brings his hand up to cover his mouth in a way that reminds me of big-league pitchers and catchers conducting clandestine strategy sessions on the mound. This brings another pang of sadness because *God,* I love baseball. Would give anything to play it again. My skills have probably gone to shit, but being able to wriggle my hand into a mitt or grip an aluminum bat would feel like coming home.

Even as I think the thought, my smile fades. Because I *have* no home. As Dr. Klinger so sensitively pointed out, my mom is dead. My — I refuse to call him my father; so, what? My sperm donor? My mom's murderer? — he's dead too.

Because of me.

You look up *patricide,* or the killing of one's father, in the encyclopedia—no Internet for Will! — and the first paragraph is devoted to Oedipus. The second, Lizzy Borden. The third entry in the *New Encyclopedia Britannica* (which isn't new at all, the 1987 version) is Ronald DeFeo. The name rang a bell, but it wasn't until I read further that I remembered where I'd heard of him: The Amityville Horror. The real one, not the movie with James Brolin or the remake with Ryan Reynolds.

Thinking of horror movies reminds me of Barley, my one remaining friend, the one whose parents wisely removed him from harm's way before the monsters showed up.

Does Barley still think of me? And if he does, is it fondly?

Just as importantly—okay, *more* importantly—does Mia remember me?

Mia Samuels, my dream girl. The one with whom I fought monsters last summer. The one I've wanted to marry since the second grade and who's probably forgotten me.

"You in a coma or something?" Pierre asks.

I blink, glance up at him. But now his lively brown eyes are broadcasting something other than annoyance.

"Just daydreaming," I answer.

"You're running out of chances. These government dudes, you think they care about you?"

"I know they don't."

"Good. You're a means to an end. And the less they believe you can help them, the worse things are gonna get."

"I told them the truth."

Pierre seems to deflate, his hands actually clapping his knees. Bent over that way, he reminds me of a baseball player catching his breath after legging out a triple. "I know you told the truth. That's the problem. The truth is insane, and unless they know what we know, there's no way they're gonna buy any of it."

As dire as all this sounds, I'm buoyed by his use of the phrase "what *we* know." Funny what you'll cling to when everything you care about has been torn away.

"Any word from Anita?" I ask.

He shoots me a look. "Man, cover your mouth when you say her name. I don't want her getting fired."

I cover my mouth. "Any word from Anita?"

He rolls his eyes. "Not now, man. You really that dense?"

I fall silent, but I keep my hand over my mouth just in case I slip again.

Pierre crouches, shields his mouth, and begins plucking blades of crabgrass with his free hand. "Anita hasn't seen anything since… what I told you about. But the critters in the barn have been restless as hell lately."

I nod. Pierre's niece, who works downstairs, experienced a firsthand encounter with the same creature I saw winging its way around the hospital a couple nights ago, a red-eyed beast with leathery black flesh and vast, tenebrous wings. The creature had seemed to hover outside my barred window, the scarlet eyes boring into me, marking me, before swooping away into the darkness.

The same species of creature had scarred the roof of Anita's car. All this would be ominous enough, yet what propelled our experiences from disquieting to downright horrifying was the massacre that took place at the Peaceful Valley Nature Preserve. What was supposed to be the grand opening of a new state park turned into a nightmare.

More than two hundred people dead.

Reports not only of the winged creatures slaughtering campers but of the Children murdering and devouring victims as well.

While my exposure to the winged creatures is limited to a nighttime glimpse, my relationship with the Children, unfortunately, is much more intimate.

But I don't want to think about the Children now. Or ever.

"I saw it last night," I tell him.

Pierre grows very still.

"The flying creature with the glowing red eyes."

He listens with the air of a man being given a terminal diagnosis. Finally, he murmurs, "Damn."

"That means Anita was telling you the truth about the thing that attacked her car."

He regards the ground sourly. "I know that."

And where does that get us? I ask myself. Absolutely nowhere. Locked in here, there's no way to spread the word. Or more importantly, to keep the people I love safe.

"How high a dose they been giving you?" Pierre asks.

I realize I've been drifting again. But I don't think it has anything to do with the sedatives. I think it's because I'm drowning in a sea of fear and regret.

"Sorry," I mutter. "When you say, 'the critters in the barn,' you mean—"

"The alpacas," he answers. "I was just trying to maintain anonymity for my niece. I'm already close to being fired. I'd rather not drag Anita into unemployment as well. She doesn't like me much anyway."

I smile a little. "How's that husband of hers?"

"Still a loser."

My grin widens. It's been so long since I've smiled that the expression induces pain in my cheeks.

"We've been out here too long already," Pierre says, "so I'll make this brief. One, you gotta start heeding my counsel, or I'm gonna stop bothering. I don't appreciate sticking my neck out only to have you go all tough guy on the doctor."

"Klinger was talking about my mom. He was talking about Chris."

"And that sucks for you. But it doesn't change a thing."

"He also—"

"—talked shit about your sister," Pierre says, nodding. "Yeah, I figured he'd do that. It's about subjugating you, showing you he's in control. He's gonna take everything you care about and weaponize it."

"But Peach…," I say, suddenly on the verge of tears. "Why can't I talk to her?"

My voice breaks, and I want to look away, but so great is my need to see my sister and so powerful is my guilt at the fact that she's alone in the world that I can't do anything but watch Pierre's face and hang on his every word.

"Don't you get it?" he asks. "Your sister is what this is all about. You need to do anything you can to get back to her."

I turn away so I can wipe the tears, but he seizes my wrist and forces me to stare down at him. "That includes doing a little pride-swallowing. I know something about pride. It can lead people to do good things and stupid things. Pride's part of why I've been a decent husband all these years. It's also why I haven't talked to..."

He brushes a blade of grass from his knee and stands.

I watch him with dawning comprehension. "You have a child?"

He shoots me a look. "How do you know that?"

"Sometimes I see things in people's heads."

I hope he doesn't press me on the issue.

"Ruben's not a child anymore," he murmurs. "Twenty-eight next month. We haven't spoken in years."

I don't know what to say, so I don't say anything. Every response I audition sounds like hollow sentiment.

"What I'm telling you," Pierre says, his voice husky, "is to let go of it. The contempt, the anger. The vendetta you have against Klinger. All of it. It doesn't do anybody any good, least of all Peach." He arches an eyebrow. "I still think that's a strange thing to call a kid."

I exhale weary breath. "Okay. Give them what they're asking for. I get it."

"That ain't all."

I glance at him.

"You know who I'm talking about," Pierre says.

I do, but I won't admit it.

"This thing with Tyler Flowers," he starts.

"Isn't my fault."

"You're not innocent."

I open my lips to protest, but he nods curtly. "Cover your mouth."

I bring my hand up, say through clenched teeth, "He's fixated on me. What am I supposed to do?"

"Stop escalating the conflict every chance you get?"

"What would you do? Let him and his buddies use me as a human stress ball?"

Pierre chuckles. "Hey, that's pretty good."

"Glad I could entertain you."

"Don't get riled up. I'm just telling you to cool it. What if Tyler and his cronies put you in a wheelchair?"

"I'd like to put them in the ground."

"That's what I'm afraid of."

I scowl at him. "What are you talking about?"

But I know already. I know and don't want to hear it.

"Dr. Fleetwood and I are worried about you."

"Don't be."

"We are. And now that Fleetwood's off your case…"

"Pierre, you're the only friend I've got, but I gotta tell you, your flair for the dramatic gets on my nerves sometimes."

But Pierre's voice isn't dramatic when he continues. Is in fact soft and uninflected and all the more chilling because of it. "There's something building in you. I've watched it. There were only hints of it when you first came here, but since then…"

I listen, unable to speak, unable to walk away.

"It's like some snarling presence," Pierre says. "Some… beast inside you. I thought at first it was just your rage over what had happened… all those horrible things you'd seen. But lately I wonder if some of the stuff Tyler says about you is true."

"You're on his side? You two gonna become pals when they ship me out of here? Make him your new project?"

"I'm gonna ignore that. We both know I care about you, even if I shouldn't."

I avert my eyes.

"There's just one more thing," he says, "and I wish it weren't true."

I listen in dread.

"Just now," Pierre says. "During your outburst?"

"Yeah?"

"Your eyes weren't brown. When you got really mad, they turned green."

T

I WENT ABOUT my day and did my best not to think about what Pierre said. The implications were too horrific to consider.

But as usually happens when I try not to think about something, I thought about it incessantly. This was the root of my insomnia. I've met people — my mom was one of them — who could talk themselves into anything.

Not me. I can't un-believe things, can't un-remember hideous events.

Can't ignore the way Tyler Flowers looks at me as I enter the cafeteria.

If I had better resources, books that specialized in the human psyche rather than a tattered dictionary and an outdated set of encyclopedias, I'd make a study of it. Is it possible that certain individuals, on a biological level, attract trouble? Are there malice magnets, forever in the crosshairs of the cruel and the violent?

Last summer there were several tormentors:

Brad Ralston.

Kurt Fisher.

Eric Blades and his brother.

The police chief and a pair of brain-dead deputies.

That all of them, with the exception of one deputy, were now dead was not lost on me. I took no pleasure in their deaths. Not then and certainly not now.

But somewhere deep in the murkiest parts of me, there are skulking creatures who lust for the suffering of my enemies. Maybe that's how last summer's events changed me. I understand hatred now, and I know how it eats away at a person.

With an effort, I broke eye contact with Tyler and weaved my way through the ten or eleven patients scattered about the over-large cafeteria. Most of my fights have taken place here. The first time it was just me and Tyler, and despite his size advantage, I bested him in that first skirmish. I call it a skirmish because it was broken up within seconds. On the other occasions, Tyler made sure his friends were participants. Sometimes I gave as good as I got. Sometimes I didn't.

But I wouldn't back down. Not ever.

But I could try to follow Pierre's advice. I wouldn't seek out conflict. I would, if possible, collect my meager lunch — the portions here suck — and scarf it down in an isolated corner. If I stayed off Tyler's radar... if I didn't return his baleful stare...

Who was I kidding? No matter what I did, there'd be another altercation. When you were dealing with the Tyler Flowerses of the world, there were always altercations.

"Extra mashed potatoes, please," I said to the plump older woman who doled out our meals.

She glanced from side to side, and the cowed look in her eyes rekindled my wrath at those responsible for creating this toxic environment. Here was a goodhearted woman who probably worked here for the crappy health care benefits, or maybe so she could bring a little kindness into the lives of troubled kids. Yet she couldn't even divvy out an extra scoop of potatoes without worrying about a consequence. I imagined Dr. Klinger shaking his head dourly and informing the woman that her wages would be garnished for misuse of facility resources.

Her hand trembling, the older woman scooped out an extra glob of potatoes and plopped it beside the first one.

"I don't wanna get you into trouble," I murmured, but then she did something amazing. She gathered a second handful of chicken nuggets and heaped them on my tray. Her jaw firmly set, she reached under the counter, came out with some honey mustard packets, and slid them under the Styrofoam plate. With a wink she pushed the tray back to me and turned to help the next customer.

"Thanks," I whispered.

"Eat it all," she said. "You're far too skinny."

I escaped with my contraband. The lunch lady was right; I *did* need to eat more. The sleeplessness was wreaking havoc on my body, creating purple half-moons under my eyes. But underneath the voluminous hospital clothes, my muscles weren't gaunt at all; they were, in fact, harder and stronger than they'd ever been. With so much time on my hands, I'd taken to working out in my room. It was amazing how many exercises you could do if you got creative. I'd heft my mattress off my bedframe and perform ungainly squats with it draped over my back. In one corner of the room, there was a curved steel rod supporting a curtain meant to give a patient privacy to change clothes when others were present. The rod was sturdy and perfectly suited for pull-ups, leg-lifts, and a couple other exercises. As a result, my back muscles were lean but striated. I could see that when I peeled off my shirt and studied my reflection in the window. I'd become a freak for pushups and dips, and whenever I got bored, I commandeered what I could find in the room — a heavy steel chair, the nightstand, even the bars on my windows — to improvise different exercises.

So yeah, I needed to put on weight. But I wasn't frail.

As Tyler well knew.

He and his pals watched me as I crossed to the far corner of the cafeteria. Even Tyler reminded me of baseball. There used to be a major league catcher named Tyler Flowers, a solid backstop and a decent enough hitter. And presumably not an asshole like his younger namesake.

This Tyler Flowers had jacked arms, a neck bulging with tendons, and though I hated to admit it, cool hair. It was light brown and wavy, like he had a personal stylist in his cell.

I gave his table a wide enough berth so no one could stick out a foot and send me sprawling. I'd seen enough movies to know that was how cafeteria fights typically began. I sat down as far away from the Flowers Gang as I could.

I was spooning mashed potatoes into my mouth when I heard the first comment. Something about Shadeland, my hometown. Initially, I thought the words were innocuous—Shadeland was nearby, after all—but the snickers that followed suggested that Tyler and his friends were starting in on me. I tried to ignore it, to focus on my tasteless meal, but soon I heard Emilio Quintana, Tyler's best friend, piggybacking on the Shadeland remark:

"There was a Bigfoot sighting there last week."

Hell, I thought. Mocking my story. Never mind that it was true.

The question was, how did they know about it? The government had whitewashed everything. There were no quotes from me in any newspaper. I certainly hadn't confided to any of my fellow inmates here at Sunny Woods.

More snickers from Tyler's table. Someone said, "I heard a werewolf ate Burgess's best friend."

My fingers curled into fists. How *dare* they joke about Chris's death?

Then it hit me: Klinger had been feeding them information. It was the only explanation. I wondered briefly why he would perpetrate such a breach of trust, but the answer was obvious: to goad me into violence. They either wanted me to change my story, or they wanted me dead. If I were killed in some bloody brawl, I'd no longer be a problem. Better yet, if I recanted my testimony, the public relations disaster would be solved; in its place they'd get a lurid tale about a psychotic teen who collaborated with his serial-killing father in a frenzy of butchery.

Screw them. I'd never change my story.

Hands seized my shoulders.

I'd been so consumed with my thoughts that I hadn't even heard my attackers sneak up on me. The glass of the cafeteria window revealed the reflections of my assailants. Three of them. Why did there always have to be so many?

Tyler was one, of course, but he was hanging back a few feet, gazing down with the passive malevolence of an underworld mob boss. Beside him loomed Emilio Quintana, his primary muscle. The kid who had ahold of me was Jett Jennings. Beady-eyed, his black hair shaved down to stubble, Jett was my age and not nearly as imposing as Tyler and Emilio. As absurd as this sounds, I was offended that Tyler had sicced his lesser henchman on me.

That's because he wants you to retaliate, a voice in my head whispered. *He knows you can break free of Jett any time you want, then he and Emilio will get the chance to beat you up and justify it later: We were just sticking up for our friend!*

I told myself not to rise to the bait, but it was *So. Damned. Hard.* Because even though the last time I'd done battle with Tyler's crew I'd ended up with bruised ribs and a gash beside my eye deep enough to require stitches, I'd been faring better and better against them.

I believe Tyler sensed this too, and it frightened him. And because it frightened him, he had to prove to himself he wasn't scared. The only way to do that was to fight me again.

All this passed through my head in an instant.

I nodded at Jett, whose fingers were cinched over my shoulders. "I don't need a massage, but it's nice of you to offer."

Emilio chuckled.

"How's the jaw?" I asked him.

Emilio's eyes hardened. The last time the dickheads attacked me, Jett swung so wildly he decked Emilio instead.

"Shut up about that," Emilio mumbled.

"I used to watch knockout punches on YouTube," I said. "Jett, yours ranks up there with the best of them."

Jett grinned.

I nodded. "Makes me wonder why you put up with the way these guys treat you."

His grin faded. "What's that supposed to mean?"

"Nothing," I said mildly. "They just treat you like a wind-up toy."

"Friend, you mean," Tyler said.

I steeled myself for what I knew was coming, but it still sank into my guts like a spear.

"But hey," Tyler continued, "you'd have friends too if you hadn't killed them."

My muscles tightened. "At least I wasn't stupid enough to run someone over."

All mirth in the cafeteria died. I didn't know the specifics of Tyler's crime, but supposedly he went for a joyride when he was fourteen and badly injured someone: an old woman, if the stories were true.

"Listen, you little fuck," Emilio rasped. "You're saying things you can't back up. You want, the two of us can go a round by ourselves. I'd love to see you run your mouth then."

I gripped the bench to keep my hands steady. I'd never gone one-on-one with Emilio. We'd tangled in group scuffles, but there'd always been too many bodies in the way for us to test each other directly. I told myself that was Emilio's good luck, but deep down I suspected it was mine.

I don't know what would have occurred had things gone on that way. Maybe Emilio and I would have thrown down right there. Perhaps Tyler would have attacked me first. In the end, neither of those things happened.

Because an attractive Black woman in a red, business-casual outfit appeared next to my table. "Are you Will Burgess?" she asked.

I looked up at her. "Anita?"

She clutched a white envelope, and her fingernails were clipped short. Probably for working with the alpacas.

"Come with me," she said.

When the goons around me didn't move, she strafed them with her frank brown eyes. One by one, they receded. Emilio, I noted with some disquiet, was the last to relent.

I rose, noticing as I did how rubbery my legs felt.

"Where are we going?" I asked, falling in beside her.

"Downstairs."

"I get to leave the ward?"

"Just the fourth floor."

Though her tone suggested this was a disappointment, for me it was like traveling to the Bahamas.

We were nearing the elevator when a wave of lightheadedness swam over me. It was the medication. Whenever they upped the dosage of whatever the hell they were giving me, I had all sorts of side effects. Vertigo, nightmares, cold sweats.

But nothing could prepare me for what happened next. Anita stepped inside the elevator, and as I made to follow, I realized at least one of the overhead lights within had burned out. This cast a shadow on Anita's face, and in the insufficient light…I could have sworn…

"You okay?" she asked.

I tottered in and leaned against the wall. "I'm fine."

But I wasn't. Because for a flickering instant, I'd been sure it was my mother in the elevator with me. My dead mother.

As we started down, a memory of my mom arose in my mind. I didn't want to think about her. Not now. And maybe not ever.

But the picture of her standing in our old kitchen wouldn't go away. She was doing the dishes and wincing a little at the pain in her back.

My poor mom. As imperfect as she'd been, I loved her. And missed her so damned much.

Then why did you let her die?

I braced a hand against the elevator wall. Anita was watching me, but I was hardly aware of her.

Because in my memory, Mom wasn't in our old kitchen anymore. She was neck-deep in our basement cistern, the black water lapping against the underside of her chin.

She drowned because of you.

I shook my head.

"What is it?" Anita asked.

You could have saved her. But you didn't care enough.

The elevator stopped. The doors opened, but Anita stayed put. "Will?" she asked.

You killed her.

I suppressed a moan.

Anita reached for me, but I shrugged her off. "I'm fine," I said.

Anita studied me for a long moment, then stepped out. Sweating, I followed her. But my mother's face pursued me.

My mother's face inside that cistern.

CHAPTER TWO

ANITA, HARRY, PORTENTS

We were accompanied by a brawny, red-haired man in his late twenties, but he took a post outside Anita's office rather than venturing inside. I suppose that was because the office was a cramped, windowless room situated on the interior of the facility, and escape wasn't an option. Not that I'd seriously pondered fleeing. There were guards everywhere, cameras on every wall. Escaping here would be like trying to escape Alcatraz.

Rather than sitting behind the slender walnut desk, Anita selected the chair next to me and crossed her legs, which glinted in the cold fluorescent light.

"My uncle likes you," she said and tapped the envelope on her knee. "I, on the other hand, think you're hurting him. He's been reprimanded three times because of you. Next time, he'll be fired."

My stomach sank. I had no idea. It really was true; I was like King Midas, only instead of gold, my touch transformed every-thing to dogshit.

Anita went on. "No paycheck, no benefits. No pension. You're spoiling what's left of his life."

I sank lower in my chair.

"And that's why," she continued, "I've spoken with Dr. Fleetwood and come to an agreement. Fleetwood has a soft spot for you. For whatever reason."

"Nice of you to withhold judgment."

"I love my uncle," she said. "I don't know you."

"But you know about the creatures."

She stiffened. "You're being transferred to Westchester Federal Prison."

I stared at her.

"That's in New York," she explained.

"I know where Westchester is," I lied. She could be making the city up for all I knew.

"There's more," she said.

"How can they send me to prison when I haven't been tried for a crime?"

"You've confessed."

"*What?*"

The door flew open, the musclebound guard filling the entryway like a ginger Kodiak bear. "You need me, Miss Myers?"

Anita smiled. "No thank you, Harry. But it's good to know you're there."

Harry colored and nodded at her, and I realized he had a severe crush on Anita. I sort of did too, and so far, she'd only been hostile to me.

Harry pierced me with a scowl and went out.

"Does he know you're married?" I asked.

"This is serious, Will."

"People can't just be sent away."

She arched an eyebrow at me. "You really are naïve, aren't you?"

"I haven't—"

"—done anything wrong," she finished. "Yeah, I know what you told my uncle. But frankly, your story stinks."

"What about the creature who tore up your car roof?"

She looked away. "I regret talking about that."

"Because it corroborates my story?"

It was Anita's turn to raise her voice. "It doesn't corroborate *anything*. Your tale about skinny white dudes that are eight-feet-tall—"

"Nine," I corrected.

"It's ludicrous. The people here want the bad press from your incident—"

"*Incident?*"

"—and the Peaceful Valley Massacre to go away."

"Of course they do."

"If they can't get you to change your story, they'll eliminate you instead."

Some of the moisture left my mouth. "What's that supposed to mean?"

She sighed. "Westchester is just one option. Everything is on the table."

"You're saying they'd kill me."

"You could have an accident."

Oh God, I thought. I'd heard about such accidents but always believed they were the stuff of conspiracy theorists. Would they really kill a sixteen-year-old kid and cover it up?

Of course they would, a cynical voice argued. *They've kept you locked up for over a year. Why wouldn't they take the next step?*

"It gets worse," she said.

"How could it get worse?"

She glanced down at the envelope, which had already been opened.

I nodded at it. "Do I want to read that?"

She handed it over. My fingers nerveless, I slid out the letter and silently read,

```
Dear Dr. Klinger,
```

Bastard, I thought.

```
My husband and I thank you for reaching
out. Our discussions have been illuminat-
ing. At first, we thought we were simply
approaching Sophia the wrong way—
```

It's Peach, *you dumb shit. Only people who don't know my sister call her Sophia.*

```
—but now we realize that Sophia's issues
stem from her dysfunctional household. How
she ever survived with an abusive older
brother, I'll never know.
```

"Will?" Anita said.

I looked up. She nodded at the letter. My fingers were punching holes in it. I adjusted my grip, aware I'd begun to sweat.

```
Thank goodness she's out of that house
now. Thank goodness her brother is confined
```

and cannot hurt her any longer.

Unfortunately, we cannot provide foster services for Sophia anymore.

"'Provide foster services?'" I said through clenched teeth. "You mean *be her parents?*"

Anita said nothing.

My husband and I have served as foster parents ten times, and in every other instance our good faith and steady guidance have borne fruit. Every one of our wards has graduated high school, and those who procured student loans were able to attend college.

Sophia, however, is different.

You're damn right, she's different, I thought. *She's better than you'll ever be.*

From the moment she set foot in our home, she's fomented unrest.

Fomented unrest? Peach is seven! What would she know about fomenting anything?

She's been a negative influence on our Benjamin.

Benny, I thought. In her letter to me, Peach talked about Benny being the only biological Westfall child she got along with.

Where before Benjamin would never talk back to us, he now questions our authority.

He's no longer a robot, you mean.

Sophia has damaged our domestic life with her constant and frequently manic attempts to contact her brother.

Atta girl. I couldn't suppress a smile.

Even worse, Sophia has captured the attention of Darcy, one of our most reliable foster children. Darcy now participates in these fantasies by communicating with the friend and girlfriend of Sophia's brother.

Barley and Mia, I thought. *Yes! Go Darcy!*

These disturbances were upsetting enough. Then Darcy came to us yesterday morning and related the hideous fiction that Sophia has been imparting to her in secret. Sophia, Darcy explained, claims that mon-strous creatures emerged from caves and are responsible for the slaughter that took place in Shadeland, murders that every-one knows were perpetrated by the serial killer Carl Padgett, and Sophia's brother, Padgett's apprentice.

"*Bullshit!*" I snapped. From outside, I heard Harry the Red-Haired Gorilla stir. If I yelled again, he'd be through the doorway in a heartbeat.

So what? I thought. *I'm tired of pretending I'm not furious.* Hearing Klinger lie about me was one thing. Having the Westfalls, the people entrusted to care for Peach, parrot those lies was worse. Had they brainwashed Peach into believing I'm a monster? The thought of my little sister being afraid of me made me want to rip out my hair in clumps.

Whatever tales Sophia has been telling have somehow convinced Darcy that these monsters exist, and the formerly reliable—

Would you quit calling Darcy reliable? You make her sound like a Honda Civic.

—young woman is now obsessed with all manner of aberrant subjects. Ted and I searched her room and discovered a stack of library books in her closet. The topics ranged from conspiracy theories to something called cryptozoology. Having never heard the word, I had to look it up. Imagine my chagrin when I discovered it involved monsters. Monsters, Dr. Klinger! Steady, sensible Darcy has transformed into a "monster hunter," and it's all because of Sophia's pernicious influence.

Call her pernicious again, I thought. *Just try it, you coldhearted bitch.*

That's not all. Darcy has been in contact with a young woman named Mia Samuels and a weirdo named Dale Marley.

I chuckled. At least Mrs. Westfall got one thing right. My friend Barley, whose real name was Dale Marley, was unquestionably a weirdo. Which was why I loved him.

These four individuals—Darcy, Dale, Mia, and Sophia—are obsessed with contacting Sophia's older brother and researching these fantastical creatures. Since the unpleasant business at Peaceful Valley—

You mean the slaughter of over two hundred people?

—their obsession has consumed our home. Even my little Benjamin is talking about these creatures as though they exist. He's experiencing nightmares. Dr. Klinger, I simply can't have it.

For this reason, I am sending Sophia to Chicago. The Mercy Home for Boys and Girls.

"You can't!" I shouted.

Harry burst into the room. I thought he'd seize the nape of my neck and hoist me into the air, but when he saw the look on my face, the hostility seemed to bleed out of him.

"It's okay, Harry," Anita said. "Really."

I realized tears were streaming down my cheeks. I wiped them away brusquely, hating myself for crying. It had always been my weakness, being too emotional. I told myself to stop it, but the prospect of my little sister being sent away was too crushing to bear.

I looked at Anita. "Have you seen Peach lately?"

She nodded at the letter. "Finish it."

I returned to the wrinkled sheet of paper.

```
     The formalities have been completed, and
we'll be driving Sophia to Mercy House this
Friday. Darcy doesn't know yet, nor does
Benjamin. The transfer will be burdensome
enough without their interference.
```

Transfer, I thought, my lips forming a sneer. *You talk about her like she's a prisoner.*

You're both *prisoners*, the cynical voice proclaimed. *You're prisoners to the government, to Carl Padgett's legacy, to the creatures lurking underground and plotting their next bloody attack.*

Maybe, I mused, it was actually better for Peach to be sent to Chicago. Maybe at the orphanage, in a city of millions, she'd be out of reach of both the Children and the winged creatures.

Or maybe she wouldn't. I remembered last night, the enormous wings flapping like a dragon's and the lurid eyes blazing at me through my window.

Would Peach be safe *anywhere?*

My thoughts a chaotic swirl, I read the end of the letter.

Dr. Klinger, my husband and I want to thank you for all your help. You've been a voice of reason, and you have a better grasp of reality than Dr. Fleetwood. It almost seems as though he believes these lies!

Sincerely,

Roberta Westfall

I reread the last paragraph, my mind racing. Dr. Fleetwood believed me? Was that the true reason he'd been taken off my case?

But this speculation faded as the reality of my situation returned.

They were not going to let me see Peach. They were sending her away.

"What day is it?" I asked Anita.

"Tuesday," she answered.

Three days, I thought. *In three days, my little sister will be sent to an orphanage.*

And I, apparently, would go to jail. Or, I thought, my airway constricting, I'll have an accident.

I held up the letter. "You got this from Klinger?"

"Who else?"

"Why show it to me? To gloat?"

She shrugged. "Wouldn't put it past him. You have a meeting with him this afternoon."

"Splendid."

"You'll recant your story, take responsibility for what happened, and tell Klinger that Uncle Pierre is the reason you've decided to tell the truth."

I closed my eyes.

"You have to do this," she said.

"What does 'more responsibility' mean?"

"You admit to participating in the killings."

My stomach clenched. "The only person I killed was Carl Padgett."

"They'll require more than that."

"So they can keep me locked up?"

"That's better than having an accident."

I swallowed.

Anita said, "You could tell them you helped Padgett because you were scared of him. That you were following his orders. No one would doubt that."

"What does Pierre think about this?"

Her chin raised slightly. "My uncle doesn't know."

"And you're not telling him?"

"He'd talk you out of it. I don't want you using his unselfishness against him."

"'Using his...' How can you say that? I care about him too."

"Then change your story. Say you fought one of those kids, Brad Ralston maybe, because Padgett demanded it. Say you killed him by accident."

I considered this. The truth was, I *did* fight Brad. I didn't do it because of Padgett. It was self-defense. But the lie would be an easy one to tell. And if it saved Pierre's job...

Then I thought of Mia. She'd been there that day and had no doubt told them the truth. If I contradicted her, I'd make her life worse.

"No," I said.

"*Please*," Anita urged. "Do it for Pierre. He'll keep his job, and you'll stay alive."

"And be sent to prison?"

She averted her eyes. "A juvenile facility."

I thought of Peach, of what she'd say when she found out I'd changed my story… how betrayed she'd feel…

Even worse, what if she *did* believe I helped Padgett murder people? She was just a little kid, and she hadn't been present for — I pored through the ghastly memories — for *most* of the killings. In a way, this was a blessing. Watching Padgett bury a machete in Brad Ralston's head would have wrought indescribable damage on Peach's psyche. But because she hadn't seen it, she had no idea how it had transpired. She and I had been separated immediately after our mom's body had been found, and we'd never had the opportunity to compare stories. She had no way of knowing what was true and what wasn't.

"It's in less than an hour," Anita said. When I looked at her uncomprehendingly, she explained, "Your meeting with Klinger."

She rose and made to walk past me, but I half-shouted, "You're helping them hurt me and my little sister."

The door whooshed open, and Harry stalked toward me.

"It's okay," Anita said.

Harry glowered at me.

"Klinger wants to crush your hope," Anita explained. "He figures if there's no sister waiting for you, the last motivation you have for clinging to your story will disappear."

"Then he'll make *me* disappear?"

She watched me for several moments. "Rehearse your story. Take partial responsibility for the crimes."

"The murders, you mean."

Harry looked from me to Anita, his eyebrows knitted.

Anita sighed. "You can take him back now, Harry. I've gotta get downstairs."

We watched Anita go, her gait not as confident as it had been. I rose unsteadily, and a wave of dizziness grayed my vision.

Harry's big hands grasped my arms until the dizziness subsided. I looked up at him, mildly astonished to see real concern in his blue eyes.

"You good?" he asked.

I nodded, knowing I should be appreciative. I made a mental note to thank him when my brain wasn't so muzzy. As it turned out, I never got that chance.

Because Harry, like so many others at Sunny Woods, would be dead within two hours.

CHAPTER THREE
RIGGS

The next hour went by too swiftly. When it came time for me to be escorted to my interview, I still had no idea what I'd tell Klinger and the other government snakes when the time came.

The nametags on the orderlies who accompanied me read BARKER and GOODE. I'd never seen them before, but the hospital was massive. Maybe they worked on one of the other floors and were filling in up here since mine was a special case.

We were nearing the conference room when I heard the clatter of sprinting footsteps. Pierre swerved around the corner, the man moving with that graceful fluidity that always took me aback. Not for the first time I wondered what kind of athlete he must have been as a younger man.

"Hold up!" he was shouting. "Don't go in there yet."

Barker and Goode, the former with a slightly crooked nose, the latter with a nose that was small and slightly upturned, stared at Pierre without speaking. Other than the disparity in noses,

Barker and Goode were like flat-topped bookends. Square-jawed and muscular.

Pierre reached us. "You can't do this, Will," he said, slightly out of breath. "I ran into Anita… knew something was up. Finally got her to admit what was happening. You can't lie to them."

"Pierre—"

"I won't let you do it."

"Hey, old man," Goode said and grabbed me by the arm, "do your job and stay out of our way."

I realized why I'd never seen these men before. They weren't just orderlies. They were guards. Hell, maybe they *were* soldiers, and they'd been brought in to throw a scare into me. If that was the case, I hated to break it to them: I was already scared.

Pierre grabbed Goode's shoulder. So quickly I barely saw him move, Barker's hand shot out and seized Pierre's wrist. Pierre flinched but didn't let go.

"You don't know this young man," Pierre said. "What's happening to him is a travesty."

Goode stared at him impassively. "Take your hand off me."

Pierre shook his head. "They're making him tell lies so they can cover their asses."

Goode reached down and flicked up his shirt to reveal a handgun.

Pierre hesitated, but only for an instant. "Will is innocent. He's trying to help me, but the stuff he's gonna tell you isn't true."

Barker's fingers on Pierre's wrist whitened, and Pierre finally let go of Goode. Barker released Pierre, but Goode's fingers didn't leave the handle of his gun.

"If you interfere again, I'll be compelled to use force," Goode said.

"You mean that wasn't force?" Pierre glanced ruefully at Barker. "I thought you were gonna crush my bones."

"Come on," Goode said, leading me forward.

"Stick to the truth," Pierre said, raising his voice as we moved away. "They'll do what they want anyway. Firing me, sending you away... they'll do it whether you change your testimony or not."

A door opened, and a booming voice called out, "There's the young fella!" An enormous man in a cornflower blue suit stepped into the doorway of Room 517. "Name's Gerald Riggs," he said. "Head of the Midwest operation."

There was a hint of Southern twang in Riggs's voice, though it wasn't strong enough to veer into caricature. Despite the easiness of the huge man's tone, I sensed a change in the corridor. Not just in the attitudes of Barker and Goode, who stood up straighter and gripped my arms a mite harder, but in the atmosphere itself, the very air charged with the smirking man's presence.

"Come on in," Riggs said. "I've heard so much about you, it'll be a treat to meet the genuine article."

We entered and I discovered Dr. Klinger and Agent Castro seated at a long rectangular table. I glowered at Castro's cocky grin. With his blond crewcut and his over-white teeth, he reminded me of Val Kilmer's character in *Top Gun*. I wagered that Castro was a decorated athlete in high school, but rather than using that renown to lift others up, he'd tormented weaker kids in the locker room. I could easily imagine him dunking a scrawny kid's face in a toilet.

Castro winked at me. I resisted an urge to fly the middle finger.

Barker and Goode led me to a chair at the foot of the table. Riggs ambled around and stood opposite, smiling benignly down at me.

The door wheezed shut. Barker and Goode took positions on either side of it. I couldn't fight the sensation that whatever hope I had of escaping had just vanished. All heads, including mine, turned toward Riggs.

He grinned. "Be at ease, young fella. This is just a friendly chat."

My disgust must've shown because Riggs glanced down at the chairback he was gripping and laughed. His brown-and-white beard fringed a large round jaw. His hair was mostly brown, with sprinkles of white.

He eyed me steadily. "Okay, son, I won't patronize you. We both know what needs to happen here, so let's get to it."

"Get to what?" I asked, though I knew too well.

His grin resurfaced. "To *what*?" A robust laugh. "Why, to the way you helped your daddy kill those people!"

—

I STAYED QUIET for what seemed like forever but was probably around thirty seconds. Seeing I wasn't going to give in easily, Riggs scooted his chair out and eased into it.

Even sitting, he was massive.

"Must be nice for you, getting a vacation from the fifth floor."

I remained silent. I could feel the eyes of everyone in the room — Klinger, Castro, Barker, and Goode — boring into me. They were used to hopping to attention when Riggs gave orders.

But I didn't work for him.

He smiled cheerfully. "You've been a fascinating study." Seeing my look, he added, "From afar, I mean. In a way, I almost feel like your daddy. I've seen you get into scraps with other boys. I've seen you cry yourself to sleep."

I shifted in my chair.

"I've even seen you try to make friends. You and that Pederson kid…what's his name, Neville?"

"Nemo," I corrected.

He nodded. "Nemo. The only boy in here who gives you the time of day. He worships you. Why do you think that is?"

I wasn't about to answer him. I wasn't going to explain that, like Barley, Nemo was a misfit no one else would talk to. He was tiny, hence the Pixar-inspired nickname. I had no idea what his real name was because he never told me. He had woeful hygiene, stunted social skills, and hair stuck in a state of permanent bed-head. But there was an honesty in him I respected, and he was never actively malicious. A low bar, maybe, but one many of the boys in Sunny Woods made no effort to clear.

Riggs drummed his fingers on the table. "You spoke with Anita earlier?"

I didn't answer.

One of his eyebrows rose, giving him a slightly satanic air. "She's a tasty dish, ain't she?"

I glowered at him.

"Don't tell me you didn't notice. I saw your eyes crawling over those cocoa-colored legs of hers every time you thought she wasn't looking. And don't forget, there're cameras in your room too. We've seen how much you like to take care of yourself at night."

Castro snickered. My cheeks burned. I was sure I was blushing furiously, but try as I might, I couldn't hide the humiliation and violation I felt.

Riggs flapped a hand at me. "Aw, don't get bashful, kiddo. We're all men here. Hell, I'd be worried if you *weren't* takin' a little personal time."

This time there was laughter behind me. *Goode*, I thought.

Klinger was scribbling feverishly in his notebook, feigning professionalism, but I could tell from the set of his mouth how much he was enjoying this.

"There's been a change of plans," Riggs said.

"Tell me," I answered through my teeth. "So I can get out of here."

"*Out* of here? Boy, you need to disabuse yourself of that notion. The rest of your life's gonna be spent in institutions worse than this. That is, if you make it that far."

"You plan on killing me?"

Riggs tossed back his head and bellylaughed. He wiped a tear from his eye. "Whew! I do love directness, and this boy here, he gets right down to business, doesn't he?" He leaned forward on his elbows. "All right then. Let's get to it. You're going to Westchester. There's no getting around that. You committed murder last summer. You know it, we all know it."

I started to protest, but he stilled me with an upraised palm. "Simmer down. You're in no position to act indignant. In fact, whether you realize it or not, you're lucky to be alive."

A chill gripped me.

He nodded. "That's right. And since you're livin' on borrowed time, you're gonna do something for us. Something that'll ensure this… problem is contained."

I thought I knew what he was talking about, but I hoped I was wrong.

"The white people," he said and lowered his chin meaningfully. "We know they're real."

"The Children," I murmured.

A wintry grin. "Call 'em what you want. We refer to the... species as the white people. It's easier to talk about 'em that way rather than using fancy names."

My experiences with the creatures rushed over me like a noxious tide. The glowing green eyes. The rapier-like teeth. The ripping claws and the leering, bloodless lips. The speed and the cunning and the appalling strength.

Living nightmares. That's what the Children were.

"You're right to be scared," Riggs said, all jocularity gone from his voice. "These things are worse than anything I could've imagined. I doubted your story until the Peaceful Valley business, but now..."

I sat forward. "You believe me?"

A sour look showed on Klinger's face, an uncomfortable expression on Castro's. Goode watched Riggs with something akin to dread.

Only Barker would meet my gaze. But his eyes were stolid. I had no idea what he was thinking.

At length, Riggs said, "You'll be accompanied by twenty of our best people. We need you to give us all the intelligence you can. Our base is situated in what was gonna be the RV area of the state park. Early next week, you'll be escorted there by Officers Goode and Barker. You will not be armed, nor will you do aught but follow orders." Riggs spread his hands. "Any questions?"

My voice was inflectionless. "You want me to go back."

"There's no 'want' to it, kiddo. You're going back."

"Have you seen the creatures?"

"Firsthand? No. But we've heard plenty of accounts."

"Then you don't know what they can do."

A grunt. "Son, we have body parts from more than a hundred campers. I think we have a *very* good idea of what these things can do."

I looked at Klinger. "You knew?"

Klinger pretended not to have heard me.

My voice trembled. "You've known all this time, and you've still pretended I'm insane."

Klinger took off his glasses and rubbed the bridge of his nose. "Your signs of mental incompetence are legion. Hostility toward authority. Repeated acts of aggression. Just this morning you spoke to your mentor about a dragon-like creature."

Damn. So they *had* been monitoring my conversations with Pierre.

"These Night Flyers," Klinger began, "are figments—"

"What did you call them?"

He agitated a hand. "Fairy tales. Just because there are smatterings of truth in your account—"

"My mom drowned. My best friend got ripped apart by one of those 'white people.' Rebecca Ralston was surrounded by them. They…they…" I broke off, aware that I was crying.

In a voice that could have almost been mistaken as sensitive, Riggs said, "This is why we need you, kiddo. Other than your sister, your girlfriend, and that other boy, you're the only one who's encountered these beasts and lived."

"That's not true. Barley's parents saw one. So did Bill Stuckey, the deputy from Shadeland."

Agent Castro said, "Stuckey denies all knowledge of the incident."

I rolled my eyes. "Of course he does."

"And Mr. and Mrs. Marley have been reluctant to discuss it," Castro continued. "Shortly after you were brought here, they hired an attorney. Getting information from them has proven difficult."

I won't lie. This stung. I understood why Barley's folks might not want to get involved — they had two children of their own to protect — but dammit, they had *seen* one of the creatures transform. Had even, I remembered, teamed up to kill it.

How could they not be involved?

Castro leaned back in his chair. "So, you're the only one who can help us."

"The only one under your power, you mean."

Riggs chuckled, glanced at Castro. "Told you he was savvy." He stood. "Agent Castro will come by in an hour or so to drop off the aerials. You can spend the evening reacquainting yourself with the area."

God. As if I needed to reacquaint myself. The horrific events of last summer had been repeating in my head on an endless loop for more than a year.

"What do I get?" I asked him.

He stared at me, bemused. "Come again?"

"I said, what do I get? You're sending me into danger, and if I happen to survive, I go to jail for the rest of my life. What the hell is my incentive?"

Riggs appeared to think it over. "Castro, would you and the others give us a moment?"

They all did, Castro favoring me with one last smirk before ambling past.

Prick, I thought.

The door closed, and Riggs approached. He eased down on the table too near me. I would have scooted my chair back, but I didn't want him to know he made me uneasy.

"I'll tell you a story that might illuminate things," he said. "Back in high school, I wanted to be an actor. Not movies or anything. Just…" An embarrassed smile. "I liked theater. But my daddy, he wasn't keen on the idea. Said acting was for queers."

"Your dad sounds like an asshole."

"He was," Riggs allowed. "We never saw eye to eye, but that's another story. What matters is this: the girl I had my sights set on, she was the lead actress in the play that year. *The Music Man*. Ever hear of it?"

I had, but opted not to say so.

"She played Marian. And the guy who ended up playing Harold Hill — the part that should've been mine and would've been mine had my dad not shamed me — he not only got the girl in the musical; he got the girl in real life. Or at least, he started dating her."

"Why are you telling me this?"

"A couple weeks after the play ended, I left a note on the kid's car — you know, the guy who took my girl."

I raised my eyebrows. "'Your girl'?"

"I pretended I was the girl in the note. Told him to meet me in the woods near the park. No cell phones back then, so the little shit stain couldn't check with the girl to confirm it was her. Hell, he probably wouldn't have bothered anyway, he was so fired up to get in her pants."

"Do you have a point?"

Riggs grinned in a way I didn't like. "Sure. Though you're too dumb to see it. You remind me a little of that kid. I've honestly forgotten his name. Harold Hill is how I remember him." Riggs must've seen something in my expression because he smiled. "Oh, I didn't murder him or anything. Just beat him to within an inch of his life. Let him know if he went near that girl again, I'd finish the job. And if he told on me, I'd kill her too."

I tried not to show how horrified I was.

"So you see," Riggs went on, "that taught me a lesson I've carried with me ever since: centralize, sanitize, cauterize."

"Excuse me?"

He leaned down, his musky aftershave strong enough to make my eyes water. "I centralized the problem. Led Harold to a quiet, out-of-the-way spot." He nodded. "I sanitized him. That beating I doled out, it was cleansing. For both of us."

My heart thumped.

"Then I cauterized the wound," he said. "By making sure he'd never go near the girl or identify me as the one who'd turned his face into lasagna, I made sure there'd be no spread of the infection, no more problems."

He grasped my shoulder, his fingers like the claws of some enormous lobster. "Centralize, sanitize, cauterize. It works every time."

I stared up at him. "I have no idea what you're talking about."

He smiled a little sadly. "You will, kiddo. You will."

CHAPTER FOUR
BRAWL, ARRIVAL

I sat in the cafeteria spooning lukewarm chicken noodle soup into my mouth and thinking everything over. I couldn't see any way around it. If I refused to comply with their orders, they might really kill me. If I did what they said, the Children would rip me to shreds and dine on my entrails. It'd been a miracle I'd survived my first encounter with them, and I knew I wouldn't be that lucky again.

My thoughts were interrupted by someone plopping down beside me. *Right* beside me.

Nemo Pederson. I untensed.

Wordlessly, Nemo set to wrestling with a chocolate milk carton. The carton was already mangled, but the milk was no closer to being accessible.

"Want me to do that?" I asked.

"Piece of crap," Nemo muttered. He jerked on a flap, and chocolate milk lapped over the torn hole, lacquering his fingers and pooling in his Styrofoam tray. He frowned at the milk swirling around his sliced peaches. "Piece of crap."

I returned to my soup. "You know, you could sit across from me like a normal person."

"I don't wanna be normal," he mumbled. "Normal here is beating each other up." He took a sip of chocolate milk, but it dribbled over his shirtfront. He glared down at it. "Stupid shirt's gonna be soggy all day."

Nemo was the scrawniest kid here, but that was the least of his issues. While many of the inmates were problem children who'd made some stupid mistake, Nemo suffered from genuine mental illness, though he never divulged what kind. He also never spoke about the scars up and down his arms, and the one time I asked, he stopped talking to me for a week. My guess was he'd been cutting himself, and because his parents didn't know what to do with him, he'd ended up here. What he needed was a supportive environment. What he got was the Sunny Woods Rehabilitation Facility, heavy doses of medication, and merciless bullying from the other boys.

The cloying odor of canned peaches brought me back to the moment. "Want me to get you another milk?"

"So I can spill it?" He attempted to spear a peach slice, but it splurted away from his fork and slopped onto the table like a stranded seal. He sighed.

I pushed my tray over to him. He accepted it without comment and stabbed one of my peach slices without incident.

"Thanks," he said.

I studied him. "How are your meds? They helping?"

"Can't tell. They keep screwing around with my dosage." He gave me a quick sidelong glance and gnawed on his lip.

"What?" I asked.

Nemo hesitated. "I think you're in trouble."

"Tell me."

"When I was in the rec room earlier, Emilio and Jett were playing a game. The one with bean bags and a wooden box?"

"Cornhole," I supplied.

"Gross name," he said. "Emilio was teasing Jett about his size. Jett got mad and said, 'Yeah? I'm gonna kick Burgess's ass tonight.'"

The soup suddenly tasted foul in my mouth. Or foul*er*.

"Why?" I asked.

"Apparently, he didn't like the way you singled him out today." Nemo glanced at me. "Did you single him out?"

I slumped over my tray. "I suppose so. I just asked why he put up with the way they treat him."

Nemo sat up straighter. "Speaking of…"

I didn't need to turn to know who was coming, but I did anyway. Tyler and Emilio brought up the rear of the procession; at the fore stalked Jett, looking eager for blood.

"Oh hell," Nemo muttered.

I was about to say something about this being a misunderstanding. Experience had taught me that angry people fed on the encouragement of a crowd, and I suspected that if I could reason with Jett one-on-one, he'd understand. But before I could say anything, he smacked me hard on the cheek.

—

NO ONE IN the cafeteria moved. I sat there, dumbstruck, and tried to process what had just happened. Jett Jennings, a kid I'd pegged as a decent human being, had just slapped me in the face. The blow had been vicious, the pain needling my cheekbone.

Emilio laughed in astonishment. "Holy shit, dude!"

My cheek hurt like a son of a bitch; that was bad enough. What was worse was the fact that Jett had *slapped* me. Being slapped was being *insulted*, being told I was less than everyone else, and dammit, I'd endured enough of that to last me ten lifetimes.

I spoke in a controlled voice. "You're better than that, Jett. Don't do this."

His eyes flared, his grin incredulous. He glanced from buddy to buddy, and I knew there was no disentangling their knot of solidarity. "You don't know me, Burgess, so don't talk like you do."

"Yell for the lunch ladies," Nemo said in a low voice. "The old one's nice. She'll get help."

I peered through the inmates and saw the younger lunch woman watching us from over the counter. The older one was nowhere to be found. Had she gone for help already?

Good luck with that, I thought. Because technically, help was already here. There were guards posted at both doors, and though they were plainly aware of what was happening, they exhibited no willingness to help. In fact, one of them, a younger guy with a black goatee, appeared to be enjoying the confrontation. He'd been present for one of the more prolonged scrapes I'd had with Tyler and his gang, and he'd behaved like a hockey referee: let 'em go at it until someone goes down, and then only break it up if it looks like the beating might turn fatal.

The sinking feeling intensified. There was no help for me. Oh, I'd live through it, and maybe after a month I'd walk upright again. But Jett and Tyler and Emilio would make sure I'd suffer properly this time. They didn't know I was about to be sent away from Sunny Woods forever, but maybe on some instinctive level they suspected their favorite plaything was about to be wrested from them.

They wanted to get their money's worth.

"You at least gonna stand up?" Jett demanded.

"He'll stand," Emilio said. I shot a glance his way and realized something. Even though he hated me, had bullied me with as much impunity as anyone during my time here, he also understood me. Maybe even respected me. He knew I wouldn't roll over. Not for anyone.

I stood.

Emilio chuckled. "Alright. Let's see it, Burgess."

"Man," Tyler said and shook out his arms, "is this sissy gonna *bleed*."

"I'll go for help," Nemo murmured.

Emilio clamped his big hands over Nemo's shoulders. "Sit your ass down."

Nemo stayed put.

"Try this one, Burgess," Jett said and swung at me.

Though he was quick, I anticipated it and deflected the blow with a forearm. My next move wasn't honorable, but then again, neither were they.

I kicked Jett in the nuts.

He let out a phlegmy *oomph*, dropped, and writhed on the floor like a garter snake in the throes of a seizure. I was sure I'd bought myself some time without his participation.

Which still left two.

Emilio regarded Jett's squirming form. "That was bullshit, Burgess."

He came for me.

I would have evaded him if not for Tyler, who stuck out a foot and sent me blundering toward a neighboring table. I landed badly, the table edge chopping into my ribs and flipping

Styrofoam trays through the air. The inmates sprang away, no doubt trying to dodge the wrath of Tyler's gang.

It was Tyler himself who pounced on me then, but I didn't know that until I was heaved onto the tabletop, Tyler springing up and landing with his knees on either side of me and pinning my arms to my sides. A cloud of yeasty breath swam over me. He reared back and belted me with a hard-knuckled fist. My face whipped sideways.

I wriggled to free my arms, but his bludgeoning fist hammered down again, this time cracking me in the brow and bouncing the back of my head off the table. Starbursts bloomed in my vision, the pain and disorientation severe.

"Hey, hey, hey! Where're *you* going?" someone called.

Nemo must've attempted to go for help. Go where, I had no idea; we were locked in the dining hall, and unless he'd commandeered a swipe card, there was no escaping. With a look I saw that Emilio had ridden Nemo down and prostrated him on the grimy tiled floor. He bent Nemo's arm behind his back and asked, "How's that feel? How about correcting my grammar now?"

"Look at me!" Tyler growled into my face.

As my head lolled toward Tyler, I remembered that Nemo did have a habit of correcting people's grammar, sometimes far too publicly. He'd never corrected mine, and I wondered if that was why he'd been drawn to me, my better-than-average grammar. Friendships had been built on less.

"*Look at me!*" Tyler thundered.

I blinked up at him.

"Aren't you gonna fight?" he demanded, spit spraying. "Or are you just gonna lay there?"

I smiled groggily.

"*What?*" he snapped.

I began to giggle. I became aware of blood on my lips, but this only made me laugh harder.

Tyler grasped my smock. "What the hell's so funny?"

I grinned with bloodstained teeth. "It's *lie* there, not lay."

His eyes flew wide. "You…stupid…mother…*fucker.*" He cocked a fist and whipped it down at my face, but I jerked my head aside and his knuckles smashed the unyielding tabletop. Tyler howled in pain and tilted sideways. I freed an arm and used it to shove him all the way over. He rolled onto his back and clutched his maybe-fractured hand, and I sprang off the table and weaved toward Emilio.

The sight of Nemo facedown and whimpering seared away my disorientation, and what flooded into its place was a raw, throbbing rage. These bastards were no different than the bullies who'd made my life such hell last summer. Brad Ralston, Kurt Fisher, the Blades Brothers. They were just like Tyler and his crew. Sadists, all of them.

I launched myself at Emilio. He barely had time to turn toward me, his mouth dropping open, the slackness of his expression igniting an even deeper hatred. When our bodies collided, something dark and slithery inside me celebrated. My momentum knocked him off Nemo. I relished the feel of Emilio's body jouncing on the hard floor.

In the wild scramble of limbs, I came out on top. I rained blows on him, blasting him in the nose, the lips. He wailed and batted at my pistoning right fist, but I kept swatting away his defenses, leaving him wide-eyed and squealing and already very bloody.

"That's enough," a deep voice said from behind me, and I was lifted bodily from Emilio's quivering form.

I writhed in my captor's grip. I shot a glance toward one door, then the other, discovered that neither guard had left his post. The one with the goatee looked on sourly, probably nettled at how swiftly the clash had been aborted. So who the hell had ahold of me?

"If I let you go," the deep voice said at my ear, "you better not go back to flailing."

"Do it," I muttered.

The arms released me. I pushed away and looked at Goode, the officer who'd no doubt been tasked with keeping an eye on me. I wondered briefly where Barker had gone, but that mystery was solved when a door opened and Barker burst through, the old cafeteria lady shuffling along beside him. She must've gone for help, I decided, and found Barker, but before they arrived, Goode had intervened.

Much too slowly.

"Thanks for nothing," I muttered to Goode, smearing blood from my underlip.

He grinned. "I'm here to serve."

Distantly, I caught a snatch of conversation between the old cafeteria woman and Barker:

"...should never have forced him to eat with the other boys," she said.

"Changes are about to be made," Barker assured her.

"He never even *did* anything," the old woman went on, "yet they've been all over him since the day he was admitted here."

"I'm sorry," Barker said, his voice surprisingly gentle. "It was Officer Goode's turn to watch Will. Otherwise, I would have responded sooner."

The old woman looked like she might still have a heart attack, but Barker's tone seemed to be working. I didn't trust Barker — I didn't trust anyone — but I wondered if he might not be a more decent sort than Riggs and the others.

A moan drew my attention. Emilio was curled up like a pill-bug and clutching his face, but he wasn't moaning. My gaze shifted to Nemo. His hair was mussed, and his shirt hung askew on his body shoulders, but other than that, it appeared he'd escaped harm.

So why did he look so alarmed?

"Hey," I said, placing a hand on his shoulder. "Emilio didn't break your arm, did he?"

Nemo moaned again. He was on his knees, gazing at something to my right. I turned that way and saw nothing but a few scattered inmates and the gigantic picture window overlooking the courtyard.

Then my insides performed a slow, horrorstruck lurch. I realized why Nemo was so transfixed.

Floating just outside the window, its vast wings slowly flapping in the deepening dusk, was the creature I'd spied the night before, the creature with the glowing scarlet eyes and the black, leathery skin.

"What on earth?" Goode murmured.

The creature flapped its wings, receding from us, and hovered in the air. It lowered its demonic-looking head.

And hurtled toward the window.

PART TWO

THE NIGHT FLYERS

CHAPTER FIVE

BEDLAM

Every eye in the cafeteria was riveted on the creature hovering outside the window. No one spoke. I don't think anyone breathed. In those moments, I experienced both an emotion and a revelation.

The emotion was unutterable terror. I was accustomed to encountering the uncanny, the unbelievable. But the look of this beast, with its glowing red eyes and its vast sable wings, recalled childhood stories of man-eating dragons laying waste to entire kingdoms. So many fairy tales seem designed to scare the shit out of you, and I'm not too proud to admit to feeling that same unadulterated panic when staring at the abomination outside the window.

Yet somehow, the revelation I experienced was even more distressing.

Because the creature *knew* me.

I understood that this monster had arrived at Sunny Woods because of me. Though I was alone and bottled up like an insect,

I was the target of the beast's wrath. Yet even though I was the target, I knew others would suffer. Those around me — particularly those I cared about — always suffered.

All this passed through my head in a space of perhaps three seconds.

Then the creature, its wingspan at least fifteen feet across, lowered its face, surged forward, and crashed into the window headfirst, the thick glass exploding inward as though it had been wired to blow. The unfortunate inmates positioned nearest the window were harrowed by deadly shards. Boys tumbled away from the window, propelled not only by the vomiting glass, but by the sheer force of the creature's entrance. The old cafeteria woman let out a shrill scream, and several boys who'd been standing in my vicinity took off running.

The creature landed on a table, enshadowing me, and I got the first good look at its face.

I wished I hadn't.

The word that tumbled through my mind was *goblin*. The ruby-colored eyes were lambent and slitted in measureless hatred. The triangular face tapered to a jutting, vulpine chin. The leathery flesh was folded and pocked with scars, the ears pointed and misshapen, like some child's attempt at sketching an elf.

It possessed a stringy mane of black hair and stood hunched over in a way that reminded me of a creepy old man prowling a twilit park.

The creature's eyes flicked down and discovered Jett Jennings staring openmouthed back at it. It beat its wings once, dropped to where Jett lay, and began to shred his body with razorlike talons.

I witnessed more than I wanted to before I turned away. Jett tossed his arms up protectively, the creature's talons cleaving the meat of his forearms like carving knives through veal. Blood bubbled from Jett's slashed arms and drizzled like burgundy wine over his gibbering face.

The inmates surged toward the door. Goode fled along with the rest of the residents. Prior to last summer, before I was disillusioned by man's capacity for evil, I would have been stunned by Goode's cowardice. After all, he was a grown adult and an armed officer of the government. If anyone could help Jett Jennings, Goode could. But all I saw of him was his back as he burrowed into the mass of boys teeming toward the exit.

Instinctively, I took a step after him, thinking only of saving myself.

But something stopped me.

I'd like to say I tried to save Jett, but that wouldn't be true. I'd seen other people mauled by berserk beasts, and I knew there was no helping him. I could hear the beast's flesh-tearing incisors all too well.

What prevented me from simply fleeing like the rest of the residents was Nemo Pederson, who'd been flash-frozen by mind-shattering terror. I knew Nemo would be unable to fend for himself.

I stepped toward him on legs I couldn't feel, bent, and hooked him under the arm. He seemed not to notice me, only gazed with disbelief at the feeding beast. I forced Nemo to his feet. He allowed me to lead him away, and as we advanced toward the doorway, we discovered Barker and the old cafeteria woman shepherding kids through the exit. I estimated that nearly half the residents had been evacuated from the dining hall, and I was about thirty feet from the exit when a strident crash echoed down the corridor. I froze, and so did everyone else. Then the screaming began.

—

NEMO STARED AT me, unbelieving. "Is there another one?"

We were nearing the door when an earsplitting cry spun us around.

The creature

(*Night Flyer. Klinger called it a Night Flyer.*)

had Emilio Quintana pinned to the tiled floor, a viscous stream of slaver stringing from its mouth to Emilio's face. So extreme was Emilio's terror that he didn't even blink as the creature's drool reached his forehead, swirled over it like ice cream from a machine, and oozed into his thick black hairline. Even from a distance, I could see bits of flesh and gristle speckling the Night Flyer's face, a scarlet scrim of blood glistening on its leathery skin. *This is about more than feeding,* I thought. *It's about the joy of the attack, the pleasure it derives from its victims' terror.*

Emilio was toast. There was no getting around it. He was as motionless as an oversized toy, his eyes glazed.

"Would you move your ass?" someone screamed at my ear.

I blinked at Nemo Pederson, my surprise stemming not only from his sharp tone but from the manner in which my own mind had retreated. *Wake the hell up, Will!*

Nemo yanked on my arm, but I broke away and circled back toward Emilio and his dragon-like captor.

"Will!" Nemo cried. "Are you *crazy?*"

I said nothing, only scanned the wreckage of the cafeteria. If overturned trays and splats of mashed potatoes were useful weapons, the situation would be less dire, but the fact was, nothing around me would help him stay alive. The creature was opening its fanged maw wider, positively leering at Emilio now. In another moment, the beast would plunge those lethal teeth into his face, and Sunny Woods would lose another inmate.

Then I saw it. Just a few feet away lay one of several overturned tables. This one had shed one of its large rolling casters, the rubber and steel apparatus abandoning its table leg like a foot bitten off by a shark.

I cringed at the thought.

I hurried over to the severed wheel, glancing at Emilio as I moved. The Night Flyer's head was descending toward Emilio's face.

"Hey!" I shouted.

No reaction from the creature. Was it any wonder? Even though the cafeteria had mostly emptied, there was still enough of an uproar to mask a single teenaged voice.

I scooped up the wheel. It felt good in my hands, its weight commensurate to a waterlogged baseball. It was roughly the same size too. I gave the caster a little toss, caught it.

"*Hey, fuckface!*" I called.

The creature snapped its head toward me. The shouting voices died. Even Emilio glanced up at me, his catatonic state shattered by my roar.

The Night Flyer climbed off him, moving with a sinuousness that was somehow obscene. Though its wings undulated and twitched, what it reminded me of most as it stalked closer was a lion dipped in pitch, the lambent red irises gleaming with hunger, the teeth glinting ferociously within a bed of obsidian gums.

"Will!" Nemo shouted. "Have you lost your mind?"

The creature stalked closer, its steps quickening as its head lowered. At any moment, it would spring.

Chris Watkins, I thought. *Be like Chris Watkins.*

My best friend had been a terrific pitcher. Who knows? With a fastball that already touched ninety miles per hour and only fifteen years old, Chris might have become a professional baseball player someday, had that monster not ended his life. But that day, as we battled the Children in the driving rain, Chris had more than once used his cannon of a right arm to hurl rocks at the creatures. And though none of his fastballs had killed the beasts, they had stunned them, and more importantly, they'd sent a message: *You might be stronger than us, you might very well kill all of us. But we won't back down from a fight. And we'll never abandon each other to save our own hides.*

I adjusted my grip on the caster and positioned my left foot in front of my right. I wasn't a future MLB pitcher like Chris might have been, but I was a good shortstop. I lifted my left knee, and as I reared back and extended my leg, the creature began to gallop toward me. *All the better*, I thought. With the Night Flyer racing and the caster rocketing from my hand, the impact would be terrible.

It still won't do any good, a bleak voice claimed.

"Go to hell," I said, and unleashed the caster with all my strength.

The force of the throw made me stumble forward, so when the caster connected with the creature's head, the distance between us was less than twenty feet. The heavy hunk of steel and rubber clocked the Night Flyer in the brow and ripped away a huge flap of skin.

I shouldn't have been surprised by what happened next, but maybe because I'd spent thirteen months in this mundane environment, the sight of what lay beneath the creature's pebbled skin took me aback. Rather than a glistening red patch of tissue and a font of scarlet jetting from the Night Flyer's head, what spewed forth resembled crude oil. *Ichor*, my horror novels would have called the foul-looking blood, and though I recoiled from the sight of it on some elemental level, the memories it brought back swept away the Night Flyer, the chaos around me, even the threat of dying.

The Children possessed the same crude-oil blood.

The Children, who had taken my best friend Chris, who had murdered Rebecca Ralston, who had slaughtered and eaten so many innocent and not-so-innocent people that day...

Then something made me forget all about the Children.

Two more Night Flyers winged through the shattered window and landed in the cafeteria.

—

THE CREATURE I'D tattooed with the caster was thrashing its head and slapping the floor in rage and pain.

I hurried toward Emilio Quintana.

Thankfully, his trance broke at about the same moment. He didn't move briskly, but at least he moved. The newly arrived creatures were about forty feet away, and though they were stalking toward him, Emilio kept the distance steady as he moved toward me. I snagged him by the arm and saw with a rush of hope that we weren't facing the three Night Flyers alone.

Officer Barker had ventured away from the exit, his gun drawn. Even in his large hands, the black gun looked enormous.

It won't stop them, my cynical side insisted.

Maybe not, I countered. *But it will sure as hell slow them down.*

Just behind Officer Barker was the older lunch lady. I chided myself for never learning her name. Here she was, risking her life to save us...

I fought off the wet heat in my throat. Sentimentality wouldn't help. If we survived, I could thank her later.

"Look out!" the lunch lady shouted.

The original Night Flyer, despite the black liquid flowing from its head wound, was staring at me with depthless loathing. I thought it would come for me then. I was certainly close enough, and I was totally unarmed.

Then something happened that told me more about the Night Flyers than I cared to know.

A voice called, "Will! Emilio! Come on!"

It was Nemo. He stood, skinny and alone, halfway between me and the exit. I shot a look at the bleeding creature, and as I did, I saw an expression very much like the ones the Children had worn during last summer's slaughter.

Sadism. Wickedness. A perverse glee at inflicting not only physical pain, but emotional suffering as well.

The Night Flyer grinned.

Then it galloped toward Nemo.

Nemo stood rigid for a second or two and had only begun to raise his arms when the creature leapt.

"Shoot it!" I called to Barker, but even as the words left my lips, I knew they were futile. To fire at the creature, Barker would have to shoot in the direction of Nemo and the seven or eight inmates piling through the exit behind him.

The Night Flyer crashed down on Nemo like a collapsing wave.

Nemo might've been knocked unconscious by the cracking of his head on the hard tile floor. I *hope* he was knocked unconscious. I hope he didn't feel the puncture of the creature's teeth in his throat or the whirring claws as they ribboned his chest.

I wanted to feel anger at that moment. I wanted to feel rage. That, at least, could be channeled, could become something other than desolation, which was what I felt: an unhelpful mixture of sorrow and hopelessness that would do no one any good, least of all Nemo, whose eyes now stared sightlessly heavenward.

"Get behind me," Barker said.

Someone hauled me nearer. Distantly, I realized it was Emilio who had ahold of me, Emilio who'd finally recovered enough to do something other than stare in shock. The three of us huddled together behind Officer Barker—Emilio, the lunch lady, and I—and though I held little hope that we'd live through the evening, the touch of the other bodies against mine was edifying, was a reminder I wasn't alone.

"When I start shooting," Barker said, "you make for the counter."

"The counter?" the lunch lady asked.

Between tightened lips, Barker said, "There's a rolling door, right? The kind that covers the gap between the ceiling and the serving counter?"

The lunch lady nodded. "It's on a chain."

"Pull it down after you three get over the counter."

"What about you?" the lunch lady asked Barker.

His voice was steady. "I'll have to find another way out."

That's your plan? I wanted to shout.

"One," Barker said.

Wait, I tried to answer, and though my lips moved, no sound issued forth.

"Two," Barker muttered.

"What if they—" the lunch lady started to say.

"Run!" Barker shouted and opened up on the pair of Night Flyers.

Emilio needed no persuading. He was halfway to the counter before I even took a step. I'd only gone ten strides before I realized I'd left the lunch lady behind.

It wasn't a question of her desire. Her hazel eyes were vast under her wireless spectacles, and her arms were chugging in terror. The problem was, she was older. Maybe over seventy. And as I've said, she wasn't a small woman. She probably hadn't tried to run anywhere for years, and now her life depended on speed.

She wasn't going to make it.

Even now, the creature who'd ripped Nemo apart was hastening toward the lunch lady, moving diagonally to head her off before she reached the counter.

It was the sight of the lunch lady that seared away my mental fog. The way her arms jiggled as she ran, the look of abject terror on her face… she was the type of person bullies like Tyler Flowers would mock. To guys like Tyler, she was just a comical figure, someone without feelings or a history.

But goddammit, I thought as I hustled toward her, this was a human being, a caring woman who was beautiful in her own way. This lady, whose name I'd been too self-absorbed to ask, had treated me with warmth and kindness for no other reason than that she wanted to. She, Pierre, Nemo, and Dr. Fleetwood were the only people who'd smiled at me in over a year; they were the only reminders that the whole world wasn't a hellscape where people lived to hurt you.

To my right, Barker's gun was roaring at evenly spaced intervals. Even though I knew nothing about firearms, the manner in which Barker was measuring his shots suffused me with a fresh surge of hope.

But deep down, I knew that hope was founded on nothing.

Because I had nothing with which to ward off the oncoming Night Flyer, no weapon, no plan… hell, it wasn't even a certainty that I'd reach the lunch lady before the creature did.

I ran harder, my stupid hospital slippers struggling for purchase as I pushed my body to its limit. I closed the distance, and as another gunshot sounded, I realized I would reach her before my nemesis did.

But I wouldn't be able to stop in time. My trajectory took me to the space between the creature and the lunch lady, and though I tried to put on the brakes, my ridiculous slippers caused me to skate right through the gap, pinwheeling my arms like a clown.

The Night Flyer whipped its head toward me, forgetting all about the lunch lady, and before I could plant my feet and pivot around to face the creature, it lunged for me. I was driven sideways as its rough hide slammed into me. Its half-furled wings enclosed me, the beast's talons clutching me by the chest. I thought for a moment we'd hang in the air that way, that the creature would swerve toward the broken window and wing away with me through the darkening sky. But in another instant we smacked the floor, the creature hissing and spattering my face with spittle.

There was no hope for me. I was pinned, the creature's girth holding me in place like a car crushed beneath a fallen underpass. I squirmed, jerked my face away from the creature, but it darted at me, that horrid sound — half-hiss, half-sigh — assaulting my eardrums.

Then the creature jolted. Its coppery, rancid breath puffed over me. I winced at the stench, but my revulsion became shock as the creature jolted again, this time jittering as though touched by a live electrical wire. I fought to move its body and was at last able to dislodge it, the creature tumbling sideways and mewling in pain.

I stared in wonderment at the lunch lady.

And the taser in her hand.

She helped me up. "They issue these to all the food staff," she explained, "in case the patients get out of line."

I grinned at her. "You saved my life."

We started toward the counter. "Then I guess we're even," she said. "Thanks for coming back for me."

Barker took the lunch lady by the arm. "Hurry. Those things aren't going to stay down forever."

I shot a glance over my shoulder and saw that Barker had downed two Night Flyers. But even at that distance I could see they weren't dead, were very much alive and preparing for another onslaught. Or at least one of them was. One creature lay on its back, its arms and legs flailing about as if catching invisible butterflies. The other had regained its feet, was shaking its head foggily as if to rouse itself into action. Ebony pools of ichor surrounded both creatures.

"You first," Barker said to the lunch lady. I joined Barker in helping the older woman onto the stainless-steel counter. I scrambled after her and into the kitchen.

Safely on the other side of the counter, I glanced at the lunch lady, whose eyes widened in horror. I turned to see what she was looking at.

The Night Flyer who'd killed Nemo was winging its way toward Barker, its claws extended in hunger, its red eyes ablaze with fury.

Barker wasn't going to make it.

—

I BENT AND scrabbled under the counter for something sharp. The whole counter jounced as the Night Flyer slammed into Barker. In the next moment, there was a whir of limbs and body parts directly over me, and as the lunch lady screamed, I realized the creature's momentum had driven it and Barker right through the opening and into the kitchen.

The entire space was maybe fifteen-by-eighteen, and with four of us in there, as well as multiple carts, stands, and food containers, the room was even more cramped. There was no sign of Emilio, but the door in the far corner of the room was open.

The creature unfurled its wings, knocking me and the lunch lady sideways. Barker had ended up on his back, and even though he was powerfully built, engulfed as he was by the Night Flyer, which had risen to a height of twelve feet, Barker resembled a small child.

I had a sudden flashback of Peach being menaced by the Children last summer and welcomed the blast of fury the memory conjured.

But before I could take action, Barker brought up his big black handgun and squeezed off two shots. I assumed the Night Flyer's head would snap backward, that its brains would paint the dingy, eggshell-colored ceiling. But it had anticipated Barker's move and leaped aside.

Placing it directly before the lunch lady, who stared up at the creature in dread.

I thought for sure it would kill her. Its face still glistened with poor Nemo's blood and viscera. But judging the danger from Barker's gun too great, it bypassed the lunch lady and scrambled to the rear of the room, overturning multiple carts and rolling steel containers between it and Barker.

Barker pushed to his feet, raised his gun to draw a bead on the creature, but before he could fire at it, the lunch lady shrieked.

Another Night Flyer, this one leaving a murky trail of ichor, was galloping across the cafeteria and was moments away from bursting through the opening we hadn't bothered to close. The creature was gathering for its leap through the aperture when I snagged the chain and pulled. The rolling door came rumbling down.

It crashed into the door, bowing it inward. One of the creature's slender black arms shot through the gap, and the rolling door bounced upward several inches.

Its virulent face glared at me, and I hauled down on the chain again. My thought was to smash its arm and maybe even slice it off, but that was when the creature seized my shirt and jerked me toward it.

The side of my head bashed the almost-closed aluminum door. I heard a guttural voice snarling, hissing, the monster so governed by its need to kill that it smashed me against the rolling door again and again. I struggled to push away, to bat at its walking-stick fingers, but so frenzied were its attempts to drag me through the tiny aperture, that I couldn't recover my balance.

Overhead, the lights flickered, dimmed. Were there other creatures in the building? Had they tampered with the power? I thought of the screams I'd heard from the hallway, judged it likely there were more Night Flyers inside.

Just like the Children last summer, a voice whispered. *They come at you in waves.*

I couldn't linger on the thought for long because the creature yanked on my shirt again, more forcefully this time. The door bent outward from the force of my body, and even more frighteningly, the door rolled upward a few inches. My God, if it rolled any higher, the creature would be able to haul me through the opening, and then it would bury its teeth in my throat. It slammed my shoulder against the rolling door, the concussion titanic enough to bring tears to my eyes. I reached down, grabbed the creature's forearm with both of mine, but there was no chance of dislodging its grip.

"Move your hands," a voice commanded.

I looked up dumbly at the lunch lady and beheld the large carving knife she gripped.

"Take your hands off it!" she shouted, with considerably less patience.

I obeyed, and the moment my hands broke contact with the creature's forearm, the cleaver came whooshing down.

The blade clipped the Night Flyer's arm off at the elbow as neatly as a celery stalk. The creature squealed, its squirting stump jerking back from the opening. I slammed the rolling door down, found the slender steel locking bar, and shoved it into place.

The lunch lady and I regarded each other. She appeared shocked by what she'd done. The lights flickered, dimmed. I opened my mouth to thank her for saving my life, but she turned, her eyes widening, and I realized I'd forgotten all about Officer Barker.

And the Night Flyer in the room with us.

Barker squinted into the increasingly poor light, his gun extended. True, the Night Flyer was enormous, its wings like stygian sails and its glowing scarlet eyes like chunks of seething charcoal. But with the flickering lights and the profusion of carts and food containers, it was difficult to discern what was a swatch of black flesh and what was shadow.

"Listen," Barker breathed. "I want the two of you to move as quietly as you can toward that door."

I glanced at it; the hallway beyond appeared even murkier.

"It might go for you," Barker continued, "and if it does, I'll take it down."

"How many bullets do you have left?" I asked.

"Two," he said. "I'm pretty sure it's two. No more than three."

Not enough, I thought.

But that wasn't necessarily true. The creature I'd last glimpsed lying on its back in the cafeteria, the one with the twitching limbs, had appeared headshot, and well on its way toward death. If Barker was able to shoot this monstrous bastard in the head too, we might be saved.

Barker yelped, his gun going off as he tipped over backward. My eyes flicked downward, and I saw the creature's wing receding, the black sail lengthy enough to snake its way under the carts and sweep Barker's legs from under him. I took a couple steps toward Barker, thinking to drag his prone body away from the creature, but before I could, the creature bounded onto a cart in the center of the room and glowered down at us.

Barker raised his gun and fired. The creature jolted. Barker tried to fire again but was met with a feeble clicking sound.

The creature had thrown up a wing to protect it, and though Barker's gun had punched a hole in the wing, the damage seemed minimal.

No more bullets, I thought. *No more time.*

The creature was lowering its bleeding wing and swiveling its face toward Barker when something drew its gaze. Its red eyes widened, glowed brighter, a look of bewilderment slackening its features. I followed its gaze, realized it had spotted the black ichor dripping from the counter, the spot where the lunch lady had severed the other Night Flyer's arm. The Night Flyer in the room with us tracked the black blood to the floor, where the severed arm had landed. Then the creature's eyes shifted to the lunch lady.

To the black-smeared cleaver in her hand.

The Night Flyer's eyes narrowed. Its teeth showed white.

"No!" I screamed.

It leaped at the lunch lady.

EVEN HAD I been quicker, I don't believe it would have made a difference. Or maybe I just tell myself that.

The creature was on her in an instant. The lunch lady threw up her arms, and as the Night Flyer crashed into her, the cleaver went skittering across the floor. I lunged for it, snatched it up, but before I could intervene, I heard something that chilled my blood. It sounded like a carton of chicken broth tipped onto its side and dumping onto the floor.

I forced myself to look even though I didn't want to, even though I knew what horror awaited me.

The Night Flyer had unzipped the lunch lady's throat, her lifeblood splashing over her apron, onto the tiled floor, onto the creature's hateful face. I watched numbly as its long, black tongue slithered out and lapped at the yawning slice in her throat. Something seized me from behind.

Barker. He dragged me toward the open doorway, not speaking. The lunch lady's unbreathing body lolled in the Night Flyer's grip. The lights overhead dimmed again, went totally black, before reviving to a sallow green hue. *The generator*, I reasoned.

As we reached the threshold, Barker gasped. He propelled me through the doorway. I shot a look over my shoulder in time to see Barker lurch through behind me, slam the heavy steel door shut, and flinch as the Night Flyer crashed against it on the other side.

Could the creature manipulate doorknobs?

I was certain it could. If it and its brethren possessed the intelligence to locate me, reconnoiter the facility, and launch an attack, then certainly an operation as simple as twisting a doorknob would present no challenge.

"The stairs," Barker said. "We can't trust the elevator."

I nodded absently. He took me by the arm and hustled me down the corridor. It was the hallway that contained the infirmary, a place I'd visited often. We angled toward a door with a wire-mesh window inset at eye level. Barker let go of me long enough to retrieve his swipe card, but his hand froze halfway to the card reader.

Together, we gazed through the wire-mesh window.

Saw the pair of Night Flyers ripping an inmate apart.

He's not an inmate, a voice reminded me. *He's a kid. A boy your age, a boy who deserved better than this.*

I looked away from the carnage, my gorge rising.

"Okay," Barker said, sounding queasy. "Plan B."

Barker was maybe an inch taller than me, but his broad shoulders, the powerful tendons in his neck, even his crooked nose kindled in me a small measure of hope. And strangely enough, it was the fear in his eyes that reassured me the most. We might not make it out of here alive, but we wouldn't die because Barker was rash or prideful. He was as scared of dying as I was, and whatever he'd do, it would be done with a healthy fear of these beasts.

We started down the hall again. "I'm out of ammo," he murmured, "but if we can get to the fourth floor, I can reload."

"Fourth floor?" I said. "Isn't that where Anita is?"

He grinned a little. "Got a crush on her, do you?"

Despite the circumstances, I blushed. "She's twice my age. Besides, she's Pierre's niece."

"My office is next to hers," he said. "The office me and Goode shared. I wonder…"

He didn't need to finish. The chances that Goode was already dead were high.

We neared the door that led to the main hallway, off of which our cells were located. We crept to the door and peered through the window, where lights flickered weakly. The corridor in which we now stood was dim; the one into which we were about to venture was nearly black.

He licked his lips, looked back at me. "Keep that cleaver ready."

I realized I was still clutching the bloody implement. A vision of the lunch lady's face arose, and I fled from it. Guilt was the last emotion I needed right now. Rage, yes. The need to survive, absolutely. But not guilt. That could come later.

If there was a later.

His fingers trembling, Barker reached out with his swipe card, passed it through the black slot. The red light was replaced with green. The lock snicked open.

He opened the door slowly. It creaked a little. He nodded at me. I nodded back. Barker stepped through the doorway.

My breath coming in shallow sips, I followed.

CHAPTER SIX

WARRIORS

My first impression of the main hallway was *cluttered*. In the murky greenish light that flickered from the dying fluorescents, I could just make out vague humps scattered everywhere, objects of various sizes and shapes strewn about as though there'd been an explosion.

Barker started left, but he'd only taken a few steps when he froze. I opened my mouth to speak, but he brought a forefinger to his lips. I surveyed the clutter around us, and even had the lights not flicked on at that moment, I would have been rendered speechless by the revelation of what I was seeing.

The hallway was a slaughterhouse.

Emilio, I discovered, hadn't made it far. His body lay face-up, his eyes gaping, his chest opened like a tropical flower and his entrails strewn around in a gruesome red snow angel.

Just a kid, a voice within me lamented. True, Emilio had treated me like crap, but that didn't mean he deserved to die.

But I'd learned a long time ago that death had nothing to do with deserving or not deserving. When death was ready for you, it came for you with both barrels blazing. Or in this case, with razor-sharp talons and scythe-like teeth.

Focus! I told myself.

But I couldn't. The abattoir staring at me deprived me of rational thought.

Bodies lay like garbage bags someone had heaved from the bed of a moving truck, their contents having scattered when they hit the interstate at seventy miles per hour. I knew I'd be able to identify most of these people if I allowed my eyes to linger on their mutilated corpses, but I didn't want that, didn't want to humanize these misshapen spills of blood and body parts. Because I could scarcely move as it was. Could scarcely *breathe.* I wondered idly if a person's involuntary functions could cease from fright.

Behind us, there were more eviscerated carcasses and three doors standing ajar, one of them torn free of its hinges and resting atop a victim.

"This way," Barker whispered, clasping my hand.

The lights flickered, then winked out entirely before returning to that sickly greenish glow. We stepped down the blood-slicked corridor, taking care not to make a sound. Overhead, the lights continued their erratic cycle.

As we crept past the corpses, mostly teenagers with a few adults mixed in, the sight of Barker's cautious face recalled another responsible adult I'd met last summer.

Officer David Wood of the Indiana State Police had risked his life to help me escape one of the Children, only to be murdered by Carl Padgett. Had Officer Wood simply saved his own hide, he might have survived that ghastly rainswept day.

But he hadn't. And his kids were fatherless because of his unselfishness.

I disengaged my hand from Officer Barker's. He glanced back at me, a hint of puzzlement in his eyes. I worried momentarily I'd have to say something by way of explanation, but he spared me by continuing through the hallway. What could I have said anyway? *I'm grateful, but people who help me have a way of dying gory deaths?*

"Ah, shit," Barker murmured. He continued around a humped shape, which I now identified as Officer Goode.

My gorge clenched. Goode's neck had been… *degloved* was the word that popped into my head, but I knew that wasn't correct. Because this wasn't one of Goode's *hands* that had lost its skin, it was his neck. One of the creatures had somehow managed to yank the skin upward from the tops of Goode's shoulders to the base of his chin, and… and…

I couldn't look any longer.

I realized we were about to pass my own cell. I glanced at the door and remembered how many nights I'd spent there thinking of Peach, Mia, and Barley.

Most of all Peach.

If this were a movie, I'd insist on Barker letting me stop at my room. My most precious possession was inside, tucked under my mattress: the letter from Peach that Pierre had smuggled in. There was a part of me that badly wanted to retrieve it.

But this wasn't a movie, and after all, it was only a damned letter. I wanted the real thing. I wanted my sister back.

I passed my room for the last time and gripped the cleaver tighter. The handle was solid, if a bit slippery from my sweat. It was a reminder that we weren't powerless. That we still might escape this nightmare.

We continued on. I heard a squelching sound. Barker went rigid and glanced down at his foot, which was surrounded by a lake of blood. Whose blood it was didn't matter. I distinguished the vague shape of an inmate's light-blue uniform, but mercifully, the lights wavered at that point, and I was able to look away before identifying the victim.

Barker lifted his dripping sneaker and proceeded down the hallway.

I realized we were moving toward the cafeteria.

"Officer Barker, I think we should—"

"There's a service elevator this way," he whispered. "They use it for food delivery. There're stairs right next to it. Now shut up before they hear us."

I shut up. But almost as if I'd witnessed it firsthand, I imagined how it had unfolded: Goode leading the inmates out of the cafeteria, the whole herd of them fleeing down the corridor, discovering more beasts in the hallway, and fleeing back the way they'd come.

Being ridden down one by one and reduced to red mush.

We were only forty feet from the service elevator. To my right, a cell door hung half off its hinges. The wire-mesh outer window of the cell had been pulverized. I remembered the other doors that had been ajar, and a thought so monstrous took root in me that the words were out of my mouth before I could stop them.

"It was coordinated."

Barker looked at me.

But I was going on, the revelation crystalizing as I spoke.

"The first creature," I said. "It burst through the cafeteria window to scare us, to flush us out. The others—" I made a quick mental count, "—four others, at least, smashed through the inmates' windows and attacked these people in the hallway."

Barker's eyebrows gathered inward. "Inmates?"

"Me. Them," I explained, flourishing a hand at the corpses.

Barker was shaking his head. "How does this help?"

I swallowed. "It doesn't. It just means…"

Barker leaned forward, eyes widening sarcastically.

I sighed. "It means they're smarter than I thought."

Barker grunted. "Terrific. Can we get moving again?"

I nodded, sure my cheeks had gone the color of overripe tomatoes.

The walk to the service elevator corridor felt like hours. We finally reached the door. When Barker raised his swipe card, I had a momentary worry the card readers would no longer work with the facility's compromised electrical system, but the red light gave way to green, and then we were creeping down the short hallway toward another steel door. The short corridor was even murkier than the main hallway had been, but to our left I made out the gleaming steel doors of the service elevator.

Perhaps sensing the direction of my gaze, Barker shook his head. "Can't risk it. They corner us in the elevator…or if it gets stuck…it'll become our tomb."

Wide-eyed, I glanced at the shiny steel doors. Barker had a point.

We reached a dreary gray door at the end of the corridor. Barker brought his face close to the square window, peered into the gloom of the stairwell, and his shoulders drooped.

"What?" I demanded.

"See for yourself," he said, moving to accommodate me.

I peered into the semidarkness of the stairwell, and what I saw almost made my bladder unleash.

The younger lunch lady had fled this way. She hadn't made it. A Night Flyer was roosting on the backs of her legs, its maw buried in the middle of her back. In the moment before I looked away, gagging, I noticed how its wings quivered as it gorged itself.

Barker sighed. "Guess we go back to the…" His words died. His eyes widened.

Together, we faced the door we'd passed through moments earlier, from which footsteps echoed. But the sound of them…

They weren't human footsteps.

I STARED AT Barker. He stared back at me.

"We take the elevator?" I said.

He swallowed, moved with even greater caution toward the elevator. The lights overhead flickered. Barker extended a finger toward the elevator button, then stopped. Under his breath he said, "When I press this button, it'll make a loud *ding*. That could bring those bastards right to us."

Yes, I thought. They *were* bastards. Murderous, fiendish bastards. The word offered a glimpse into Barker's mind. While I'd been thinking of them as monsters or beasts, Barker merely regarded them as adversaries. And adversaries were things you fought, not things you feared.

This is a battle, I told myself, *not a bloodbath.*

I remembered the young lunch lady in the stairwell and amended my thought: *Okay, not just a bloodbath.*

From the main hallway came more squelching noises. I couldn't be sure, but it sounded like there were several creatures out there.

Barker whispered, "When I push the down button, you go through first and press G."

When I didn't answer, he explained, "G for Ground."

"I know."

"Just making sure."

I was too frightened to feel disrespected.

"You ready?" he asked. "When they hear it, they'll come at us hard. You saw what they did to those doors."

I swallowed.

He brought up a hand, extended an index finger.

Pressed the down arrow.

Nothing happened.

Barker frowned, depressed the button again.

Still nothing.

We were trapped. To our left, creatures prowled the main hallway. To our right there was a stairwell with at least one Night Flyer feeding. Before us was an elevator that didn't function.

I thought briefly of prying apart the double doors and muscling our way inside. I imagined Barker boosting me toward the ceiling so I could climb onto the roof of the elevator like Bruce Willis in *Die Hard,* and then…

It was stupid. We couldn't pry open the doors, and if we tried, we'd make enough noise to attract the creatures. Furthermore, there might not be an escape door in the ceiling of the elevator, and even if there was, what then? I'd be stuck on the roof in a pitch-black shaft, and we were on the highest story of the building. Where the hell did I think I was going to go?

A hand touched my chest.

I glanced at Barker, who was peering toward the main hallway door. I swiveled my head, knowing what I'd discover even before I beheld the face in the window.

A Night Flyer was watching us, its luminous red eyes glowing like hellfire.

"Stairwell," Barker breathed.

"But what about—"

The creature banged on the door. A baseball-sized knot appeared.

Shapes moved in the corridor window. Even as we backpedaled toward the stairwell door, I understood Barker's thinking: In the main hall there were several creatures. In the stairwell there was only one.

Barker didn't ask if I was ready. What was the point? I wasn't ready, could never *be* ready for such an insane maneuver. We were entering a stairwell — a confined space with almost no lighting — to confront a creature straight out of myth, a flying beast with dragon's wings and an insatiable appetite for human flesh.

Behind us, the creatures banged against the hallway door again, and both Barker and I jumped. This time the bottom of the door bowed inward. Barker raised the swipe card, hesitated.

"Cleaver," he said.

I handed over the cleaver with more than a little regret. I knew he'd be better with it than I would be, but it was still painful to relinquish the only weapon I had.

He adjusted the cleaver in his right hand, while with his left he brought up the swipe card. When the door opened, we'd have to fight our way past the creature on the landing. The Night Flyer had the dead lunch lady flayed open directly in our path to the stairs. Sure, we could attempt to clamber up the single stretch of stairs leading to the roof, but even if we made it, what then? We'd be exposed, fully within the creatures' domain. After all, they were Night *Flyers*. It would be madness to seek refuge high in the open air. And Sunny Woods was, of course, in the woods, which meant there'd be no waving our arms and shrieking for help. I had no idea how remote the facility was, but if the views out the windows were any indication — there wasn't another building as far as the eye could see — we were effectively in the middle of nowhere.

It was down the stairs or death.

At the same moment Barker swiped the card through the reader, the door behind us boomed again. The door had begun to come loose of its housing. Any moment the creatures would swarm through the doorway.

The stairwell card reader glowed green. The lock clicked. Barker crammed the card into his pocket and wrenched the door open.

The feasting creature leered up at us. Blood dripped from its pointed chin.

Barker lunged at it.

The creature, perhaps thinking Barker would be easy pickings, rose to its full height. It was at least eleven feet tall. Its tenebrous shadow swallowed us as its wings unfurled in the tight space.

But Barker never hesitated. He swung the cleaver in a tight, upward arc, and its sharp blade chunked between the creature's legs. I had no idea what gender it was or if it even had a gender. All I know is that the crotch is a tender area, and this one had a cleaver embedded there.

It slapped down at Barker's shoulders, not to assault him, but in an agonized, reflexive movement. It squealed shrilly enough to make my ears ring. The main hallway door crashed open. I whirled, realizing I hadn't bothered closing the stairwell door behind me. In the sallow, intermittent light, I couldn't tell how many creatures flooded through the main doorway, but there were enough of them to galvanize me into motion. I slammed the stairwell door shut.

A half-second later, the tide of beasts smashed into it, bowing it toward me.

Barker had gripped the squealing creature by its upper legs, was driving it backward toward the stairs. As its feet blundered over the descending steps, Barker's sneakers slipped in the blood surrounding the lunch lady's body.

It saved his life.

Rather than tumbling down the stairs with the Night Flyer, Barker landed on the first step. Instinctively, I snagged both his ankles to prevent him from sliding down the stairs after the squalling beast. On my stomach, my arms wrapped around Barker's ankles, I heard a snapping sound from below.

I hoped it was the creature's neck.

Something boomed behind us, and I knew the stairwell door had half-shattered off its hinges.

"Fast," was all Barker said as he scrambled to his feet. Cleaver in hand, he hustled down the stairs with me trailing him. The paltry light of the landing below us revealed how the creature's head was cocked at an unnatural angle, one wing mangled and trapped beneath its dragon-like body.

Barker had evidently seen the same horror movies I had. Or maybe he was just naturally cautious. Whatever the case, rather than stepping onto the landing and continuing around to the next flight of stairs, he leaned on the handrail, vaulted over it, and landed nimbly on the steps leading down.

I made to follow his example and was halfway over the handrail when something seized my ankle. I gasped. My upper body continued with my momentum, and I found myself dangling over the descending stairs, the creature not dead at all, the bastard still spry enough to snag my ankle like a martial artist snatching a housefly out of midair with chopsticks.

Above me, the door exploded inward and crashed against the stairwell wall.

The creatures were coming.

And I was dangling upside down. And being hauled upward again.

Cursing, Barker clattered up the steps, cleaver raised above his head. He chopped down with it as though splitting a cord of firewood. It severed the creature's arm and sent me dropping onto the unyielding concrete stairs. I had time to get my arms up, but it was still an awkward fall. Yet the pain scattered like a puff of smoke when I heard the noises overhead.

The creatures were spilling through the open doorway onto the landing.

They would be upon us in seconds.

Barker was already moving. I clambered down the stairs with him, and when we reached the landing, we beheld a sight that made us both freeze.

Shadows were cavorting up the stairwell below us.

More Night Flyers.

Barker didn't hesitate, merely growled, "Hold this," and shoved the handle of the cleaver into my chest. He produced his swipe card, fed it through the slot, ripped open the door to the fourth floor, and shoved me through.

Right into the arms of another Night Flyer.

I had no idea where Barker was, and it didn't matter. The only one who could save me now was me.

The creature's grip was viselike, the face leering down at me lambent-eyed and savage.

I freed my right arm and swung the cleaver at the creature's side, but the thing had drawn me too close, and I wasn't able to get much force behind the blow. The creature grasped me by the shoulders and jerked me hard into the air. Pain blossomed in my skull as I crashed into the ceiling. I dropped the cleaver. Then the creature dropped me.

I landed on all fours, my knees erupting with bright pain. I caught a glimpse of Barker struggling to close the stairwell door.

The creature clutched the back of my shirt. I suspected it wouldn't bash my head again, would instead take a bite out of my throat.

I was lifted from the floor. Frantically, I threw out my arms, and my fingers brushed the cleaver handle. Impulsively, I seized hold of it and brought it down on the only part of the creature within reach:

Its foot.

Even as the keen blade clipped off two of the creature's talons, I marveled at how long they were, how curved and lethal.

Ichor spewed from the severed stumps straight into my face.

Spluttering and spitting, I crawled away, having no idea at all where I was heading. All I knew was that I'd gotten that monster's filthy blood in my mouth, more creatures were on the way, and Barker might be in even bigger trouble than I was. I seized the belly of my shirt, mopped my stinging eyes, and blinked away the blood. The creature flopped onto its side, its mouth hinged open in a horrible wail. A figure raced toward me. I'd just identified it as Officer Barker when his hand hooked me under the armpit. He hauled me to my feet, and together we stumbled toward the fourth-floor corridor. He had his pass card out.

Barker swiped the card. I twisted the knob, flung open the door, and together we burst into the main fourth-story hallway.

And froze.

The lighting here was as dreary as it had been in the short hallway we'd just vacated, but it was bright enough to see we were about to die.

Dead teenaged girls lay all around us, the carnage even more severe than it had been on the fifth floor. There were Night Flyers ahead of us and behind us.

We were surrounded.

There was no escaping this time.

—

I JUMPED AS the horde of creatures in the short elevator corridor pounded the steel door beside us.

"You have the cleaver?" Barker asked.

"Sorry," I said. "When that thing's blood shot into my mouth, I…"

I let the sentence die. What was there to say?

The creatures ahead of us and behind us stalked closer. The Night Flyers in the short corridor boomed against the door again. One more blow, and they'd spill out right on top of us.

It was over. Barker and I were going to die, and I was never going to see my little sister again. Here at the end, staring death in its red-eyed face, I was surprised to find that my dominant emotion was frustration. *I want to see Peach!* a voice in my head screamed. *I want to see—*

Movement from my right made me gasp.

"*Move*," a voice demanded.

It was Pierre.

He seized me by the arm, dragged my numb body toward the doorway of what I now realized was a janitor's closet.

Pierre and I piled into the closet with Barker right behind us. The moment we slipped inside, the creatures in the hallway surged toward us. Barker was just able to ram home the door before the creatures banged against the other side, and though I was grateful for Pierre's intervention, our hiding in here seemed futile. I'd already seen them smash through multiple steel doors. What was different about this one? If anything, we'd ensured that Pierre would die a horrible death too.

A flashlight clicked on, the beam brilliant in the gloomy janitor's closet. When the first dazzling moonburst dissipated from my vision, I discovered Pierre on his knees before an opening near the floor, a square vent with the grate removed.

"Get inside," he ordered. "They can't follow us through the vents, not with those big-ass wings of theirs."

I didn't want to enter the ventilation shaft, but we were out of options. As if to accentuate this point, the door jumped in its hinges. Ten seconds, twenty at the most, and the creatures would be inside the closet with us. And then it truly would be game over.

I climbed inside the sheet metal vent and began to army-crawl.

Pierre said, "You next."

Barker didn't argue. In a moment he was right on my heels, and though I knew I should be scuttling forward like mad, I couldn't help but peer behind me, beyond Barker's straining face and broad shoulders, in the hopes that Pierre had made it into the vent too.

Pierre's flashlight beam stabbed my eyes, then began to bob as he crawled forward.

There came a brain-rattling *boom* as the closet door was projected inward. I heard the squalls of the Night Flyers, but this time the quality of their voices was different. It wasn't pain or hunger I detected, but rage.

It seemed Pierre was right. The creatures couldn't fit into the narrow shaft.

I'd actually begun to think we'd make it when I heard Pierre yelp.

I turned as much as the tight space would allow and screwed up my eyes to see beyond Barker. I only caught a glimpse, but that single glimpse caused my stomach to clench.

One of the creatures had ahold of Pierre's foot.

The flashlight had tumbled from his grip and lay sideways in the narrow shaft, but it broadcasted enough light to reveal the single, spidery arm extending from the closet to Pierre's foot, and what was more, Pierre was slowly losing ground. *My God*, I thought. *That closet is full of monsters. If they tow Pierre back inside…*

I couldn't allow that.

"Grab my shoe," Barker told Pierre.

Pierre's white teeth shone as he groped for Barker's sneaker. "Can't… reach it."

Barker scooted backward a couple of feet, and for no more than half a second, Pierre let go of the walls of the shaft with which he'd been bracing his body, and in that half-second I was sure the creature would simply yank Pierre backward into the waiting throng of Night Flyers.

But Pierre's fingers clutched Barker's shoe, and Barker began towing him forward. They'd made up the ground they'd lost when Barker jolted. His eyes widened.

He began to slide backward.

Holy crap, I thought, squirming toward Barker. Were the Night Flyers forming a chain just as we were?

Barker and Pierre lost another couple of inches. Using my toes, I shed my slippers and extended a bare foot toward Barker.

"Grab hold," I commanded.

It was dark in the shaft, but I could see well enough the look Barker was giving me: *I know you mean well, but c'mon. You're just a kid.*

I banged a fist on the flexible metal. "Grab ahold, dammit!"

Barker grasped my ankle.

I strained against the creatures' force. For a couple delirious seconds, all three of us were dragged backward. Pierre uttered the queen mother of all obscenities.

No, I thought. *No!*

My toes seemed to adhere to the smooth metal. My hands found purchase. Groaning with the effort, I pushed forward with all my strength.

Barker and Pierre slid forward with me.

"The *hell*?" Pierre murmured.

Beyond Pierre, I heard a screech of anger, and our linked bodies tremored as the creatures gave a tug.

But I'd braced my limbs in the shaft and kept us moored in place. Before they could haul us backward again, I dug in and lurched forward. This time the resistance was even greater, but it didn't prevent us from gaining more ground. With a straining grunt, I lunged forward, and this time we moved almost two whole feet. Just before I landed on my face, I experienced an extraordinary sensation, a rough jolt that told me we'd been released.

I didn't allow myself to celebrate; I clambered forward like the world's biggest toddler, and I could hear Barker and Pierre doing the same.

"Take a left up here," Pierre said in a gravelly whisper.

I couldn't see a thing. I said so.

"The turn should be about fifteen feet in front of you, give or take," Pierre said.

"Can I hold the flashlight?" I asked.

Pierre heaved an annoyed sigh. "There *is* no flashlight."

"You didn't pick it up?" Barker said.

"You two critics might not have noticed," Pierre answered, "but that monster was trying to kill me back there. I was more concerned about getting the hell away than I was about a five-dollar flashlight."

"But it's pitch-black," I said.

Pierre's voice rose a notch. "You wanna go back and get it, that's fine by me. But I am *not* gonna save your dumb ass again."

"He's right," Barker said.

I know he's right, I thought. But that didn't mean I relished crawling through a coffin-like space in complete darkness.

I set off again. The metal bent and flexed as we moved. From below, I fancied I heard a rustling sound. But I kept going. At any moment I expected a set of those wicked talons to puncture the metal under me, tear away a huge flap of the vent, and send the three of us plummeting into a sea of Night Flyers.

I was thinking this when my forehead cracked the metal wall. The gonging sound reverberated through the shaft.

Barker was chuckling softly. "I think Will found the turn."

"Shut up," I muttered. Damn, it hurt. I reached up and discovered a knot the size of a Brazil nut at my hairline.

"Unless you're unconscious up there," Pierre said, "I can't think of a good reason for us to stop. I feel like I've been buried alive."

Barker tapped one of my feet. "He's right, Will. This sucks."

I started to move again. It was uncomfortable navigating the bend in the ventilation shaft, but I managed it, and judging from the grunts and moans behind me, Barker and Pierre did too.

"You alright, Pierre?" I called.

"Keep moving," he answered, his voice surly.

"For a second it sounded like you were constipated, all that grunting."

"If we get out of this shaft, I'm gonna whup your ass," Pierre said.

I grinned and kept crawling.

We'd been at it for thirty seconds or so when Pierre said, "Ahead and to your left, you'll happen upon another opening. That's the one we want."

"What is it?" I asked, my voice hushed.

"The portal to another dimension," Pierre answered.

I tried to look back at him, but it was too dark.

Pierre sighed. "It's my niece's office, you dipshit, now get moving."

Cheeks burning, I set off again.

Anita, I thought. I didn't see how making it to her office would help, but I didn't say anything. Pierre had gotten us this far. We'd undoubtedly be Night Flyer food if not for him. I figured he and Barker had earned my trust twenty times over. *At least there are two adults in the world I can trust,* I thought.

But as it turned out, there were several.

I just wish they'd all lived through the night.

CHAPTER SEVEN
SACRIFICES

When I neared Anita's office, I could clearly discern the square opening where the ventilation grate had been removed. At first, I worried that was because someone in the office had left on a light, but when I reached the opening, I realized the subtle glow was emanating from under the hallway door. I was just about to climb into the room when a voice, shockingly loud in the otherwise soundless space said, "Please tell me that's you, Uncle Pierre."

Anita sounded as terrified as I was. That was good. After our first interaction, I'd come to view her as a soulless automaton.

Hands fell on my shoulders and dragged me out of the shaft.

Someone hoisted me to my feet. "Anita?" I asked, surprised by her strength.

"Harry," a voice answered.

Something bumped into the backs of my knees.

"You mind?" Barker asked.

I shuffled forward, brushed noses with someone else. I caught a whiff of a familiar cologne.

"Hey, Will," Dr. Fleetwood said.

"The son of a gun did it," Harry remarked.

Behind me, Pierre was cursing.

"Keep it down," Fleetwood said.

"You take care of you," Pierre answered. "If you were a fifty-seven-year-old man crawling around like an earthworm, you'd be salty too."

"You're always salty," Anita said, but she crossed to Pierre and wrapped him in an embrace. My eyes had almost adjusted to the meager light, and I could see tears gleaming on Anita's cheeks.

"We told him he was delusional," Fleetwood said to me, "but Pierre insisted you were still alive."

"How'd you find them?" Harry asked.

"I'd planned on taking the stairs to the fifth floor," Pierre said. "Obviously, my plans changed."

I thought of how choked with creatures that area had been and marveled that Pierre had not only survived, but somehow managed to lead us to safety.

"It was dumb luck," Anita said. "Anyway, we don't have time for a post-mortem now."

"Do you have to use that term?" I asked.

Anita ignored me. "If those things run out of victims, they're gonna start knocking down the doors to get at us."

"Anita's right," Pierre said. "We've got to move."

"Move where?" Barker demanded. "The stairwells are crawling with those things."

"We don't know that," Fleetwood said.

"We *do* know that," Barker answered, his voice raspy. "Will and I tried two staircases—"

"There are five stairwells in this building," Anita said.

"She's right," Harry said. There was excitement in his voice, and not just the species brought on by being near Anita.

"But how do we get to them?" I asked. "The hallway's filled with those bastards."

To punctuate the point, we heard a hissing sound from under the door. In the ensuing silence, I held my breath, certain the others were doing the same. We heard the click-scrape of a Night Flyer's talons. The creature was moving from left to right, away from the janitor's closet.

Fleetwood whispered, "The door to the central artery—"

"The central what?" I asked.

"The hallway reserved for doctors and other big shots," Pierre explained.

Fleetwood didn't contradict Pierre. "Logic would dictate they'd keep the patients centralized and devote the perimeter to safe passage for the employees. But Sunny Woods was designed counter-intuitively—"

"Stupidly," Pierre remarked.

"—with the patient areas around the outer layers of the building and the administrative areas in the center."

Fleetwood turned to me. "You know the courtyard where you and Pierre have your private talks? The interior windows overlooking the courtyard belong to the doctors and administrators."

"Klinger," I said, the name tasting sour in my mouth.

I wondered idly if Klinger had been working tonight. It was an ungenerous thought, but part of me hoped he *had* been working.

If the Night Flyers had preyed on him, at least he wouldn't be able to torture future patients.

Anita picked up Fleetwood's train of thought. "The doorway we need is only what? Ten yards from this office?"

"Fifteen," Fleetwood corrected. "Give or take."

"About three doors down?" Pierre asked.

"That's right," Fleetwood answered.

"The five stairwells you're talking about," Barker said. His parched-sounding voice reminded me of how thirsty I was. God, if we made it out of here, I'd never take water for granted again. "Four are on the corners of the buildings?"

"And the fifth," Anita said, "is in the dead center."

"Off the central artery," I said, then felt a little stupid. The statement seemed a trifle obvious, and the words *central artery* still sounded too grand for a hallway, but if anyone thought I was a dumb kid, no one said so.

Harry broke in. "Then we run for it. If those monsters attacked from the outer windows, they may not have bothered knocking down doors to get to the building's center."

"They found plenty of victims around the edges," I said.

"And this wasn't a random attack," Pierre added.

This was met with a stunned silence.

"What are you talking about?" Harry finally asked.

"Those things," Pierre said. "I think they came here for Will."

"That's preposterous," Fleetwood said, for the first time sounding like the other doctors here at Sunny Woods.

Anita asked, "Why would they kill all these people if they were only after one?"

"Fringe benefit," Pierre answered. Anita made a disgusted sound, but Pierre pushed on. "Will, you wanna tell them?"

"This is all interesting," Harry said, "but I'd rather discuss it after we've gotten the hell away from this place."

"So would I," Barker said. "But I think this is important. Tell us, Will."

I swallowed, but there was no saliva, only a sandpapery scraping in my throat. "I saw one of the Night Flyers last night. It… hovered outside my window."

"You *saw* one?" Anita said, something cold seeping into her voice. "And you didn't tell anyone?"

"He *did* tell," Pierre snapped. "But as usual, no one listened."

"There's more," Barker said.

"How much more could there be?" Harry asked, his voice nearly a moan.

"When that thing had ahold of Will," Barker began. "Just before Pierre saved us." He hesitated. "The creature could have killed him. Every other time they've encountered people, they've gone berserk, biting and ripping and—"

"We get it," Pierre said.

"—but when it grabbed Will, I got the funniest sensation. I was sure for a moment that it was wrapping him up to…"

"To what?" Pierre demanded. "To slow dance?"

"To *take* him."

A couple of us started to talk, but Anita hushed us. We shut up quick, and it was a good thing, too.

The click-scrape of a Night Flyer had paused just outside our door.

—

FOR AN EXCRUCIATING period of perhaps twenty seconds, we waited. I could hear the creature's breathing outside the door.

The only other noises were the distant growls of the Night Flyers, the clatter and bump they made as they moved from corpse to corpse, tearing gobbets of flesh from the dead. I was reminded of one of my favorite movies. Chris, Barley, and I had watched it at least five times, munching popcorn and high fiving when Sigourney Weaver kicked ass:

Aliens.

Though there was nothing remotely entertaining about our current situation, the guttural rasp of the Night Flyer's breathing outside our door, the somehow ravenous huff of its breath… it sounded to me like the aliens had.

I became aware of an itch in my throat, the overwhelming desire to cough. I hated coughing. Not only because it hurt, but because the need to cough overtook me at the most inopportune times. Sitting in church during a sermon. Taking a test at school and knowing you'd irritate your peers. At night, when I knew I might wake up Peach, who shared a bedroom with me in my old life.

Or now, when you were trying not to get slaughtered by monsters.

After an eternity, the Night Flyer moved on.

Anita waited until it was well down the hallway before speaking. "To hell with this. We have to make a break for it, or we're gonna be creature food."

"We could wait for help to come," Fleetwood suggested.

"Anita's right," Barker said. "We can't rely on outside help. If they send cops here, what do you think's gonna happen to them?"

"I go first," Pierre said.

"*I* go first," Harry answered.

"Harry's right," Anita said.

"Why do you—" Pierre started.

"Because he's faster," Anita snapped. "The one who takes the lead has to get there before the rest of us so he can open the door."

"Who says I'm not fast?" Pierre demanded.

"You're almost sixty," Anita said. "Now shut up and listen to the plan."

Pierre tapped me with the back of his hand. "You hear the way she talks to me? It's that jerkwad husband of hers. He's a bad influence."

"Harry goes first," Barker said. "Pierre goes second."

"Why not Anita?" Harry asked.

Barker's tone was not unkind. Maybe he, like the rest of us, understood how lovesick Harry was for Anita. "After Harry gets the door open, the first one through the doorway's got to face whatever is there, right?"

"I can fight as well as you all can," Anita said.

"Okay," Fleetwood said. "Harry first, Pierre second. Who follows Pierre?"

"I do," Anita said before anyone else could answer. "Will goes after me."

"Who's next?" Fleetwood said, and though he didn't explicitly say so, I could tell he was hoping to be named. I couldn't blame him. I sure as hell wouldn't want to pull up the rear in our lame escape attempt.

"You do," Barker said to Fleetwood. "I go last."

"Okay," Harry said. "Let's do it."

I admired his bravery, though I didn't give our plan much chance of succeeding. Hell, it wasn't even a plan. We were making a run for it and hoping we got lucky. What if there were creatures between us and the central artery door? What if there were Night Flyers waiting for us beyond that door? I imagined Pierre entering the stairwell and being immediately beset by snarling creatures.

I clamped down on the thought before it could steal what little resolve I'd mustered.

Harry went to the door. Reached for the handle.

"Wait," Anita said.

She moved past Pierre, who'd lined up behind Harry. Anita placed a hand on Harry's shoulder, raised up on her tiptoes, and kissed him on the cheek.

It wasn't too dark to see Harry's grin. "Thanks, Miss Myers."

She returned his smile. "It's Anita, you goofball. Now be fast. You've got the swipe card?"

Harry nodded, his eyes like black marbles. "Everyone ready?"

No, I thought.

"Here we go," he said, turning the handle.

Then he was lunging through the doorway and pounding down the hall. Pierre burst through too. The creatures squalled. Anita was sprinting like an Olympic athlete, and though I couldn't feel my feet or any other part of my body, I took off after her.

Peering ahead, I could see we'd caught a break. There were plenty of creatures in this corridor, but the majority of them were feeding at the far end of the hallway, well beyond the door to the central stairwell. One Night Flyer was halfway between us and its brethren, but Harry was barreling forward at full speed, and the lone Night Flyer was just beginning to move in our direction. I was certain Harry would reach the door first.

I heard the slapping of rapid footfalls, and I threw a look over my shoulder, sure a Night Flyer was bearing down on me. But it was Dr. Fleetwood, moving faster than I would have guessed he could move.

He's only thirty-seven, a voice reminded me.

Let's hope he lives to see thirty-eight, I thought.

The hallway was a hell-tunnel of screeches and growls. Harry was nearly to the door, but I realized with a sinking heart that he was in trouble. The lone Night Flyer had reacted slowly, but now that it had gathered a head of steam, its long legs and half-extended wings were propelling it rapidly toward Harry's charging body.

He wasn't going to make it.

We weren't going to make it.

Then something happened that made me want to cry, cheer, and vomit all at the same time. Likely sensing the end was upon us, Harry changed course. Rather than veering to his right, where the swipe pad was and the door we hoped would lead to our salvation, Harry kept chugging straight ahead. He saw that he wouldn't be able to operate the swipe card and open the door in time for the rest of us to pass through the threshold.

So Harry sacrificed himself.

No! my mind screamed. *I know you're in love with Anita, but you don't have to die for her.*

But if he didn't do this, we were all dead, and Harry knew it. The other Night Flyers were converging from ahead and behind. Ten more seconds and we'd all be torn apart.

Harry lowered his head and launched himself at the Night Flyer's midsection. Like an NFL linebacker, Harry crashed into the creature, lifted it off its feet, and planted it on its shoulder blades.

Pierre had his swipe card out, passed it through the reader, and the red light was swapped with green. Pierre lunged through the door; Anita followed. I was a few feet away when I chanced a look at Harry, hoping against hope that he'd managed to push away from the creature and follow us through the doorway.

But that hadn't happened. The creature might have been surprised by the aggression of Harry's tackle, but it had possessed the presence of mind to seize hold of him after they'd hit the ground. In the moment before I looked away, I saw Harry's face pointed skyward, his neck and shoulders straining to push away from the creature. But the Night Flyer's claws striped the front of Harry's uniform, the blood spuming over the creature's face.

Fleetwood crowded against my back, his momentum shoving me through the doorway. Then something happened I didn't expect, something that made me gasp in horror.

"Run!" Barker shouted from behind us, and amidst the screeching and the clattering of the approaching Night Flyers, Barker reached out and slammed the door shut.

With him on the other side.

Not you too, I thought weakly. *Don't sacrifice yourself too.*

"Come on!" Anita shouted, taking hold of my arm and dragging me away.

From the other side of the door, I heard Barker scream.

CHAPTER EIGHT
THE DESCENT

"The hallway's clear," Fleetwood said, but I scarcely heard him. I kept seeing Harry's head thrown back with his eyes squeezed shut and his teeth bared in agony, kept hearing Barker's scream echo. On some level, I realized that the door behind us hadn't boomed yet, a sign that the Night Flyers were currently glutting themselves with their victims, or Barker had somehow led the creatures in the other direction.

But if he'd led them away, why had he screamed?

I didn't know, and I didn't have time to think about it. Because we were nearing where I thought the stairwell would be located. As I hustled along, I noticed how extravagant the central artery was, how expensive the furnishings. Unlike the fifth floor I'd called home, this corridor was a riot of finery: wainscoted walls, fancy prints every dozen feet. One painting, "Woman with a Parasol — Monet and Her Son," reminded me powerfully of my best friend Chris. But for once, the recollection didn't bring me to tears.

I was too busy trying not to die.

"That one!" Anita called.

"I know," Pierre answered as he stopped before a windowless door. He swiped his card, but instead of twisting the knob when the green light glowed, he looked at us. "No way of knowing what's beyond here. If the hallway's full of them, we gotta close this door and hide in one of the offices."

"Then what?" Anita demanded. "Wait for them to kill us?"

"Better than offering ourselves up," Pierre countered.

I tended to agree with Pierre.

"Let me go first," Fleetwood said.

The light still flickered, but the sallow glow was stronger than it had been in the other corridors.

Pierre's expression soured. "Why the hell would you do that? I'm first, you're last, and Anita and Will are safe in the middle."

"I wouldn't say 'safe,'" Anita said.

Pierre gave her a flat look. "Fine. Safer."

"I'm part of the reason we're in this nightmare," Fleetwood said. "Had I listened to Will... taken him more seriously..."

"You'd be fired by now," I said. "It's not your fault."

Fleetwood shook his head. "Will, I—"

"Screw it," Pierre said and opened the door.

We stared into the darkness. The stairwell appeared empty.

"Come on," Pierre said. "Four stories down. We can do this."

And then we were descending the stairs, our footfalls as light as we could make them.

The trip down took forever, and many times I was sure I heard a stirring in the stairwell. But sound was funny during that interminable descent. Amplified. More than once, I mistook the chuff of my own breathing for one of the creatures.

We finally made it to the ground floor.

"Now what?" Fleetwood asked.

"Pretty simple," Anita answered. "We go through the door, turn right, and hope we make it. The lobby's straight down the hallway, through the double-doors."

"Another swipe pad?" I asked.

"To get to the lobby, yeah," Pierre said. "But the doors leading outside are regular doors. No keycard necessary."

He passed the card through the reader. The door opened and we piled through the doorway after him. We weren't walking, but we weren't jogging either. More like an accelerated speedwalk, the kind of clip you'd achieve when hustling to the bathroom, a palm clamped over your mouth, just before vomiting.

Each doorway we passed guttered with greenish light. And each one, so far, was barren. We were nearly to the double doors when Fleetwood said, "What now? Just run through the lobby?"

"You got a better plan?" Pierre whispered back.

Fleetwood didn't answer, and it wouldn't have mattered if he did. Because Pierre was swiping his card and pushing through the doors, Anita after him, me a step behind Anita, Dr. Fleetwood crowding my back.

The lobby was spooky as hell.

It shouldn't have been. After the claustrophobic spaces I'd inhabited — stairwells, corridors, Fleetwood's office… most of all that wretched ventilation shaft, a space so tight and smothering I suspected I'd simply get wedged inside it and die — the soaring, window-fronted atrium should have felt like freedom.

But it didn't. What it felt like was *exposure*.

We'd broken into a jog and were nearing the outer doors when Pierre said, "You do have your car keys, don't you, Anita?"

Anita froze. "I thought we were taking your car."

Pierre winced. "They make the serfs like me and Harry park in the rear lot."

The moment the words left his mouth, I could see he regretted them. It was obvious Anita had never reciprocated Harry's massive crush on her, but it was equally obvious she was shaken by his death.

"We'll take mine," Fleetwood said. "It's closer anyway."

We shuffled to the doors and peered out. "Which one is it?" Pierre asked.

"The Mercedes," Fleetwood answered, sounding sheepish. "The white one in the front row."

"It's okay," I said. "Unlike Klinger, you earn your money."

Fleetwood smiled.

"We ready?" Anita asked.

We scanned the sky above the parking lot. It was mostly dense forest, but above that the heavens were that velvety blue-black that only seems to occur in July. It was warm in the atrium, the cooling system having failed in the power outage, but I suspected the night would be even warmer.

I longed to be outside at night. It would be the first time in over a year.

Pierre pushed on one of the double doors. Frowned.

"What?" Anita demanded.

"Oh no," Fleetwood said.

Anita's expression went tight. "Don't tell me it's locked."

Fleetwood massaged his brow and talked as though he were lecturing himself. "Of course it's locked. The facility cares more about security than it does comfort—"

"Which is why," Pierre said, picking up the thought, "these doors automatically lock in a power outage."

"Can't you use your swipe card?" I asked Fleetwood.

"This one doesn't work like that," he answered.

Anita clenched her fists. "*Fuck.*"

"This isn't a big deal," I said. "We just break the glass."

Anita gave me an acerbic look. "With what?"

I glanced around. "One of those chairs."

Pierre spread his arms. "That's brilliant. While we're at it, why don't we find a bullhorn so we can announce to those creatures exactly where we are?"

I glared at him. "Or maybe we should just stand here and wait for the power company to arrive."

Pierre leveled a finger at me. "You're startin' to piss me off."

"Will's right," Fleetwood said. "Once that window's shattered, it's only thirty yards or so to my car."

Pierre passed a hand over his face. "Okay, which one of us is gonna—"

He cut off in mid-speech. Anita was already dragging a heavy chair toward the glass doors.

I frowned at the chair, which had squat wooden legs and puffy burgundy fabric that made me think of rich dudes in smoking jackets. "Isn't that too big?"

"You and Pierre are gonna hoist it together."

I opened my mouth to point out I was only sixteen, but I caught myself, remembering how I'd somehow managed to haul both Barker and Pierre away from the Night Flyers in the ventilation shaft.

A phrase drifted through my mind: *unnatural strength.*

I shrugged it off because Anita was still talking. "...and I'll kick away any residual glass. Doc goes through first, then me. Will, once you two let this chair fly, you get on Pierre's back—"

"Huh?" I asked.

She looked at me like I was a moron. "Your feet. You really wanna run barefooted through broken glass?"

I swallowed, realizing how right she was. If you were, say, Bruce Willis in *Die Hard*, you could go sprinting blithely through a glittering carpet of broken glass and still manage to fight bad guys. But something told me it wouldn't work the same way for me.

"Hold on," Pierre said to Anita. "Why do you need to go second? Wouldn't it be better if you went after us, so we knew it was safe?"

"*Safe?*" she said. "Are you serious? This is about as unsafe—"

Anita stopped talking.

We all stopped breathing.

There was a screeching sound coming from the hallway we had just exited.

The Night Flyers had found us.

—

PIERRE AND I grabbed hold of the oversized chair. Fleetwood extricated his keys from his hip pocket. I didn't know what Anita was doing, and I didn't have time to check because Pierre was rocking the hefty chair backward and bending his knees. I followed suit, and when we'd cocked the chair back as far as we could, we heaved it toward the glass door. I was certain it would deflect harmlessly off the glass, which I suspected was reinforced.

But reinforced or not, the glass shattered.

For a moment, all we could do was gape.

Then Anita was ushering Fleetwood through, and Pierre was beckoning me impatiently toward him, his eyes fixed on the door behind us.

The one reverberating with the creatures' rabid screams.

"Get on, dammit," Pierre said. "If I'm gonna lug your sorry butt around, I'd just as soon get it over with."

I climbed on. "Fine. But only far enough to get past the glass."

Pierre adjusted his grip on my calves. It occurred to me as he stepped awkwardly over the big chair that I hadn't ridden piggyback since I was a little kid. My mom was shorter than I was, and anyway, she'd had a bad back, hence her addiction to prescription drugs. My dad... well, when your dad is one of the most notorious serial killers in American history, you didn't tend to ride him piggyback very often.

From the hallway, a Night Flyer brayed. My skin broke into gooseflesh, but Pierre didn't hesitate. Moving with an ease I admired, he navigated the chair and the shattered glass spangling the sidewalk and managed to get us to the lawn.

"That's far enough," Pierre said, letting go of me. "For a scrawny kid, you weigh a lot."

"Maybe you're just getting old," I answered as we started running side by side.

"I'll show you old," he said, and we both grinned.

Our grins vanished when something swooped around the corner of the building and made a beeline for us.

"Down!" Pierre shouted, draping an arm around my shoulders and dragging me to the grass. A split second later, the space we'd just vacated was cleaved by a screeching Night Flyer. Rather than doubling back to grab us, the creature beat its wings once, twice, a deep *whumping* sound that reminded me of the ringwraiths in *The Lord of the Rings*, and the creature was almost to Anita, who'd turned and stared up wide-eyed at it. I was sure it would claim her, that this brave woman would fall victim to the monsters, but she too hit the ground and covered the back of her head.

Dr. Fleetwood wasn't fast enough.

He was nearly to his white Mercedes when he discovered what was bearing down on him, and by that time it was too late. The Night Flyer extended its taloned feet and seized Fleetwood by the shoulders, and then they were rising above the parking lot, the creature winging toward the forest. Beneath the triumphant screech of the Night Flyer and the approaching cries of the creatures behind us, I heard the soft tinkle of steel on concrete and understood that Dr. Fleetwood had, even as he was consigned to an unimaginable fate, given us a chance to survive.

Glittering like gemstones, his car keys lay a few feet from Anita.

Anita clambered to her feet, snatched them up, and Pierre and I hoofed it after her. She was a few feet from the Mercedes when I heard the familiar *beep-beep* and saw that blessed double flash of headlights indicating the doors were unlocked. Anita tore open the driver's door and plopped down behind the wheel. She was gunning the engine when Pierre jerked the passenger door open.

I heard the shriek of a Night Flyer and glanced back in time to see a creature climb through the shattered glass door of the lobby and take flight. Numbly, I opened a back door, and before I'd even sat down, Anita was backing out of Fleetwood's parking space.

I grasped for the open door, but as Anita swung out of the space and gunned the engine, my door crashed shut, and soon we were knifing through the parking lot. As we reached the end of the row and skidded a hard left turn, I spun in my seat to take in the front of the Sunny Woods Facility. I was sure I'd spot the Night Flyer who'd just climbed through the broken door, but it was nowhere to be found. This should have reassured me, but it didn't. Seeing a Night Flyer was bad; not seeing a Night Flyer until the last moment was worse.

Just ask Fleetwood.

Anita motored past a stretch of vehicles, and then we were swerving to our right, onto the slender-but-paved road that led to Sunny Woods, our backend fishtailing as the Mercedes's tires toiled to grab the asphalt.

"You wanna take it easy?" Pierre said, his voice uncharacteristically tight. He was squeezing the door handle with one hand and the drink holder with the other.

"You look for those creatures," Anita answered. "I'll do the driving."

The forest swallowed us up, the road as murky as the hallways had been.

"Headlights, maybe?" I asked, leaning forward between Anita and Pierre.

Anita's eyes flicked to mine in the overhead mirror. "I was thinking we shouldn't alert them to—"

"I don't think it matters," I said. "Those eyes of theirs... they're used to hunting at night."

"He's right," Pierre said.

Anita compressed her lips, but a moment later, the road lit up.

I relaxed a little. The Night Flyers still might murder us, but at least we wouldn't die in a head-on collision with a tree.

"You've got a lead foot," Pierre remarked.

Anita said nothing, but the Mercedes accelerated. We rumbled around a curve; I clutched the leather seats on either side of me as the car groaned.

"How many speeding tickets you have?" Pierre asked.

"None in almost a year," she answered.

Pierre glanced back at me, eyebrows raised. "That's reassuring."

We were nearing a curve, this one looking even more treacherous.

"Hey, look," Pierre said, shrinking against the seat, "you don't have to prove what a capable driver you are. Just slow down and I won't say another—"

The Mercedes jolted. Above us, something clattered on the roof.

"Jesus!" Anita gasped.

I was staring up at the ceiling when three yellowish hooks punched through the beige fabric.

"Oh hell," Pierre muttered.

I had begun to scoot my body to the floor when another trio of hooks punctured the metal.

"*Ohmygod*," Anita breathed.

"Brakes," Pierre said, but we continued to skid along the curve.

I was afraid of crashing into the forest, but I was even more frightened of the creature on the roof.

"*Brakes*," Pierre repeated.

There was a grating squeal of metal, and then a flap the size of a manhole cover was ripped away above us. The Night Flyer cast the ragged scrap of metal aside and leered at me, its scarlet eyes like seething coals. A taloned hand reached into the Mercedes, the hooked nails descending like a malevolent arcade claw game.

"Hit the damned brakes!" Pierre shouted.

This time the message broke through. Anita stood on the brakes just as we reached a straight span of road. One moment the creature's claws were fastening onto my shirtfront, the next, a swatch of fabric tore away as the creature nosedived over the hood of the Mercedes. It tumbled twenty more feet in a tangle of limbs and leathery flesh. One wing had been ripped in half and a flood of what looked like Indian ink was spraying over its body. The creature's strident wail hammered my eardrums, its whole body vibrating in a paroxysm of agony. Its mouth was stretched wide, its incandescent eyes glazed with suffering.

But Anita didn't hesitate. She stomped on the accelerator, bore down on the broken creature. The Mercedes bounced violently as we crunched over the Night Flyer.

Instead of driving on, Anita threw the car into reverse and rumbled toward the creature again.

This time the Mercedes didn't roll over it, merely bulldozed it behind us, grinding the Night Flyer into the asphalt.

"I think it's dead," Pierre said.

Anita goosed the accelerator one last time, maybe to prove a point, and something snapped under our back bumper. One of the creature's legs, maybe.

"Hey, Anita?" Pierre said.

Anita stopped the Mercedes, glowered at her uncle.

"You killed it."

Anita continued to glower.

Pierre's voice was weary. "Can we please go home now?"

Anita returned her gaze to the road. "Okay. My alpacas need fed."

She slid the car into drive. With a last jounce, we left the mangled Night Flyer carcass behind.

Anita still pushed the Mercedes faster than necessary, but neither I nor Pierre criticized her. I gazed at the skies behind us but distinguished no dragon-like shapes.

It was ten minutes before the woods gave way to cornfields. Another five before the cornfields became forest. No one said anything. The fact that I had finally escaped Sunny Woods provided no solace. There'd been too much carnage for me to be happy. Besides, I was sure that once the bloodbath became public and the dead had been counted, the authorities — Riggs mainly —would realize I was alive.

They would hunt me. They would find me.

I was free now, but it wouldn't last. I didn't know the first thing about living as a fugitive, and I sure as hell wasn't going to let Pierre help me. I didn't want to be responsible for ruining anyone else's life.

A face scudded through my memory. A kind face, framed by curly gray hair. Smiling at me when almost no one else did.

"The lunch lady," I said.

Pierre glanced back at me.

"The lunch lady," I repeated. "The older one. Short gray hair, always nice—"

"Rose," he said.

I looked at him.

"Her name was Rose," Pierre said.

I was short of breath, but this time it had nothing to do with physical exertion. My vision blurred.

"They got her too," Pierre said. Not a question.

My voice was barely a whisper. "She saved my life."

Pierre didn't say anything, but I knew he understood how I felt.

Unable to bear his sympathetic look, I stared into the black summer night. I should have been worried about the Night Flyers swooping out of the sky. But I couldn't think about them anymore. I could only think of the people who'd died.

Nemo Pederson. Rose the lunch lady. Harry. Most of all, Officer Barker.

The tears spilled over my cheeks then, and I was grateful for the darkness of the backseat.

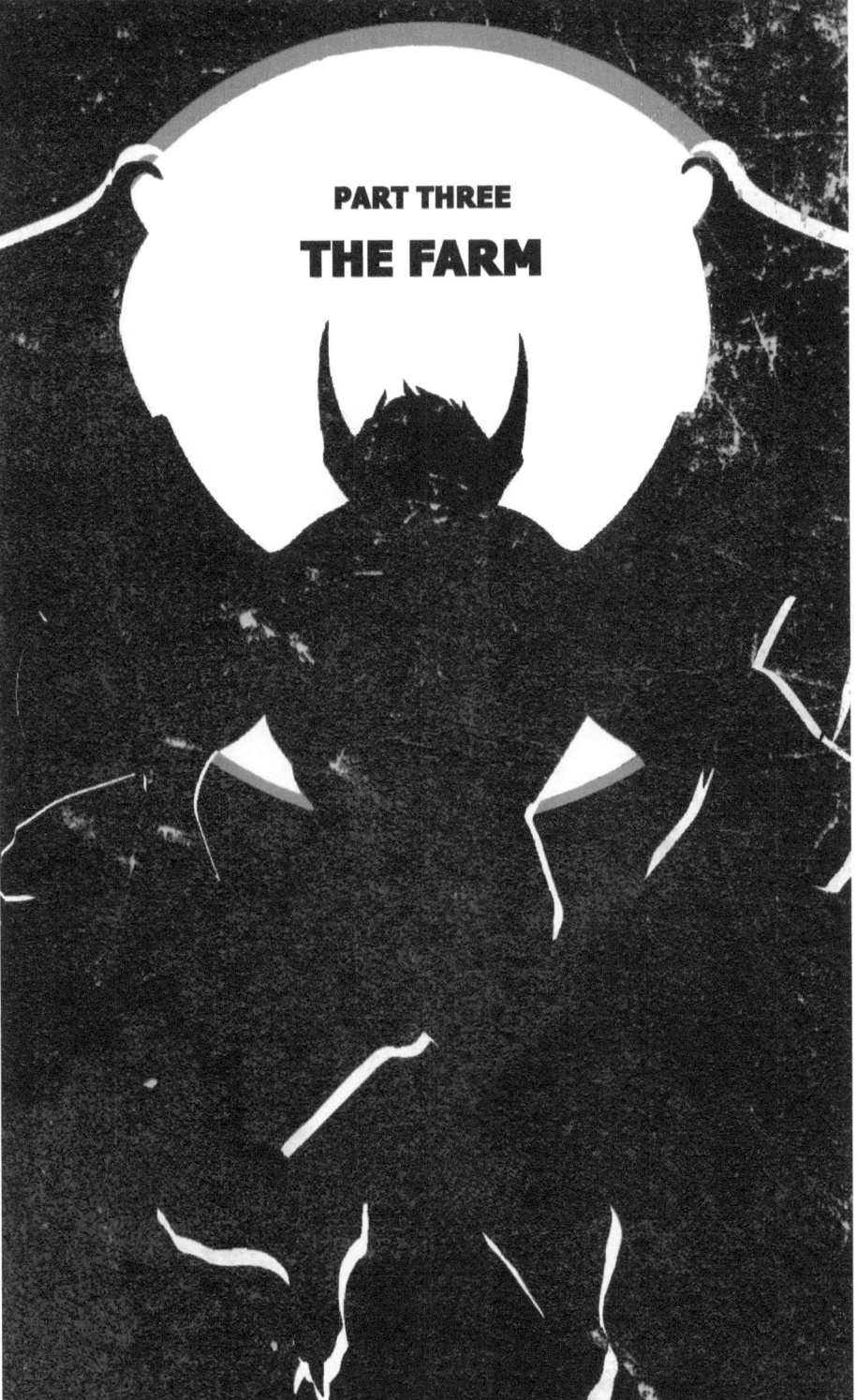

PART THREE

THE FARM

CHAPTER NINE

HOPPER, DESIREE, AND THE KILLER

I don't know what I expected an alpaca farm to look like. I guess I figured it'd be a dreary place with junker cars strewn about the lawn and weeds threading through the property like malignant tumors. This was probably owing to my uncharitable feelings about Dave Myers, Anita's shiftless husband. Granted, I hadn't met the man yet, but I trusted Pierre, and if he viewed Dave as a deadbeat, I was willing to accept that judgment.

What I hadn't taken into account was Anita's influence on the property. Like her uncle, Anita was undoubtedly a hard worker. And like her uncle, Anita possessed an unwavering pride that wouldn't allow a homestead to fall into disrepair.

Of course, it was difficult to tell for sure in the pitch-blackness.

We rolled into the valley at a little past ten P.M. Our headlights spotlighted a short, guard-railed bridge, the creek that it traversed no more than fifteen feet across as it squiggled through the Myers's property. Ahead lay a two-story farmhouse, white siding with black shutters, and beyond that an old but sturdy-looking red barn. At the rear of the property, where the ground began a gradual climb up the valley, rose a legion of trees. They looked like oaks and maples, but with the way the headlights bobbed on the uneven lane, it was difficult to tell.

Anita parked in the gravel driveway and killed the headlights.

"We gonna wake the lord of the manor?" Pierre said.

Anita faced straight ahead. "Don't start."

Pierre glanced at me but didn't push it any further.

Anita slipped the key from the ignition. "Will, we'll put you in the basement. There's a futon there. Uncle Pierre gets the guest bedroom."

"Smells like weed in the basement," Pierre said.

I looked at Anita. "You guys smoke weed?"

Her lips thinned. "We do not smoke weed."

Pierre shrugged. "Smells like it."

Anita glowered at him. "Dave makes his own beer. You know this."

Pierre glanced out the passenger window. "Goes well with the weed."

She swatted her uncle on the shoulder. "Stop trying to bias Will against my husband."

"Will won't need any biasing," Pierre said. "Moment he meets that loser, he's gonna see why I don't like him."

"That is so unfair."

"Unfair is making your wife work all day and come home to take care of twenty animals—"

"Fifteen."

"—while he sits around playing Xbox and making smelly beer."

"He tends the animals all day!"

"Then why do you have to go out there in the dark?"

"He gets headaches. You know that. By nightfall he can barely open his eyes, the pain is so bad."

"Poor fella," Pierre said.

Anita's eyes looked moist. "He's a good man, Uncle Pierre."

"Was one, you mean. Now he's a leech sponging off the system while his wife works herself into the grave."

Anita was out the car door so fast Pierre barely had time to finish his sentence. We watched after her in awkward silence as she bypassed the house and headed for the barn.

"Gotta feed the alpacas," Pierre muttered, shaking his head. "Pitch-black out here, and she's still got chores to do."

"What happened to her husband?" I asked.

"It's late. You need some sleep."

"Really? You're gonna say that?"

Pierre turned in the seat and scowled at me. "What part didn't you understand?"

"Just like the movies. Characters go through something terrible… and the moment they get to safety, they say, 'Let's get some sleep.' Like it's a switch they can flick on and off." I looked at him. "Are *you* tired?"

"We're not talking about me."

"Right. And for the first time in over a year, I'm not locked in a cage. Sleep is the last thing on my mind."

Pierre waved me off. "Whatever. You do what you want."

He opened the door, hauled himself out, and headed for the house.

I got out and savored the night air. I didn't enjoy arguing with Pierre, but the fact that I was free — if only temporarily — overrode any unpleasant residue from our conversation.

After doing a slow 360 and examining the property, I started toward the barn. I knew sleep would be a long time in coming. I'm an insomniac at the best of times, and after witnessing the gruesome murders of people I'd known, I was anything but drowsy.

On the way to the barn, I heard the persistent drum of a woodpecker and scented the gamy odor of large animals. There was a tangerine glow filtering under the barn door. I slid it open and went in.

I immediately regretted it.

Not because of the barn itself. In fact, the smell of hay brought on a wave of pleasant associations. I had a friend back in fourth grade named Steve Gottschalk. His folks had owned a farm with cows instead of alpacas. Chris and Barley and I used to love it there until Steve's dad got a job at the bank in the next county over, and they sold the farm. But the space in which I now stood, with its animal pens and its hayloft, reminded me forcibly of games we used to play in Steve's barn. Mainly jumping from unsafe heights into beds of straw.

The reason I regretted entering Anita's barn was Anita. She was leaning against a support post, forehead on arm, sobbing almost silently. My first instinct was to backpedal to the door and recede into the night. But some impulse made me approach her and ask if she was alright. A stupid question, I knew, but it was what you said when you wanted to help but didn't have the words. At least I wasn't making fun of her husband the way Pierre had.

She swiped a hand over her nose and recommended dumping food from a five-gallon bucket into a trough. "The basement stairs are off the main hall," she said. "You'll find blankets and a pillow in the closet."

"I'm not tired," I said.

"Harry didn't even turn thirty until next month."

I chewed the inside of my mouth. "He cared about you."

She wiped her eyes. "I never did anything with him."

"I didn't say you—"

"He never tried to either," she went on. "He was just a... sweet soul. I can't believe he..." She trailed off, a fresh tear spilling down her cheek.

"I'm sorry he didn't make it," I said.

She didn't respond, only moved on to the next pen.

I kept pace with her and glanced at the animal she'd just fed. There was a nameplate drilled into the top slat of the pen, the sign about eight inches long and six inches high. FRODO, the plate read.

I ran a finger along its length. "That copper?"

"Bronze," she said. "Pierre had them made."

"Must have cost a lot of money."

"He can be a nice person when he's not being an asshole."

I tried to get a look at Frodo the Alpaca, but the animal's face was buried in its food trough. The chewing sounds were very loud in the otherwise quiet barn.

She poured food into the next trough, and I read the name on the second bronze plate: MALORIE.

Like Frodo, Malorie was too immersed in her food to notice me.

When Anita reached the third pen, I ventured closer, hoping to cheer her up. Problem was, I had no idea how to do that. I'd tell her a joke if I knew any. I guess I knew a couple, but they were crude ones I'd heard from Chris, and the prospect of telling a beautiful woman penis jokes made me blush.

For something to do, I reached between the slats to pet the top of the animal's head.

"I wouldn't do that," she cautioned.

I froze. This animal was larger than the others and was staring at my hand with an emotion I couldn't identify. I guess I hadn't spent enough time with alpacas yet to properly read their moods, but the giant snow-colored animal didn't appear pleased with my attentions.

"Hopper's a llama," Anita explained. "He doesn't like people. You put your fingers near his food, you're likely to lose them."

I pulled my hand away. Hopper began to munch his food pellets.

She regarded me again, her look softer. "You wanna feed Desiree?"

"Desiree?"

Anita stepped over to the next pen. "My other llama. My favorite animal."

An alpaca bleated loudly from across the barn aisle. "Sorry, Pennywise," she called. "I love you too, boy."

I grinned. "Did you name them, or did your husband?"

She grunted. "Dave thinks it's silly to name them. Or at least he does now. Back when we first met…"

"What happened to him?"

She pursed her lips and made a little kissing noise. Out of the darkness wandered the tallest, broadest animal I'd seen so far. Nearly six feet tall, the neck and chest muscular-looking, Desiree had brown fur that was splotched with black and white. Though Anita had already filled Desiree's trough, the animal ignored her food and instead poked her furry face over the gate and looked hopefully at Anita.

"There's my girl," Anita said and surprised me by placing her forehead against Desiree's. For the first time that night, Anita smiled. "Desiree, I'd like you to meet Will Burgess."

The giant llama turned and, honest to God, she smiled at me. Better still, Desiree's toothy grin was lopsided, the bottom jaw shifted to the left, so that it appeared she was clowning for my benefit.

Laughing, I reached out, but paused with my fingers a few inches from her fluffy head. "I won't get bitten, will I?"

"She might lick them," Anita said, "but no, I've never known her to bite. She's too ladylike for that."

As if to refute this, Desiree trumpeted a loud fart.

We both laughed. I don't know why, but it surprised me that a llama could break wind.

Anita scratched the llama's neck, "Where are your manners, girl?"

Desiree flashed her toothy grin again and dipped her head toward me. I scratched her behind the ears, figuring this animal, like the dogs I'd known, would enjoy it.

"She likes you," Anita said.

"What's not to like?"

Anita rolled her eyes. "Dork."

From our left an alpaca bleated. "Keep your pants on, Rapunzel. There's enough for everybody."

I tried to keep my voice casual. "Lots of farms have four wheelers and dirt bikes."

"I know what you're thinking, and you can forget about it."

"What?" I demanded. But she'd seen through me.

"Riggs will figure out who lived and who died tonight." Anita emptied what pellets remained in the bucket, and a jet-black alpaca — RAPUNZEL, the nameplate said — began to gobble them up. Moving toward the barn entrance, Anita continued. "The entire agency will cordon off Sunny Woods and start the cover-up, just like they did after Peaceful Valley."

I wondered how many people had died tonight. Had it been more than the two hundred who'd been slaughtered at the state park? I supposed there could be survivors hiding in Sunny Woods, but the victims would far outnumber the survivors.

Why didn't anyone come to help? I wondered.

The question stopped me. Sure, Sunny Woods was in the middle of nowhere, but it had phones, didn't it? And nearly every adult who'd worked there would have owned a cell phone.

Yet when we were driving away on that tortuous country road, we hadn't seen any vehicles approaching. How could that be?

"The last thing you need," Anita said, "is to be seen. That house where your sister's living?"

"Yeah?" I asked, an edge to my voice.

"That'll be the first place they look. They'll be sure to monitor those friends of yours too."

"Leave them out of it," I muttered. "How far is the Westfalls' from here?"

"Ten miles at least."

Ten miles, I thought. It didn't seem so far.

"What about Shadeland?" I asked.

"Forget Shadeland," she answered, opening a giant wooden box and retrieving a metal scoop.

"Look," I said, trying to keep my voice level, "I appreciate all you did tonight. I wouldn't be alive if not for you and Pierre."

"You want to do me a kindness?" she asked, stopping in mid-scoop. "Grab one of those buckets and help me feed the animals."

I did as she instructed, snagging the handle of a blue five-gallon bucket and placing it by the food box.

"I understand your need to see your sister," she said.

"Oh you do, huh? You know how that feels?"

She rested her arms on the edge of the stomach-high box. "No, I don't. And I'm sorry you've had to endure all this—"

"Prove it then," I said. "Let me borrow your four-wheeler."

"We don't have a four-wheeler." I opened my mouth, but she overrode me. "*Or* a dirt bike. Or a golf cart or a hang glider." Her eyes shifted downward. "Don't do that."

I stared at her for a moment, then glanced down at my right hand, which had bunched into a fist and was punching my hip in frustration.

I compressed my lips. "You don't wanna help me, fine. I'll get on your computer and look up the Westfalls' address."

"It's password-protected."

"Then I'll hitchhike to Lafayette," I half-yelled.

"There's anger in you."

"Of *course* there's anger!" I spun and heaved the empty bucket across the barn. It cracked the wall and clattered on the floor. I ran a hand through my hair. "Everyone treats me like I'm either unstable or something... freakish."

"Your eyes," she said.

"I know they turn green," I said through gritted teeth. "I know something's wrong with me. But being locked up isn't going to make me better."

"Being institutionalized has nothing to do with what's happening inside you."

I spun and saw her recoil. "Don't you think I know that?"

"You're scaring me, Will."

I tapped my chest. "*I'm* scaring me. But you know what scares me even more?"

She didn't retreat from me, but she looked like she had an urge to.

"Never seeing my sister again!" I shouted and was appalled at the hoarseness of my voice. "I'm going to find her, with or without your help."

"It's late."

"I don't care if it's three in the morning—"

"It will be by the time you get there," she cut in, "and that's if you take Dave's bike."

I felt a leap of hope. "Is it a motorcycle?"

"It's a ten-speed. Before his accident, he used to ride it everywhere."

I looked around. "Where is it?"

"It's stored away and will be until morning. I'll get it down for you then."

I opened my mouth to argue, but Anita's words sank in. "You'll help me see Peach?"

"I can see you're gonna do this whether I help you or not. I might as well give you a nudge in the right direction."

My emotions have gotten weird since last summer's horrible events, and at that moment, the weirdness all gushed out. I began to laugh and smile so widely my jaw ached. I also started to cry. And to blush. Weeping uncontrollably in front of a beautiful woman wasn't high on my list of favorite activities.

But to her credit, Anita didn't seem embarrassed by my behavior. Instead, she nodded. "Let's finish feeding the animals, and I'll give you something to help you sleep. In the morning, I'll show you the route to the Westfalls'."

"Can you drive me there?"

"Hundreds of people are dead. A banged-up car belonging to one of the victims is sitting in front of my house. At some point tomorrow, Riggs and his agents are going to descend on the farm, and my uncle and I are going to have to lie like hell in order to keep you safe."

"Lie about what?"

"About how you got killed last night."

At my thunderstruck look, she explained, "The only way those bastards are gonna stop chasing you is if they think you're dead."

—

I WAS SKEPTICAL about sleep, but whatever Anita gave me — the pill was gigantic and got lodged in my esophagus long enough to make me fear choking to death — made me lethargic within ten minutes.

Within fifteen, I was zonked out on Anita's futon.

When I awoke, sunlight was blowtorching my face. I shielded my eyes from the basement window and wondered if this was how a vampire felt when caught outside at dawn.

I threw my feet onto the carpeted floor, stretched, and yawned. I winced at the horrible taste in my mouth and hoped Anita had a spare toothbrush.

The thought was swept away in a tide of recollection.

The Night Flyer attack.

The brutal murder of Rose the Lunch Lady.

Harry and Officer Barker sacrificing themselves.

Dr. Fleetwood being borne away like a baby rabbit in a hawk's talons.

By the time I reached the top of the stairs, I was running. I rounded the corner, my bare feet slipping on the hardwood floor, and stumbled into the kitchen.

Where Pierre, Anita, and a man I assumed was her husband sat eating at a round table.

Sometimes appearances are surprising, but not in this case. Dave Myers looked exactly as I would have guessed. Pale complexion, sad eyes. His hair was trimmed short, but it still managed to seem disheveled. There was a salting of chalk-white hair mixed with the black, and I wondered how old he was. Anywhere from a poorly preserved thirty-five to a decent-enough fifty. He wore a black *Star Wars* t-shirt with the iconic yellow lettering, and he had too much arm hair.

They all stared at me, Pierre and Anita with good humor, Dave with an expression I couldn't interpret.

I looked at Anita. "Where's the map?"

She merely gazed back at me.

"The route to Lafayette," I prompted. "You said the Westfalls live on the outskirts—"

"Sit down and have some eggs," Pierre said.

"I've gotta go to my sister. I don't have time—"

"You're right, Will," Anita interrupted. "We don't have much time. Which is why you need to trust us."

Trust wasn't my strong suit.

"You didn't get the kid some clothes?" Dave said, leaning back in his chair. "He looks like an escaped mental patient."

I stared at him. He winced. "Sorry," he muttered.

"Why don't *you* help him?" Pierre asked Dave. "You two are about the same height."

Dave patted his belly. "Not the same waistline."

"Well, he's not going to wear anything of mine," Anita said, enunciating enough to show her impatience, "so maybe you could find some things that are tight on you."

Dave stared back at Anita, eyes hooded. I could practically feel the tension crackling between them. Pierre sipped his orange juice, unperturbed.

For something to do, I ambled toward the empty place setting. When I pulled back the chair, Dave asked, "Is that blood?"

I looked down at my clothes, which were spattered with the creatures' ichor, my own blood, and some stains that belonged to other victims.

Dave had stopped chewing. "You know what? You do need some new clothes. C'mon."

He pushed away from the table, and I trailed after him, noticing as I did how badly he limped. I followed him up the stairs.

We entered the owner's suite. There were pictures on the dressers. I saw a much younger Pierre dancing with a woman I assumed was his wife, the picture maybe taken at some wedding reception.

"Nah," Dave said from the closet. "Those pants are big even for me."

The closet was modest, but it was a walk-in. One corner appeared to be Dave's, while the rest was packed with Anita's clothes. I stood outside and watched Dave rummage.

"It doesn't have to be anything special," I said.

"That's good," he answered. "Because I don't have anything special." He dragged a heavy-looking coat from the back corner, held it up. "Don't suppose you want my high school letter jacket?" He grinned and chucked the jacket aside.

I'd noticed there were several faded gold bars on it. "What sports did you do?"

"Football, wrestling, and baseball."

He held up a pair of jeans that looked like they'd been gnawed by rats. "These are a thirty-two waist. Haven't fit me for fifteen years." A mirthless chuckle. "Don't know why I haven't thrown them out. Probably telling myself I'll lose weight."

"They're great," I lied.

He slid them off the hanger, tossed them to me. "With the heat outside, all those holes will give you extra ventilation." His eyes lowered, and he frowned. "Uh, do you need something to wear beneath…"

"My underwear are fine."

He gave a relieved nod. He crossed to his dresser, wincing whenever he put weight on his bad leg. "You'll want a short-sleeved shirt."

It was July, I remembered, what used to be my favorite month.

I was about to tell him to grab any old shirt when he glanced at me over his shoulder. "Don't suppose you're a Cubs fan?"

My grin must have been huge because he smiled back. He fished a blue T-shirt out of the dresser, wadded it up, and flung it toward me. I caught it, grasped it by the shoulders, and let it unfurl. The name on the back was HOERNER.

Nico Hoerner. The Cubbies' second baseman. My favorite player.

"Hell of a hitter, isn't he?" Dave ventured.

"He is," I said, examining the Cubs' logo on the front. "At least he was when I got put away."

"One of the best gloves in the league, too," Dave said. "And fast. Stole over forty bases last year."

I smiled at this, but the smile was short-lived. I hated the negative run of my thoughts, but I couldn't help it: the reminder of all the games I'd missed watching… all the arguments Chris and I would have had because he'd been a Cardinals fan… all that time we'd lost… it made me want to scream.

If Dave picked up on any of that, he didn't let on. "Come to think of it…" He slid open a drawer at knee level. "Here," he said, retrieving a pair of cargo shorts. "These have a drawstring, so it doesn't matter that my waist is twice as wide as yours."

I gladly accepted the shorts.

"Need anything else?" He started toward the door.

"I don't suppose you have any shoes, do you? I mean, this stuff is great and all—"

He put up a hand, limped toward the door. "Yeah, yeah. I get it. You don't have to be artificially nice just to wrangle an old pair of sneakers from me."

"I wasn't being artificial."

He stopped at the door. "Sure you were, kid. Everybody's artificial. Pierre hates my guts but keeps it to himself most of the time. My wife thinks I'm worthless. I know you've had a rough time of it, but you're not the only one. When your wife thinks you're a failure… that's a hell of a way to live."

I struggled for some kind of response, but Dave saved me the trouble. He went out.

I moved down the stairs in my new clothes and found a pair of ancient Asics running shoes awaiting me. I sat on the bottom step and slid them on. Slightly snug, but without socks on, the fit was acceptable. I caught the aroma of fried meat and realized my stomach was growling, so I headed to the kitchen, where I found Pierre.

"Good thing you came when you did," he said as I sat down next to him. "I was about to steal the bacon off your plate."

My mouth watered at the sight of bacon strips, even if they were cold by now. I tore into one and decided it was the best I'd ever tasted. Rose the Lunch Lady had tried her hardest, but she was limited to whatever food the higher-ups at Sunny Woods ordered. But this… this was proper breakfast food. Bacon, scrambled eggs, and orange juice. Even the triangle of soggy toast gave me chills.

Pierre gestured toward the front of the house. "Anita's on the phone with that Castro prick."

I heard Anita's voice. Though it was muffled, I could tell her tone was frosty. It made sense that Castro had called instead of Riggs, who'd believe himself above such pedestrian fieldwork. He'd have his underlings do the investigating, and once everything was squared away, he'd lumber in and take the credit.

I swigged orange juice, wiped my mouth. "How am I going to get—"

"Dave's taking you," Pierre answered. "Castro instructed all of us to remain here — me, Anita, Dave… as far as we're concerned, you got killed last night — but I'll be damned if I'm staying here at Alpaca Land all day. My wife needs me."

I studied Pierre's face. This morning he looked his age, the seams in his forehead deeper. "Is your wife healthy?"

He turned to me, eyebrows raised. "Why, how nice of you to ask. Only took you a year."

I cringed, realizing he was right. It's funny. No one thinks of himself as self-absorbed, but pretty much everybody is.

Chastened, I asked, "What's wrong with your wife?"

"Arthritis," he said, looking like he'd tasted something foul. "She's had it for ages. Used to give piano lessons, but now she can barely hold a fork. It's worse when it's humid. Like today."

Pierre made to rise, but I said, "Why do you hate Dave so much?"

He looked at me then, and in his look I could see the internal debate of the adult who doesn't know what a kid is ready to hear. He must have decided I was old enough for whatever it was because he nodded. "I'll tell you, but only if you promise not to ask questions."

"Okay. No questions."

Pierre leaned toward me and said, "Dave murdered my sister."

CHAPTER TEN

THE CRASH, THE GROVE

I opened my mouth, but Pierre stilled me with a patented Pierre glare. "No questions," he reminded me.

"But—"

He raised an index finger, his eyes fierce.

I slumped in my seat. After a beat, I asked, "So you're fifty-seven, huh?"

"You got a problem with that?"

I shrugged. "I thought you were younger."

He finished off his coffee and wiped his lips. "I aged twenty years last night."

"What are we going to do?"

"I'm gonna see my wife." He rose and pointed at me. "Don't do anything stupid."

Before I could respond, he went out, and moments later, he was motoring away in Dr. Fleetwood's battered white Mercedes.

When I got done showering and brushing my teeth — neither activity had ever felt better — I stepped onto the front porch, where Dave Myers waited for me in a white rocking chair. He rose and waved me toward the detached garage on the other side of the driveway. When the garage door trundled up, my skin broke into goosebumps.

Dave noticed my expression and frowned. "Something wrong with the Highlander?"

Nothing, I thought. *Nothing at all. Except for the fact that it's the same make, model, and color of the vehicle in which Carl Padgett held me hostage last summer.*

"Hey," Dave said with a nervous smile, "we could ride bikes, but that'd take forever."

I swallowed. "I thought that was the plan anyway."

"My wife doesn't want me to get involved, but when she brought you here, she involved me. Whether I loan you my old bike or drive you there myself, I'm still aiding and abetting an escaped delinquent, right?"

I tried to return his smile but couldn't. An icy scrim of sweat had broken out on my neck. Knowing how irrational I was being but unable to dispel the feeling, I climbed into the Highlander. Dave fired it up, reversed out of the garage, described a tight half-loop in the driveway, and drove up the lane.

He winced. "God, the sun's bright. Forgot my shades in the house."

We rolled over the bridge and the short span of creek. I was scanning the slow rise of the land, the meadows, the intermittent spray of trees, when something drew my attention. Something dangling from an oak tree in the middle of the meadow.

"Stop," I said.

"Need to take a leak?"

"Stop the car," I repeated.

He did. "What's up?"

"That," I said, pointing. "Do you guys ever use it?"

"Oh, that thing. I put it up when Anita got pregnant. We lost the baby. And every baby since." He sighed. "I guess I never bothered to take it down."

I swallowed. "I'm really sorry about the miscarriages, and I know this is a weird thing to ask right now. But… do you have a knife?"

He shrugged. "I keep a Swiss Army knife in the glove box."

"Perfect."

He leaned over, peered through my window. "Hope you're a good climber."

<hr>

WHEN THE JOB was finished — it *had* been a difficult tree to climb, and I'd almost broken my neck trying to saw through the rope — we set off again and made it to the country road.

No sign of any government vehicles yet.

Dave glanced at the object in my lap and said, "Don't know what you're gonna do with that thing. Camelot isn't exactly in the middle of nowhere."

"Camelot?"

"The neighborhood your sister's foster parents live in," he said. "Anita looked them up this morning."

As we rolled down the lane, I chewed my lip. What exactly *did* I plan to do? The Westfalls considered me a menace. Hell, they considered Peach a danger to their family, and she was only six.

Seven, a voice reminded. *She's seven now.*

The thought knocked the wind out of me. I'd lost more than a year of her life. She'd lost her mom and her big brother. And she'd been going through everything alone. The realization set my throat aflame. I turned toward the passenger window, hoping Dave hadn't noticed my frustration.

It wasn't fair. Peach had been struggling to begin with. No money, a crappy house, shabby clothes. Her peers had made fun of her at Shadeland Elementary, and she'd been self-conscious about it. How much worse would it be for her now, without a family that loved her? Without her big brother to remind her how amazing she was? Goddamn it…

"Pierre tell you why he despises me so much?" Dave asked.

I used the shoulder of the Cubs shirt to dry my eyes. "Uh-uh."

"You wondered though."

"Sure," I said, glad of the subject change. "Wouldn't you?"

He didn't answer, instead halted at a stop sign that divided the country road from Highway 25, the main route between Shadeland and Lafayette. I expected to spy a caravan of black SUVs approaching, but there was only a single pick-up truck, hunter green with rust showing around the wheel wells.

When the pick-up passed, Dave pulled onto the highway and said, "Christmas Eve. It must've been… oh, four years ago? Pretty sure it's been four. By the time the night I'm talking about happened, Anita's parents would've been in their late sixties. Not old or anything, but… I don't know. Overly cautious? Neither one liked to drive in bad weather."

I remained silent, but a pall of foreboding had crept over me. A part of me didn't want to hear the story. I was sure it was going to be unpleasant.

"In spite of what Pierre might have told you about me, I'm not an evil person. Oh, I've got my imperfections, and I know I've sort of…" A brittle laugh. "…what, let myself go? Since the accident, I mean. But…" He passed a hand over his mouth. "You go through something like that, it never really leaves you, you know?"

I said nothing.

"I volunteered to pick up Anita's parents in Lafayette on Christmas Eve. You know, trying to be nice. Anita's mother, she pretended to like me, but I could tell she was just being civil for her daughter's sake. Anita's dad, he never trusted me. Bill was his name. Bill Raines."

A black SUV rumbled past in the other direction; Dave watched it recede in the overhead mirror. Apparently deciding it wasn't part of some covert government agency, he asked, "Where was I?"

"Christmas Eve. Bad weather."

"It *was* bad weather. Dreadful, when I think back on it. But I'd never had a wreck. And the Nissan Sentra I drove, it was ultra-reliable. I told Anita's folks I'd pick them up around noon and drive them home around nightfall."

"Was Pierre there?"

Dave looked at me dourly. "Of course he was there. Pierre and his wife, Bill and Janet, and Anita and me. Six of us." He smiled, but there was pain in it. "Or seven, depending on how you count it."

I frowned at him.

He turned that doleful smile on me. "Anita was four months pregnant at the time. The second time we were expecting."

Oh man, I thought.

Dave rasped a hand over his chin stubble. "We'd also invited Pierre's boy Ruben like we always did, but like always, Ruben refused."

I could see how sore a subject it was and decided not to press him on the estrangement. If ever a family was cursed, it seemed that Pierre and Anita's was.

And you're adding to their misery, a voice in my head murmured.

I shifted in my seat.

"The irony of it is," Dave continued, "we were having a great time. Everyone but Anita's mom was playing euchre — she considered card-playing un-Christian — but even she sat beside Anita at the table, talking about whatever moms and daughters talk about. Bill actually laughed at a few of my jokes, and when we opened presents and he saw the smoker I'd picked out, he howled with delight."

"Smoker?"

"For cooking ribs and—"

I waved him off. "Yeah, yeah, I got it."

Though I didn't. Not really. Mom hadn't been too invested in the culinary arts. If it wasn't mac-and-cheese or something microwaveable, Mom would have judged it beyond her abilities.

I still missed her.

We'd reached a long, curving hill on Highway 25. Three-Lane Hill, I remembered it being called. So many accidents had occurred there, and so many lives had been lost, that they removed the extra lane and forbade cars from passing. Common sense, really, but sometimes it took terrible events for common sense to prevail.

Dave sighed. "When it was nearly dark, Janet started making noise about heading back to Lafayette. She was always a worrier, and the conditions worried her."

"Were the roads bad?"

"What do you think?" He shook his head. "What do they call that stuff on pennies? That green stuff—"

"Patina?"

He looked at me. "Anita told me you were a smart kid. There was a patina of snowfall, and I figured that would give me traction. You know, snow's not such a difficult thing to drive in. Not if it's just snow.

"Despite Janet's nerves, we stayed at the farm. Anita's dad, he was thawing toward me, and I guess I wanted to press my advantage." He tapped the wheel with his thumbs. "Naw, that isn't quite right. I wasn't trying to get anything from him. I just... my father and I were never close and having Anita's dad like me — or tolerate me, at least — felt good. Like having a dad, you know?"

I nodded. I knew the longing well.

"Bill normally didn't drink, but that night he was drinking Budweiser with me. Nothing earth-shattering, but... we were bonding."

Some atonal chord inside me began to sound.

"Anita got restless. She *is* her mother's daughter, after all. She pulled me aside and said we needed to get going, but I said what's the problem? We're all having fun. At some point Bill and I started watching *A Christmas Story*. You know the movie?"

"'You'll shoot your eye out,'" I quoted.

"That's right. Ralphie and the leg lamp. I didn't realize anything was wrong until Pierre stalks in and stands over me. 'We've got a problem,'" he says.

"'Are we out of beer?'" I asked.

"Pierre shook his head. You know that judgmental look he gets?"

I knew it well, but in this circumstance, I fully commiserated with Pierre. Driving at night in an Indiana winter is nothing to take lightly.

Dave went on. "The point is, Anita was pissed at me for upsetting her mom. Janet was crying, and Pierre told me it was time to go. *Now.* It wasn't a request."

"What time was it?"

"Almost ten. I didn't realize it was that long after dark, but like I said—"

"You were having fun."

He shot me a stony look. "Don't do that, kid. Don't sit there in judgment. They gave me a breathalyzer afterward, and I was below the legal limit."

How far below? I wondered.

"You can guess the rest. We were going too fast. The roads were worse than I thought. Under that snow, there was a lot of ice." He ran his tongue around his mouth. "Some of it was black ice."

"Where did it happen?"

"Up here," he said, nodding.

We were coming to a steep hill, one I'd always pretended was the first large drop of a roller coaster, the kind that gave you butterflies in your stomach.

"Bill and I were talking. Janet wasn't speaking, but I could tell she was mad at me. I guess I resented that. Maybe that was why I was going so fast.

"We were halfway down the hill when I began to lose control. First, there was a wobble from the back end of the Sentra. Then, the road in front of us started to slide. I fought the skid, did exactly what you're supposed to do. But I overcorrected."

Dave took a breath. "We spun toward the shoulder. Only there *was* no shoulder. Just a steep drop-off."

I realized we were approaching the hill. But rather than slowing down, Dave bore down on the pedal, the Highlander accelerating to nearly seventy. "The crazy part of it was, I didn't have a seatbelt on. That's how impervious I felt." He shook his head. "So stupid..."

We crested the hill and began the long descent. I noticed a guardrail to our right, on the other side of which lay a deep, sunless ravine.

"They've fixed it since," he said. "But... here's where we went off the road."

The butterflies in my stomach had nothing to do with the steepness of the hill. I felt like I might be sick.

"I was thrown free of the car," he said. "Right through the windshield." He rubbed his head, just above the hairline. "There's a plate up here. And of course, I've got the limp."

"Bill and Janet?"

"What the hell do you think? The Sentra tumbled end over end I don't know how many times. By the time it came to rest, upside down, they were dead."

A firestorm of thoughts blazed through my mind, some of them sympathetic. But among the many thoughts, I have to confess, was this: *I don't blame Pierre for hating you.*

He propped an elbow on the door and stared miserably ahead. "You religious, Will?"

I supposed I was. The teachings of Jesus always rang true to me, but frankly, I think Jesus would be appalled by the behavior of many who claim to follow Him.

"Yeah," Dave said. "I suspect you are religious. Everybody around here is. So let me ask you, why does God let things like that happen?"

I didn't know what to say.

He stared at me, his eyes red-rimmed. "I mean it, kid. Why the hell would God let a stupid, silly accident like that take the lives of two good people and leave me broken and... *hated* by my own wife?"

"I don't think Anita hates you."

His mouth curdled into an ugly grin. "You don't, huh? The teenaged expert?"

"I didn't say I was—"

"A hypocrite? Because that's what you are, kid. That's what everyone is who claims there's some higher power out there." A bitter laugh. "I take that back. Maybe there *is* a higher power. Maybe it's those flying dragons that killed all those people last night. Or the white monsters who slaughtered everyone at Peaceful Valley."

I decided not to answer. What was there to say?

And if I didn't say anything to piss Dave off, maybe he'd get me to the Westfalls. And if we got there, maybe I could catch a glimpse of Peach.

I dug my fingers into my legs and stared straight ahead.

I'm coming, Peach. Please be there when we arrive.

—

WE'D RIDDEN IN uneasy silence for several minutes when Dave yelled, "Camelot!"

I jumped, adrenaline pumping through my limbs. I glared at him.

Dave smiled. "Haven't you seen *Monty Python*? That's what King Arthur yells right before the musical number."

I knew the scene well. Chris, Barley, and I had watched *Monty Python and the Holy Grail* a couple years ago, rewatching the part with the killer rabbit about twenty times. The thought of Chris, dead, and Barley, inaccessible to me, cast a darker cloud over my mood.

"Luck's on your side," Dave said.

I looked at him, uncomprehending. He nodded. "The Westfalls are at the end of that cul-de-sac. One of those big houses, backing up to the trees."

He didn't need to explain. If I could approach from behind… hide in the forest at the rear of the property, maybe I could catch sight of Peach. It was still early, but the day was warm. It was possible she'd head outside to play.

You won't be that lucky, a cynical voice said.

"Piss off," I muttered.

Dave looked aggrieved. "Hey, I drove you here. You don't need to—"

"I wasn't talking to you. I was… never mind. Where do we park?"

Dave cut a left turn. "Next road over. Maybe it's a dead end too." We drove for a spell, and he turned right. We parked at the end of a road that paralleled the Westfalls'.

My mouth was dry. I estimated we were about sixty yards from the Westfalls' property. Dead ahead lay a pair of vacant lots.

Dave was watching me. His voice was softer. "You know, kid, this probably isn't going to work. If those government guys figure out you escaped last night, they're going to be hunting for you. They'll tell the Westfalls. Your sister might not even be here.

They might have taken her into custody. You know, to protect her from you."

"What the hell's your point?"

He shrugged. "Guess I don't want you to get your feelings hurt."

I searched for irony in his eyes, but after a few moments, I gave up trying. I reached for the door handle.

"Will," he said.

That stopped me. Since we'd left the farm, I'd been "kid."

"Have you thought about what this might do to your sister?"

"What's that supposed to mean?"

"I'm only saying…" He gestured. "Maybe she's returning to normal. You don't want to bring all her pain back, do you?"

I wanted to tell him how wrong he was. How time wasn't always a healer. How time could be the fingernail that scratches the scab. How time keeps it bleeding and raw and only digs the wound deeper. I thought of Chris. Of my mom. Of the pit inside me that deepened and spread every time I remembered I'd never see them again.

I opened my door and got out.

"Wait," he said, leaning toward me. "You're really taking that with you?"

I redoubled my grip on the rope.

"I'll wait for you," he said.

"It might be hours."

"I've got time." He rummaged through the glovebox, fished out a snatch of magazines. *Craft Beer and Brewing*, one cover said. "I'm considering dry-hopping a stout."

Having no idea what he was talking about, I flipped the door shut and set off across the vacant lot.

There was no discernible path, but the forest wasn't that dense. Not like Savage Hollow, the woods that bordered my old home.

The last place I'd seen my sister.

Dave's right, a voice cautioned. *Peach won't be here, so it's best not to get your hopes up. And even if she is, what then? She'll be with her foster parents. The moment you show your face, they'll be on the phone to Riggs, and then it's Westchester Prison for you and an orphanage for Peach. In other words, the end.*

I brushed the thought away and padded through the woods. It was risky to pass so close to the subdivision, but I was afraid if I ventured too far, I'd lose my bearings, and then I'd never locate the Westfalls' property.

I needn't have worried. Even moving briskly, I was able to maintain a uniform distance from the forest's edge. Soon, I reached the cul-de-sac and the broad, pie-shaped lots that bordered the woods. The house, I remembered, had been a brick two-story, with a three-car garage. A couple properties down, I caught glimpses of the dark brick through a screen of spruce trees.

I cut a diagonal path toward the yard. Then I received a shock: the layout of their backyard was similar to that of my old house. There was a shed on the western side of the property, a large sandbox. And behind that, about twenty feet from the forest, loomed a giant sycamore with down-hanging branches as broad as my waist.

It was perfect.

Without delay, I broke from my place of concealment and leaped to snag hold of the lowest branch. I climbed higher, and soon, I had the rope fastened securely. I made for the forest's edge. There, I waited.

Had I thought the situation through, I might have brought a paperback with me. So I had to content myself with observing the house from the woods. After maybe a half-hour, the sun began to dim, a drab flotilla of clouds creeping over it. With the clouds came the speculation:

Had the Night Flyers attacked Sunny Woods because of me? As I wondered this, I felt a peculiar mental tug somewhere in the base of my skull.

(...are you...)

I twitched at the voice. The forest around me, relatively quiet to begin with, had grown hushed. No birdsong or cicada sounded; no animals scuttered through the undergrowth.

(Where... are you...)

This time the voice was louder. There was a sinister quality to it, a hunger.

(...coming for you, Will...)

I put my hands on my temples. "Stop it," I murmured.

(We're coming for you)

"Stop it!" I yelled and clamped a hand over my mouth. God, what was wrong with me? What if someone heard? What if they followed my voice and discovered me here, a shaggy-haired kid in a Cubs shirt, sweating and talking to himself—

I saw her.

The figure descending the back steps onto the paver patio was a couple inches taller than I remembered, but it was unquestionably my sister. My leg muscles tensed as though they would take control of me and leap out of the forest. There was another figure with her, this one maybe my age, with flowing black hair. But I barely registered her presence.

I could only stare at my little sister and feel my heart break at the injustice of our separation. She moved into the yard, where a rainbow-colored ball lay in the grass. Peach bent, picked it up, attempted to punt it, but shanked it off the side of her foot. Rather than chasing after it, she made a fist and punched herself in the thigh.

I felt a twinge of disquiet.

"It's okay, Peach," the other girl said, and the use of Peach's preferred name made me turn and really study the other girl for the first time. She was tall, of Asian descent, and her bespectacled eyes were filled with concern.

This could only be Darcy.

I'd never met her, of course, but the letter Pierre had smuggled to me from Peach had been transcribed, with a few editorial comments, by Darcy. I felt a rush of affection for her.

Peach sank to the grass.

"Hey," Darcy said, striding toward her. "You don't need to—"

"I'm terrible at kicking!" Peach snapped.

"Take it easy. You're not terrible."

"*You* don't miss," Peach countered.

Darcy laughed. "Of course I do. And I'm almost ten years older than you. I should be a little better, right?"

Darcy stopped and stared up at something.

I hunkered down in the weeds so Darcy wouldn't see me.

"What is that?" Darcy asked.

"What?" Peach answered.

"That thing in the tree." Darcy took a step forward. "Is that a swing?"

This time Peach did look up, and when she did, her features went slack. She got slowly to her feet, her eyes never leaving the swing, and began to walk toward it.

"Did Ken put it up yesterday?" Darcy asked.

Ken, I assumed, was Mr. Westfall, but I didn't have time to think about that. Because Peach had uttered the magic words.

"What did you say?" Darcy asked, striding after her.

"Goon-goon," Peach said.

"*Goon-goon,*" I whispered to myself.

Darcy was scowling. "What the hell's a goon-goon?"

"It's this," Peach said, smiling in disbelief. She grasped the rope, ran her fingers over it. She examined the faded blue circular seat, the one Anita and Dave had hung from a tree in the hopes that their children would one day swing from it.

Darcy stood beside Peach. "I wonder who put it up?"

Peach froze. Her smile disappeared, in its place a look of astonishment. Her face swiveled toward the woods. Her eyes began to sweep the tree line.

"Will?" she asked in a hushed voice.

You can't let her see you! the voice in my head shouted. *If she does, she'll be in as much trouble as you are.*

I turned away and jogged stoop-backed through the undergrowth.

"Will?" she called, louder this time.

I moved faster, the brambles plucking at my cargo shorts. Something whipped me in the face, and my eyes watered. There were two voices behind me now, Peach shouting after me and Darcy calling to Peach. I crashed through a pair of trees, tripped, and did a header in a bed of pine needles. My vision was blurred, and my airway had constricted to the width of a coffee straw. I made to stand, but the toe of my sneaker hooked on a vine and sent me sprawling again.

I landed on my forearms. Wincing, I pushed to my hands and knees, and that's when I heard Peach's voice, just on the other side of the trees. I looked up, heart slamming, and realized I'd fallen in a small glade in the center of a pine grove.

"Will?" Peach called.

Maybe, I thought, if I waited here and didn't move, they'd continue on. Or return to their expensive brick house where Peach wouldn't have to worry about having that scab ripped open. Losing me, I decided, had been a gift. I was tainted, poisonous to others, and Peach would be better off—

"Is that you?" Peach's voice asked.

The pine boughs stirred, parted, and then my little sister, my amazing little sister, whose lips were trembling and whose eyes were brimming with tears, stepped through.

On my knees, I gazed back at her.

"Will?" she said.

My face must have broken into a smile because hers did too.

"Hey, Peach," was all I could say.

And then she was in my arms and sobbing into my neck as hard as I was sobbing into her soft brown hair.

CHAPTER ELEVEN

PEACH

I don't know how long we hugged each other and wept. But I did remember to take the advice of a Billy Joel song my mom used to play: "Leave a Tender Moment Alone."

To Darcy's credit, she left the moment alone as well. I wasn't even aware that she was watching us from a respectful distance until I'd sobbed and rocked with my little sister for well over a minute. And when I did finally notice Darcy, with snot slicking my upper lip and my cheeks soaked with tears, I didn't feel as embarrassed as I probably should have. After all, I was a total mess, and Darcy, I realized as my eyes refocused, was quite pretty.

She wasn't what I'd expected.

I know how stupid this sounds, but it occurred to me that I'd been picturing Velma, the bookish young woman from the old *Scooby Doo* cartoons. Nothing wrong with Velma, of course, but Darcy had the sort of looks that made you do a double-take. Not supermodel looks; she wasn't six feet tall, and she wasn't wearing some weird futuristic outfit. But when she smiled, you could see she meant it.

It's fair to say I liked Darcy right away. Mainly because she had taken care of Peach.

I closed my eyes and kissed Peach's head. She'd rested her cheek on my shoulder, facing away from me, so I was able to inhale the scent of her hair. I frowned. It smelled like it did when she avoided baths. Oily. The odor of neglect.

I kissed her head one more time and mustered a smile. "Don't they make you shower at the Westfalls?"

Peach swiveled her head to look at me, and seeing her that close, seeing the tearful eyes and the heart-shaped chin, my heart nearly broke.

"Only on Thursday nights," Peach said.

I stared at her. "What's only on Thursday nights?"

"Showers," Darcy said.

I glanced at Darcy.

Arms crossed, she gave a one-shoulder shrug. "The Westfalls run it like a factory. My nights are Wednesday and Saturday — I get two showers a week since I'm older. Peach's are on Thursdays." A barely perceptible curling of her lips. "Roberta likes to conserve water."

I thought of the gigantic brick house on a huge lot with a three-car garage. "Doesn't look like they're hurting for money."

"They're not," Darcy said. "Not when it comes to their biological children. Agatha can take baths whenever she wants."

"Agatha?"

"Benny's sister," Peach said, her face close to mine. From force of habit, I inhaled her breath to test whether or not she'd brushed her teeth.

She had. I suspected Darcy had something to do with that.

"Are you free now?" Peach asked.

Oh God, I thought. I sat back on my haunches. I'd been mulling over what I'd say to my sister for thirteen months, but now that the moment was upon me, I had no idea how to answer. Then again, the circumstances weren't what I'd expected them to be. I'd figured I'd be permitted to leave the facility at some point, so that Peach and I could start a new life together in some uncomplicated way.

This was as complicated as it could get.

Perhaps sensing my struggle, Darcy said, "I heard there was an incident last night. At Sunny Woods."

My mouth went dry. "What did you hear?"

"I don't have much Internet access," Darcy said, sweeping a black lock of hair from her brow, "but the local news said there'd been a security breach."

"Security breach," I repeated.

She nodded. "It said residents in the area needed to be careful. That some patients might have escaped."

"That's why you brought Peach out here," I said in a faint voice.

One corner of Darcy's mouth lifted.

"What's a security breach?" Peach asked.

When a bunch of winged monsters descend on a mental asylum and slaughter almost everyone inside.

"Something bad happened last night," I said.

Peach's eyes widened. "Are you okay?"

My chest tightened. God, what a kid. Always worrying about me. So rarely asking for anything. She deserved a better life.

"I'm fine," I said. "But I think they're looking for me."

Her hands, which had been resting on my shoulders, dug in painfully. "Don't go. Don't leave me again."

That single word — *again* — tore me in half. My chest shuddered. I opened my mouth to explain how much I loved her, but no words would come.

Darcy rescued me. "Will isn't going away for long."

Tears shone in Peach's eyes. "Last time, he did."

Darcy moved closer. "He has to hide for a while. Then, when he thinks it's safe, he can come back. Isn't that right, Will?"

I glanced at the pine needles underfoot so Peach wouldn't see my eyes. "That's right. When things cool down, I'll come back to get you."

Tiny fingers touched my cheek. I allowed Peach to lever my face up so she could make eye contact with me.

"What if they catch you?" she asked.

"They won't," Darcy said. "Will's going to find a good hiding place."

Peach gasped. "The fort!"

Confused, I glanced in the direction she was indicating and discovered, at the base of one of the great pine trees, a ratty blue tarp supported by an assortment of branches.

"Darcy helped me and Benny build it," Peach said, her eyes shining. "You can sleep there tonight, and every few hours we can bring you food and be with you. Maybe I could even spend the night out here."

Her face was so full of joy that I didn't have the heart to tell her the plan would never work, that this was the first place Riggs and his men would look for me. In fact, I couldn't shake the suspicion they'd staked out the property already, that they were, even now, recording everything we said.

"Where'd you find that swing?" Darcy asked.

"Goon-goon," Peach corrected.

Darcy smirked. "I can't tell you how nice it is to finally know what a goon-goon is. Peach has been talking about it since she came to live here."

I looked at my little sister, saw how her face was glowing with hope, and for the first time, I realized how sunken her cheeks were, how much weight she'd lost. It wasn't like she'd been over-fed back when I was taking care of her, but I always made sure she wasn't hungry.

Aren't they feeding you? I wanted to shout. *Don't they care enough about you to make you wash your hair? Or are they only keeping you here because of the monthly check?*

And on the heels of that thought, the stark truth rammed home: *They're not keeping her here, remember? They're sending her away this week.*

My heart began to gallop.

"What's wrong?" Peach asked. "Aren't you going to stay? The fort is awesome. Come see it." She grasped my hand and attempted to haul me up.

Darcy looked like she was going to say something, but a rustling sound made us all whirl. From the direction of the Westfalls' house, a freckled, sunburned boy about Peach's age burst through the screen of pine branches. I knew who this was even before Darcy said, "*Benny.* You scared the crap out of us."

"Mom's looking for you two," Benny said, out of breath. "She got a call a minute ago and started to yell at everyone."

Shit, I thought. *Riggs.*

Peach flung herself at me, her arms squeezing my neck in a death grip. "Let's leave. Roberta won't let me see you. She won't even let me talk about you. I hate her!"

I hugged Peach back and looked up at Darcy, whose gaze seemed to acknowledge every horrible word my sister had uttered.

"It's true," Benny said. He licked his lips. "You're Will, right?"

I returned the boy's gaze. He had freckles on his cheeks, his chestnut hair trimmed in a straight line across his forehead. "Peach tells me you're nice to her," I said.

Benny blinked at me. "She said that?"

Darcy mussed his hair. "You *are* nice," she said. "Most of the time."

Benny ventured a timid smile, but a moment later we all jumped. A voice had called in the distance.

Mrs. Westfall.

"Benjamin!" the voice shouted. "Sophia!"

A bitter taste tinged my mouth. Peach hated her real name. It didn't surprise me at all that Mrs. Westfall insisted on using it.

"If I find you three in the forest, there will be consequences!" the voice shrilled. "Do you hear me, Darlene?"

I glanced at Darcy.

She leveled a forefinger at me. "Don't you dare call me that."

Despite the circumstances, I had to swallow a grin. "Of course not."

She must've picked up on my amusement because she flashed me a warning look before taking Benny by the hand. "Run along the wood line until you get to the cul-de-sac," she told Benny.

Benny frowned at her. "Huh?"

Darcy's tone remained patient. "You're going to pretend you're returning from a walk."

Benny's frown deepened. "I don't go for walks."

"Today you do. That will divert Roberta's attention away from the woods."

Benny wasn't getting it. "Why do we want to—"

"To give Peach and Will time to say goodbye," Darcy snapped.

Peach gasped again, but this time it was a wet sound, a heartbroken sound. "No! You can't leave!"

It was like someone had taken one of those carnival mallets and bashed me in the breastbone. I couldn't breathe.

I was sitting on the forest floor, and Peach had curled into my lap, the way she'd done when I was eleven years old, and she was only two. The memory of how often we used to sit like that on the living room floor, her clinging to me and burrowing her head into my shoulder, reminded me how happy we used to be, despite our poverty, despite our mother, whose drug addiction cast a shadow over our lives.

"Benjamin!" Mrs. Westfall's voice repeated, closer this time. I pictured her in the backyard, in the general area in which Peach had tried to kick the ball.

The memory made me hold Peach tighter.

"Does Will really have to go?" Benny asked.

"*You* have to go," Darcy said, fixing Benny with a stern look. "Or Peach and I will get in big trouble."

Benny's face drained of color. "The naughty room."

I had been stroking the back of Peach's head and rocking her, but at Benny's words, my limbs went rigid. "The naughty room?"

Darcy didn't turn, but I could tell she'd heard me perfectly well.

"What the hell is the naughty room?" I asked.

Darcy swallowed, squeezed Benny's shoulders. "Just go. Okay?"

Benny nodded faintly, and with one last glance at me, took off at a jog.

"It's an unfinished room in the basement," Darcy explained. "Clean enough, though there are a few cobwebs. It's... it's a corner of the basement where there aren't any windows. Just a single wooden chair." Her tone was lifeless. "When we break Roberta's rules, we have to sit in the chair, with the door locked, for whatever time Roberta deems appropriate."

I could feel Peach burrowing closer. Fury and horror battled inside me. "Is there a light in there?"

"Sometimes," Darcy answered. "There's a single bulb on a pull string. Sometimes Roberta lets us turn it on." She swallowed. "If the infraction isn't too severe."

I imagined Peach in a dark room, locked up like an animal, terrified and alone. At least at Sunny Woods, I'd been permitted a light. But here… Peach's foster mother… that ghoulish, beastly woman…

I buried my face in Peach's hair. She was weeping soundlessly.

"Darlene!" a voice called, much closer this time, from about the place where I'd hung the goon-goon.

Darcy blanched. "I'm sorry, Will, but we have to go."

I knew she was right, but I suspected I was physically incapable of releasing Peach. And even if I could let go of my little sister, I doubted I'd be able to detach her from me. Her arms were locked around my neck like a horse collar.

"Hey, Mom," a new voice called from the distance.

Benny, I thought. The kid had listened to Darcy.

Mrs. Westfall's voice, moving away from us: "Where have you been? I've been calling you for twenty minutes."

That, I thought, was an absurd exaggeration, but then again, people like Roberta Westfall were adept at distorting the truth. Anyone who could lock a child in a lightless dungeon wouldn't think twice about telling shameless lies.

"What do you know about that swing?" Roberta demanded, far enough away now that we had to strain to hear her.

"I've never seen it before," came Benny's reply.

Roberta's answer, patronizing, cold: "Of course you've never seen it before. The hideous thing wasn't *here* before."

It's called a goon-goon, I thought. And though I knew it was childish, that I'd all but given myself away by hanging the swing from the Westfalls' tree, I experienced a perverse thrill in angering the woman.

"I... um...," Benny began, but Mrs. Westfall was going on.

"Where are Darlene and Sophia?" Mrs. Westfall demanded. "A great deal has happened, and they can't be outside today."

Darcy crouched before me. "I don't want to go, but we have to."

I knew she was right. I kissed the top of Peach's head. Peach snuggled deeper in my arms.

"When can we see you again?" Darcy asked.

"I don't know," I said, and as I spoke the words, I realized how limited my options were, how we were at the mercy of Riggs and Klinger, people who cared nothing for this remarkable little girl in my lap.

I just want to be with my sister! I wanted to scream. *Is that too much to ask?*

And at that moment, crazily, I was reminded of a sign hanging in Barley's family room. His mom wasn't much of a decorator, and Barley had remarked more than once that her taste was too old-fashioned. But deep down, I'd always admired her simple desire to spend time with her family, her unwavering devotion to her husband and her kids.

The sign, which was painted with ivory script on a rectangular wooden board, read THE BEST PLACE TO BE IS TOGETHER.

Jesus, it was true.

Tears were leaking down my cheeks, but I didn't care. Something about Darcy made it seem okay to cry.

She rubbed Peach's shoulder, but it was to me she spoke. "Where did you stay last night?"

Had this been a movie, I would have said something unselfish or enigmatic: *I can't tell you. The less you know, the better.*

But I was no brooding movie hero. "At an alpaca farm," I said. "Not far from Shadeland."

"Anita's place," Darcy said.

I looked up at her, stunned. "How do you—"

"She and Pierre are the only ones who answer me."

"You've talked to them?" I asked, unable to believe it.

"I talk to Barley and Mia on email when I can, and they said Pierre and Anita have answered them too."

Peach mumbled something I couldn't make out.

I looked down at her. "What?"

She peered up at me, her eyes puffy from crying, and said, "You were like Merry and Pippin."

"Huh?"

Darcy smiled. "She means like in *The Lord of the Rings* when the hobbits get taken by the Uruk-Hai. Peach loved the parts where Aragorn, Legolas, and Gimli tracked them." An embarrassed shrug. "We pretended we were like that, chasing after the bad guys to save you."

Maybe it should have amused me, Peach likening me to a hobbit, but instead the comparison reached inside my chest and ripped more of my heart away. I'd just started reading Peach *The Lord of the Rings* last summer when our lives had gone to hell. Evidently, Darcy had picked up where I'd left off, and though a better person would have been grateful to her for reading with Peach, I couldn't help but feel as though I'd been replaced.

Thirteen months, I thought. Thirteen months of missing out on everything. On Peach, on Mia, on Barley, on baseball and even, God help me, school. What I wouldn't have given to sit through a boring math class, if it meant I could also read books with my sister.

My thoughts scattered as Darcy's eyes shot up and a large hand fell on my shoulder.

I sucked in air and jerked my head around, certain Riggs had found me.

Dave Myers peered down at me, his expression apologetic, but his posture tense enough that I was sure something had gone wrong.

"I'm sorry," he said, "but it's time to go."

I shook my head.

"I saw a police car pass where we're parked," he explained. "The cops might have already spotted the Highlander."

"Sorry, Will," Darcy said, arms outstretched for Peach.

I made to pry Peach's arms off my neck, but she redoubled her grip, clung to me as though letting go meant death.

In a way, it does, I thought. But I brushed that away as the unhelpful notion that it was. This wasn't the end. It couldn't be. Peach and I had been through too much to never see each other again. One way or another, this would all be made right, and we'd be allowed to start our life over together. Without fear. Without pain and separation.

The best place to be is together, I thought.

With a sob in my throat, I broke Peach's hold on me and pushed her thrashing body toward Darcy.

CHAPTER TWELVE

APPEARANCES, AFTERSHOCKS

know I should've been nervous during our ride home, but I could only peer glumly out the passenger window with my chin in my palm. I scarcely registered the scenery whooshing by, and when Dave finally spoke, I didn't respond. What was the point?

I'm not a quitter, and I've never given in to despair. Granted, over the past thirteen months I'd been dwelling in a pretty gloomy mental space, but I suspect anybody in my position would have. Yet now... now things were different. As I sorted through my feelings, it became clear what the problem was.

Riggs and his cabal represented the engine of this infernal machine. Yet the fuel... the substance that ensured the machine would never stop pursuing me...that fuel was poverty.

With money, I could buy plane tickets for me and Peach. With money, I could buy a car the way they did in movies — *I'll pay all cash if you don't ask questions.* With money, we could move to Mexico, to Singapore, to any damned place, and we could be a family, an honest-to-goodness family, the way we'd been before. It hadn't been perfect, and I suppose I'd been guilty of that dreaded condition known as teenage angst. I had focused too much on my mom's drug habit, on my worn-out clothes, on everything I didn't have. Instead of appreciating what I had.

What I had was a mother. More importantly, I had Peach.

And that's all I really wanted. Sure, freedom would be nice, and having friends and a girlfriend would be added bonuses. But if you had family, you had a foundation. Having a family meant having a *life*. And was that really too much to ask?

Evidently, it was.

Dave spoke again, and again I ignored him.

"You know, taking it out on me won't help," he said.

"Nothing will help," I mumbled.

"Pierre said you were a fighter. Doesn't sound like it to me."

I turned to him, aware I was being baited, but unable to avoid the bait. "When you lose everything, you can talk to me about fighting."

"You don't think I lost everything?"

An image of a car overturning flitted through my head, but I elbowed it aside, not wanting to feel sorry for him. "You still have Anita."

He stared straight ahead. "Do I?"

I had no response for that.

We'd driven for several minutes when Dave's cell phone rang, causing my sphincter to tighten, and my belly to buzz with a horde of crazed dragonflies. I didn't recognize the song he'd set for his ring tone, but I thought the voice belonged to Johnny Cash. The Man in Black. The

(color of the Night Flyers)
singer Barley's dad used to listen to at his store. I'd always sort of liked those songs, though most of my peers made fun of country music.

Dave was talking to someone. Mostly, he just listened, but I caught scraps of the conversation:

"Yeah… yeah, he's fine."

A pause.

"He saw her." A glance at me. "Good, I guess. I mean, you know…"

A longer pause.

"You did? Good. He'll be—" A quick glance in my direction. "Look, we'll be home in a few minutes."

Silence, Dave nodding. A hint of a smile maybe. "I won't say anything. Okay. Bye."

I stared at him. "Care to let me in on the secret?"

"It was Anita."

"Yeah, I got that. What aren't you supposed to tell me?"

Dave grinned crookedly but only kept driving. We neared the turnoff.

My hands balled into fists. "If you guys told Riggs I'm with you, the least you can do is drop me off here to give me a chance to run."

Dave's brow knitted. "Huh?"

"Your wife was ready to send me away to protect her uncle. I have a hard time believing she suddenly decided I'm worth jeopardizing everybody's safety for."

"You always this suspicious? What does she have to do to gain your trust?"

As we made the turn, I half-expected to discover a blockade of vehicles stretching across the country road, but as before, we were the only car in sight.

I said, "Maybe it's not Anita I don't trust."

Dave shrugged. "I can respect that. You don't know me. I probably wouldn't trust me either. Think I'm gonna sell you out?"

"It isn't that."

"What then?"

I blew out weary breath. "People take care of their own. They don't care about others. Especially those who don't have families."

"Come on, Will. You've got a family."

I looked at him.

"That kid sister of yours." He ventured a smile. "You've got her, at least."

I stared straight ahead. "Do I?"

—

WHEN WE PULLED into the drive, we spotted Pierre drawing the door of the detached garage down with a rope. My first thought was to wonder why Dave and Anita didn't have an automatic garage door opener.

My second thought was why Pierre had bothered to close the garage door.

Were Riggs and his men already here? Had Pierre and Anita cut a deal with them?

Dave brought the Highlander to a stop and turned off the engine. Pierre passed in front of our car on the way to the house.

"Aren't you going to park in there?" I asked with a nod at the garage.

"Pierre likes to use it sometimes," Dave said. But I noticed he wouldn't make eye contact. My nerves stretched tauter.

I started to speak, but Dave opened his door and slipped out. He limped around the back of the Highlander. By the time I got out, he was almost to the front door.

"Dave?" I called. "What's waiting for me in the house?"

He stopped, one hand on the screen door, and when he looked at me, the early afternoon sun brought his face into clearer detail. The seamed forehead. The salt-and-pepper stubble on his cheeks. The nose that, I now realized, must have been broken at some point. Maybe during the crash.

But his eyes were full of sympathy. "I get that you're hurting. But at some point, we all have to trust somebody."

I watched him several seconds longer. He opened the screen door and stood waiting for me.

I drew even with him and peered into the empty foyer, the stairs leading to the second floor. I couldn't see anyone, but I could make out muffled voices. Soft laughter. As I drew closer to the doorway, the voices became clearer. A couple of them were familiar. I picked out Pierre's, Anita's. And one other...

My nerves thrumming, I passed through the threshold. When I turned toward the living room, the voices went silent. Were Riggs and that bastard Klinger waiting for me, handcuffs at the ready?

I made it to the doorway and discovered a familiar figure across the living room, seated in a rocking chair.

Mr. Marley, owner of the Hilltop General Store, father of my only living friend. Nearer me, on the couch, Mrs. Marley turned, her round face full of emotion, her eyes shimmering with latent tears. "Will," she said.

I didn't have time to move before she crossed to me. She enfolded me in her arms and squeezed, her head buried in my shoulder. Funny, but until then I'd never realized how short Barley's mom was.

She was crying and hugging me and telling me how sorry she was. It occurred to me she was not only happy to see me, but she felt guilty as well. For what, I couldn't imagine. She'd always gone out of her way to treat me like I was her own son.

It choked me up. I returned her hug and fought back the tears. How much could one person cry in a day? I had to be approaching that limit.

"You've been all alone," Mrs. Marley said. "I hate so much that you've been alone. I wish—"

She broke off. Drew in a shuddering breath. Anita had appeared behind her, her hand on Mrs. Marley's shoulder.

I said to Anita, "You brought them?"

Anita smiled. "Pierre did."

I gave Pierre a grateful look. He winked at me.

"He brought someone else too," Anita said.

She nodded to my left, and standing there, looking as unsure of himself as always, was Barley. He hadn't grown much, and his acne had worsened. His hair was longer, and he'd put on weight. But behind the black-framed spectacles, his brown eyes looked the same as they always had. The embarrassed smile was the same too.

"Hey, Will," he finally said. "It's good to see you."

Mrs. Marley gave me one last squeeze and moved away to provide a clear path to her son. I took a couple steps in that direction, and on Barley's face I read a rapid succession of conflicting emotions. He extended a hand.

I ignored it and threw my arms around him. He was stiff for a moment, but as I lifted him off his feet and shook him, he let out a half-groan, half-laugh, and then everyone in the room was laughing and he was hugging me back. I realized I was laughing as well, and tears were streaming down my cheeks. Amazingly, Barley had buried his face in my shoulder and was weeping too. The best part was that standing in the middle of a room full of people and crying together with my friend didn't feel unnatural at all. It felt as natural as breathing.

I guess it was just a day for tears.

———

MRS. MARLEY SPENT the next ten minutes fretting over me, demanding to know why they hadn't fed me better at Sunny Woods, claiming she was going to drive over there now and tell someone off. It was so nice to have someone care for me that I didn't have the heart to remind her that everyone at Sunny Woods was dead.

I caught Mr. Marley's eye during his wife's harangue, and he shook his head affectionately.

"…his basic needs," Mrs. Marley was ranting. "It's bad enough they locked him away like a criminal, but to not even care for him, a growing boy—"

"I'm sorry, Mrs. Marley," I broke in, "but I was wondering…" I looked at Anita. "Has it been in the news?"

Anita exchanged a glance with Pierre. "A few details. But they can't hush it up forever."

Pierre gave his niece a grim look. "Did a pretty good job hushing up Peaceful Valley."

We lapsed into an uneasy silence.

Mrs. Marley said, "I expect you and Dale would like some time together."

I glanced at Barley, slouching beside me on the couch. "Yes, Dale. I'd love to spend some time with you."

Barley rolled his eyes, but his mom tapped me on the knee. "Oh, Will. Are you ever serious?" I returned her smile, thinking to myself how awesome Barley's parents were.

"You can use the basement if you want," Anita said.

Barley rose and followed Anita to the basement door. I followed too, but before I got there, Mr. Marley said, "I want to apologize."

"For what?" I asked.

"For…" He sighed. "We tried to get you out of there… I mean, we talked about getting a special lawyer… but everybody we asked… they said there was no way we'd win." He glanced at me, then lowered his eyes. "You know how expensive lawyers are. We couldn't afford another…"

I nodded, understanding perfectly. *Money*, I thought. *It all comes down to money.*

He must have misread my expression because his voice sounded miserable. "I hope you forgive us someday. I swear, if it was in my power to get you out—"

"You would have," I finished. He looked at me hopefully, and I nodded. "I know you would have."

He favored me with a small smile. "You're a good kid. Please understand… I'm thankful you're friends with my son."

I realized with some alarm that he was fighting back tears. "Mr. Marley, you don't need—"

"I should have helped you more," he said. "Not with money. With… time. All those days you came into my store… you weren't just buying food for you and your sister. You may not realize it, but I think you were looking for someone to talk to. You know, the way a dad might talk to you."

I started to tell him this was ridiculous, but before I could, I had a memory of a summer's day, one when Chris and Barley had both been away at some camp we couldn't afford. This was when I was maybe ten years old, and Mom was home with Peach. I'd wandered around the neighborhood, imagining scenarios that involved Jedi knights and Sith lords, and somehow ended up at Mr. Marley's little store. It hadn't been busy — it rarely was — and the Cubs had been playing on the boxy old television behind the counter. I'd stood there talking to Barley's dad long enough for him to stack some plastic soda crates for me to sit on. We'd watched most of the game that day, the Cubs getting spanked by the Nationals. But the lopsided score hadn't mattered. What mattered was how fun it was to sit there with this kind man and talk about batting averages and coaching decisions. When a Cubbie would strike out, we'd both groan and grumble, and I'd taken to mimicking some of his sayings: "Hit the ball, Rizzo!" or "Throw strikes, Kyle!" But he was always quick to smile afterward, and I was too. We spent the afternoon cheerfully pissed off, and it was one of the happiest days I could remember.

Mr. Marley was looking at me now like a person who's failed someone and feels it's too late to make it right.

"I'll make you a deal," I said.

His eyebrows went up.

"Take me and Barley to a Cubs game when this is all over, and we'll be square."

For a moment, he looked at me like I'd lost my mind. Then he started to laugh.

I realized Pierre and the others had been watching the whole exchange. I said to Pierre, "Thanks for bringing them here."

"Tried to get that girlfriend of yours, too," Pierre said, "but no one was home when I drove by."

Mia, I thought. Man, how I longed to see her again.

Pierre nodded at me and said to Mr. Marley, "Look at that. You ever seen a kid blush that much? He's got it bad."

I realized I *was* blushing.

"Now go talk to your friend," Pierre said.

"Don't touch any of my equipment," Dave called.

I stopped at the doorway. "Equipment?"

"His beer-making stuff," Anita explained, her expression rueful.

I looked at Dave. "You mind if Barley and I sample some new formulas?"

"Funny," he said.

I followed Barley to the basement. As we entered the carpeted space, I caught a glimpse of his face, and what I saw I didn't like. His features were the same as they'd always been, but they weren't quite the same. I dismissed it as fancy, but there seemed to be some shadow overhanging him, a sort of parasitic energy. The brown eyes were lusterless, the set of his mouth sullen, as though some authority figure had punished him unjustly. There was the faintest suggestion of a beard, just straggly hairs really, but they furthered the impression he was not himself, or not the Barley I'd known thirteen months ago.

He isn't, the voice in my head reminded me. *How could he be?*

I looked around, for the first time noticing the basement was done up in a combination of western, sports, and movie geek decorations, the main room low-ceilinged and about twenty-by-twenty. There was a bar on the far side of the room cluttered with jars, casks, boxes, and machines. Had I been less excited to see my friend, I might have examined the beer-making equipment. As it was, I only wanted to talk to Barley.

I smiled, the connection finally occurring to me. "Hey," I said, "I wonder if there's—"

"Barley in one of those boxes?" he said. "Yeah, I wondered that too."

There was an edge to his voice, but I tried to keep it light. "How's it going?"

He faced me. "Are we really gonna make small talk? Act like this is normal, me visiting you like you're some prisoner?"

I mustered a smile. "I'm out now."

"For how long? It's *bullshit*, Will. I can't believe what they did to you."

"I'm as mad about it as you are. But we need to enjoy the time we have."

He cocked an eyebrow at me, and I winced. Even to my own ears, what I'd said sounded inane. Like some teacher advising his students to seize the day.

I agitated a hand. "What am I supposed to say? Of course I'm pissed off."

His scowl softened.

"What?" I asked. "You thought I was happy with all this?"

"I didn't know," he said. "It's been so long since we've seen you."

We, I thought. A face appeared in my mind, a face with sun-browned skin and electric blue eyes.

Barley picked up on it. "Mia really misses you."

"Yeah?"

For the first time, Barley grinned the goofy grin to which I was accustomed. "Oh, come on, man. Stop trying to act cool."

"Okay, I'm dying to know. Tell me."

"What do you want to know?"

"Everything," I said. "How she is, what's she's been doing for the past year?"

"Other than pining for you?"

It was selfish, but Barley's words sent a warm, tingling wave through my body. "Has she… you know…"

"Been dating anyone?"

I waited, holding my breath.

I expected Barley to make some joke then, or else obliterate me with bad news — *She's married and expecting twins* — but apparently, he understood how vulnerable I was. "She hasn't dated anyone since they took you away. She hasn't had time." At my puzzled look, he explained, "She spends every moment trying to get you out or doing research."

"Research?"

His grin faded. "About the creatures."

Oh God, I thought. *The Children.*

Into the silence, he said, "I talk to her a couple times a week. I'm telling you: she's obsessed."

"She's doing okay, though, right?"

A grunt. "Depends on your definition. I mean, she's not locked up like you, so there's that. But she lost her best friend."

Rebecca, I thought. *Poor, brave Rebecca.*

"She dropped out of everything to focus on you." His expression darkened. "And them."

I ignored that for now. "She still swims, doesn't she?"

"She quit the team, dropped out of Honors English and math. She's really…" He shook his head. "I'm worried about her."

"Pierre said he went by her house, but no one was there."

"Wednesdays are her therapy days. Her parents take her to Indianapolis." He crammed his hands in his jeans' pockets. "Her parents believe she has split personality disorder or something. They've talked about moving to Indy to be closer to the clinic."

I felt hollowed out. Again, it occurred to me how selfish I'd been. Yes, I'd wondered obsessively how Mia was doing, but it had always been in connection to our relationship. I'd never considered the trauma *she'd* been through, the toll it must have taken on her psyche.

I looked at Barley, who'd gone over to inspect a silver canister. "What about you?"

"What about me?"

"How are you dealing with it? I know you miss Chris as much as I do."

"I don't want to talk about that."

I stepped closer. "*Have* you spoken to anybody about it?"

In an almost inaudible voice, he answered, "Mom and Dad try to. They've taken me to see a couple of people. They had a woman come to the house. But talking is no good. I don't feel any better."

I put a hand on his shoulder. "Hey—"

"Don't," he said, shrugging me off. "Anyway, Mia's got it worse than I do."

"You mean the Indianapolis trips?"

He glared at me, his eyes red-rimmed behind his thick lenses. "I mean *everything*. She's not sleeping. I guess neither one of us sleeps. But at least the people at school leave me alone."

Heat kindled between my shoulder blades. "What do they say to her?"

He uttered a withering laugh. "Call her a whore, say she was dating both you and Brad. They call her a lesbian. That her and Rebecca were lovers."

I shook my head. "Why would they—"

"Because it's Indiana," Barley said, "and half the kids are homophobes. She's got that short hair—"

"I love her short hair."

"So do I!" he yelled. "But the girls, they're jealous of her. And the guys...you know how merciless dudes can be, especially when they ask a girl out and she turns them down."

"So because she won't date anybody, they make fun of her."

"Make fun of her? They *torment* her. Nobody at school talks to her, and online… the stuff they say…"

I could feel my heart ramming my chest. "How's it affecting her?"

"How is it not?"

"What does that mean?"

"It means I'm *worried* about her. She hasn't tried anything yet, but if it keeps up… if it doesn't get better…"

The dreaded word hung in the air between us, unspoken, yet as clear as if it were pulsing in giant neon letters.

"You don't think she'd hurt herself, do you?" I asked.

Barley just looked at me.

I ran my hands through my hair. "We've got to go to her. If she ever did anything…"

"She's made it this far."

"That doesn't reassure me."

"It doesn't reassure me either," he snapped. "But this is how life is now, and it's not like we can change it."

The basement door *whish*ed open above us. "Everything okay down there?"

Anita.

"I heard yelling," she said.

"It was just me," I said. "Barley was telling me about a movie, and I got excited."

"You sure?"

"I'm sure. It's a romantic comedy. Barley loves those."

"Uh-huh," Anita said. A moment later, the door closed.

I turned to Barley. One side of his mouth twitched. "You're an idiot, Burgess."

CHAPTER THIRTEEN

THE SCOUT AND THE HORROR

Barley and I talked on, our conversation focused on Mia, Peach, and what we could do. Before I realized it, Anita was calling down the stairs to let us know it would soon be suppertime.

When we came up, Barley branched off to the living room, but I went the other way, thinking to use the bathroom off the kitchen. It was occupied, so I went outside to piss in the woods. I'd just unbuttoned my cargo shorts and gotten ahold of myself when a voice called, "Don't get poison ivy on your winky."

I gasped, damned near pissed on my sneakers — Dave's sneakers. I guessed that was poetic justice since it'd been Dave who'd startled me. I glowered over my shoulder and found him slouched in an aluminum lawn chair woven with fraying yellow polyester. I hadn't spotted him because the chair was nestled beside the trunk of a great red oak. He was munching sunflower seeds and spitting the shells into the grass.

"Sorry about that," he said, not sounding particularly sorry.

My urine stream had dried up, and I doubted I'd be able to get it flowing again. Not with him behind me chewing seeds like some overgrown rodent. I buttoned my fly and asked, "Aren't you helping with dinner?"

"Anita prefers I stay out of the kitchen."

"You sure about that?"

He stopped in mid-chew. "What's that supposed to mean?"

"Seems like she does a lot of the work around here."

"I do plenty."

I don't know where the words were coming from, but they wouldn't stop. "She cooks, tends the animals. She works full time."

"I work too," he said, his tone plaintive. He leaned forward in his chair. "Where the hell do you get off telling me—"

"What happened to Anita's parents wasn't just about you."

The early-evening sun gave his eyes a reddish tint. "You don't have any idea what you're talking about."

"No? You told me how guilty you feel, how much Anita resents you—"

"Don't you dare—"

"—but she's the one who lost her parents. It was her tragedy, not yours."

Dave rose from the chair. "Listen, goddammit…"

"I did listen. You told me the whole story." I stepped closer. "Now I'm telling you what I see: a man too self-absorbed to get past himself and be there for his wife."

"Shut up."

I pointed toward the house. "She's in there right now making food for us, even though she damn near died last night. And all you can do is sit here eating seeds?"

Dave was staring at me now, appalled and maybe even a little sick. But the words wouldn't stop. They flowed out of me like poison from a punctured abscess. "Why don't you help her a little? Be there for her? Feed the animals or shovel out their pens?" I moved closer, so we were nearly nose-to-nose. "Or how about this? Spend a little more time talking to her instead of screwing around in the basement making beer?"

"You don't know what you're..." His eyes looked more bloodshot than ever. His upper lip twitched in a sort of snarl. Just when I thought he might punch me, he shook his head and strode off, not in the direction of the house, but toward the lane. Beyond him stood the tree from which the rope swing had hung.

A couple minutes later, I went back inside.

—

WE GATHERED IN the dining room, Dave entering last and not making eye contact with me. I felt guilty for what I'd said, but I didn't really regret it. Soon enough though, dished up and drinking strawberry lemonade I was sure Anita had home-made, the conversation started to flow.

Yet as I shoveled in green beans spruced up with little scraps of bacon, the heaviness inside me began to descend. Beneath Pierre's jokes and Mrs. Marley's maternal warmth lurked the undeniable truth: I wasn't free. Riggs would be coming for me. I forced myself to be polite, to remember that these people were my allies. Yet the simple fact was that they weren't the ones who were hunted. They weren't the ones whose freedom could be stripped away at any moment.

I sat there as long as I could, but after devouring Anita's sausage-and-gravy and mashed potatoes, I excused myself and headed outside.

I was moving toward the backyard when I heard Barley call out, "No wonder you're so thin." As he caught up to me, I could see he was winded even though he'd only run about ten yards. "I could've eaten for another hour. Even the green beans were good."

A subtle breeze whispered over us, maybe the first breeze I'd felt in over a year. Funny how many things I took for granted before being locked up. I closed my eyes and savored the sensation. Then the good feeling vanished.

"I've gotta get moving," I told him. "I've got to find a way to take Peach with me."

"In what? Do you even have a license?"

I gave him a flat look, and he lowered his eyes. "Sorry. I guess they don't do driver's training at the hospital."

"It wasn't a hospital," I muttered. "It was a cage. When they find me, they'll put me in another cage, and this time they won't let me out."

Barley let loose with a sneeze so loud I clamped a hand over my chest.

"Damn, Barley," I muttered.

"Allergies," he explained. "So how *did* you escape?"

I was totally at a loss. Just how did you explain a wholesale slaughter like the one that had decimated Sunny Woods? And how could you describe the Night Flyers, creatures that had no business being real, much less roaming the skies of Northern Indiana?

We moved toward the rear of the barn, from which extended a fenced-in area where the alpacas and llamas were loitering in the summery air. Nearing the gate, I made out Frodo, Pennywise, and Malorie. In the far corner of the dusty space stood Hopper, a head taller than the alpacas and a good deal broader.

"Wait," Barley said, "you're going in?"

I drew open the gate and stepped aside to allow him to pass. "After you."

Barley lingered a few feet from the opening, his bespectacled eyes huge. "Do they attack?"

"Only if you show fear."

"That's not funny, man. I've seen YouTube videos."

I lowered my nose at him. "Of alpacas killing people?"

"Maybe not alpacas, but all sorts of animals. There's one of an elephant trampling people at a circus. She killed like five people. They finally had to put her down."

At that moment, Desiree the Llama appeared over my shoulder and started to sniff my hair. I reached out and scratched her forehead. She closed her eyes and nuzzled into my fingers. "I don't think Desiree's going to trample you, Barley."

He let out pent-up breath and, still not looking convinced, waded through the gateway.

I closed the gate behind me and double-checked the latch. I had no desire to lose any of Anita's animals.

"It's person versus nature," he murmured.

"Look at her," I said. Desiree looked positively rapturous as I scratched her. "It's not anyone versus anyone."

"I don't mean them," Barley said. "Or them *necessarily*."

"What the hell are you talking about?"

His shoulders slumped. "What if they all decided to attack at once?"

"The alpacas?"

"*Any* group of animals."

"Barley, you're not—"

"I should have been with you!" he said, his voice raw. "I shouldn't have let you and Chris go into Savage Hollow alone." He turned away. "It's my fault. Chris, Rebecca. Even your mom. If I hadn't have been such a coward, I could've helped you guys. I could've made a difference."

I put a hand on his shoulder, but he pulled away, staggered a little, and sank to his knees, head in hands. His sobs weren't loud, but his torso tremored with them. About six inches to his left lay a flyblown splat of alpaca shit, but I decided now was not the time to inform him of the fact.

I crouched before him. "You didn't go with us because your parents wouldn't let you."

"I could've argued with them."

"They were right," I said. He started to snuffle out another argument, but I overrode him. "Chris shouldn't have been allowed to go. If his dad hadn't been a gutless abuser, Chris wouldn't have been with me either."

Barley looked at me. "But he was. He was with you when they came. He was with you when Carl Padgett was kidnapping your sister—"

"Padgett's dead."

Barley blinked at me.

I realized my voice had gone hoarse. "Chris is dead. Rebecca is dead. And you'd be dead too if your parents hadn't been so responsible."

The emotions warred in his face. Wanting to believe me but not wanting to let himself off the hook.

"You love your mom, right?" I asked.

"Of course."

"How would she feel if you'd died that day? Can you imagine her grief?"

His eyes had come unfocused. I could tell he was imagining it.

"What about your dad? He might not say it, but I know he cares about you."

Barley wiped his nose, stared at the ground. "He does say it. He still comes into my room and kisses me goodnight." Barley shot me a look. "You'd better not tell anybody."

I gave him a wry smile. "Who am I gonna tell?"

"You *wouldn't* tell anybody. You and Chris always made fun of me, but you never meant it. You've always been a…" He swallowed, and when he spoke again, his eyes were pleading. "I'm so sorry I wasn't there."

I smiled at him to show it was okay.

Then a plangent cry filled the night.

I spun, expecting to see a horde of crazed alpacas bearing down on us. But the alpacas were fleeing in the opposite direction, away from the barn and toward the far corner where Hopper stood. I turned and saw nothing at first, just the open sliding doors and the darkness within.

My eyes crawled up the chipped red paint of the barn, past the window to the hay mount, all the way to the peaked roof, forty feet above the barnyard.

Perched up there, outlined by the royal-blue gloaming, stood a black shape, its scarlet eyes blazing.

Then the tenebrous wings unfurled, and the Night Flyer dived at us.

—

THOUGH THE SIGHT of the Night Flyer caused my bowels to roil, I had the presence of mind to do one thing: I slung an arm over Barley and drove him to the ground. A split second later, the air above us was rent in two, the Night Flyer's talons missing us by inches. Its great wings splayed, the creature rising to clear the fence, then knifing higher to avoid the bordering forest. The alpacas were shrieking and stamping, the whole mass of them congregated around Hopper, who was tracking the Night Flyer as it rose above the trees.

"Will?" Barley said. "What do we do?"

A smell hit me then, and when I looked down to identify it, I realized I'd driven Barley straight into the pile of alpaca shit. One of his elbows was buried in it, but he didn't seem to notice, and anyway, there were more pressing matters to worry about.

Like the Night Flyer winging its way toward us.

My thoughts started racing. The Night Flyer screech had been loud, yes, but I didn't think it'd been loud enough to rouse the adults in the house. And anyway, I wasn't sure I wanted them to come. I'd seen what these creatures could do, and they didn't discriminate with regard to age. That meant Pierre, Anita, Dave, and Barley's parents would all be in grave peril if they hurried out here, and my conscience was already burdened enough by those I'd lost.

But now Barley was in harm's way. I had to protect him.

Protect him? a scoffing voice demanded. *You can't even protect yourself.*

But I could. I *knew* I could.

But not without a weapon.

"The barn," I said.

He goggled at me. "What about it?"

"Run for it!" I growled. "Now!"

We broke into a sprint, but within moments I realized we were in trouble. Not only was the Night Flyer making a beeline for us, but Barley was no athlete, and unless he found another gear, there was no way we'd make the safety of the barn before the creature descended on us.

Safety of the barn? that same hectoring voice said. *There is no safety. Wherever you go, they'll find you. They'll never stop hunting you.*

"*Move*, dammit," I said, a hand on Barley's back. Behind us sounded a faint whistling, the creature's wings scything through the sundown air.

We weren't going to make it.

"Down!" I shouted, but I knew I was too late. Something snagged my T-shirt, tugged, and I was hurtling forward, toward the open barn doors. I was only three feet off the ground, and a quick glance at the opening made me doubt the creature could make it through, but of course I'd forgotten my experiences of the night before, the many ways in which these monsters could contort their bodies.

The Night Flyer's wings retracted, and we swept inside the darkened barn. It released me, and I skidded awkwardly along the straw-strewn floor. The Night Flyer landed smoothly deeper in. My momentum carried me toward the creature. I stuck out my arms, but this only sent me into a thudding barrel roll.

When I came to a stop, the creature was poised directly over me. Leering. Slaver stringing from its open maw.

I stared up into the creature's bloodred eyes. Its leer widened.

"Get away from him!" a voice shouted.

Upside down, I craned my neck, and there, in the open barn doorway, stood my friend, severely winded but resolute.

It wouldn't be a stretch to say I loved Barley then.

Not that his intervention would make a difference. The creature's gaze was returning to me. The maniacal gleam in its eyes swelled.

"*Wendigo!*" Barley shouted.

The creature looked up, and this time I rolled away.

"I've read about you, you stupid bastard!" Barley was shouting.

I hightailed it toward the front of the barn, knowing there'd be little there to aid me. It was murky, but I could dimly discern the alpaca pens to my left and right. Ahead, I spotted the feed bin and the shovel leaning against it.

A hissing sound made me whip my head around, and what I discovered caused my testicles to shrink.

The Night Flyer was stalking toward Barley.

To his credit, my friend was holding his ground. Faced with such an abomination, most people would have run away screaming.

I scanned the darkness feverishly for something that might save us. I grimaced. Dammit, I couldn't *see*.

The Night Flyer hissed again, louder this time.

It's hungry, I thought.

That decided me. I lurched toward the barn door, scrabbled in the dark for the light switch. I found it, flipped it on, and the overhead bulbs cast their amber glow.

The creature had stalked closer to Barley, who'd begun to back away.

I spotted a broom — too feeble — a rake — not sharp enough — an old-fashioned wagon wheel — too bulky and too round!

Then I saw it: the pitchfork.

I seized it and set off at a sprint. I remembered Anita tossing straw with it, imagined its sharp tines puncturing the leathery flesh of the Night Flyer.

The creature was accelerating, stalking Barley with more insistence, no longer toying with him but preparing to sate its wicked hunger. Barley was backpedaling faster, but soon the beast would be on him, ripping and tearing.

I wasn't about to lose another friend to these monsters.

"Hey!" I shouted.

The Night Flyer paused, its wings quivering.

"Yeah, you," I called, rushing toward it. "Fight me, you ugly fuck."

It snarled at me over its shoulder.

Barley chugged toward it, heaved a double-handful of straw at its face. The flimsy fragments scattered over its head, a few of them sticking on its hide. It turned back toward Barley, and I heard a growl deep in its throat.

I raised the pitchfork, surged forward, and plunged it into its back.

Its body went ramrod straight. Its squall made my legs liquefy, but I knew I had to keep up my assault. I hauled back on the pitchfork handle, but the tines had sunk in too deep. It spun around to face me, the handle whipping toward Barley. He ducked at the last instant, the wood whistling over his head. Barley bent, scooped a golf-ball-sized rock off the floor, and chucked it at the Night Flyer's back. The rock missed and cracked me in the forehead. I stumbled back, my vision blurring. "What the hell, Barley?"

"Sorry," he answered.

The Night Flyer strode toward me. It was growling loudly now and stalking me on its hind legs. It was reaching back to unseat the pitchfork, but its wings were in the way. I wondered if I could make it to the front of the barn and use the shovel to defend myself, but at that moment, the creature stopped and screeched again, its arms thrown up, its wings shivering in pain. It blundered sideways, and I spotted Barley, grasping the pitchfork handle and driving it in deeper.

Yes, I thought.

I knew it was a risk, but I wouldn't do us any good empty-handed. I bolted toward the shovel leaning against the grub box. When I got ahold of it, its weight feeling good in my hands, I turned to discover the creature staggering away, dragging Barley toward the open doors and the dusty barnyard beyond. I sprinted toward them, part of me wanting Barley to simply let the creature go, the other part of me wanting to keep it here, to kill it. Nearing the struggling pair, I wondered if Barley had the same idea, that the Night Flyer was merely a scout, sent here to kill me if it could, but if it couldn't, to communicate word of my whereabouts to the other Night Flyers.

It was the thought of the horde descending on the farm that quickened my steps. If this beast got away, if it led the entire throng of Night Flyers to this farm, everything here that lived and breathed would be dead by sunup.

I couldn't let it escape.

At the open barn doors, the creature bucked. Still grasping the handle for dear life, Barley was heaved into the air. The back of his head cracked the door lintel, and he dropped to the ground like a sack of feed.

I was almost upon them when the creature spun and eyeballed me. I was sure it would kill my friend then. Or bear him away into the night the way Dr. Fleetwood had been.

But this monster had other ideas. With a satanic leer, the creature set off across the barnyard. With a mixture of relief and dread, I watched it approach the wood-and-wire fence. But just when I was sure it would wing away into the night, it veered to the left.

Straight at the alpacas clustered in the corner.

No, I thought. The Night Flyer was going to slaughter innocent animals.

As I pelted toward the baying alpacas, the shovel handle squeezed tight in my hands, I longed for Anita and Pierre to arrive on the scene. I began hollering at the top of my lungs, knowing they probably wouldn't hear me, knowing I was too late to save the animals.

The Night Flyer reached the mass of alpacas and llamas and raised one taloned hand. The animals cowered. I was nearly there, but I wasn't going to be fast enough. The Night Flyer's claws were already whipping down, and I realized with a sick heart that Desiree was the monster's intended victim.

"*Don't—*" I started to yell, but then the talons bit into Desiree's woolly body, just above her left foreleg. A thick swatch of wool went spinning away, and a soupy gout of blood sprayed from Desiree's hide.

"*Son of a bitch!*" I screamed. I swung the shovel at the Night Flyer's face, but it was an ungainly swing that glanced off the beast's shoulder. It spun and aimed a backhand at my face. Its leathery talons drilled me flush on the cheek, and I went tumbling into the mass of animals.

Desiree was squealing in pain, but the Night Flyer was abandoning her, was turning its attention back to me, and this time I was weaponless and dazed. The Night Flyer stalked closer, eyes slitted in hatred.

Then it was bowled over and rolling in the dust. I pushed onto my elbows and gaped in shock at the swirling tangle of wings and wool.

Hopper had tackled the Night Flyer. The llama had saved my life.

But Hopper had paid a dear price for saving me. The Night Flyer had its maw buried in the side of Hopper's long white neck, its black muzzle sprayed by Hopper's blood.

"Get off of him!" I shouted, rising and staggering toward the shovel. I grasped it, but my vision carouseled, and I had to lean on the handle to prevent going down. The creature growled like a feral dog as it chomped and shook Hopper's neck.

I knew the Night Flyer would attack me next, but I didn't care. I strode forward and was less than ten feet away when the barnyard lit up, a deafening fusillade of gunshots hammering my eardrums. The Night Flyer jittered, brayed in agony, and convulsed as it rose on its hind legs. Then, with a last glance in my direction, it twisted and keeled onto its back, right beside its final victim.

I stumbled over to Hopper. The llama didn't move. His eyes gazed sightlessly at the indigo sky. I touched Hopper's reddened fur, discovered bullet wounds in his side.

I turned and glared at the gun-toting men who'd killed the Night Flyer but caught Hopper in the crossfire.

"Well, Burgess," Riggs said, nodding at the dead llama, "looks like we can add another victim to your list of casualties."

He patted the barrel of his rifle. "Sometimes I wonder why I don't just use this on you. It'd sure as hell save everyone a world of trouble."

PART FOUR

THE CAULDRON

CHAPTER FOURTEEN

ERNESTINE AND MIKEY

Reclining next to me in the backseat of an SUV, Riggs said, "I reckoned you and I could use some time alone." I hadn't seen the make or model of the vehicle, and frankly I didn't give a shit. I wanted to strangle Riggs for the way they'd treated me, for the way they'd treated my friends.

Moments after his goons murdered Hopper, an armada of men swarmed the farmhouse. By the time Agent Castro dragged me out of the barnyard, the driveway was clogged with vehicles. Before I was stuffed inside the black SUV, I saw too much:

Barley, expressionless and pale, being force-marched to a black Jeep.

Mr. and Mrs. Marley separated into matching silver sedans.

Dave Myers, an ugly purple bruise on his cheek, forced to his knees in the front yard. A smirking man stood behind him with a gun pointed lazily at his back.

Though nightfall and the heavy window tint conspired to blot out my view, I'd glimpsed two more figures being led to separate vehicles: Anita and Pierre. Anita was thrashing and shooting elbows at her captors. Pierre was staring fiercely in Anita's direction, but there wasn't much he could do.

Not with handcuffs on.

Riggs might have picked up on my thoughts because he said, "Quite a scene, wasn't it?"

"Will Desiree be okay?" I asked.

He squinted at me. "Who the hell is Desiree?"

"The other llama. The one with different-colored spots on her hide."

He shrugged. "She'll be fine. That creature barely scratched her."

We were nearing the end of the lane, the country road coming into view. Riggs's scent wafted over me, a combination of musky aftershave and deep-fried food.

I nodded at the Plexiglass divider between us and the driver. "Can he hear what we're saying?"

Riggs glanced at the armrest on the door, which housed a dozen buttons. "If I want him to."

"Do you want him to hear me call you a heartless jackass?"

Riggs's whiskered face spread into a grin. "You know, I'm glad you didn't buy the farm last night." He put a mischievous pair of fingertips to his lips. "Oh, not that farm." A nod over his shoulder at the Myers' homestead. "Must have been a hell of an ordeal. I'm surprised you made it out of Sunny Woods alive."

I stared at the smoky Plexiglass divider, which showed not a speck of dust or a fingerprint. There were subtle light sources back here, a couple glowing orbs on the seatbacks, amber-colored bars above the doors. Everything was pristine. The windows, the charcoal-cloth bench seat. Even the floor mats projected the same antiseptic neatness, not a single pebble or scuff mark anywhere.

Riggs was giving me a funny look.

"What?" I asked.

"Just trying to figure out what makes you so special. Why a teenaged kid should live through two such dangerous events. Oh, pardon me. Make that three dangerous events. Must've scared you to death to find that dragon in the barnyard."

"Night Flyer," I muttered.

"How's that?"

"Nothing."

Riggs sighed. "Young man, it's time you and I came to an understanding."

"I understand you perfectly."

And I did. In fact, as we trundled down the gravelly road, I couldn't shake a dreadful sensation of déjà vu. Just over a year ago, a ghoul named Carl Padgett had held me hostage, and he'd spoken in the same maddeningly reasonable tones that Riggs used. He'd grinned the way Riggs was grinning. And though I didn't believe Riggs was infected with the same insidious virus Padgett had acquired from the Children, I did read the same viciousness, the same sadism in Riggs's remorseless eyes.

"You ever hear of Ernestine Beck?" he asked.

"The girl who ditched your ass for the Music Man?"

Riggs made a face. "To hell with her. She was nothin'. But Ernestine... she was the real deal."

"I don't give a shit."

He rubbed his jaw and closed one eye. "Let's see. This would've been... oh, back in 1988."

"How old were you then?" I asked. "Sixty?"

Riggs snorted. "That's a good one, kiddo. Glad to see you haven't lost your sense of humor."

But his sarcasm scarcely registered. A chill had settled into my bones. *Kiddo* was one of the names Padgett had called me. The notion that Riggs was every bit as dangerous as The Moonlight Killer deepened.

"I was only a pup back then," Riggs went on. "Twenty-two and just starting out with the bureau."

"You're with the FBI?"

"Kiddo, this is about as far from the FBI as you can get. They're the public face. We do the real work."

For a moment, it was like I was talking to Barley, the biggest conspiracy theorist I'd ever met. "So you're with the shadow government. The guys who covered up Area 51."

"Ernestine was my first case, but I've never forgotten it. It's eaten away at me ever since. Course, part of that could be because I was in love with her."

Did this asshat actually want me to feel sorry for him?

He glanced out his window. "I know you view me as some kind of monster." He donned a snooty British accent. "Bereft of warmth or empathy." He glanced at me. "That about right?"

"How would you feel if you were me?"

"Fair enough. But I *do* feel. Too much sometimes. And it's gotten me into trouble."

"Can we skip—"

"No we cannot," he said and shot me a glare.

I fell silent.

"Ernestine was a single mom," Riggs said. "Young. Not yet twenty. But she was working two jobs and trying to support a three-year-old son." He rubbed his jaw, the stubble rasping audibly. "She contacted the local police because she'd been attacked by something with red eyes. Something that swooped down from the night sky."

That got my attention.

"She was leaving the restaurant where she waited tables when the beast came for her. One moment she was reaching for the handle of her beat-up Oldsmobile, the next she was lying on the ground bleeding from the scalp. By the time she realized she'd been attacked, the creature was looping back toward her." His eyebrows went up. "Sound familiar?"

He paused. "She got away somehow and summoned the cops. They didn't know what to make of it, and nothing else might have come of it had she not shown up at the station a week later and told the sheriff she was having dreams about eating her son."

I stared at him.

A nod. "Eating him raw. Just tearing him to pieces and—"

"I got it."

"As you might imagine," Riggs went on, "that got the sheriff's attention. He began to worry about Ernestine, but he worried even more about the child. He contacted a friend at the state police post, and that's how we were brought in."

Riggs placed his big hands on his knees and sighed. "By the time I got involved, they'd already put Ernestine through a whole battery of psychological tests, none of them worth a damn. What she had wasn't psychological. It was a disease."

My face burned. I didn't want to hear the rest.

"I don't know when I started to care about Ernestine, but at some point, I did. What struck me about her was how much she loved that boy of hers." A fond smile. "Mikey. That's what she called him. Like that old cereal commercial."

I didn't know the commercial he was referencing. I just wished he'd shut up.

"Ernestine was a good mama. Everything she did was for that boy. Mikey didn't have many toys or new clothes, but he had love. Yes, sir, he certainly had that."

I was stunned to see tears glistening in Riggs's eyes.

"I enjoyed playing with that kid. By God, I did. Matchbox cars, hide-and-seek. I even got him a little train set."

"You were dating Ernestine?"

He glanced at me. "I wouldn't say we were dating. We never could've gone out in public without me getting fired." He chewed his lower lip. "But we did spend time together."

"Did she hurt her son?"

He shook his head. "I won't say more about it — hurts too much. But there is another connection to your situation."

"The only thing that matters—"

"Kiddo?" he interrupted, eyebrows raised. "She lived a half-mile from your old house."

—

I SHIFTED IN my seat. "So what? That was decades before I was born."

"True enough," Riggs allowed. "But the bloodbath at the hospital was last night. The massacre at Peaceful Valley was this summer. And what happened to you last year—"

"I don't want to talk about that."

"You don't have to." A cold grin ghosted across his mouth. "At least, not yet."

I slumped in my seat and closed my eyes.

"That's right," he said. "You just sit back and listen. Kids don't do that enough these days. They're all rebels and activists, but they've got no idea how the real world works."

Go to hell, I thought.

"After the Ernestine case, my supervisor was fired, and I was reassigned to Colorado. You ever been?"

I didn't answer.

"Pretty enough place," he said, "but the people out there… they're not centered. Bunch of granola eaters."

I opened an eye and looked at him. He peered out his window, as if there were more to see than night-swept cornfields and forests. He stifled a burp, and I caught a whiff of what might have been baked fish. "They bounced us around quite a bit. I've worked in almost every state and a goodly number of foreign countries. But every now and then I'd hear of something involving Shadeland."

"Let me guess. You think the town is cursed."

"Don't be stupid. It's beneath you, kiddo."

The comment took me aback, though I tried not to show it.

"It's not the town," he said. "Or not *just* the town. But I do think Shadeland's near the center of it."

"The center of *what*?"

"The cauldron," he answered. "That's how I think of it. This area… it's like a giant black pot. Like something out of a fairy tale. You and me, our driver… we're all skimming along the surface. But underneath us, it's boiling, heating. Getting ready to send up another bubble."

"What kind of bubble?"

"Jesus Christ, kid, it's a metaphor! Didn't you learn anything before you dropped out of high school?"

I looked away. I wanted to tell him I understood what a metaphor was. I wanted to tell him I was one of the best students in my English class, that I wanted to be a writer when I grew up. And I hadn't dropped out of school, for God's sakes, I'd been locked away in a mental institution!

But Riggs was pressing forward. "There've been too many abnormal occurrences around here to keep track of. I never said anything to the head of my division about it. He was an unimaginative dolt, which I suppose was why so little got done. The guy who replaced him, he wasn't much better. But the current leader... *he* understands the forces that exist here. He understands the chaos."

"He's the one who let you take this case?"

"In a manner of speaking," he said. "The man we're talking about... it's me."

I stared at him. "You're the leader of the shadow government?"

Riggs's belly shook. "Would you quit calling it that? I feel like I'm on one of those idiotic television shows. The ones with all the UFO freaks?"

"UFOlogists," I corrected.

"Crackpots. They have no idea about the truth."

"And what is the truth?" I asked, trying and failing to disguise my interest. A part of me wished Barley were in the SUV with us. This would have been his dream come true.

"The cauldron spans about seventy miles," he explained. "It touches nine different counties."

"You're talking about the caves."

"The caves are part of it, sure. But it's more than the land. The cauldron, it isn't passive. It isn't merely there. It's also a beacon."

"Like the Overlook Hotel?"

He blew out a disgusted puff of air. "Don't get me started on that crap. Stephen King has contributed to the delinquency of more kids than anybody alive." He drummed his fingers on the armrest. "Everybody's worried about the massacres. Did you know a news crew showed up at Sunny Woods this morning and had the audacity to shove a microphone in my face?" A slow grin. "Those reporters will be released in a couple weeks. If they're lucky."

I wanted to tell him this was un-American, that he couldn't just incarcerate people. But I knew too well he could. He could do whatever he wanted. Look at how he'd treated me.

"What folks don't talk about," Riggs said, raising his hips and reaching into the pocket of his slacks, "is the source."

"Which is…?"

Instead of answering, he extricated a can of snuff. *Copenhagen*, the little green can read. With an unnaturally long thumbnail, he began to shred a slender tear between the hockey puck-shaped can and its lid. When he'd completed his incision, he removed the lid, reached into the packed snuff, which resembled glistening coffee grounds, pinched a wad the size of a monarch cocoon, and deposited it between his lower lip and gum.

"You know that's bad for you," I said.

"Kiddo, we're all gonna die of something. I'd just as well have a say in the matter."

"Just tell me where we're going," I muttered. Then I froze.

Riggs grinned around his distended lower lip. "He gets it! The kid finally gets it!"

I wanted to tell him off, but I'd seen the brown sign flicker by, knew exactly where we and the rest of this unholy caravan were heading.

The Peaceful Valley Nature Preserve.

—

THE PARK WAS spooky at night. According to Pierre, the massacre had occurred only weeks ago. And though there were no bloodstains or other signs of violence along the meandering lane or the old-growth trees that canopied our passage, I could easily imagine dreadful things happening here.

How would anyone ever know?

Though most of the world was connected by cell phone towers and satellites, the Peaceful Valley Nature Preserve was as far off the grid as you could get. Maybe it was because our windows were rolled up, but the night seemed so still that the park felt devoid of life, as though some monstrous plague had steamrolled through, killing fish and mammals, birds and bugs, even microorganisms.

Riggs said, "Welcome to the center of the cauldron, kiddo."

I tried not to shiver.

We drove on through the darkness, the approach so lengthy I was reminded of the one and only time I'd been to Disney World. Chris's parents had taken us when we were in the fourth grade, and I remembered how interminable that approach into the park had seemed: off ramp after off ramp, parking lot after parking lot. Then a long walk. And the trolley. And another long walk followed by a monorail. And though the elevated train had been neat the first time we'd ridden it, by our third day there, it had become just another trial to be endured before we reached the actual park, where another hike awaited us.

At last, the SUV coasted to a stop. It was too dark to see the structure looming beside us clearly, but what I could discern resembled a gigantic log cabin. "What is this place?"

"The main shelter," Riggs explained. "We've equipped it to serve as our headquarters."

"You've set up *here*? Even after what happened?"

Other vehicles were crunching to a stop around us, but Riggs settled back and showed no desire to leave the SUV. "When I took over the division, I knew there'd come a point when I'd need to deal with this problem. In many ways, it's why I wanted the job. A few teams had been dispatched here over the years, but no one had come close to solving the puzzle."

"That's what this is to you? A puzzle? You're endangering all these people — my friends — to prove something to yourself?"

"You ever hear of the greater good?"

"Oh boy."

"Yeah, to a brat like you, that phrase probably sounds antiquated. Maybe even sinister. But the truth is, it's how a government operates. It's what my branch is all about."

"Cover-ups," I said. "Wrongful imprisonment. Maybe even murder."

"If it's necessary, sure. But something tells me we won't have to lift a finger against you."

My mouth felt moistureless. "Why is that?"

"Never mind," he said, and gave me a look I couldn't interpret. "There's someone in there waiting for you."

CHAPTER FIFTEEN
THE ACOLYTE

To my surprise, the SUV was unlocked. I elbowed open the door and scrambled toward a steel entryway flanked by a pair of grumpy-looking sentries. I thought they'd bar my passage, frisk me or something, but they merely watched me rush toward them. I tore open the door, veered right, and burst into a large gathering hall.

Every head turned in my direction. Under other circumstances, I would have felt awkward, like one of those dreams where you find yourself in the school cafeteria wearing nothing but your tighty-whities. But I didn't care about awkwardness now. All I cared about was the small figure seated across the shelter, the one munching on what might have been a peanut butter-and-jelly sandwich, the only face that hadn't turned to goggle at me.

My heart swelled, but a complication tempered my joy. I glanced at the guy closest to me — I'd never seen him before, but he looked like he'd rip the heads off kittens for fun — and said, "Why'd they bring my sister here?"

The guy, who was massive and had a deep, pitted scar running from his temple to the corner of his mouth, only favored me with a smirk.

I bypassed the kitten decapitator and hastened to where Peach sat. She looked up just as I arrived and called out my name through a mouthful of sandwich, little flecks of bread tumbling out of her mouth.

Chuckling, I wrapped her up and kissed the top of her head. "Have you been brushing your teeth?" I asked.

"Only when I threaten her," a voice answered.

Darcy approached us, a bottle of water in each hand. She handed me one, twisted the top off another and placed it beside Peach's plate.

"You know," I said to my sister, finally breaking our embrace, "you could make life easier on people if you'd take care of yourself without being scolded."

"But it stings," she answered.

I didn't need to ask what she meant. Peach only liked kids' toothpaste, the kind that tasted like cotton candy or overripe grapes. The Westfalls didn't strike me as the type to accommodate delicate brushing habits.

"You're stubborn," Darcy said to Peach, but she smiled as she said it.

Peach swigged water and wiped her mouth in satisfaction. "Can you brush my teeth?"

"I just got here," I answered.

"Please? You haven't done it in forever."

I averted my eyes so Peach and Darcy wouldn't see them. But Darcy must have intuited how I was feeling because her voice was gentle. "I've got her toothbrush. It was one of the few things I was able to grab before they took us."

I stared at Darcy. "'Took' you?"

She lowered her eyes, and I realized she was scared. Scared deeply and trying not to show it.

I knew quite a bit about that.

"Hold that thought," I said, rising. I squeezed Peach's shoulder. "Come on, knucklehead."

She grinned toothily up at me. "*You're* a knucklehead."

Darcy knelt before a *Star Wars* backpack and rooted around inside. She came out with a fuchsia toothbrush and a tube of Colgate and handed them to me.

Peach and I started away, but I hesitated, glanced back at Darcy, who was zipping up the backpack. "Have I thanked you for taking care of my sister?"

"I don't do it because of that. I do it because—"

"—you care about her," I finished.

Darcy stood. "That's right."

"It's just...," I started. I shook my head, unable to find the proper words.

"You don't have to—"

"I do," I interrupted. "They took everything from us last summer. If you hadn't been there to help my sister..."

"Darcy?" Peach said. "Why are you looking at Will like that?"

Darcy blushed.

Peach grinned. "Do you like my big brother?"

"Go brush your teeth," Darcy muttered. To spare her further embarrassment, I tugged on Peach's hand and led her away.

As we walked, I took a moment to survey the gathering hall. It was rustic but homey in here, the walls comprised of logs, the concrete floor painted brown. I estimated the space was sixty-by-sixty, though from the outside, the building had appeared larger than that. I guessed there were smaller rooms off the main area. Maybe that was where Riggs had made his temporary office.

I counted around thirty people milling about, some of them in soldier's fatigues, others in civilian clothes. All of them looked tough as nails. There were more men than women, but there were more women than I would have guessed. For whatever reason, I assumed Riggs wouldn't hire women. Probably because he was reprehensible in every other way.

As we neared the RESTROOMS sign, I was disconcerted by how broad the soldiers were, how hardened their expressions. Whether this toughness was genuine or feigned, I didn't know, but I'd never been more aware of my own lankiness. True, I'd matured some in the past year, and there was more strength in me than met the eye. But among these soldiers, I felt puny, like the manager for the football team, the kid who scurries around filling water bottles.

I thought Riggs's goons might prevent us from entering the bathroom, but no one got in our way. The men's room was long and rectangular, with stalls and urinals on the left and sinks on the right. It was a testament to Peach that she didn't bellyache about using the men's room. She'd had plenty of experience with that growing up with me.

"Anybody in here?" I called.

When no one answered, we crossed to a sink. I had the wild notion that we might try escaping, but when I saw how high the windows were — the ceiling was probably eighteen feet tall, the windows situated near the apex of the wall — I realized how foolish the idea was. Besides, the park was crawling with soldiers. Peach and I wouldn't make it far before they caught us.

I turned on the hot water and began to splash it over my face. God, it felt good to remove some of the grime and perspiration from the day. The incident with the Night Flyer and poor Hopper replayed in my head. I supported myself on the counter to keep my body from shaking, then twisted off the sink and used the front of my shirt to dry my face.

Peach was watching me.

"Are you gonna brush your teeth?" I asked.

"I thought you were gonna do it."

I cocked my head. "Seriously?"

"Like you used to," she added in a small voice.

I wetted her brush under the tap and squeezed out some paste. She opened her mouth dutifully, and I started in on her back teeth, the ones she neglected when she brushed them herself.

"So Darcy's pretty cool," I said.

"Uh-huh," she said through a mouthful of foam. "Eelikoo."

I took the brush out of her mouth. "Huh?"

"She likes you," Peach clarified.

"Open up," I said. "Cheesy."

Peach gave me her cheesiest smile so I could brush her front teeth. I graduated to her molars. When she began to groan — she always grew antsy toward the end of a brushing — I said, "Alright, go ahead."

She lurched toward the sink and ejected her spit as messily as possible, only managing to get half of it into the basin.

When she straightened, she said, "Did they tell you what Barley's parents did?"

"They finally got him potty-trained?"

Peach beamed. "You're a dork."

"What did they do?"

"They want to adopt us."

I looked down at her, speechless.

"They have an extra bedroom, remember?" she went on. "Right beside Barley's room. We can do bunk beds!"

I couldn't even begin to humor her in this fantasy. Riggs was going to ship us both off soon.

"Aren't you excited?" she asked.

"Here," I said, grasping her by the waist and depositing her on the counter between a pair of sinks. "My mouth tastes like I ate a dead raccoon."

"Gross!"

I rinsed Peach's brush, squeezed out a goodly dose of paste, and started in on my teeth. Peach didn't fuss about my using her toothbrush.

When I finished, I placed my palms on the counter on either side of Peach's knees and spoke to her face-to-face. I kept my voice low, figuring the bathroom was bugged: "I want more than anything for us to be together."

Like someone had pulled a lever, her eyes welled with tears. "We can't?"

I bit my lip. I didn't want to give her false hope, but I didn't want to crush her either. I feared she was nearing a breaking point. I recalled the way she'd crumpled to the ground in the Westfalls' yard when she'd missed the ball. These days it took very little for her to feel hopeless.

"At some point," I said, choosing my words carefully, "we'll be able to stay together."

She blinked at me, a tear spilling out, but the shine of hope there too.

"There's nothing I want more," I said. "Do you believe that?"

Her lips quivered, but she nodded.

"But first I have to... help these people. I have to give them what they want. Then we can be together."

If I'm still alive.

She searched my face. "What do they want?"

"I'm about to find out."

Her eyes widened. "Don't leave me again."

"Peach—"

"Don't tell me we can't be together!" she said, and now the tears were rolling, her slender shoulders quaking. "Please don't tell me that anymore."

Dammit, I thought. Riggs, Klinger, the rest of them. I wished they'd die for what they were doing to my little sister.

"Come here," I said, wrapping my arms around her.

She buried her face against my shoulder. "Promise, Will. Promise you won't go away."

"I—"

"*Promise!*" she yelled and pulled away from me. She grasped the front of my shirt. "You *have* to promise. I won't let you leave."

I cleared my throat. "I promise I won't go far."

She began to shake her head, but I hurried on. "I have to give them something. Without that, they won't let me go."

"You have to cooperate?"

For some reason, this made me sadder than anything she'd said. A year ago, she couldn't have pronounced the word *cooperate*.

I kissed her on the forehead. "Come on. You're gonna hang out with Darcy for a little while."

"Where are you going?"

"To see Riggs. He and I are gonna make a deal."

—

AFTER ACCOMPANYING PEACH back to Darcy, I found Agent Castro and told him I needed to see Riggs.

Castro had been talking to a woman, one whose gray muscle shirt revealed biceps twice as large as mine. Her sable hair was trimmed short, her eyes as dark as her hair. She watched me balefully as Castro spoke.

"He's in the conference room."

I glanced at the doors. "Which one is it?"

Looking put out — maybe Castro had the hots for the ripped soldier — he ran a hand through his blond crewcut. "Give me a minute," he said to her. Then to me, "Move it."

I followed him, nodding at the ripped soldier as I passed. She didn't nod back.

I said to Castro, "Can I ask you a question?"

"Wanna know how to score with the ladies?"

I grunted. "No. What I'm wondering is how it feels to be such a shitty person."

His cocksure expression didn't waver. "Hell," he said. "You're the one who gets everybody killed."

I wanted badly to fire back but couldn't think of anything. I felt like I'd been kicked in the balls.

We passed several knots of people on our way to the door, and I sensed numerous sets of eyes scrutinizing my every move. I felt like some rare and dangerous species of animal they'd captured, one they'd soon dissect for the advancement of science. When Castro opened a door and led me through a short hallway, I heard raised voices.

One man: "Why would you risk my people's lives?"

A smooth, cozening voice that could only belong to Riggs: "They're *my* people, Haddad."

The first man, Haddad apparently: "You assured me I would have autonomy. Otherwise, I'd have never—"

Riggs: "The Marines were deploying you all over the globe. You wanted to be closer to your family. Haven't I given you that?"

Haddad: "You've given me a rogue's gallery of sadists and lunatics."

Riggs, through hearty laughter: "Sadists and lunatics! That's priceless."

Haddad: "If what the boy says is true—"

Riggs: "It isn't. Oh hey, Castro! Come on in."

Castro led me inside a conference room. There were charts and maps all over the baby blue walls, but behind Riggs's desk, where the man himself reclined with his feet propped on a blotter, historical artifacts hung, framed collections of arrowheads, arcane-looking photographs of Native Americans and pioneer families. Even some rusty tools, one of them the sort of thing you'd see the Grim Reaper clutching.

"Will Burgess," Riggs said, "this is Colonel Haddad."

Haddad didn't look at me. He wore a beige military uniform, looked north of fifty and fit, had brown skin and tiny moles on his cheeks.

"The boy seems ready to cooperate," Castro said.

Riggs's eyebrows rose. He laced his fingers over his belly. "That right, kiddo?"

Remember Peach, I told myself. *Focus on her, not these bastards.*

I nodded.

"Well, this is a dandy way to end my night," Riggs said. "Castro, please bring in our special guests."

Castro frowned. "You mean—"

"That's right," Riggs said and fixed Castro with a meaningful look.

With a whatever-you-say shrug, Castro went out. Riggs gestured toward an empty chair next to Haddad's. "Take a load off, kiddo. The colonel and I were just working through some issues. He doesn't trust you much."

Haddad shifted in his chair.

"Colonel Haddad regards your... connection to these creatures with suspicion," Riggs explained. "But *I* say it's precisely what we need."

I clutched my thighs to stop myself from fidgeting. "What do you want from me?"

"Guidance," Riggs answered.

Haddad remained silent.

Riggs studied the ceiling. "Haddad and his team will enter the cave network beneath Peaceful Valley with the intention of locating the creatures that have caused all this ruckus."

"Ruckus," I repeated.

"You will accompany them into the caves," Riggs went on. "Or as I like to think of it, the Lair of the Beasts."

My mind raced. All along it was where I assumed the Children lived. Perhaps the Night Flyers too. Last summer, in rescuing Peach from Carl Padgett, I had descended into the catacombs in the forest behind my house and had encountered a number of cave drawings, ones that depicted both the Children and the Night Flyers.

Now Riggs was telling me to seek these creatures out.

"That's suicide," I said.

For the first time, Haddad looked at me.

I stared back at Haddad. "You and your people… me too, if I go… we're all gonna die."

"Ungrateful," Riggs remarked. He made a tutting sound. "I could threaten to kill you, but I tell you what… just to prove what a softhearted guy I am, I'm gonna incentivize this. If you do what we ask… *everything* we ask… I will sign the adoption papers for you and your sister."

I couldn't conceal my excitement. "To live with Barley's parents?"

Riggs nodded magnanimously. "They've already agreed. And I'll expedite the process."

At that moment, the fact that I would probably die a gruesome death in the caves seemed a distant concern. I'm afraid I even smiled.

"We got a deal?" Riggs asked.

I glanced at Haddad, whose expression hadn't altered.

I turned to Riggs. "Deal."

He clapped his hands together, slid his feet off his desk, and perched his elbows on the blotter. "Hot damn. This is gonna be a blast." He raised his chin toward the door. "Y'all can come in now."

The door opened, and my smile shriveled.

It was Dr. Klinger, looking disheveled but no less haughty than usual. I considered showing him my middle finger but somehow restrained myself. Castro entered next, followed by a figure that made my jaw drop.

It was Barker.

He favored me with a wan smile. "Hey, Will."

Impossible.

I shook my head. "I thought… I thought—"

"Me too," he said.

The others in the room were watching the exchange closely, but at that moment the only fact I could process was that Barker had somehow survived.

"I was sure they got you," I said.

He gave me an embarrassed smile and muttered something about being lucky.

"I heard you scream," I said. "That hallway was full of creatures."

He glanced from Klinger to Riggs, then said in a quiet voice, "I'll fill you in later."

Barker moved behind me, but before I could question him further, someone else entered the room, someone who made me climb to my feet, my jaw dropping another couple inches.

Mia Samuels.

She smiled more dazzlingly than I'd ever seen her smile. The most beautiful smile I'd ever seen. She stood there a moment, then rushed forward and gave me a fierce hug. I squeezed her back, unable to trust the feeling of her in my arms. It felt too wonderful to be true.

From far away, I heard Riggs say, "Ain't that sweet. Now if you two young lovers are ready, we've got plans to discuss."

Mia drew gently away, gave me a look that made my insides flutter, and strode around the desk toward Riggs.

"Well, hey there, darling," Riggs said, grinning up at her. "Do I get some sugar too?"

Mia slapped him with enough force to whip his face sideways, the sound like a thundercrack. A scarlet handprint on his cheek, Riggs gaped at Mia as though she'd transformed into a Bengal tiger.

Looking utterly at ease, Mia rejoined me and said to Riggs, "Let's negotiate."

—

BACK BEFORE MOM had gotten injured in a car accident and well before she'd become addicted to the painkillers that haunted our family, we'd attended a tiny Lutheran church on the edge of Shadeland called St. Mark's. I didn't like some of the people there, but some of them were nice to us. In particular, there'd been a pastor who'd taken an interest in me and Peach. Pastor John was kind and fair and willing to give people a chance, even poor ones who most Sundays couldn't leave anything in the collection plate.

But Pastor John had a problem.

It wasn't like he was that old, though at the time I thought he was ancient. I'm guessing he was in his late sixties, but a congenital heart defect gave him the stamina of someone twenty years older.

No one at St. Mark's knew about Pastor John's heart condition until he started getting woozy in the middle of sermons. But when folks noticed and he was forced to disclose his heart condition, the parishioners did what people always do: Some showed compassion and the rest turned on him. Though I was only ten at the time and young for the job, I was the acolyte for Sunday morning services, which meant I had a prime view of the entire affair.

Resting in a side room after one of his dizzy spells, Pastor John told me, "It won't be long now, Will. They've already contacted the synod."

Having absolutely no clue what a synod was, I just nodded.

"I can't save my job," he said, "but I can hang on a few months longer."

"Save your job?" I repeated dumbly. I'd been so naïve back then, thinking that the people at St. Mark's might take into consideration that the heart condition wasn't Pastor John's fault and that maybe, just maybe, they could make the situation work if they showed a little grace.

Like I said, I was terribly naïve.

"Would you be willing to help me?" he asked. "I'll understand if you say no."

"Sure," I said and meant it.

He unfolded a metal chair, which I sat on and awaited instructions. It was all mysterious to me; I felt like some underage superhero being given a top-secret mission.

"I won't last long," he said. "They'll say it was because of my health, but the truth is — and I want you to remember this — if someone wants to fire you, they'll do it, one way or another."

"They can't," I said with all the resoluteness of a stupid kid.

A sad smile. "I ran afoul of one of the elders last fall because I agreed to baptize little Luis Villegas."

"What's wrong with that?"

"Nothing that I could see," he answered. "Except... well, it's complicated."

I hadn't pressed him, and it was just as well. Looking back, I know it was because Ana Villegas, Luis's mother, had never gotten married — reason enough for some of the more Puritanical parishioners to deny the child baptism. More problematic for many was the family's immigration status. By agreeing to baptize Luis, Pastor John was, in the minds of his detractors, encouraging both pre-marital sex and illegal immigration.

But explaining all that to a ten-year-old would have taken awhile.

Instead, Pastor John asked me if I'd take on extra duties during the service. I'd be holding the tray of glasses while he distributed them during communion, bringing him bottled water when necessary, and performing several other small but crucial jobs to help him soldier through each Sunday morning.

The system worked for a few months, but there were a couple of scares. One Sunday during a hymn, he began to sway ominously, and just before he'd toppled backward, I was there to prop him up, my movements so stealthy from my chair to the pulpit that only a handful of parishioners witnessed what I'd done.

On another occasion, Pastor John had lost his train of thought, and amidst the murmurs and shiftings of the crowd, I'd hurried over and pointed to the spot in the Gospel of Luke from which he'd been reading. He nodded at me gratefully, but I sensed that sadness again, the same resignation I'd seen the day he'd asked me for help.

You see, I was only the acolyte, but I was the one who made sure the service ran smoothly. There at the end — this would have been about six months after our initial talk — I was performing nearly all the physical duties. My mom joked, not really joking, that he would have me delivering sermons soon. And I would have, if it would have helped Pastor John, whom I'd come to view as a sort of father figure. God knows how badly I needed one. And Pastor John possessed the character necessary for the job.

Until it all fell apart.

I pushed the memory away and glanced at Mia. Because sitting there now, in the conference room of the Peaceful Valley Nature Preserve, I realized that Mia and I were very much like I and Pastor John had been. His name was on the black-and-white placard out front, but I was the one who'd kept the show going.

I looked around at all these people. Riggs, Haddad, Dr. Klinger, Agent Castro. They all thought I was the key to unlocking this riddle, but the truth was, Mia had been the reason we'd survived last summer.

Or Mia and Peach. It was the pair of them that had given me courage, the two of them who'd fought bravely beside me and kept us alive long enough to escape that nightmare. Like Pastor John, I was weak, I was failing. Look at what happened back at Sunny Woods. What good had I done there? Had I saved anybody? Made any difference at all?

No. In the end, the Night Flyers had slaughtered nearly everyone. And these people, these foolhardy, pompous men believed they could stop these monsters? Even more ridiculously, they believed I could help?

Without Mia and Peach, I was nothing. I was a scared, troubled kid who was destined to lose everyone I loved.

I looked at Mia. My acolyte. My strength.

I had to get her, Peach, and the rest of the people I cared about as far away from here as possible.

Riggs nodded at Haddad, who rose and moved to where several maps hung. Barker brought a chair over so Mia could sit next to me. Wordlessly, Mia threaded her fingers through mine. I racked my brain to remember whether or not we'd ever held hands, but if we had, I couldn't think of when. My heart thumping pleasantly, I directed my attention toward Colonel Haddad.

"We are here at the moment," he said, pressing an index finger onto a vermilion dot. The map was four feet high and six feet wide, with a beige surface and numerous squiggly lines and tiny text printed on it. Haddad leaned onto his tiptoes. "One entry point is here," he said, tapping the map.

"The most practical way in," Castro said.

Riggs smiled an apology. "I forgot to mention that my right-hand man here is an expert on numerous subjects. Geography, Cartography—"

"That's the study of maps," Dr. Klinger said to Mia.

"I know what it is," Mia answered.

Castro rose and brushed past Haddad. "There's an aperture broad enough for two men to climb through." He traced a line on the map with his forefinger. "From there, we believe the passage to the lower caves is unobstructed."

I gaped at Castro. "You've sent people down there?"

"Sonogram equipment," he explained, "and infrared imaging. We can't be sure until we see it for ourselves, but yeah, the passageway appears to be clear."

Mia scowled at Castro. "How'd you find a passageway?"

Riggs shifted. "I guess we should clue our newcomers in. After all, they're gonna be part of the expedition."

I shook my head. "You mean *I'm* going to be part of the expedition — not Mia."

He smiled without humor. "I mean what I said. Things are liable to get hairy below ground. You might be apt to renege on our agreement."

"I won't—"

"Which is why," he interrupted, "we're taking Miss Samuels here as insurance."

Castro smirked. "To make sure you don't get any dumb ideas."

I looked at Mia. "You agreed to this?"

"She did," Riggs answered.

Are you all insane? I wanted to scream. Maybe Mia caught my wavelength because she gave my hand a squeeze.

"I'm not surprised you're enjoying this so much," Riggs said to Mia. "You being a conspirator yourself."

Mia looked like she'd been slapped.

"We got it all on tape," Riggs went on. "You told Klinger everything last summer."

"I told him the truth," Mia said.

"And we've been monitoring you ever since." He made that *tsk*-ing sound that gave me an urge to strangle him. "You've been one busy lady."

"Your search history is troubling, young woman," Dr. Klinger agreed. "Monsters, conspiracies. Even looking us up by name. What did you plan to do with that information, Miss Samuels?"

"So naïve," Castro said and leaned over the desk toward Mia. "Don't you know we can monitor your computer usage at the library? At your school?"

I remembered what Barley said about Mia being obsessed with setting me free. Now they were using that against her. I knew it wasn't my fault, but I couldn't help feeling responsible.

In a thin voice, Mia said, "You have no right."

Riggs belly laughed. "Darling, we have *every* right. We're your United States Government."

And sitting there, I had a premonition. My body went cold all over.

Riggs pushed away from his desk. "Meeting's over, folks." On the way toward the door, he flicked a hand in my direction and muttered to Castro, "See that they're looked after. I gotta check how the pavilion's coming."

He swept out the door, and Mia and I looked at each other.

"Did you miss me?" she asked.

"God, yes."

But my smile was half-hearted. I couldn't banish the memory of the images I'd glimpsed in Riggs's head.

Hell, I might as well admit it.

Last summer's encounter with the Children had not only given me occasional strength, a hellacious temper, and a penchant for glowing green eyes.

It was sporadic and infinitesimal, but I had acquired a trace of telepathy too.

And if what I'd seen had been accurate...

My friends and I were in far worse trouble than I'd assumed.

—

WHEN WE EMERGED from the stuffy conference room, I noticed that a change had come over the shelter, not only in the vibe out here, which was more subdued, but in the arrangement. Where before there'd been picnic tables lined up the way they'd been in the Sunny Woods cafeteria, there were now pockets of cots and sleeping bags situated where some of the tables had been. It didn't look comfortable, but it was an improvement.

At the spot where I'd sat earlier with Peach and Darcy, the tables had been rolled away, and there were now five sleeping bags, which I assumed were for Barley, Mia, Darcy, Peach, and me. At the notion of sleeping beside Mia, my body went a little rubbery. For thirteen months, I'd been thinking about her, about our single romantic moment in a moonlit creek. And now...

Peach spotted me, scampered over, leaped into my arms, and all carnal thoughts fled like wind-blown smoke.

"Were they mean to you?" she asked as I arranged her on my hip. Maybe she was too old to be held that way, but the carry felt natural, and Peach obviously craved the closeness. Truth be told,

I did too. If it were possible, I would have tethered Peach to me with unbreakable chains.

"About what you'd expect," I answered.

"They were mean," she said, scowling. As we moved toward Barley and Darcy, who were reclining atop their sleeping bags, Peach asked, "You want me to tell them off?"

"What would you say?"

"Bad things," she said solemnly.

"But not bad *words*, right?"

"What if they deserve it?"

"They do deserve it," I said, "but you still can't say bad words."

"You say them sometimes."

"That's because I'm awesome," I answered and lowered her to stand by Darcy.

"You need to settle an argument for us," Darcy said. She was cross-legged on a lumpy midnight-blue sleeping bag. "Barley and I were discussing werewolf movies."

"She's out of her mind," Barley said. "She claims *Ginger Snaps* is better than *An American Werewolf in London*."

"*Ginger Snaps* is a heck of a movie," I answered.

Barley gawped at me. "But better than *American Werewolf*? Come on, man. Don't tell me that hospital took your sanity."

Mia laughed breathlessly. "*Barley*."

He blinked at her. "What?"

Darcy popped a Cheeto into her mouth. "I think she's calling you insensitive."

"*Insensitive?* Insensitive is crapping on one of the best werewolf movies ever made."

I eased down on a sleeping bag, a musty olive-green one that looked older than I was. Mia took a spot beside me.

"Saying it's not the best werewolf movie ever made is hardly crapping on it," I pointed out.

Barley gestured at Darcy. "She said it was dated."

I looked at her. "Whoa, whoa, whoa. That's blasphemy."

Mia gave me a backhanded swat on the shoulder. "She can have an opinion if she wants."

"Not if her opinion sucks," Barley argued.

Staring at Barley, Darcy reached up and scratched the corner of her mouth with her middle finger.

Mia and I laughed.

Peach frowned. "What's so funny? 'Sucks'?"

I opened my mouth, but Darcy beat me to it. "*Sucks* isn't a great word, Peach. Will and Mia were laughing because Barley was so rude."

Barley gaped at Darcy.

Peach crawled over and swatted Barley the way Mia had swatted me. "Don't be rude, Barley," Peach said.

I laughed harder. So did Mia.

Barley opened his mouth to say something, but Peach raised a warning forefinger and said, "Be nice."

"So?" Darcy said to me. "Which movie's better?"

"Honestly? I prefer *Dog Soldiers*."

"That's a copout!" Darcy said, but Barley shrugged, accepting it.

"When I can I watch a werewolf movie?" Peach asked.

"When it won't give you nightmares," I answered. "Come here, knucklehead."

She crawled over and leaned against me. I slid my arm around her and was reminded of the time, two summers ago, that Barley's family had taken Peach and me to an amusement park in Southern Indiana called Holiday World. Peach had never been to Disney, had never been much of anywhere, but our day at Holiday World had been one of the greatest times of our lives. Eating junk food and riding the smaller rides — Peach had only been five at the time — had, at least momentarily, made up for the deprivation, the unfairness of our situation. Sitting beside Peach and howling with joy as we were spun around on the Scrambler, I could almost forget that there was very little waiting for us back in Shadeland. Just a drugged-out mom and a shabby little house we could barely afford.

But we'd had each other. Peach and I always had each other.

I squeezed her little body against me. Whatever Riggs was plotting, I couldn't let him separate us again. I'd rather die than be without my sister.

After a time, I realized the others were watching me and Peach in silence.

I didn't speak. I couldn't. Nor did I want to. All I wanted was right here beside me.

The best place to be is together, I thought.

Please, I prayed. *Please let us be together.*

CHAPTER SIXTEEN
BRIGHT SEGMENT

To say I slept fitfully that night would be an understatement. The kaleidoscope of thoughts that swooped through my head would have troubled even the most seasoned psychologists. As I lay there with Peach snoozing against my side — she'd insisted on arranging our sleeping bags like a mattress and a blanket rather than zipping ourselves inside them individually — I recalled the positive developments of the past twenty-four hours:

The reunion with Peach.

Pierre surviving the Night Flyers.

Barker's unlikely reappearance.

Getting to know Dave and Anita.

Returning to the farm to find Barley and his parents there.

Seeing Mia again. Yearning to kiss her for the first time.

But then an avalanche of horrific images crashed over me:

The attack on Sunny Woods. The massacre of nearly everyone inside. Nemo Pederson. Poor, misunderstood Nemo being eaten alive by a Night Flyer. Likewise for Rose, the kind-hearted lunch lady. Likewise for Dr. Fleetwood, who'd been carried away to experience who knew what kind of hellish tortures. And Harry, the lovelorn orderly who'd given his life to save a woman he could only pine for. And Hopper, the badass llama who willingly sacrificed himself to protect others.

I felt guiltier than ever. As I lay there with my sister's slender arm slung over my chest, not a bit drowsy and listening to the susurrant breathing of the people I cared about, I asked myself, *Why the hell are you still alive? What gives you the right to live when others are dead?*

I brought ruin to everyone I knew.

Was I endangering people by remaining here? What if I attempted to escape? Would Riggs's men shoot me, and if they did, would that ensure that no one else I cared about would suffer?

And what of the images I glimpsed in Riggs's brain? All of us screaming. Me, Pierre, Anita, Mia…

I'd lost the reel of faces then, but what I'd seen had made me queasy. Was it simply Riggs's anger at me, his desire to see me suffer? Or was there something more concrete, some plot designed to destroy us?

I didn't know. But these thoughts kept me on the uneasy edge of sleep until dawn.

By five-thirty there was enough light showing in the upper windows that sleep was an impossibility. Barley still slumbered peacefully, his mouth open and a string of drool darkening the plum-colored sleeping bag under his shaggy head. Next to him, Darcy stirred, her black hair lying in a tumble across her forehead. She looked angelic.

"She likes you, you know," a nearby voice said.

Heart pounding, I discovered Mia watching me with an imp-ish smile. She was propped on an elbow, only her upper body visible within the sheath of her cardinal-colored sleeping bag.

I shook my head. "I wasn't looking at her, I was—"

"It's okay," Mia said, her smile widening. "She *is* attractive. She tries not to show how into you she is, but I can tell."

"Mia—"

"Relax. I don't feel threatened."

"You don't?"

She shrugged a shoulder, the strap of her electric blue tank top slipping down a couple inches.

I forced myself to maintain eye contact.

Something new entered Mia's gaze, a knowingness that made my throat burn and my head dizzy. She glanced behind her — we were near the wall, and as far as I could tell, everyone in the shel-ter was still asleep — then moved her shoulder a little, so that the strap descended a trifle more.

I watched, my whole body tingling. It occurred to me that this was extraordinarily weird, given the fact that my little sis-ter was dozing behind me. But dammit, I'd been incarcerated for over a year, and not a night had passed that I hadn't thought of Mia.

She seemed to pick up on my thoughts. "You remember the creek?"

I swallowed. Nodded. How could I *not* remember the creek? That glorious moon-bathed night early last summer, only days before our world crashed down around us, back when my mom and best friend were still alive. Mia and I had splashed around in the water, her in her sports bra and underwear, I in my cargo shorts and no shirt, so that my bony, unmuscular chest shone white in the moonlight. Yet Mia hadn't cared, had liked me anyway, had acted as though she was as attracted to me as I was to her.

"I think of the creek all the time," she went on, her voice soft enough that only I could hear it. "One thing I appreciate about you is how…" Her eyes went away, returned to mine. "People think a girl is too forward if she shows she's into someone."

"People are idiots."

"But you never… even when I was dating Brad… you never made me feel like a slut—"

"You're not—"

"—or a fool for making bad decisions."

I chuckled. "You're not a fool."

"I *am*," she said, her words loud enough to worry me that Peach would awaken. "I'm a fool. I wasted all that time dating Brad, and when I finally realized how much I cared about you, it was too late. You were gone. They took you away and…"

But I had slithered, as stealthily as I could, from under my sister's arm. I slid my arm around Mia, drew her closer. Her eyes glimmered slightly despite the darkness.

I didn't know what to say. With every fiber of my being, I wanted to kiss her, but I felt unworthy. All I'd brought her was pain.

I looked into her eyes. "God, I missed you."

Her mouth curved in a close-lipped smile I found irresistible. There was a searing heat in my throat, my chest. She placed a hand there, her fingers closing on the fabric of my T-shirt. She drew me to her, her eyes lingering on mine, and our lips touched for the first time.

I thought I might die of happiness.

Though I'd kissed a couple girls before, this was my first *real* kiss, one so sublime that it eclipsed the others the way a floodlight would drown a votive candle. I'd been waiting to kiss her since the second grade. The fact that we were surrounded by people didn't matter. In that moment, Mia was the entire world. My mind spun, but I reminded myself to enjoy this. Given the way things had been going, I might never experience anything so glorious again.

She paused a moment to catch her breath, then we moved our bodies closer, pushed together, the only barrier between us Mia's sleeping bag.

"I'm so sorry, Will," she said into my mouth. "I'm sorry for not getting you out of there."

I kissed her, my hands on her back, and though I wanted to tell her she didn't need to be sorry, that her apologizing for something completely out of her control was ludicrous, I let my actions show her how I felt. Our hands roved over each other, our kisses deepening. The heat between our bodies grew unbearable, and though some rational region of my brain cried out, *What the hell are you doing? You're four feet from your little sister and there are dozens of people in this room,* my dominant impulse was to kiss Mia, to caress her warm, dark flesh, to get as close to her as possible. I had no idea how far things would have gone had they continued that way, but a loud *brrrlat!* jolted us out of our passion and made us stare, wide-eyed, at the person in the sleeping bag between Peach and Darcy.

Barley murmured in his sleep and smiled contentedly, having ripped the world's loudest fart.

Our foreheads pressed together, Mia and I devolved into laughter. A few minutes later, everyone around us was awake.

—

SOMETIME LATER, I pulled Mia aside. Darcy and Barley were helping Peach dish up from a breakfast buffet, and the adults seemed not to notice Mia and I as we hurried to a little alcove between the men's room and what might've been a utility closet.

"I need to tell you something," I said.

"I've got a lot to tell you too," she answered.

"I'm afraid if I don't say it now, they'll swoop in and take you away from me. And I don't..." I broke off, unable to articulate how much she meant to me.

She must've misread my silence because her features went hard. "Are you breaking up with me?"

I gaped at her. "Are you kidding? God no. I can't believe you waited for me this long."

She drew back. "What did you think I was gonna do? Start dating everybody in the school?"

"Why would I—"

"They *all* say it," she snapped. "Everyone but Barley and Tristan."

I hate to admit this, but I felt an immediate tightening at the second name. "Who's Tristan?" I asked. "Does he like you?"

She pitched a sigh. "Yes, but that's irrelevant." Before I could interject — probably with some juvenile plea for reassurance — she said, "It's his influence on Barley I don't like."

Someone passed by very close to us — the massive soldier with the pitted scar — and I lowered my voice. "How's he influencing Barley?"

"Tristan's rich," she said, "so he can afford whatever he wants."

Does that include you? I thought, then suppressed an urge to slap myself in the face. *Stop being such an insecure asshole!*

"When you say he can afford things, what are we talking? Cars? Alcohol?"

"Alcohol," she agreed, "and drugs."

I shook my head. "Whoa whoa whoa. You're telling me Barley's doing *drugs*?"

"I'm not sure what they're into. They smoke weed and drink a lot, but I think they do harder stuff than that. And they take chances. Tristan drives them around while they're high. He drives too fast. And they like to break things, to scare people."

I opened my mouth to assure her this couldn't be. Barley was the sweetest, most innocent guy I knew. He would never…

Then I remembered last summer. How he'd lost his two best friends, one to the Children, the other to a psychiatric ward. I thought of the things he'd seen… how guilty he felt for not being with us in the end…

I thought of the shadow I'd detected in Barley's face, the harder edge in his eyes.

"Damn," I murmured.

She studied me. "What was it you wanted to tell me?"

I hesitated. "It's hard to put into words."

"I swear to God, if you tell me you're breaking up with me—"

I kissed her. She sucked in breath, frozen that way for a moment. Then her hands went to my shoulders and her lips softened. God, the taste of her mouth, warm and citrusy, sent a thrill all the way through me. Not a sexual thrill, just a…

Love, a voice supplied. *The word you're looking for is love.*

I pulled away and she looked up at me, a little dazed.

"Mia," I said, "I'm so sorry for what you've been through."

She started to shake her head, but I grasped her by the shoulders. "You've gone through hell. People have hurt you, lied about you, and you haven't deserved a goddamned bit of it."

I thought there might be latent tears forming in her eyes, but I had to get it out, had to say it. "You lost Rebecca and Kylie Ann. Chris too. You lost me. Even Peach." Now she did look away, a tear sliding down her cheek. I went on, "The stuff that's happened to you, no one should have to go through. But in spite of all of it, you've never stopped caring, never stopped trying to help. You've kept going when anyone else in the world would've quit."

She wiped away tears. "It's okay. Really."

"It's *not* okay," I said. "You haven't deserved any of the stuff that's happened… the way people have talked about you…"

A wry smile. "Barley told you?"

"Mia, I…" I broke off, words failing me. "Nothing I can say will take away your pain. But I've thought of you every day since they locked me up in that fucking place. It's thinking about you and Peach that's kept me going."

She smiled through her tears. "Yeah?"

I nodded. I knew we should be getting back, knew Peach would be wondering about us. But seeing the look on Mia's face and the warmth in her brimming eyes, I couldn't stop myself. I wrapped my arms around her and kissed her again. She laced her fingers behind my neck, and even that, the light brush of her fingernails on my skin, sent a wave of euphoria through me.

"There're people trying to eat here," a deep voice said.

We looked up at the massive, scarred soldier, whom I now realized had been dispatched to watch me.

"Come on," Mia said, taking my hand and leading me past him.

"Dick," I muttered.

He snagged my arm, his grip so viselike I'm afraid the pain showed in my face. "Call me that again, and I'll throw your skinny ass across the room." He nodded at Mia. "See how impressed she is with you then."

I glared back at him but knew I was beaten. He gave my arm a final, brutal squeeze, then let go. Mia led me away, and I'm not too proud to admit I was relieved. Because I'd seen the kind of look he'd given me from other people. Carl Padgett had looked at me that way.

There'd been murder in the soldier's eyes.

—

"WHAT'S THAT SOUND?" Mia asked.

We were seated at one of the lengthy rectangular tables that had been wheeled out for breakfast. Mia sat to my left, Peach to my right, with Barley and Darcy across from us. At a table a couple aisles over, Pierre, Anita, and Dave were talking to Barley's folks.

I returned my attention to our table, where Barley kept stealing glances at Darcy. I tried not to think of what Mia had told me, tried not to think about the things Barley been doing, the chances he'd been taking. But the name echoed in my head: *Tristan.*

I'd never even met him, and I already despised him.

"There it is again," Mia said, head cocked to listen. "What *is* that?"

"You mean the rain?" Barley asked.

She looked at him dourly. "Not the *rain*, Barley. I mean that high-pitched buzzing sound."

"Masonry saw," Darcy said through a mouthful of eggs.

We all stared at her.

Darcy held up an index finger while she chewed her food. She swallowed, took a sip of bottled water. "It's a masonry saw."

"How the hell do you know that?" Barley asked.

"The Westfalls had their driveway fixed this spring." She shrugged. "I watched."

"Darcy wouldn't let me go outside with her," Peach said. I noticed she hadn't touched her food.

"That's because you weren't wearing protective eyewear," Darcy explained.

"Neither were you."

Darcy tapped her glasses. "I already had mine."

"That's not technically protective," Barley said. "An errant fragment of concrete could have shot under your frames and lodged in your eye."

Smooth, I thought. *You're a real sweet talker, Barley.*

Darcy looked at him mock-seriously. "I appreciate your concern for my safety."

Barley smiled at her with a tinge of amazement. Man, he had it bad. I also noticed he had a bit of sausage lodged between his front teeth.

"Well, kiddies," a voice boomed from our left, making us all jump.

Riggs.

"Time to show you what we've been working on," he said.

I exchanged a look with Mia.

Darcy asked, "Does this have to do with that sawing sound?"

Riggs cocked his head. "As a matter of fact, it does." He looked at me. "I always appreciate a smart lady, don't you?"

"Go to hell," I muttered.

Peach tightened at my language. But I wasn't going to sit here and pretend we were anything other than what we were.

Prisoners.

"Oh, yeah," Riggs said, as though remembering something. He laid a big paw on Darcy's shoulder. "Time for you to head home."

Darcy glowered up at him. "I'm staying with my friends."

Riggs laughed. "Friends? These losers? I'd have thought you'd be more discriminating than that."

"Don't you—"

"Hush, darling. Your mama's here."

Darcy frowned. "Mrs. Westfall?"

Riggs nodded. "Nice woman. Feisty too. I like that."

"Darcy's leaving?" Peach asked. I started to speak, but a thought kept me silent: Darcy was better off leaving here. For that matter, maybe Peach would be better off too.

Darcy glanced at us as Riggs led her toward the exit, and in the next instant she was gone.

Peach gazed up at me with huge brown eyes. "Is she gonna be okay?"

"Yeah," I answered. I put a hand on the nape of Peach's neck, massaged it so the little muscles would untense.

Riggs was back within moments. He stood before us and clapped his hands once. "You lead the way," Riggs instructed me. "You come, they'll follow. Isn't that how it works?"

"They can think for themselves."

He chuckled softly. "If you say so."

A quartet of soldiers materialized around us.

Overkill much? I thought. Three teenagers and a seven-year-old hardly required a horde of armed gorillas.

I took Peach's hand; Mia took her other hand. The three of us followed Riggs, with Barley trailing. We moved toward the exit, where we found Colonel Haddad, Castro, and Barker.

"Wait," I said. "Where are Barley's parents? Where's Pierre?"

"They're already inside the membrane," Castro said and flashed a sharkish smile.

"Inside *what*?" Mia asked.

"Come on," Riggs said, his tone easy. "You'll see."

With more than a little misgiving, I followed Riggs and his entourage into the muggy, overcast morning. The rain had ebbed, and the cicadas had begun to chirr. Peach trembled against me. Did she sense something that I couldn't? I knew I had some sort of telepathy, but whatever terrible gift I'd gotten from those monsters was dormant as we moved through the eerily silent campground.

We passed through a screen of spruce trees and followed a broad trail winding left, then right. When we emerged from the thicket and I saw where we were headed, a chill gripped me with implacable fingers. I shivered, but caught myself when I remembered I was supposed to be brave. I glanced at Mia, who was staring at our destination in dread.

The membrane, as Riggs had called it, was a large outdoor shelter, roughly fifty feet wide and eighty feet long. It was situated in a slight depression and surrounded by a ring of dense forest. Because the trees that reefed the shelter were so old and tall, the structure was overlaid with shadows, so that despite its newness — I was sure it had been built for the ill-fated state park — it projected a woebegone, neglected aura, like a shuttered hospital or an abandoned amusement park. But the chill within me had little to do with the shelter and more to what Riggs's people had done to it.

Riggs grinned back at me. "Like it?"

"What's all that stuff around it?" Peach asked.

"Plastic sheeting," Riggs said. "My men picked it up at Home Depot."

"But why—" Mia began.

"No questions," Riggs cut her off. "Come on, now. Time's wasting."

And before Riggs turned, I caught something in his face that frightened me more than anything had since Barley and I had almost been murdered by the Night Flyer. Instead of cruelty or scorn, there was an unaccustomed tightness around Riggs's eyes, a peculiar set to his mouth. The truth slammed home to me:

Riggs was scared.

My heart racing, I moved with my sister and my friends toward the shelter.

No, a voice in my head corrected.

The membrane.

—

"WELCOME TO YOUR home for the morning," Riggs announced, his voice overloud in the plastic-encased shelter. Entering it, I spotted Pierre, Dave, Anita, and Barley's parents. Of course, it wasn't difficult to spot them; other than the guards stationed around the perimeter, they were the only people in the enclosure. No tables, no benches, not even a solitary charcoal grill stood within the gaudily illuminated space. But despite the brilliance of the overhanging lights, the membrane was creepy as hell.

I caught movement from the far corner of the enclosure and realized I'd been wrong. There *was* one other object. Riggs's soldiers were wheeling a large implement out between the plastic sheets.

"Masonry saw," Mia said.

A pair of soldiers knelt before a square hole in the floor. One was grasping what looked like a steel door; the other was affixing it to hinges.

Noticing our gaze, Riggs explained, "Tornado shelter. It's large enough to accommodate a couple hundred people. More in an emergency. The problem is," he continued, moving toward the center of the shelter, "there's a major design flaw."

"The fact that the walls are made of plastic?" Barley said.

"Smartass," Castro mumbled.

Riggs waved them off. "The walls don't matter. Hell, you think walls are gonna prevent a tornado from ripping this entire structure off the ground and flinging it into the heavens?"

"Hey, Pierre," I said when we reached where they stood. Barley's mom went immediately to her son and wrapped him in a bear hug. I glanced at Barley's dad, who was eyeing Riggs as though the big man were some hostile alien species bent on annihilating us.

Actually, I decided that might not be far from the truth.

The chill within me deepened.

"They tell you anything?" Pierre asked me under his breath.

"Just some stuff last night."

His eyebrows went up, and I realized I hadn't debriefed him after we'd been taken to the conference room. I was about to share what little I knew — the caves, the discord between Riggs and Haddad — but Riggs's voice intruded before I could speak.

"How in the world," he said to no one in particular, "did the makers of this place decide that one entryway into the bad weather bunker was sufficient for a whole shelter full of people?"

"Fools," Castro said.

"Remember, kiddo," Riggs said to me, "always leave yourself another way out."

The sounds of a scuffle made us all turn.

"Don't... touch me!" a man's voice demanded.

Barker. He was being prodded forward by a pair of Riggs's goons. All told, there a dozen soldiers in the enclosure, and that wasn't counting Riggs, Castro, or Haddad. Klinger was conspicuously absent.

Yet all these soldiers seemed... excessive.

"You doing okay?" someone asked. It was Dave Myers, who'd crouched in front of Peach.

"I don't like this place," she said.

He smiled ruefully. "Me either. It gives me the willies."

Peach nodded, but she crowded closer to me. I could tell she wasn't ready to trust Dave, which both reassured and saddened me. On one hand, she'd always been too trusting, so much so that I used to worry about her going off with some stranger. On the other hand, she'd seen me interact with this man, yet she still didn't trust him. Just another sign of how all this had changed her. Soon, she'd have no innocence left.

"My guys worked all morning long," Riggs said, then placed a hand on his mouth and glanced at Mia in mock contrition. "Whoops. I should say 'My *people*,' shouldn't I? Don't wanna discount the ladies under my command."

"Let these people go," Colonel Haddad said.

Everybody turned and stared at him.

"Hell, Colonel," Castro said, "you know we can't do that."

"Let them go," Haddad repeated.

I realized I'd been fooled by his stolid demeanor. He didn't emote a lot, but that didn't mean he didn't feel anything.

Riggs eyed Haddad. "Now why the hell would we do that?"

"Because it's the right thing to do," he answered.

Riggs's features relaxed, the serene sadist reappearing. "Shit, Colonel. To think I almost let bygones be bygones. I must be going soft in my twilight years."

"Told you we couldn't trust him," Castro muttered.

Haddad stepped closer to Riggs. "What are you talking about?"

"New Hampshire," Riggs answered. "The White Mountains."

A look of incredulity spread on Haddad's face. "*That's* what this is about? It was a disagreement—"

"Disagreement, my ass. It was straight-up insubordination. You contravened my orders."

"That was twenty-three years ago," Haddad said. He glanced from face to face as if to locate some sanity. "You're telling me this is about settling some old score?"

"Oh, it's settled already," Riggs answered. "You just don't realize it."

Anita broke away from her uncle and addressed Riggs. "Will someone tell us what in the hell is going on?"

"Gladly," Riggs said, his eyes not leaving Haddad's. "There are now two doors to the tornado shelter. That means seven people to a door."

"Your twelve guards," I guessed, "plus you and Castro."

Riggs glanced at me. "You're smarter than I thought, champ."

Voices sounded from outside the enclosure. Quite a few of them.

"Wait a minute," Anita said. "Why would you and your men need to take shelter?"

"Why, to keep us safe, darlin'," Riggs answered.

"Safe from *what*?" she demanded.

But I thought I knew. My throat constricted.

Riggs's mantra echoed in my brain: *Centralize...*

"What are those men doing?" Anita asked.

Silhouettes moved and shifted outside the translucent sheeting.

"What are they *doing*?" Barley's mom demanded, her voice teetering on the edge of panic.

Riggs's voice in my head: *...sanitize...*

One of the men bumped the plastic sheeting and smeared a red streak on the translucent surface.

"Paul?" Barley's mom asked, and it took me a moment to realize she was addressing her husband. I'd never thought of him as Paul before. He was always just Barley's dad.

Dave Myers spoke, and though I could tell he wanted to sound authoritative, his voice came out tight. "Tell us what those men are doing."

"Chumming," Pierre answered.

We all looked at him.

A moment later, a gout of red liquid splashed the plastic. Twenty feet down the length of the shelter, more of the red substance splattered the sheeting.

"What do you mean, chumming?" Mia asked.

Red splashed the walls on all sides.

"They're attracting the monsters," Pierre said. "Isn't that right, Riggs?"

...cauterize, I thought. *Jesus Christ.*

Riggs and his people were edging toward the shelter doors, moving as though they'd planned this already, each soldier going directly to a pre-designated spot. I longed to sweep Peach into my arms and make a break for it, but the soldiers had their weapons drawn. In the center of the shelter, we clustered together: me,

Peach, Mia, Barley, Barley's parents, Pierre, Anita, Dave, Barker, and Haddad. Eleven of us.

Eleven people who were about to die.

Castro and Riggs reached the nearest trapdoor. Castro drew it open and climbed inside. The shelter must not have been deep because I could see the top of Castro's blond head within the bunker. Riggs fetched a walkie talkie from his belt, muttered something into it. It sounded like, "Almost ready."

Haddad was shaking his head. "All that stuff about the caves, about taking a team underground…"

"Horseshit," Riggs said and beamed at him. "Bona fide, one hundred percent horseshit. I can't believe you bought it."

"What about Ernestine?" I asked.

All mirth fled from Riggs's face, and he stared at me, dead-eyed. "What about her?"

"You can't be completely heartless. You cared about her and her son…" I sought for the name. "…Mikey. You can make amends now, by setting us free."

"Make amends," he repeated tonelessly.

"Peach is just a kid. She deserves better than this."

He let out a soft, bitter laugh. "You know what happened? They found Ernestine hanging from a tree in her backyard. She must've done it after she… after she became herself again."

My stomach roiled.

Pierre stepped forward. "I don't know who you guys are talking about, but you can't go through with whatever you're planning."

Riggs went on, those dead eyes of his fixed on me but not really seeing, the scene in his head from 1988 replaying: "I got there first. I'd been spending a lot of time with Ernestine and her boy…"

I shook my head. "You don't have to—"

"She did it," Riggs said in little more than a whisper. "They found pieces of Mikey sprinkled around his bedroom. Ernestine must've mutated… must've become one of them."

"That's enough," Haddad said.

Riggs's gaze on me was pitiless. "That's what you'll do. What you'll become."

I began to shake my head.

"You know it's true," he persisted. "You think you're protecting your kid sister? As long as she's near you, she's in danger. I'm doing her a favor."

Anita stepped toward him. "You can't do this. You can't just—"

She leapt back as a barrage of bullets tore a line through the concrete six inches from where she'd been. Instinctively, I thrust Peach behind me as chips of concrete sprayed us. I saw a huge soldier—the one with the facial scar—approaching with an assault rifle. His hands were slick with blood.

"Take it easy, Montana," Riggs said. He moved to the open trapdoor and settled down on the rim.

It took a moment for the connection to snap into place, but then, despite the terror of our predicament and the adrenaline pumping through me, I realized Riggs had given the scarred man that name because of the Al Pacino character, Tony Montana in the movie *Scarface*. At the end of that movie, I remembered, Pacino had snorted a mountain of cocaine and unloaded a hellstorm of bullets.

As he leveled the gun at us, Montana looked no less unhinged than Pacino had in the movie.

"Don't get too bent out of shape," Riggs said to our group. "By the time the Children get inside, my people will be tearing this place apart with their M16s. It'll happen so fast, you'll barely feel a thing."

Barley's mom spoke, her voice barely more than a whisper. "You're using us… you're using these children… as *bait?*"

Riggs grinned. "It's a hell of a big fish we're after."

Before Barley's mom could reply, a chorus of voices sounded from the forest, the cry somehow guttural and shrill at the same time. I felt my insides liquefy. Beside me, Peach whimpered. I didn't blame her. We'd heard the same hellish war cry last summer.

The Children had come.

PART FIVE
THE CHILDREN

CHAPTER SEVENTEEN
AS ABOVE, SO BELOW

"Watch 'em, Montana," Riggs called.

"They're not going anywhere," Montana answered. His machine gun, assault rifle, whatever the hell an M16 was, was trained straight at us.

Riggs slithered down into the hole. Only his eyes were visible as he said, "You know what to do, right?"

"Breeze," Montana said, and I saw with mounting disbelief that the scarred man was grinning.

"You know you're being sacrificed, don't you?" Anita asked Montana.

Montana shifted the muzzle of the machine gun a notch, so that it pointed toward Anita's chest. She was shorter than I was, but as she stepped forward, she seemed to swell to twice my size.

"Just look," she said, flourishing a hand at the trapdoor nearest us, which had swung closed. "They're leaving you up here to die."

Montana's grin widened. "I'm not the one dying."

"Have you *seen* them?" I demanded. "The Children… they're like an elemental force. Your weapons aren't going to make a difference."

"Not *weapons*." Montana patted the M16. "*Weapon*. Lizzie is the only protection I need."

"Oh, Jesus," Barley said. "He actually named his gun. Like a crappy eighties action hero."

But Montana seemed not to hear. With a narrowing of his eyes, he swung the gun ninety degrees toward the sheeting. I didn't detect any movement there, but I was swept up in that horribly familiar acceleration. That nightmarish sensation of events spiraling out of control, my brain and body too sluggish to keep pace.

"I'm scared, Paul," Mrs. Marley said.

Mr. Marley slid an arm around his wife. "Come here, Dale," he said softly. Barley did as he was told. It's crazy, but even in that moment, I envied Barley his parents. Their solidity. Their simple love for him and each other. It occurred to me their other son must be staying with Barley's grandparents, and even that seemed beautiful. I had no grandparents of which I was aware.

But dammit, I had Peach. I drew her closer to me. She wrapped her arms around my waist. Her little body was quaking. Sure, she'd grown some since last year, but she was still only seven. Seven and needing someone to protect her.

"Come here," I said, bending a little. Without argument, she laced her hands behind my neck, and I hoisted her up so that she could bury her head against my shoulder instead of facing the ghostly ivory walls, which undulated lazily in the warm July breeze.

I remembered reading a play in eighth grade called *The Miracle Worker*, the one about Helen Keller. There'd been a line in there about how parents don't just keep kids safe, but kids keep their parents safe, too. At the time, the sentiment had struck me as nonsensical. How the hell could a kid keep her mom and dad safe?

But holding Peach at that moment, feeling her soft cheek nuzzle my shoulder, I finally understood. She gave me courage as much as I gave her reassurance. Without my sister, my life felt purposeless. But with her in my arms, I felt like I mattered. If I could keep this wonderful little soul safe, my life would have meaning.

I looked at Haddad. "What's our plan?"

His eyes shifted from me to Peach. "Let's close ranks."

Wordlessly, we all backpedaled so that our bodies touched. Our group felt much larger, much *stronger*, massed together like that. Peach was latched onto my neck like the world's largest tick. Mia crowded against my left side. Someone pushed closer on my right, and a hand grasped the shoulder Peach wasn't occupying. I looked up to find Pierre, his slender frame next to mine. He didn't speak, but he did gaze down at me, and in that moment, I remembered all the times over the past thirteen months he'd made me feel like something other than a pariah. He'd made time for me every day. Sometimes it had been just a quick hello. Other times he'd visited my room. And the courtyard discussions, the long walks to and from the bathroom. Pierre was the only one who'd bothered talking to me as I struggled through my soul-killing exile.

"Thanks," I said to him.

His stoic expression never wavered, but he gave my shoulder a squeeze. Maybe I didn't have a mom or a dad. But I had Pierre.

More figures crowded in behind me, and with a glance I realized Anita and Dave had filled in the gap there. Dave smiled at me, and I smiled back.

The creatures outside bellowed and all my good feelings vanished.

"Stay calm," Haddad murmured.

Dave grunted mirthlessly, and I couldn't blame him. How could we stay calm with monsters amassing around us?

But Haddad continued, his words a gruff whisper. Whatever he had to say, he didn't want Montana to hear. "We need a diversion."

"From the Children?" Mia asked.

"From Montana," Haddad answered.

"I'll do it," Barker said.

I swiveled my head to look at him. I'd forgotten he was there. We hadn't really spoken since our ordeal with the Night Flyers, and I noticed with misgiving that he looked unwell. His skin was ashen, his hair... my God, was his hair longer? Only a couple of days ago it had been militaristically short. Now it appeared shaggy, almost frizzy at the tips. And there was something else. Something that couldn't possibly be.

His crooked nose... it didn't look crooked anymore.

I pushed away the thought.

"I can do it," Barker told us.

"You sure?" Pierre asked Barker. "You're a young man with your whole life ahead of you. And I can run like hell."

What Pierre said was true, but the thought of him risking his life made me sick in the pit of my stomach. I held my breath, hoping Pierre wouldn't get the job, hoping even more that this was a nightmare from which I'd soon awaken.

"It has to be me," Barker said. "It doesn't make any difference now."

Whatever that meant, we had no time to consider because Haddad was pressing on. "Fine. Barker, you break toward the north wall, draw Montana's fire. I'll rush him from the flank, try to catch him off guard."

"Got it," Barker said, but Dave was shaking his head.

"That won't be enough. Montana will cut you down—"

"No time to argue," Barker interrupted, wincing.

I frowned. What was the matter with him?

Peach burrowed deeper into my shoulder.

"I'll rush him with you," Dave suggested.

"No offense," Pierre whispered, "but with that limp of yours, you're not rushing anybody."

"I can still run," Dave said. Anita started to speak, but before she could protest, he added, "I have to do this."

My throat tightened. I'd seen this behavior before. Rebecca Ralston, Mia's best friend, had felt responsible for the death of her little sister. Because of that guilt, she'd sacrificed herself last summer to save us. I thought of how the Children had circled Rebecca, how they'd taunted her before ripping her apart.

"Listen, Dave," I said, my voice thick, "you don't have to—"

"I *do* have to," he interrupted. "You were right. I've been a miserable excuse for a husband." He took Anita's hands in his. "It's no consolation, but I'm sorry. You deserved better than what I gave you. You deserved the best."

"Please—" she started, but Haddad broke in.

"We've got to move. Barker, draw Montana's fire. Dave, you swing around with me and attack from behind. One of us is bound to get him."

"Then what?" Anita demanded. "He'll tear you to shreds."

"Let's all rush him," Barley suggested.

"You're staying right here," Haddad told him. "So are the rest of you. Once the firing starts, I want you to hit the floor. Gather as close together as you can, and stay low."

Mia shook her head. "But you haven't explained what happens once you reach Montana."

"I've got my knife," Haddad said.

"But—" Mia started to protest.

"Once we have the gun," Haddad cut her off, "we'll have a chance of getting out of here."

"You don't have to go," Pierre said to Dave. "It's better if I—"

"No more time," Barker interrupted. "Look."

We looked. Along the northern wall, where Barker was supposed to stage his suicidal diversion, a shadow had appeared. It was difficult to tell with the translucent plastic undulating the way it was, but the shadow appeared to be very tall and very thin.

It wasn't the sort of shadow a human would make.

"It's time," Haddad whispered.

"I'm going with you," Pierre said.

"You're staying here to protect these kids," Haddad said.

I heard a kissing sound, half-turned to see Dave pulling away from Anita, who had tears in her eyes. "You don't have to—" she began.

But she stopped when a figure broke from the group.

Barker was charging across the shelter.

Montana was indeed diverted. The massive soldier leveled his M16 — *Lizzie*, I remembered with a sick roll of my stomach — and began to fire.

—

IT WASN'T UNTIL they'd closed half the distance that I realized Dave and Haddad had looped around and were approaching Montana from the rear.

The machine gun roared again, and I whirled to see if Barker was dead yet.

He wasn't, but in slow motion I watched the bullets spang off the concrete, pursuing Barker like a sparking trail of gunpowder in some old cartoon. Hunks of concrete and puffs of dust leapt off the floor as Montana honed in. Bullets cracked ten feet behind Barker... five feet... one...

Blood splashed from Barker's calf, more from his hamstring. *No!* my mind screamed, but in the next moment, Barker somersaulted and sprang up in a crouch, hands and feet planted beneath him like some jungle cat.

His eyes glowed red.

Holy Mother of God, I thought.

"Will?" Mia asked, sounding as stunned as I was.

Montana was staring in dismay at Barker, but I was sure at any moment he'd regain his composure and finish Barker off.

Barker glowered at him, red eyes blazing, teeth bared in a snarl.

"What the fuck is happening to him?" Montana murmured.

I shot a glance at the duo approaching Montana. Dave was chugging along, but he was laboring several steps behind Haddad, who was only fifteen feet away. Montana's eyes widened and he spun just as Haddad extended his arms to tackle him.

Haddad's momentum and sheer courage propelled him into Montana, who was caught off balance. He went blundering backward with Haddad on top of him, the M16 spraying its lethal fire at the ceiling, where the sheet metal sparked and pinged.

Dave had faltered, was on his knees, a hand cupped against his shoulder. Not fatal, I thought, but not good either. Blood pulsed through his fingers from the errant M16 slug.

I threw a glance at Barker, but now the man's head was lowered. Garbled words issued from his mouth. His arms twitched unnaturally as he crouched a few feet from the plastic barrier.

Montana writhed beneath Haddad, who'd drawn his big knife. He pumped the blade into the meat near Montana's collarbone, Montana emitted a surprised grunt, and Haddad scrambled on top of him to wrest the gun away. One of Montana's massive hands had swung up to grab the knife handle protruding from his shoulder, but the other was still miraculously gripping the M16.

Evidently, he was disinclined to part with Lizzie.

Haddad grappled with him. Dave staggered slowly to his feet, his blood pattering on the floor. At any moment, the Children would swarm the shelter.

Pierre broke toward Montana, realizing perhaps that if Montana were able to retain possession of the gun, he'd no longer bother with orders. He'd simply open up on us and massacre the entire group.

"Weren't we supposed to lay on the floor?" Peach whispered.

I swallowed, realizing she was right. It had all transpired so rapidly that I'd been too stunned to react.

Haddad was succeeding in prising the weapon from Montana. The gigantic soldier looked disoriented as hell. Haddad rose to his feet, his hands hauling up on the weapon. He braced a foot on Montana's prone form for leverage, and just when the weapon appeared ready to yank free, Pierre arrived, reared back like an NFL placekicker, and booted Montana's arm above the elbow. Haddad went stumbling away, but he had the M16. Montana rolled over, both hands on the knife embedded in his shoulder. Pierre rushed over to Dave Myers.

"Okay," Haddad called to us. "Everybody follow me. If we hurry, we can…"

He trailed off, his expression going slack.

The little hairs on my forearms rising, I turned and discovered what had silenced Haddad.

A pair of Children had torn through the plastic wall.

—

"OH MY GOD," someone whispered. It was Anita, I realized. Anita, who had never encountered these monsters.

I recalled my first experience with them. It had happened near a cave in the forest, and though there'd only been one of them, and there'd been three policemen accompanying me, we hadn't stood a chance.

That was the terrible, unholy truth about the Children. There was no withstanding them. Even now, they were stalking toward us, their leering mouths full of mottled, tapered teeth, their huge green eyes fraught with hunger and triumph.

"Everybody down!" Haddad bellowed.

This time we listened.

I placed a hand under Peach's head, so that as I fell on top of her, she wouldn't be concussed on the concrete. I positioned her little body under my own, so that any misplaced bullet would hit me instead of her. Mia had also draped her body over Peach, forming a shell with me.

Haddad was opening up, the M16 spitting thunder at the Children. An answering shriek told me he'd hit at least one. When I raised my head, I saw a creature writhing on the floor. But any satisfaction I might have felt at the sight of the fallen Child evaporated instantly.

Two more Children were ripping through the plastic sheeting not far from where Pierre and Dave stood.

"Look!" Mia said to me, and following her gaze, I discovered something so grisly and fantastical that I forgot to breathe.

Barker was sprouting wings.

He was screaming, too. The pain must have been immense. From either side of his ribcage, glistening sable wings were extending, quivering, bursting through his flesh as though it were wet paper. And as horrifying as this was, it didn't compare with Barker's face, which was rupturing in a dozen places, the pale flesh peeling and curling in gooey strips to reveal oleaginous black flesh.

Barley murmured, "Night Flyer."

I nodded faintly.

One of the Children had been riddled by Haddad's M16, but the other had branched off. Pierre and Dave were hemmed in on both sides by the creatures.

"Get down!" Haddad shouted at them, but before they could follow his command, a flurry of movement drew everyone's attention.

Barker, half-transformed into a Night Flyer, had taken flight.

His progress through the air was both pitiful and awe-inspiring to behold. His wings were encumbered by that mucus-like substance, and his wingbeats were labored and unwieldy. Yet it was clear that this transformation had brought with it incredible strength. Barker's arms were undergoing that same hideous molting, and the leathery black flesh beneath was corded with muscle. The Barker-thing beat its wings harder, rising above us, moving in a gradual arc toward the Children, who glowered at the newborn Night Flyer with loathing. As the Barker-thing passed over us, I saw with a sense of unreality that his new feet had torn through his shoes, that his toes had become talons.

The Children faced the Barker-thing.

Having flown to a height of twenty feet, the Barker-thing lowered its head and winged straight at a Child. The Child leaped at the Barker-thing, its tensile legs vaulting it ten feet off the ground. The creatures collided in midair and immediately began tearing at each other.

The other two Children rushed at us.

I knew at once we were screwed. Haddad was shouting at us to *stay down, stay down*, but because there were so many of us, it was difficult for him to get an unobstructed shot at the creatures.

Pierre and Dave broke toward the onrushing Children.

Lunatics! I thought, but even as I thought it, I experienced a wave of affection for them. Though my view of humankind had dimmed considerably since last summer, the realization that there was still decency in the world imbued me with a desperate flare of hope.

I started to rise.

"What are you doing?" Mia demanded, her fingers grasping my shirt.

"Helping," I answered. "Stay with Peach."

But by that time, it had happened. I knew it even before Anita's scream. Dave had attracted the attention of a Child. The other was still pounding toward our group, with Pierre in close pursuit. But Dave had accomplished his goal; a nine-foot-tall Child stalked toward him.

No, I thought feebly. Anita pushed to her feet, moving to intervene, but Barley's mom had gripped her around the waist.

As Dave limped toward the creature, his gaze flicked toward Anita. There was a sad smile on his face, a look that said *This might not be good enough, but it's the best I could do.*

In the moment before the creature leapt at him, I spotted a Swiss Army knife in Dave's hand, pitifully small but ready for action.

The creature leapt. Dave swung the pocketknife. The blade pierced the creature's side as it slammed down on top of him. Dave's head cracked the concrete.

"Look out!" Mia shouted.

I'd forgotten about the other creature, which was closing in on us. Pierre was sprinting with everything he had to catch it.

He wasn't going to make it. The creature was twenty feet away. Fifteen. Ten feet away it leapt, its yellowish fingernails extended and its green eyes glowing, and as its shadow swept over us there came a roar of gunfire, Haddad opening up with the M16.

His aim was true. The creature was already jetting blood from half a dozen wounds when it crashed into our group. I just had time to scoot Peach's body under my own before the spraying torso walloped my back. Someone grunted in pain — Barley's dad? — and then the creature tumbled over and lay squalling.

I heard an anguished cry and remembered Dave. He was pinned under the Child, whose snapping jaws and whirring nails ripped his upper body apart. But still he pumped the pocketknife into the creature's side again and again, trying to inflict as much damage as possible.

Anita broke free of Barley's mom, but Pierre was there immediately, wrapping his niece up and dragging her out of Haddad's line of fire.

Haddad shouted, "Over here!" at the creature mauling Dave.

The creature's head snapped around to glare at Haddad, its mouth slick with blood. I felt a surge of hatred for the monster. Beneath it, Dave had stopped moving, his valiant last stand ended.

"Take me on, you son of a bitch," Haddad growled.

Leering, the creature pushed to its feet, blurred into motion, but before it could reach its maximum speed, Haddad opened up, and this time his aim was even better. Its milky flesh burst at the shoulder, the neck, and, just before it dropped like a sack of butcher shop offal, its right eye exploded, the glowing green orb winking out like a shattered headlight.

From across the shelter sounded a shriek. The Barker-thing had severed the Child's jugular, was in the process of tearing strips of flesh from its chest.

Beneath Anita's keening and Pierre's attempts to console her, I heard a meaty thumping sound, Barley's dad pounding on the steel door under which Riggs had taken refuge. Barley was shouting curses at the soldiers and demanding they open up, but there was no answer. I considered reminding Barley that Riggs no more cared for our safety than he did for the Children's, but it was Haddad who spoke first.

"Let Riggs stay down there," he said.

Barley looked at Haddad incredulously. "Are you insane? That's our only hope."

But Haddad gave him a knowing smile. "The shelter's no safer than up here."

"What do you *mean?*" Mia demanded. "If we can get underground—"

"Underground," Haddad said, "is where those things live."

I nodded. "The park is honeycombed with caves. If they find a way through—"

A muffled scream sounded beneath us. Then several more.

"They found a way into the bunker," Haddad murmured.

Gunfire *burr*ed from under our feet, followed by the squalling of Children and bellows of pain from the soldiers.

"What is happening?" Barley asked. The door beneath him jolted. He and his dad pushed away, and it was a good thing. At that moment, Riggs and Castro muscled the door open, the heavy slab of steel crashing down on the concrete. Barley just had time to dance away from it before it crushed his toes.

"*Let me the hell out—*" Riggs was muttering, but the rest of his terrified words were lost in a strident shriek. A red-haired soldier had climbed up beside him, was attempting to wriggle out of the bunker, but a pair of freakishly elongated hands clamped onto his shoulders and dragged him screaming into the darkness.

Riggs was half-in, half-out of the opening. His eyes were vast, and he was having a hell of a time hauling his bulk out. In the darkness of the opening, I glimpsed a series of flashing lights, the soldiers down there doing battle with the creatures.

A figure passed in front of me — Montana, bleeding badly but still alive — and seized Riggs by the shoulders. In moments, Montana had dragged him to safety. Riggs was breathing hard and had spittle flecking his lips. He gesticulated at the open door. "Close it, Montana! Close it!"

"What about the rest of your men?" Haddad demanded.

"Those things are down there!" Riggs shouted, as if that settled the matter. "They burrowed their way to us."

He made to close the door, but Haddad spun Riggs around by the shoulder, reared back, and punched him in the nose. Riggs landed on his ass a few feet from the trapdoor. A moment later, a soldier appeared in the gap — a woman with short black hair — and then another, a man almost as pale as the creatures. I remembered them both from the night before. The black-haired woman made it through the door. Grudgingly, I hustled over and offered the pale soldier my hand. He took it. I hauled back, but he was so damned heavy, it took everything I had to keep my feet planted. He was nearly through when I chanced a look down and saw what had befallen the red-haired soldier: He was being eaten alive by a pair of creatures, his blue eyes staring sightlessly as the Children tore gobbets from his mutilated body.

"Close the door," Riggs commanded.

"Too late," Barley's mom said.

We followed her gaze and saw the other door opening. Castro emerged, his blond hair streaked with blood. Just after he escaped, a long arm snaked out of the hole. Then a loathsome white face with more hair than I'd ever seen on a creature. Its green eyes seemed to pick me out of the crowd.

It grinned at me.

"Let's run for it," Mia said to the group.

"Good idea, kid," Pierre answered. Then to Anita, whose head was buried in his chest, "Come on."

"It's no good," Riggs said. He seemed on the verge of hyperventilating.

Mia squared up to him. "We have to get out of here. More of them will come."

"You don't understand," Riggs said. "My men have orders to kill anything that leaves this shelter."

CHAPTER EIGHTEEN

GAME TIME

"*What?*" Barley's mom asked.

"You heard me," Riggs muttered.

"Doesn't matter," Pierre said. "We gotta make a run for it."

"He's right," Haddad agreed.

As if to accentuate this point, the creature emerging from the trapdoor made it the rest of the way out and was promptly replaced by another creature. The soldiers who'd escaped — the black-haired woman and the pale man — had staggered over to join Montana. The pale man handed Montana a pistol.

"Come on," Pierre said to me. "Keep Peach close."

Our group migrated toward the northern wall.

"But my gunners—" Riggs began.

"To hell with your gunners," Pierre snarled. "I'd rather get shot than be eaten alive by those motherfuckers." He jerked a thumb at the creatures, who were stalking slowly closer. The soldiers and Agent Castro leveled their guns at them.

Riggs shook his head. "We stand a better chance—"

"Would you *look*?" Mia shouted.

I followed her pointing forefinger and felt my stomach clench. Not only were two more creatures emerging from the trapdoors, but from the south and the east, several tall, spectral shapes were materializing on the other side of the plastic.

Soon, we'd be surrounded by Children.

"What are your people's orders?" Haddad asked Riggs.

The soldiers exchanged uneasy looks, but Riggs remained close-lipped.

"What are their *orders*?" Haddad snapped.

The nearest Child was twenty feet away and closing.

The woman soldier cleared her throat and said, "They're supposed to open fire when enough of those creatures take the bait."

"The bait," Anita repeated. "You mean us."

Pierre glanced at the pale soldier. "You. Casper the Friendly Ghost. You lead us out."

I thought the pale man would refuse, but he nodded and moved toward the plastic sheeting with his M16 poised before him.

"It's suicide," Riggs said.

"Staying here is suicide," Mia answered. She'd taken Peach by the hand.

"Once they see you," Haddad said to Riggs, "your people will stop firing."

"The hell they will," Riggs said.

"Haddad is right," Agent Castro argued. "This is the only chance we have."

As if to verify these words, the Children who'd climbed through the trapdoor broke toward us.

"Shit," the woman soldier said.

"Stay focused, Mesecar," Castro said.

"It's game time," Montana said, and at any other moment I might have appreciated the *Aliens* reference. But things happened too fast for me to appreciate anything.

And so many good people were about to die.

—

"NOW!" PIERRE SHOUTED.

Galvanized by his voice, our ragtag group bolted toward the sheet-plastic wall. Both Haddad, who carried Montana's M16, and the pale soldier reached the plastic and lifted it to afford the group passage. At the same moment the shelter erupted in gunfire. Montana fired his handgun and a Child tumbled, tried to crawl forward, then jolted as Montana nailed it in the forehead with a perfectly placed bullet. He might be partial to Lizzie, but he seemed to be a better shot with the smaller weapon.

A flurry of movement drew my gaze. The Barker-thing had finished feeding on the Child and was winging its way along the A-framed ceiling. I noticed Mesecar, the woman soldier, tracking the Barker-thing and was about to tell her, *Not him! He's not the enemy!* But she fired anyway, and the Barker-thing jerked, flailed, and smacked the floor in a jumble of wings. I watched numbly as Mesecar strode forward and fired three more times before a shadow swam over her. Mesecar turned.

Half a second too late.

A pair of Children slammed into Montana and Mesecar, the ravenous white creatures attacking with a vigor that made my stomach lurch. Montana managed to squeeze off two shots, but they both went wild. Montana moaned as the creature's teeth inched closer to his larynx.

Mesecar was faring no better. She managed to graze the creature mauling her, but it pinioned her down and sank its teeth into her forearm. She shrieked as blood frothed over her skin.

I spared a glance at the Barker-thing, but it lay face down, not moving, not stirring at all. *Damn it,* I thought.

"I'm scared," Peach said. I drew her closer and moved with the others past the plastic sheeting. We emerged into the overcast day, but before I could celebrate our escape from the shelter, a teeth-rattling snare drum erupted from the forest.

Machine-gun fire.

"Stop!" Haddad bellowed, but there was no way the gunner heard him.

"Get out there and talk to them!" someone behind me shouted. Barley's dad seized Riggs by the collar and shoved him toward the front of the group.

Casper returned fire at the machine gunner.

Pierre grabbed Riggs by the arm, and aided Barley's dad in thrusting Riggs to the fore of the group. "Tell him to stop shooting!" Pierre demanded.

The machine gunner did stop for a moment, but before Riggs could shout his orders, the shooting resumed, and this time the gunner's aim was better. A trail of mulch leapt into the air as the bullets plowed toward us. I grabbed Peach and dove to the side. Someone cried out, and when I looked up, I saw Casper juddering as the slugs riddled his big frame.

A few feet away, Haddad bent, drew a bead on the machine gunner, and fired. A split second later there was a scream and the hail of bullets ceased. From the shelter behind us, Mesecar was shrieking.

Damn them, I thought. *Damn these accursed creatures.*

"You got a soldier stationed on each side?" Pierre shouted at Riggs.

Riggs nodded, his expression blank with shock.

"Then we go straight through," Pierre said and nodded north, toward the place in the forest where Haddad had sniped the machine gunner. The soldier who'd been firing at us was still alive — his high-pitched caterwauling made that clear — but I doubted he'd be shooting at us again.

Haddad hustled over, retrieved Casper's gun, and glanced at Pierre. "You know how to handle this thing?"

"Never shot a gun in my life," Pierre said.

"I can do it," Anita said. "Sometimes wolves come sniffing around our stock. I'm a good shot."

Haddad handed her the bulky M16. "You'll have to lead the group. When we get closer to the tree line, the shooters Riggs stationed on the east and west sides of the shelter will spot us, and they'll start firing." Haddad glanced at Riggs. "You owe us. I'll cover us to the east; you return fire to the west. With any luck, your man on that side will see it's you and stop shooting."

Riggs shook his head, his eyes huge.

Pierre stalked over to him and wrested the handgun from his grip. "You're worthless. I'll take the west side."

Haddad nodded. To Anita he said, "You move fast and hard into the woods. Don't stop. There'll be more creatures out there. Shoot anything that moves."

Anita nodded. "I'll cut a path."

"Guys?" Barley said. "I think we have a problem."

"We've got to go," Peach said. I picked her up and glanced at Barley. "We don't have time to—"

"Will!" Mia shouted.

The plastic sheeting rose behind us. One of the Children, its body drenched in blood, emerged from the shelter.

Behind the sheet, five more shapes materialized.

"Go!" Haddad ordered.

We ran.

As we picked up speed, I was reminded forcibly of last summer, of my flight with Peach from the Children. I knew we'd be faster if I allowed her to run alongside me, but an illogical belief told me that Peach would be safer in my arms than on the ground.

We were forty feet from the woods. Anita was chugging ahead of the group, the M16 clutched in her grip. Mia was slightly ahead of me. Haddad and Pierre flanked us, their guns ready but as yet unfired, and behind me staggered Barley's family. Behind them I glimpsed Riggs and Castro, both looking horror-struck. Before I turned again toward the forest, I discovered the sheet-plastic wall being shredded in a dozen places.

The creatures were swarming out of the shelter.

Hellfire blazed from Riggs's gunners to our right and left. Haddad and Pierre returned fire. We were almost to the forest. I had no idea if the machine gunner Haddad had knocked down was still incapacitated, but I hoped so. If he'd recovered, we were sprinting straight toward our deaths.

Someone behind me gasped. I threw a glance that way and discovered Barley's dad clutching his elbow.

"Keep moving," Barley's dad shouted, but I could hear the strain in his voice.

Anita made it to the forest, Mia ten feet behind her. As Peach and I dashed into the shadowy woods, someone behind us yowled in terror. The creatures were closing in on Castro and Riggs. Just as a creature leapt at Riggs, another ripping barrage sounded from the forest, the machine gun embedded within the pine trees blazing, saving Riggs's life.

"Look out, Will!" Peach shouted.

I swiveled my head in time to realize we were about to smash into the trunk of an oak tree. Moving by instinct, I jagged to the right, but that put me squarely on a trajectory to crash into a downed elm that I'd either have to duck under or dodge altogether.

Machine gun fire thunked to my left, the oak tree we'd side-slipped riddled by one of Riggs's gunners.

The sons of bitches. Even with the Children in plain sight and swarming toward Riggs and Castro, the gunners were still attempting to take us down, to make sure we'd be silenced forever.

"Will!" Peach cried.

I remembered the downed tree in our path; Peach and I were about to smash into it. The tree was mossy and chest-high. As we closed on it, a pair of slugs chewed through its scum-slicked surface.

I couldn't dive under it, not with Peach in my arms. I couldn't turn and run in a different direction because the gunner from the west was firing at us.

I jumped.

We were only in the air for a couple seconds, maybe not even that, but even as we landed on the velvety bed of soil beyond, I understood how impossible it was. I shouldn't have been able to hurdle that tree, which rose more than five feet off the ground. How much more improbable was it that I'd accomplished the feat with a seven-year-old in my arms?

As if echoing my wonderment, Peach said, "How'd you do that?"

But I ignored her, my attention shifting to Mia, who'd witnessed my leap over the tree and was staring at me with a mixture of fear and wonder.

"Keep moving!" I shouted. The leaves of a low-hanging oak danced as the hot slugs tore through them.

The shooting cut off and a high-pitched screaming began. A couple seconds after that, the other machine gun gave a last, abbreviated cough, and another soldier began to wail.

The machine gunners had fallen.

The Children had reclaimed Peaceful Valley.

—

THE ORIGINAL SHELTER, the one in which we'd spent the night, wasn't far, yet sprinting madly through the forest and pursued by bloodthirsty beasts, it seemed miles away. My back ached from carrying Peach, and whatever adrenaline had enabled me to leap that downed tree had worn off and left me enervated.

Behind us, I heard Pierre and Anita hurrying the Marleys along. Barley's dad was bleeding badly from the elbow. Barley's mom limped along beside her husband. Neither had been a paragon of physical fitness. But now, one of them injured and both of them winded, they were making extremely poor time.

"I can run," Peach said, and as I set her down, I suppressed an urge to mutter *Thank God*.

Haddad shouted, "This way!"

Mia got on the other side of Peach, and though a dreadful foreboding had begun to creep into my heart, I was grateful for the way Mia prioritized my sister's safety above all else. I wanted to tell Mia this, but there was no time.

A voice behind me said, "Almost there." I spun half around and discovered Pierre. "Well, look at you," he said, grinning. "Last time you were this worked up was when I told you the Cubs wouldn't make the playoffs."

"Don't remind me," I said, trying not to smile.

"There's the shelter!" Mia said.

The trees were thinning. Not only could I make out the painted brown logs that comprised the shelter, but I could also discern the asphalt, which had taken on a slate-colored hue in the increasingly gloomy midmorning.

Pierre fell back to wait for the Marleys. Haddad exited the forest ahead of us. I wanted to tell him not to go toward the shelter, that taking refuge was akin to suicide. There were too many creatures, too little help.

An ululating cry scattered my thoughts. The Children were closing in.

Mia, Peach, and I broke through the screen of leaves, our shoes slapping asphalt. Haddad pounded down the sidewalk between the shelter and the parking lot, and I thought, *Go for the vehicles! Don't go inside!*

Haddad went for the vehicles.

But in the next instant I realized that was probably a mistake. Only in movies do people leave their keys in the ignition, or more eye-rollingly, in the overhead visor.

Haddad yanked open a Jeep door. "Get in!" he shouted.

We hurried to the black Jeep he had chosen. Mia climbed into the backseat, and half-dragged Peach in after her. Rather than joining Haddad in the front, I chose the back too, so that Mia and I flanked Peach.

"The keys are in it?" I asked.

"Riggs knew they might have to leave in a hurry," Haddad said, firing up the engine. "I doubt he considered it might be us driving out of here rather than them."

Holy crap, I thought. *It makes sense. It's incredible good luck, but it actually makes sense.*

Pierre, the Marleys, and Anita were emerging from the forest. The sight didn't encourage me. Judging from the amount of blood soaking Barley's dad's side, his wound was worse than I'd assumed. Barley's mom was moving in a tottering lurch, a hand pressed against her lower back.

Instinct drew me toward them, but no sooner had my sneaker touched the asphalt than someone snagged my arm.

Peach was staring up at me, her eyes wide. "Please don't leave me."

I nodded and settled back inside.

Pierre stopped at the first vehicle he encountered — a black Jeep without a roof or windows — and leaned over the passenger's door. Evidently satisfied by what he saw, he opened that door, then the back door, and a couple seconds later Anita and the Marleys came shuffling toward the Jeep. Pierre helped Mr. and Mrs. Marley into the back, while Anita hurried around to start the engine. Barley climbed in next to his mom, and Pierre rode shotgun.

Just before Pierre closed his door, I spotted a dark patch of blood on his side, just above his belt.

No, I thought.

Haddad only waited long enough for the Jeep with our friends in it to start rolling, then he gunned our Jeep and took the lead. I glanced out the window, sure the Children would explode out of the forest, but for now it seemed we were safe.

I was thinking this when my window shattered.

It was so sudden that I didn't have time to throw up my arms, but I'd closed my eyes before the chunks of glass hit me, a reaction that might have saved my vision.

"Give me the gun," Mia growled.

"No time," Haddad answered.

Mia stared fiercely out the back window, both her hands pressing Peach downward, out of range of whomever had shot at us. Though my eyes were blurry, and we were nearing a curve in the lane, I caught a glimpse of a couple figures scurrying toward a black Hummer, and thought, *Of course. Riggs and Castro.* They climbed into the Hummer, and then, though I couldn't be sure, I thought I glimpsed another figure shambling behind them. Then our Jeep rumbled around the bend, and I lost sight of both the other Jeep and the Hummer.

"It's okay, Peach," Mia said as she stroked my sister's hair, "but stay down for now."

I put a hand on Peach's back, and I wondered if this was what being a parent felt like: wanting to protect your family but feeling incapable of doing so.

I didn't have time to linger on the thought. Ahead of us, the forest encroached on both sides. Narrow to begin with, the ribbon of asphalt now felt like a one-lane road. The forest reached out for us, the branches hungry to claw at us, to draw us into the darkness. The rumors I'd heard about the Peaceful Valley Massacre flickered through my mind. Two hundred people murdered. More missing. A bloodbath beyond reckoning.

And on the heels of that I remembered our own experience last summer. How the Children had claimed Chris and Rebecca. How the remorseless beasts had treated them like playthings. How their jaws had ripped and chewed, how their hideous white faces had reveled in the blood spray.

Stop it, I told myself. *In ten minutes, you'll all be safe. Sure, you might have Riggs and Castro to deal with, but at least you'll be out of range of the Children.*

And what about the Night Flyers? a voice answered.

The thought made me suck in breath. I shivered and attempted to fight off my growing dread. No, I didn't know for sure that the Night Flyers hunted exclusively at night, but my experiences with them *had* been at night — or twilight, at least.

"Uh, Will?" Mia asked.

I glanced dumbly at her, then followed her gaze toward something ahead of us, something at the end of a lengthy straightaway.

Something in the trees.

"Hey, Colonel?" I said to Haddad. What Mia had glimpsed, what I now beheld with dawning horror, was the sway of a maple tree, one large enough to crush a man if it landed on him.

Also large enough to block a road if it fell.

And that was precisely what the Children were attempting. They'd cut across the forest, knowing there was only one roadway out of here, the other boundaries of the park comprised of the Tippecanoe and Wabash Rivers. The creatures gathered in the uppermost section of the tree, the part that loomed over the narrow road. On the ground were a pair of creatures, both of them muscular specimens shoving against the trunk with all their might. I watched, appalled, as the tree trembled and leaned toward the road. Its roots twanged out of the ground, and then the weight of the creatures near the top took over.

"Go faster," Mia said, but I could tell Haddad was already pushing the Jeep harder than he wanted to. We were doing sixty, and on a narrow road like this, that was risking a crash. A crash meant certain death; even if the impact didn't kill us, the creatures would.

The tree tilted toward the road, and though it didn't fall, it was clearly going to, if not before we reached it then just after.

Which meant that Anita's Jeep wouldn't be able to pass, and we'd be cut off from our friends.

Our Jeep accelerated.

A glance at the speedometer showed we were up to seventy. That was fine for the moment. The roadway hadn't yet been obstructed, and we had maybe sixty yards to go on the straight-away. But beyond the slowly falling tree, the road curved left, and at the speed we were traveling, there's no way we'd make that turn.

With a final shove, the two muscular Children pushed the tree over.

Only thirty yards away, Haddad had no choice but to stomp on the brakes. Our back end skidded, the whole car describing a slow, sickening revolution as the tires did their best to grab the road.

Our Jeep shuddered to a halt ten feet from the felled tree.

The creatures stalked toward the Jeep.

"Take the gun," Haddad ordered. He jerked gearshift into reverse.

I reached into the front seat, grabbed Lizzie, and realized I'd need both hands to lift it. The gun felt ridiculously heavy in my hands. The Jeep vibrated and bounced as Haddad motored backward, away from the creatures, who were leering at us, their green eyes alight.

"Watch out!" Mia yelled.

I glanced over my shoulder and saw the other Jeep bearing down on us.

Haddad made a hissing sound and jerked the wheel. The other Jeep rumbled to a stop as we drew even with it. Somehow, Haddad's crisp reflexes had permitted us to veer past our friends. For a brief second, I glimpsed Barley staring out the back window at me, his eyes comically magnified by his glasses and his terror.

The Hummer came into view behind us.

I dragged the huge weapon into the backseat with me, careful not to point it anywhere near Peach or Mia.

Haddad had an arm thrown over his seatback, was reversing at twenty-five miles an hour. "Make sure the safety is off," he said.

I shook my head. "I have no idea where the safety is."

He clenched his jaw. "Never mind. Just pull back the charging handle—"

"*What the hell's a charging handle?*" I shouted.

"Dammit," he muttered, applying the brakes. We skidded to a stop.

"Here," he said, shoving the gearshift into park. "You drive. I'll shoot." He climbed into the passenger's seat and wrested the gun from my grip. I was glad to relinquish the M16, but I'd never driven a car. I climbed behind the wheel.

"Drive," he said.

"Drive where?"

"There!" Peach yelled from over my shoulder. I discovered a pair of wheel ruts leading into the forest, what might have been a path the park rangers used for a shortcut. I pushed the Jeep into drive. Peripherally, I saw Anita guiding the other Jeep in a U-turn, and it was a good thing too.

The Children who'd blocked the roadway were sprinting toward her with ungodly speed.

Move! I thought, my insides squirming.

Though I tried to stay locked on the road ahead and our impending entry into the forest, I remained aware of the other Jeep. And the creatures dashing in Anita's direction.

Focus on driving, a voice in my head reminded. *You can't control everything, but you can keep Peach and Mia safe.*

A thunderous noise made me jump. It was Haddad, opening up on the creatures before they reached Anita's Jeep.

"Watch it!" Mia shouted, and I jerked to attention a half-second before we plowed into a tree. Haddad was on that side of the Jeep, leaning out and firing at the creatures, and as our vehicle swerved, he nearly lost his grip on the gun. I heard him cursing, but all my attention was on driving. I'd made it onto the twin wheel ruts, and though the weeds underneath flogged the chassis with relentless animosity, the path was wide enough for us to motor along safely.

The question was, would our friends make it to the wooded lane as well?

I kept the Jeep steady at twenty miles an hour. That might not sound particularly fast, but on the uneven terrain and with the weeds whacking the Jeep's underside, the speed felt hellacious.

"Where are they?" Peach asked.

I flicked my eyes to the overhead mirror. I'd been wondering the same thing. Anita's Jeep should have appeared by now. For that matter, so should have Riggs's Hummer.

"There!" Mia said.

Peach gasped and actually clapped her hands in delight, and when I glanced in the mirror, I saw it was true. The other Jeep had reached the path.

It seemed like too much to hope that the Hummer hadn't made it.

A second later, the Hummer appeared on the path behind the Jeep.

"Concentrate," Haddad reminded me.

I forced my eyes back to the lane, which trended to the left.

Haddad was fiddling with the M16. I hoped he had enough ammunition to hold those creatures off. I was certain there were legions of them converging on us. This was, after all, their home.

I asked, "How many of them did you hit?"

"Three of the five," he answered. "But only one stayed down. The other two just took it and kept right on coming."

Sounds about right, I thought.

"Do we know where this goes?" Mia asked.

There came a loud *chick-chick* as Haddad readied the M16. "Not precisely," he said. "But I'm pretty sure we'll come out at the river."

My fingers tightened on the wheel. The Tippecanoe River was broad and because it had been raining a lot recently, it would be deeper than usual.

Peach wasn't much of a swimmer. How could she be? The only times she'd gotten to swim were the occasions I'd walked her down to Deer Creek, and even then, I'd been so paranoid that I'd let her do little more than wade.

My spirits sank a notch lower, but I kept my eyes on the path and hoped we wouldn't encounter a downed tree. If we did, there'd be no escaping.

The forest would become our tomb.

CHAPTER NINETEEN
ORPHANS

I knew the Children were linked telepathically, knew it even without that vague chatter that sometimes drifted in and out of my mental hearing, like someone twisting an A.M. radio dial and picking up snatches of news or some preacher warning about damnation. I didn't want to consider the implications of this hearing, nor did I want to think about the overturned tree I'd leapt while carrying my sister. But the guttural words still came through, like distant shouts from a contentious schoolyard kickball game:

...meat... no escape... find them... kill them...

Then the word that made my stomach perform a violent lurch:

...river...

I swallowed and gripped the wheel tighter.

They were coming.

"I think we outran them," Mia said, but I knew her well enough to know she was just trying to reassure Peach. Or herself.

"Marshaling their forces," Haddad muttered.

I shot him an angry look. Didn't he understand the importance of self-deception?

I shifted in my seat and took a steadying breath. The day was growing gloomier. The forest path, already dark, made it feel like ten at night rather than ten in the morning. I cast occasional looks in the mirror. Anita was keeping pace with us, maybe thirty yards back.

Too easy, a voice whispered. *You won't get away this easily.*

Stop, I thought, but the voice pressed on.

You haven't suffered enough. You know from last summer, there has to be more pain. More death.

Tell that to Barker, I thought ruefully. *Tell that to Dave.*

God. The thought of Dave being ripped apart made me short of breath.

"It's opening up," Mia said.

I peered into the screen of forest ahead.

"I do believe you're right," Haddad murmured.

The trees *were* thinning, glorious daylight peeking through. Oh, it was dingy daylight, the dispiriting hue of chain-link fences, but the woods appeared to be coming to an end, at least for a time.

A macabre thought occurred to me: this would be where the Children would ambush us. A clearing.

But it was more than a clearing, I realized as we rumbled nearer. It was a long stretch of open field, fringed on either side by tall prairie grass, the kind that Peaceful Valley prided itself on. You couldn't miss the bronze plaques drilled into boulders all over the park proclaiming the preservation of the native flora.

I compressed my lips. *Wish they'd put more effort into preserving the lives of the people who camped here.*

That wasn't entirely fair, and I knew it, but I was beyond charitable thoughts. The Children were coming, of that I was certain. As for the Night Flyers, I said a silent prayer that they were indeed limited to the night.

One species of monster was more than enough.

The Jeep emerged from the forest into a hundred-yard stretch of prairie grass.

"We made it!" Peach yelled, and I mustered as much of a smile as I could. She was leaning forward between the seats, a hand perched on my shoulder.

"We made it," I agreed.

On the far side of the prairie grass began another thicket of trees, and if my sense of direction was any good at all, somewhere beyond that stretch lay the Tippecanoe River.

Could the Children swim?

Almost certainly, I decided. In fact, I suspected they would be expert swimmers. Long, lean, and powerful, their tensile bodies might scythe through the water like eels.

Stop worrying about that, I told myself. *Focus on now. There are no trees to contend with, so gain some ground on the bastards.*

I depressed the accelerator, the Jeep juddering but grabbing the dirt with no trouble.

"Can probably get away with thirty," Haddad said. "I wouldn't risk much beyond that."

I glanced at the speedometer. I was sitting at thirty-two miles per hour.

I didn't ease off the gas.

I scanned the top of the prairie grass for glowing green eyes but found nothing. I reminded myself that the Children could lope along on all fours like bizarre human-panther hybrids, but that wasn't their preferred style. When they came for you, they advertised it plainly. They were too arrogant for stealth. Besides, if you didn't see them coming, they couldn't fully savor your terror. Something told me they enjoyed that aspect of the hunt as much as the meat they devoured.

The pursuit. The anticipation. The emotional torture.

We were nearing a rise when movement in the overhead mirror drew my gaze, and at the same moment a deep thunderclap rattled the Jeep. I looked up, hoping it was merely the grumble of an impending storm, but a pall of smoke told me otherwise.

Anita's Jeep had overturned, was shrouded in a thick ashy haze. The Hummer's front left corner was badly dented, the squat vehicle having veered into the prairie grass. The Hummer, too, was spewing smoke.

Oh my God, I thought. *Riggs or Castro, whichever had been driving, had rammed Anita's Jeep.*

I let off the gas.

"Let me out," Haddad said.

I didn't answer. My sister clutched my arm.

"Stop here," Haddad said. "You three go ahead. The river's not far."

I brought the Jeep to a stop. "I can't leave Barley."

"This is not a debate," Haddad answered, shifting the M16 in his grip. "Your duty is to protect your sister."

"Mia will do that," I said, and the instant I said it Peach was between the seats, her arms around my neck and her face jammed against my shoulder.

"You can't leave!" she said. "You can't leave me again!"

The tears were already scalding my eyes, and I wrapped my little sister up and buried my face in her hair.

"If you go," Mia said, "we all go."

I clutched Peach tightly. She needed me to take care of her.

So take care of her!

I fought back a sob. I *wanted* to take care of her, dammit, wanted it more than anything in the world, but Barley was back there, and so was Anita. And Pierre, who'd been more of a father to me than anyone ever had. Not to mention Barley's parents, two wonderful people who deserved none of this.

I couldn't leave them.

You can't leave Peach!

Haddad pushed open his door. "Drive on. When you get to the river, swim across as fast as you can."

"I can't—" I started to say, but Haddad continued as though I hadn't spoken.

"On the other side of the river, there'll be a road. Highway 25. If you're lucky, there'll be a lot of cars on it."

"I'm coming with you," I said.

"No!" Peach cried into my shoulder.

"Hail the first vehicle you see," Haddad said. "They may not stop for you, but they'll sure as hell stop for Peach. I know I would."

"You drive," I said to Mia and began the job of detaching Peach's arms from my neck.

"We stay together," Mia persisted.

"Don't make this any harder," I said.

"Listen to your girlfriend," Haddad commanded, half out of the Jeep. "She's a lot smarter than you."

I didn't respond. I *couldn't* respond because I was crying now, and Peach wasn't letting go. I reached for the door handle, fumbled it open, but that only made her redouble her efforts. She was strong for a seven-year-old, so strong that I had to back out of the Jeep with her dragging over the seat, still attached to me.

Mia was out of the car, fencing me in between Peach and the open Jeep door. Mia clutched the front of my shirt. "This isn't some stupid save-the-women-and-children thing. You belong with your sister."

Don't you think I know that? I wanted to shout, but I couldn't form the words. My throat was burning, my breathing reed-thin. Did Mia think I *wanted* to go back and face Riggs and Castro? For that matter, did she actually believe I wanted to encounter the Children, who were almost certainly closing in?

Part of me cried out to go, to drive on and save Mia and my sister, and with almost all my heart that's what I yearned to do.

But I couldn't forsake Barley. I couldn't consign him and Anita and Pierre to a bloody death. Even now, Riggs and Castro might be herding them from the overturned Jeep, lining them up for execution.

I had to go back.

Haddad spoke to me across the roof. "There's brave, son, and then there's stupid. Your desire to help your friends is admirable, but these two need you."

I swayed a little, realizing Peach was standing on the running board of the Jeep, so that we were almost the same height. She was battened onto me in a death-grip, and Mia's hands were on my shoulders, Mia speaking at my ear.

"He's right," Mia said. "If anyone can save them, it's Colonel Haddad. Your sister needs you."

I thought of how it had been last summer, how the three of us — Peach, Mia, and I, along with Peach's friend Juliet — had banded together to make a last stand against the Children, a dozen of the creatures congregating under the tree house and clambering up after us. I thought of how fiercely Mia and Peach had fought. I remembered what a great team we'd proven, how in the end we'd vanquished the vile bastards and made it to safety.

Yes, I thought. I *did* belong with Peach and Mia. If we drove on now, we'd stand a decent chance of crossing the river unscathed.

Then I remembered how Pierre had saved me two nights ago at Sunny Woods, how he'd risked his life by crawling through the airshafts.

I kissed the side of my sister's head and turned to Mia. "You're an awesome swimmer," I said.

Mia's eyes widened. "Don't even—"

"You're gonna put my sister on your back," I told her, "and ferry her across the river."

"*No!*" Peach yelled, and clung to me even harder.

"Stop trying to—" Mia started, but I pulled her to me and stopped her with a kiss. It was clumsy and a little off-balance, but I kissed her hard and squeezed her body to mine, and when I pulled away, her face was crumpling.

"Take care of her," I said.

Mia's lips bunched together, the tears streaking her cheeks. "Will..."

Before I could lose my nerve, I turned and wrapped my arms around Peach's waist. I lifted her out of the car, got my forearms under her rear end, and carried her around to the passenger's seat.

Haddad's gaze was steady, but he backed away from the open door to allow me to place Peach inside. She showed no signs of releasing me. Somehow, I managed to get a grip on the seatbelt and draw it across her body. As soon as it clicked, she began to thrash and reach for the release button, but I covered it with a hand and spoke into her ear. "Listen to me, Peach. Listen to me."

"No!" she was shouting, her voice broken by sobs. "Don't leave me again."

"Listen," I repeated, my voice just as broken as hers. I spoke into her ear, my cheek pressed against hers, our tears merging. "You are the most important person in my life."

"*You promised*," she said, but I was going on.

"No one matters more to me than you. If something happened to you, my life would be over."

"Don't go," she said, her voice a brokenhearted whisper.

"I love you, Peach. You've made my life worth living."

"Don't go," she repeated, her body shuddering.

I kissed her roughly on the cheek, and even as I did, I noticed how her cheekbone was more pronounced than it used to be. She'd wasted away in the year we'd been apart. Who would make her eat if I wasn't around? What would become of her if I didn't survive? If Riggs lived, he'd make sure Peach was sent away.

I froze.

Would Riggs be content with sending Peach away, with letting Mia go on with high school, given all they knew?

I thought of the massacre they'd staged in the shelter. The gunners.

My muscles hardening, I pushed away from my sister and shut her door before she could clamber out.

She took off her seatbelt right away, of course, but I was pushing against the door, holding her in. Mia watched me from the driver's seat. I stared back at her and tried to put as much of a plea as I could into my gaze. Whatever she saw there, she evidently understood I'd made up my mind.

Mia reached out, drew her door shut. Her hand went to the door lock button. I heard the dull click of the locks.

Go, I mouthed at Mia, and moved away from the Jeep. She gave me one last look, and then they began to roll forward. Peach threw herself against the door, battering the window with her palms. I heard her crying, imploring Mia to stop.

My eyes swimming with tears, I hustled to catch up with Haddad. The overturned Jeep was fifty yards away.

Haddad sped to a trot, and as I drew even with him, he said, "Gutsy decision, kid. A dumb decision, but a gutsy one."

I didn't answer. I couldn't.

It was likely I'd never see my sister again.

"We enter here," Haddad said, and nodded to his left.

I followed him off the path. Together, he and I ducked into the tall prairie grass.

—

IT WAS THE *quality* of the wailing that brought chills to my spine.

People only wept like that when someone was dead or terribly injured.

Please don't be Barley, I thought.

And on the heels of that: *Or Pierre.*

Or, for that matter, Anita or Mr. or Mrs. Marley. There was no one in that vehicle whose death I wouldn't be affected by.

Maybe it's Riggs who's bawling, I thought. *Or Castro.*

But this thought was swept aside as soon as it had arisen. The voice was too high-pitched for Riggs, and unless Castro's rose an octave when he was grief-stricken, I doubted it was him either.

"C'mon, Will," Haddad growled.

He was trudging through the prairie grass, hunched over and gripping his weapon like he was about to attempt a beachhead landing. I hurried to keep up with him, but as I did, I realized how conspicuous we were in this wide-open prairie. Sure, we were running stoop-shouldered, and that shaved a few inches off, but the grass itself was swishing with our passage. We might as well be carrying neon signs that read HERE WE COME!

Haddad swerved left.

"Walking trail," he murmured. Someone had taken a riding mower and carved a four-foot swath of prairie grass, a path that would bring us to within twenty or so yards of the crash site.

But then what?

A harsh shout came from ahead, about where I judged the overturned Jeep would be. The keening continued.

Haddad slowed, brought up a hand, and I promptly decelerated. He hesitated, then hastened forward another fifteen feet before raising a hand again and skidding to a halt. He regarded me over his shoulder. "You don't have a weapon, do you?"

I didn't answer. He could see well enough I was unarmed. Unless you counted my breath, which tasted like a mixture of gastric juices and motor oil.

I said, "Are they—"

He brought an index finger to his lips, and I quieted. If Riggs and Castro heard us, it would come down to a firefight, and since it was two weapons against one, I didn't like our chances.

What about Anita? I wondered. *She had a gun earlier. So did Pierre.*

It sounds like Anita wailing.

The thought enveloped me like a freezing tide: If Anita was weeping, there could only be one person who'd make her feel that way. With her husband already murdered, it could only be Pierre who was injured.

Or worse.

No!

Haddad jabbed a finger at the dense prairie grass. "They're right through there," he whispered. "I'll go first. You follow single file."

I hurried after him. Even now they might be lining up our friends for execution. I had zero doubt that was their goal. Hell, they'd attempted to exterminate us all back at the shelter.

Haddad stopped and leaned forward, head cocked. I listened too. Though the wailing had abated, there was still weeping.

"Get over here," a male voice snarled. Riggs?

I knew it was ill-advised, but I couldn't take it any longer. I clambered past Haddad until the prairie grass began to thin.

"*Will*," Haddad whispered.

I crouched and beheld the scene.

It was worse than I'd anticipated. The wailing was coming from Barley's mother. She and her son were okay, but they were hunched over Barley's father, who was not.

Barley's dad wasn't moving. His face was coated with dust, and though the only sign of trauma was a trickle of blood issuing from the corner of his mouth, the truth was plain. I'd seen many dead people over the past thirteen months, and I'd never been surer of someone's death than I was now.

Barley had lost his father. A good man. In many ways a great man. He'd been murdered by two sons of bitches who were trying to cover their tracks. I thought of the afternoon I'd spent watching the Cubs game in Mr. Marley's store. He'd been so kind, so generous with his time. Not once had he made me feel like a nuisance. He'd always looked at me like I mattered. Hell, he'd even laughed at my jokes, which I'm sure weren't funny. I was only ten at the time, after all.

And now, Riggs was gripping a handgun and glowering pitilessly down at Mr. Marley's dead body.

My hands balled into fists.

"I said, get over here!" Riggs commanded. "Now, goddammit!"

When neither Barley nor his mother moved, Riggs stalked over to Barley, grasped a handful of his shirt, and jerked him to his feet. Barley blundered along as the big man dragged him away.

"*Easy*," Haddad said in my ear. I realized I'd been tensed for a spring. Every fiber of my being cried out to attack now, before Riggs could hurt Barley, but in the next instant, I discovered another problem, one that made our situation exponentially worse.

My view had been screened by the overturned Jeep, but when I'd crawled a few feet to track Barley's progress, I'd discovered the others.

Agent Castro had Anita and Pierre on their knees, their hands folded behind their heads. Castro's weapon was poised no more than six inches from the base of Pierre's skull.

No!

I started forward, but Haddad collared me and spoke directly into my ear. "You do it, we all die. Riggs and Castro are facing us. We've either got to steal around behind them—" I began to shake my head, but he tightened his grip on me, "—or wait until they aren't looking this way. And since there's no way to flank them, and since we're almost out of time anyway, we wait until one of them turns."

"What happens then?" I asked.

"Whoever turns away, you rush. I'll mow down the one facing us. I've barely got ammo left, but I can get one for sure."

"What do I do after I tackle him?" I asked.

Haddad gave me a flat look. "What do you think?"

I shrugged. "Take his weapon away?"

"If you can. At the very least, keep him occupied until I can get there. Then I'll disarm him."

"How you gonna do that without a gun?" a deep voice said from behind us.

I gasped. Haddad jerked the M16 around, but before he could level it at the soldier who'd snuck up on us, the sleek barrel of a handgun was jammed into Haddad's forehead.

"Please try it," Montana said. "I'd love an excuse to kill you."

—

HOW THE HUGE soldier had accomplished it, I had no idea. I was sure he'd died back there in the shelter. Then I remembered the shambling figure, the one that had neared the Hummer before I lost sight of it. Somehow, Montana had broken away from the creatures and climbed inside the Hummer with Riggs and Castro.

Now here Montana was, herding me and Haddad into the clearing at gunpoint. I'd only gotten a brief look at him before he'd instructed me to turn around and walk, and what I'd seen hadn't been pretty. Not that he'd been photogenic to begin with. But now, his face was slathered in blood, he exuded a sewery stench, and his black hair was caked with what might have been the noxious ichor that pulsed within the Children's veins. At that moment, Montana reminded me of Bruce Campbell in the latter stages of *Evil Dead II*, after his character has been through hell and back. Only with Bruce Campbell, there'd been that underlying likability no matter how bedraggled he got.

With Montana there wasn't a hint of likability. He'd come here to carry out orders.

He'd come here to murder us.

"Move your ass," he snapped, and shoved Haddad forward with the muzzle of the M16 he'd reclaimed. The big black pistol had been pocketed.

Did Montana know how low on ammo his weapon was? I hoped not. I didn't count many advantages for us, but if we had one, that might be it.

We emerged from the prairie grass and beheld the scene. Barley's mom was draped over her husband's body and sobbing. Seeing her that way ignited a torrid ache in my throat. It had always been like that; when people I cared about cried, I did too. Over the course of my life, it had been a nuisance — to be truthful, it had been a major pain in the ass and a source of constant embarrassment for me. The world acted like boys weren't supposed to cry, so any boy who did was contemptible and weak — but now, in what I was sure were my last moments on Earth, I didn't try to hold back the tears. Hell, I'd already been crying with Peach, so my eyes hadn't had the chance to dry.

"Don't worry, ma'am," Montana said on the way past Mrs. Marley. "You'll join your husband soon."

She looked up slowly, her eyes at first bewildered and glassy. Then her gaze focused, and I could see her comprehending the awful words the huge man had uttered.

She bared her teeth. "*You… fucking …bastard.*"

I gaped at her. To hear her use those words, even under extreme circumstances, was a shock.

"Unbecoming language for a lady," Riggs said. He had Barley by the neck of his tee shirt, but his eyes were peering down the long, dusty roadway.

You know the Children are coming, I thought. *They'll be here any minute.*

"Your husband was ejected from the Jeep," Castro told Mrs. Marley. "It's not like we killed him."

"Dumbass should've buckled up," Montana said, and he shoved me forward. I stumbled and went down about ten feet from Barley.

Barley pushed his glasses up his nose, which was runny and red. "Don't call my dad a dumbass. He's worth a thousand of you."

"*Was,*" Castro corrected. "*Was* worth."

"Jesus, Castro," Montana said, but he was chuckling.

Montana's grin made something inside me snap. "It's hilarious, isn't it?"

"Will?" a voice said. I recognized the voice as Pierre's, but those blinding sheets of flame were engulfing me, the ones that came from the cruelest side of my nature, the side that seemed to be controlling me more and more.

I got to my feet. "A good man dying is the funniest thing in the world, isn't it? You callous motherfucker?"

Montana leveled the M16 at me. "On your knees."

I took a step toward him.

"Do what he says," Pierre commanded, but I continued forward.

"What if I don't want to?" I asked.

Montana looked delighted. "You actually think I won't do it, kid?"

Another step. Very close now.

"*Will!*" Pierre snapped.

"Stop it!" Anita said.

"One more step and you're done," Montana informed me.

"Do it," I said.

Montana hesitated for less than a second, but it was enough for Haddad to leap at him. As he slammed into Montana's side, the M16 spat thunder, the blast so close to my ears I went momentarily deaf. The massive soldier twisted sideways, Haddad bulldozing him. They grappled for the gun, Montana the stronger of the two, but Haddad grimly determined and much more seasoned.

They struggled wildly. Both Riggs and Castro were shouting at Haddad to stand down and for Montana to *Drop! Drop!* But Haddad wasn't about to stop now.

My paralysis broke. I dove forward and got Montana around the hips. He didn't so much as bat at me because he was so absorbed with Haddad. I reared back and punched Montana in the groin. He let out an *oomph*, doubled over, and Haddad came away with the M16.

He leveled it at Montana, who threw his hands up as if he could ward off the bullets. Haddad's expression was obdurate. I was certain he was going to blow Montana away when Riggs yelled, "STOP!"

Haddad tensed, his finger a shade lighter on the trigger, but he didn't fire.

"You do it," Riggs said, "and the boy dies."

I turned, assuming Riggs meant me.

It was Barley, however, that he held at gunpoint.

No, I thought. *Please God, no.*

I took a step in that direction, but Barley's mom cried, "Stop, Will! He'll do it!"

She was right. Riggs was responsible for countless deaths. Why would he scruple about one more, even if the victim was an innocent teenage boy?

"Let him go," Haddad said.

Haddad hadn't shifted the M16 from Montana's chest. That was good, I decided. If he relinquished the weapon, we'd be dead within seconds.

You'll be dead soon anyway, a voice reminded me. *Remember the Children?*

Holy shit, I thought. *The Children.*

I glanced at Barley, whose eyes were huge and terrified. *Don't kill him*, I thought. *Losing Chris was bad enough. Don't kill my one remaining friend.*

"Please," Barley's mom said, her voice breaking. She had risen, was moving in a shell-shocked stagger toward Riggs. "Please don't hurt my baby."

Riggs watched her impassively.

"It's over, Riggs," Haddad said.

Riggs chuckled. "Hell."

Mrs. Marley's hands were wrestling with each other, her face puffy from crying. "Please let my son go. Please don't take him too."

"Mom...," Barley said, "...don't—"

But Riggs tightened his forearm on Barley's throat, Barley standing on his tiptoes to breathe.

"Please, let my son go," Barley's mom begged.

Riggs's voice was surprisingly gentle. "What do you propose I do, ma'am?"

New hope dawned in her eyes. "Take me instead."

"Alright," Riggs said, turned the gun on her, and pulled the trigger.

The blast was deafening. Barley's mom spasmed and pressed a hand to her chest as though to stem the gush of blood. Barley screamed. Montana lunged at Haddad, and Haddad opened up on him. But even as the massive soldier went floundering backward, his great arms jagging, my attention remained on Barley's mom, who sank to her knees, her eyes never leaving her son. In that moment, I remembered the dozens of times she'd been there for me when my own mother hadn't, the nights she'd let me stay over and the mornings she'd made us pancakes. The time I got in trouble in the fourth grade for using profane language toward a school bully in defense of Barley, and after the principal had gotten done disciplining me, how Barley's mom, a secretary at the school, had wrapped me in a hug and thanked me for sticking up for her son. I remembered all her hugs. Her after-school snacks and her patience with me and Barley and Chris, even when we were acting like shitheads. I remembered all these things as Barley's mother drew her last breaths.

I remembered these things and hated Riggs.

I sprinted toward him.

And Riggs turned the gun on me.

CHAPTER TWENTY

SWARM

I should have been scared as I stormed toward Riggs. But a mist of crimson rage had surrounded me.

Unlike Barley's myopic eyes, my own vision was very keen. I wasn't a power hitter at the plate, but I always saw the baseball extremely well. Especially when I was locked in and confident. Oftentimes, the world seemed to slow down when the ball was hurtling toward me, and in that moment, I could discern the tight red stitches, the cursive blue *Wilson* stamped on the pearly leather. Honest to God, I could.

So in that moment, I saw Riggs's sweat-soaked shirt, the tuft of gray chest hair poking from the collar. I saw his broad bull neck, the clenched jaw above it. Riggs's cheeks gleamed with perspiration and cast silvery glints in the overcast light. His eyes were suffused with a churning brew of hatred, fear, and self-preservation.

Yes, I saw Riggs very well.

And I saw Barley. Him most of all.

That was good, I decided. Because *he* was the reason I was doing this. Oh, there were other reasons — to avenge Barley's parents, to save Anita and Pierre, to be reunited with my sister and Mia — but at that moment, rising above all others, the reason I was charging toward a ruthless gunman was because I wanted to save my friend. And, if possible, I wanted to kill Riggs.

Riggs fired.

And would have nailed me had I not seen his lips draw back from his crooked teeth, the unconscious snarl that telegraphed his murderous intent a half-second before he squeezed the trigger. When those lips twitched, I instinctively changed course, still barreling forward, but darting to my left. In doing so, I saved my life.

Even though my endurance was shit, my speed was still there, better than ever. I was faster than I had any right to be — unnaturally fast — and when I caught a glimpse of Barley's face, I knew he was seeing what the others had seen back at Sunny Woods.

"Your eyes," Barley breathed.

I didn't care that my irises had turned green. At that moment I was happy to accept the blur-quick movements that accompanied the Children's infection.

I grinned as I sprinted at Riggs.

I was ten feet and closing when he fired, and by the time he shifted the gun to pop me in the face, I was launching myself at him.

I knew I couldn't go in high — that was suicide. Riggs was no slouch with a gun, and if I placed myself anywhere near his crosshairs, I'd be a goner. So I went for his legs.

More specifically, I went for his right knee.

He fired again. I heard — even *felt* — the whistle of the slug as it strafed the valley between my shoulder blades.

Then I struck Riggs's knee at maximum speed, my shoulder pounding his patella like the world's dirtiest linebacker attempting to ruin a quarterback's career. Riggs was a tough son of a bitch, but when I crashed into that kneecap, his leg hyperextended a good three or four inches before the rest of his body caught up and floundered backward. I expected the gun to erupt again, but it didn't.

I did hear voices though, several of them, as Riggs landed on his back. I scrambled to my hands and knees. Riggs had let go of Barley as he'd gone down, and though Barley, too, had fallen, I could see my friend was safe.

Something thumped down in front of me. I stared at it, unable to comprehend what I was seeing.

Riggs's gun.

Flabbergasted by my luck, I snatched it up, pushed to my feet, and took aim at Riggs, who was grasping his knee with one hand and extending the other toward me.

I wasn't about to show him mercy. I drew a bead on his pain-racked face and prepared to fire.

"You might want to think about that," a voice called.

Castro. Maybe he'd fire on me the moment I killed Riggs, but I didn't care. Let him shoot me. At least I'd save Barley and Pierre and Anita. At least I'd—

"Don't, Will!" Anita shouted.

Her urgency broke through my fury. I swiveled my head and saw what I didn't want to see: Castro holding Pierre hostage the same way Riggs had held Barley hostage.

So we're back to that, I thought. *Dammit.*

"Stand down, Castro," Haddad commanded. "I've got you covered. It's two to one."

"The hell it is," Castro said, an insane grin contorting his face. "Yours emptied when you killed Montana. I heard it."

I didn't want it to be true, but I could see from Haddad's expression that Castro was right. There was no use pretending otherwise.

Which meant it was me and Castro.

My heart thundered in my chest. My breathing thinned. Why did it always have to come down to this? Why did I always have to make some choice between two unspeakable options?

If I shot Riggs, Pierre would die too. I had no doubt about that. Sweat dripped from Pierre's face as the muzzle dug into his temple. Castro had cinched his forearm around Pierre's throat so tightly that Pierre was struggling for air.

"Do it," Barley said to me.

I glanced at my friend, and at that moment, I scarcely recognized him. He was staring grimly down at Riggs in the way of one who has lost all regard for right and wrong, who's only governed by vengeance. I didn't blame him — the son of a bitch had just murdered Barley's mother — but I couldn't consign Pierre to death.

But if I gave up the gun, we'd all die.

Like he'd heard my thoughts, Barley said, "He'll kill Pierre anyway. You know he will."

"Last chance, kid," Castro said.

Pierre was watching me, but because Castro was gripping him so roughly, his eyes were slitted, and I couldn't make out the emotion written there. But Anita, a few feet to Pierre's right, was easy to read. She was imploring me with her eyes to put the gun down, to negotiate her uncle's deliverance. I didn't know what to do, but I knew I couldn't let him die.

I was about to speak when the hackles on the back of my neck rose. I knew what that meant, knew it even before Castro's expression went from triumphant to confused. Castro stared at me for a moment. Then he swiveled his head toward the forest.

Pierre's eyes widened, and I knew the pressure from Castro's grip had slackened just a bit. But it was enough to allow Pierre's eyes to blaze at me.

Castro was gazing toward the forest when Pierre pumped an elbow into his captor's stomach. Castro doubled over, Pierre slipped away, and I swung the gun around to aim. I was about to fire — *would* have fired — when an alabaster shape exploded from the high prairie grass and landed on Castro.

In a movie, Anita would have shrieked bloody murder — the women in movies always did. But it was Pierre who cried out, "*Oh my holy God!*" as the creature began tearing Castro's face off.

I realized my mistake too late. As Castro's gun tumbled in the dirt and Anita began to scramble toward it, I remembered Riggs, the bastard I'd been about to kill.

The bastard I'd left uncovered while I witnessed Castro's murder.

Riggs chopped at my wrist, and the gun skittered away. I took a step to retrieve it, but then I saw them. Two more shapes scything through the prairie grass, their luminous green eyes bright with bloodlust.

The Children had found us.

And we were hundreds of yards from the river.

"Will?" Barley said.

"Run," I answered.

"They're gonna—"

"We've got to get to the river."

But deep down, I knew it was impossible. Three creatures versus a group of mostly unarmed people.

This was going to be a bloodbath.

The creature had buried its maw in Castro's throat, was ripping and tearing like a tiger shark.

The other two closed the distance with appalling speed.

My only thought at that moment was of Peach.

Please get away, I thought. *Please don't die too.*

The thought vanished as the Children raced toward us.

—

ANITA FIRED CASTRO'S gun, and one creature staggered. The prairie grass around it tremored, but it regained its balance, and its companion leapt out of the grass, straight at Anita.

Anita planted her feet wide, took aim, and blasted the creature in the face.

The white head jolted, and the creature took a nosedive. It skidded to a stop at Anita's feet.

A shrill cry split the day. The other creature had reached the edge of the grass and was about to leap at us. But beyond that, where the woods met the prairie, there were three or four more shapes loping toward us. Our chances, already slim, dwindled to zero.

"The gun," someone behind me said.

I stared stupidly back at Barley.

"The gun!" he repeated.

Somewhere, in the recesses of my overtaxed mind, I wondered why Barley didn't just retrieve Riggs's gun himself. But the thought was gone as soon as it had arisen, and I lurched toward it. I'd only moved a half-step when my body jerked — someone kicking my ankle — and I went down. I spun on the ground and discovered Riggs, the treacherous bastard, grinning at me. Worse, he was retrieving something from his pocket. He gave a practiced flick of his wrist, and a wicked-looking blade, six inches long, appeared. Riggs hammered down with the knife.

Straight at my shin. A primal fear of pain surged through me, and I jerked my leg from Riggs's grip. The blade sliced through the heel of my tennis shoe and stuck in the ground. I kicked out at Riggs, nailed him a good one on the knuckles. He gasped, wrenched his hand back, but with his other hand he was already swinging around, wrenching the knife free. He lifted it, teeth bared and eyes glinting maniacally, and was about to stab at me again when his eyes twitched up and clouded.

I spun around as the creature crashed into me. It was the third Child, the one Anita hadn't shot, and it was on me, pinning my shoulders to the ground and breathing its pestilential breath into my face. The stench was so rank, I almost retched. I pushed against its chest with all my strength. But the creature's face was stretching in a monstrous leer, the green eyes and the scimitar teeth reveling in my helplessness. It lowered its jaws toward me, the mouth yawning wider, a putrid string of slaver stringing over my forehead.

Then it jolted as a gunshot cracked the day.

Another. The noises were thunderous.

The fingers relaxed their grip, the creature craning its head around to see who had shot it.

It was Barley.

Oh, he was no marksman. His cruddy vision and the fact that he'd never operated a gun guaranteed that. But he'd fired from less than three feet away, and at that range, his aim had been true.

The back of its head sluicing ichor, the creature sagged sideways and thumped down next to me. I scrambled to my feet. Barley turned the gun on Riggs, and though I didn't blame Barley for focusing on his parents' murderer, we had much graver problems than a psycho with a pocketknife to consider.

The herd of Children was almost upon us.

"Barley?" I said, but then Barley was firing again. I heard a surprised cry and saw Riggs grasping his shoulder, his knife tumbling at my feet.

Barley strode forward, grinned horribly, and aimed the gun at Riggs.

Click.

"Shit!" Barley shouted. He brought the gun toward his face, stared furiously into it, and I had time to think, *Be careful with that thing!*

Riggs lumbered forward. I plucked the knife from the ground. Riggs roared as he lunged for me.

In that moment, the beast inside me rose up. I remembered all the evil that Riggs had perpetrated. Thinking of how he'd murdered Barley's mother, I swung the knife with all my strength.

And buried it in his left eye.

Riggs howled. I yanked the knife out and Riggs clamped his hands over his ruined eye and spun around in a shrieking, ungainly pirouette.

When he faced me again, I slashed him in the belly. A foot-long burgundy stripe appeared in his shirt, and rills of blood dribbled over his trousers.

"Holy shit," Barley said. He started to say something else, but I wasn't listening, wasn't even myself in that moment. I could only think of punishing Riggs, of spilling his blood.

I raised the knife to jam it in Riggs's throat, but someone seized my arm.

Haddad.

"Those things are coming," he said. "We gotta run."

I blinked at him. Barley was staring at me with something like horror. Like he didn't know me. It scared me, that look, and it succeeded in bringing me back from that awful mental place.

The truth of our situation sank in. Anita might still have ammunition, but when that was spent, we had no more protection. We were beaten up, wounded, and we had maybe three hundred yards before we reached the river. And the Children were fast approaching. They'd easily overtake us.

We started running anyway. It was the only choice. I paused long enough to fold up Riggs's knife and cram it into the pocket of my cargo shorts. Behind us, Riggs was blubbering, one hand gripping his bloody eye socket, the other swinging wildly from side to side as if trying to hail a helicopter. But there were no helicopters, no help at all. Just us and this vast open space and a horde of bloodthirsty creatures.

We staggered on, but it was no use. We'd only gone twenty yards when the first of a larger wave of Children burst from the prairie grass. They were closing the distance rapidly, running us down like baby antelopes separated from the pack.

A warbling screech of agony filled the day. I glanced backward and watched Riggs being swarmed by the creatures. One moment he was on his feet, pleading with us to turn around, the next instant, they were tackling him, riding him down with no effort at all. He clambered to his feet, but they moved with him, snarling and clawing. There were three of them, and through the blur of their slashing nails and snapping teeth I glimpsed Riggs's upturned face, his mouth hinged wide, his remaining eye shuttered open in anguish. The blood bubbled over his teeth and sprayed in fine, cherry-red droplets, and then, through some ghastly miracle of physics, his body stayed that way, upright and spewing blood, as the creatures beset him from all sides. They ribboned his shirt and tore strings of cartilage and gristle from his chest. He wailed. One creature clamped down on his left nipple, wrenched its head, and swallowed the doughy hunk of meat like some ravenous seabird.

Sickened, I turned away.

"*Faster,*" Anita commanded. Pierre faltered, his wounds sapping his energy. Anita made to get her head under his arm, but he pulled away, grimacing.

"Don't do that," he said. "You're gonna get yourself killed."

"But they're…" she started but let the thought trail off. There was no need to finish it anyway. Because there were now roughly half a dozen Children ripping and tearing Riggs's body to pieces, three or four others feasting on Castro's ruined carcass, and though I did my best not to look, there were other Children feeding on Barley's parents' bodies. Montana's too, though I didn't give a shit about him.

I had no idea how many Children were in pursuit, but I'd counted at least a dozen more pounding the path behind us, forsaking the dead for fresher meat.

Our time was almost up.

"Faster, damn you," Anita said.

I glanced over and felt my heart sink. Not only had Pierre fallen behind, but he looked ready to lose consciousness.

"Over…" Barley said between wheezing breaths. "It's over."

I slowed down, grasped his shirt at the shoulder, and dragged him with me. I was easily the fastest member of our group, but I knew it didn't matter. My maximum speed paled in comparison to these monsters. The beast at the fore was only ten yards from Pierre and Anita. As I debated what to do, Anita's gaze shifted. Her eyes widened.

"Oh my God!" she shouted.

From our left, the Jeep rumbled out of the prairie grass with Mia white-knuckling the wheel and Peach staring out the windshield beside her.

—

THE JEEP BROADSIDED the nearest creatures, one of them mowed down under the wheels, another cartwheeling upward, crashing into the windshield hip first, and barrel-rolling over the roof. The third creature was only clipped by the bumper, but because the beast had been racing so swiftly, when the collision occurred it performed a brutal nosedive, its head catching the road and its body folding backward with a brittle crunch.

The Jeep, marauding full bore across the roadway, veered back in the direction of the crash site.

Back in the direction from which the Children were pouring.

What are you doing, Mia? I had time to wonder. But an instant later, it became evident what she was doing.

The Jeep rattled into the prairie grass, but several seconds later, it emerged again more than a football field behind us, angling back toward us after having described a wide loop. We'd begun to sprint again, but from over our shoulders we watched the Jeep thunder toward us. I was reminded of Simba in *The Lion King*, the moment when the wildebeests stampeded the valley. The Jeep swerved left and right to pick them off. I grinned as Mia plowed into a pair of creatures, their arms splayed out like marathoners at the finish line. They ate dirt as the Jeep bounced over their bodies, the sounds of cracking bones beautiful percussion in my ears. The Jeep veered right, catapulting another creature into the tall grass.

The Children near the Jeep had finally clued in to the slaughter taking place — what a shock it must have been to be on the receiving end — and they took measures to dodge it. But Mia was clever, and she hated these fuckers as much as I did. Beside her in the passenger's seat, I glimpsed Peach gesticulating and exhorting Mia on. Even with that savage expression, Peach looked sort of cute, and for the first time since the Jeep had reappeared, it occurred to me that the two of them had totally ignored my order to escape. I won't lie — I was happy as hell to see them; we would have been ripped apart had they not undertaken this desperate rescue mission — but I was also worried. What if the Jeep overturned?

I was thinking this when one of the creatures vaulted toward them and made a grab for the roof. *No way*, I thought. The creature's angle was all wrong, and the Jeep was rumbling along too rapidly for the creature to latch onto it. But just before its feet hit the ground, it snagged the roof rack and clambered on top of the Jeep.

The vehicle lurched — Mia slamming on the brakes — and the creature atop the roof somersaulted forward in a whir of limbs. The Jeep marauded over it, the space between the front wheels seeming to devour the creature like the hungry maw of some swift ocean fish, and before two other Children could leap onto the vehicle, Mia took evasive action. She veered right and left in a zigzag and succeeded in fending the creatures off. She accelerated then, the path between us devoid of monsters.

It was a good thing too.

Pierre was gasping and staggering, Barley doing the same. Haddad had slowed considerably. Only Anita appeared unfazed by our grueling flight.

The Jeep approached.

"Pierre gets in first," Haddad called. "Then Anita."

We continued to shamble along as the Jeep drew nearer, but even though there was a fifty-yard gap between the Jeep and the Children, I was doubtful we'd be able to board everyone without being overtaken.

The Jeep swept past us, and for a surreal instant I thought it might continue on, Mia deciding this rescue mission was doomed after all and returning to the original plan. But then the Jeep was skidding to a stop, and I realized how shrewd she'd been. She'd put as much distance as possible between us and the creatures, and now it was a race against time to climb inside the vehicle before the Children overtook us.

Just before the Jeep ceased its forward progress, a back door flew open, and Peach's face appeared in the aperture. She was shouting at us to *Come on! Come on!* and despite the severity of our plight, I couldn't suppress a grin at her guts. Damn, but I was proud of her. Whatever hell she'd been through, she was a fighter. And as Peach's presence often did, she helped center me.

I joined Anita in helping Pierre into the back of the Jeep.

Once we'd deposited him inside, I glanced over my shoulder and felt my stomach plummet. The creatures were only fifty yards away. In a few seconds, they'd be upon us.

Someone hauled me into the Jeep. I landed on top of Anita, who'd been the one to drag me inside, and as I registered the presence of Barley in the back seat beside Pierre, and Haddad in the front seat next to Peach, I realized we'd started moving again.

But the creatures were right on our tail.

One of them leaped, its claws missing the rear bumper by inches.

We accelerated, but another creature — this one taller and more muscular — vaulted at the Jeep, banged against our back window, and managed to hang on.

We topped a rise, and as I beheld the valley spreading out below us and the lowlands leading to the river, I realized how dramatically the path narrowed. Where before it had been thirty feet wide, it was now a mere ten. Mia had to be cautious, for if she veered too wildly right or left, she'd consign us to the marshy vegetation, where we'd get bogged down.

The creature punched through the back window, the glass spraying. Mia jerked the wheel, the Jeep shimmying convulsively. But the creature held on, its sinuous arm snaking inside the hole it had made. I reached into my pocket, extracted Riggs's knife, and was climbing over the back seat into the storage area when the creature's other fist crashed through the back window. Though the whole window was spiderwebbed from the dual impacts of the creature's fists, I could still make out its loathsome face grinning at me through the glass.

It snatched at me. I sucked in my stomach as its talons whickered by, and then I brought the knife down, slashing at the monster's fingers.

The Jeep rocked as something landed on the roof. It could only be another creature.

"Move!" Anita shouted. She was leaning over the back seat, both hands on the gun she'd taken from Castro, and I had time to wonder, *Why didn't you use that thing earlier?*

Of course, there hadn't really *been* an earlier; all of it was happening so fast. Anita had been more concerned with keeping her uncle safe than going on the offensive, but she looked more than ready to do damage now, her eyes narrowed, the pistol coming to rest at a spot equidistant between the creature's groping hands.

Anita fired, a jagged hole appearing in the already-damaged back window. Black liquid jetted against the glass. She fired again, and this time the creature's arms tremored so spasmodically that, above its squall of pain, we heard the ear-grinding squeal of the window splintering out of its frame. The entire window came loose with the creature, and both disappeared on the dusty path behind us.

The Child on the roof shrieked, a high-pitched sound that froze my blood. Anita glanced at the ceiling, raised the gun, and fired. There was no way to tell if she'd shot the creature or not, but there'd been no answering screech, no ichor dripping through the hole in the roof. She fired again, and a split second later, a fist-sized section of the ceiling crumpled downward. Anita took aim, squeezed the trigger, but the gun clicked empty. We stared at the ceiling in dread, waiting for the creature to batter the metal again, but a cry from Peach told me the beast had other ideas.

I turned toward the windshield and saw, upside down, its demonic white face leering at us.

—

I DON'T KNOW what decided me. Maybe it was the fact that we were almost to the river. I could see the murky water roil beyond the creature's upside-down face, maybe a hundred yards from our current position.

What compelled me through the Jeep's missing back window was the sight of Peach shrinking away from the creature. Seeing the two that close together — the little sister I loved and the beast who yearned to hurt her — made something inside me snap.

"What the hell are you doing?" Haddad shouted, but I was already climbing onto the roof. Like a pirate in some old swash-buckler, I had the knife clenched in my teeth. I crawled onto the roof, pushed myself to a crouch. The Jeep wobbled, and I damn near tumbled off. Steadying myself, I grasped the knife and crept toward the creature. The one thing I had going for me was the element of surprise, and the longer I waited, the less likely it was that I could take the creature unawares.

The Jeep bounced, and I landed with a thud on both knees.

The creature spun around, its face twisting. It scrambled to its feet and faced me, its arms thrown out for balance. The creature had slender, pendulous breasts and didn't possess a phallus like the majority of the Children seemed to.

The beast roared at me.

I raised the knife and hammered it down. The blade skewered its foot and chunked into the metal roof. The creature tossed back its head and squalled. I wrenched the blade free, and the beast lashed out at me. I threw my shoulders back, and for a moment I was sure I'd leaned too far, that I'd simply tumble off the roof, land in the road, and be torn apart by the pursuing swarm. I windmilled my arms to keep from toppling over, and the creature advanced. It tore down at me just as I regained my balance, and this time, there was no avoiding the swipe. Fire seared my chest. I glanced at my torso and was aghast at the diagonal red stripes blossoming there.

I realized my mistake too late. In the instant it had taken for me to assess the damage, the creature had readied itself for another attack. I looked up in time to see the wicked claws rise, the maniacal expression on the creature's face, the wind whipping its stringy hair toward me like greasy black streamers celebrating some devil's Sabbath. I flung up a hand, knowing I was too late, but the creature's expression changed, its body tilting sideways, and then it was whamming down on the roof, its elbow clanging on metal and its head jarring violently.

"Kill it!"

I spotted Haddad's head and shoulders above the roof. He was perched in the open passenger's window and grasping the creature's ankle. I turned back to the beast, raised the knife, and before it could repel my attack, I plunged the blade into the side of its throat. Shrieking, it grasped my wrist, but I was inexorable. I jerked on the blade, unzipping its throat, and as the noxious black blood spilled over the roof, I started to slide forward. We were decelerating.

We'd almost reached the river.

With a backward glance I discovered the path behind us was clear. Oh, the creatures were still in pursuit, but Mia's aggressive driving had given us some breathing room.

The creature on the roof with me was still twitching and batting feebly at my arm. I tore the knife free, and as we rumbled toward the edge of the river, I shoved the creature's dying body off the roof.

A few moments later we coasted to a stop and beheld the Tippecanoe River.

It was sixty yards across.

I pocketed the knife, climbed off the roof, knelt, and spread my arms.

Peach was in them less than a second later.

CHAPTER TWENTY-ONE
ALL YOU LOVE WILL BE TAKEN

Though I relished the feeling of Peach clinging to my neck, we had no time for sentimentality. The Children were racing toward us, and they were more motivated than ever to destroy us.

Peach showed no sign of wanting to leave my arms, and that was fine with me. We were on the crest of a short decline leading to the riverbank, a stretch of rye grass and cattails followed by seven or eight feet of sandy shoreline.

I was lugging Peach toward the river when I noticed a commotion from the driver's side of the Jeep. Barley and Mia were right behind me with Haddad in tow. It was Anita and Pierre who were shouting at each other.

"Hold on," I said to Peach, setting her down at the river's edge.

She protested, but Mia stepped in and instructed her to take off her shoes. That was smart, I decided as I climbed back up the bank. Waterlogged shoes were heavy. I made a mental note to do the same as soon as I got Pierre and Anita down this hill and into the water.

The Children are coming! a frantic voice shouted.

You don't think I know that? I answered, hustling up the hill. *But Pierre is injured. He must need help. That's the only explanation for...*

My thought trailed off when I saw how hard Anita was sobbing.

I hurried the last few strides, sure Pierre's injuries were much worse than I'd thought. But he was alive and sitting in the still-running Jeep. He had a hand out, caressing Anita's arm.

"What's wrong?" I asked.

Anita shook her head, but Pierre merely smiled and said, "I can't swim."

I gaped at him, the words not yet fully registering.

He chuckled and I noticed how ashen his skin had become. "I always meant to, you know? One of those things you tell yourself you're gonna do. I made sure Ruben and Anita got lessons, but..." He shook his head, his smile fading. "Too late now."

I swallowed, knowing the truth but unwilling to accept it. "The river's not that deep. You can wade across. And if —"

"I'm bleeding to death."

I shook my head and reached for him.

He caught my hand and gave it a squeeze. "Stop, Will. You're a good kid." He coughed, wiped blood from his lips. "A hell of a good kid. But you know this is it. You can either die here or save your sister."

I started to protest, but my eyes flicked to Pierre's midsection. His clothes glistened a dull crimson. *No,* I thought. *Please no.*

"Pierre's right," Haddad said. He took me by the shoulder and tried to do the same to Anita, but she shrugged him off and wrapped her uncle in a quaking embrace.

"It's okay, Pumpkin," Pierre said. "It's okay."

Anita's shoulders spasmed as she clung to her uncle. I was tearing up too.

"We have to go," Mia called up to me. I backpedaled as Haddad led me away.

"Come on, Anita," Haddad said.

Moving sideways down the bank, I saw Pierre push her out of the doorway as gently as he could. Anita backed away and descended the hill, her expression shell-shocked. She'd already lost her husband and was about to lose the man who was even more a father figure to her than he was to me.

"Hey, Will?" Pierre called as I reached the sandy bank.

I stopped and gazed up at him. He closed the Jeep door, rolled down the window. "Take care of Anita, will you?"

My throat burning, I nodded. I could barely see his wan smile because my eyes were so blurry.

"And tell my wife and son I love them," he said.

The words were like daggers to my heart, but I nodded. The last I saw of Pierre was the way he looked at Anita as he shifted the Jeep into gear. He was in pain, but he was smiling a soft smile.

He drove away.

I knew what he was doing, and it made me love him even more. If he could mow down more creatures with the Jeep, he'd buy us more time. How much, I had no idea, but any time would help.

With Peach on one side and Mia on the other, I waded into the river.

—

"IS PIERRE GONNA die?" Peach asked.

I wiped my eyes with the heel of my hand but didn't answer. We didn't have time for mourning. For the first fifteen feet or so, the water didn't reach my knees, and I wondered if it might be shallow all the way across.

Then the bottom dropped out, the river at shoulder-level. I snatched Peach out of the water and told her to grab onto my neck, which she did. She'd learned last summer not to question orders at pivotal moments, and she could hear in my voice that obeying now was imperative.

Behind us, the first thump sounded: Pierre smashing into a creature.

I hoped he'd make it out alive.

Another thud. *Give 'em hell,* I thought.

In the deeper water, Mia began to stroke with practiced regularity, easily pulling ahead of us. Barley dog-paddled at a lethargic pace, and I knew he was in trouble. He wouldn't drown — at least I didn't *think* he would drown. The river was still shallow enough for us to touch bottom, but the current was increasing.

I realized I'd left my sneakers on. This had been helpful at first because the river bottom was littered with jagged rocks and, I was sure, sharp objects like beer cans and fishing hooks. But now the same shoes that had protected my feet were like anchors. Each step cost a mammoth effort, and two or three times I almost stumbled.

"Can you swim for a few seconds?" I said over my shoulder to Peach.

"I think so," she answered, but she didn't sound convincing. It occurred to me how much she'd been deprived of. No swimming lessons, no vacations where she could splash around a pool.

So much she hasn't done, I thought. *So much.*

And on the heels of that: *You have to keep her alive. You have to give her a chance to do everything.*

Peach let go of me, and I reached down to peel off one shoe and then the other. Peach was paddling frantically, her eyes huge and her mouth spitting water. I grabbed her forearm and resituated her on my back.

But swimming was a lot harder than I'd anticipated. Peach wasn't heavy, but that added drag made for slow going. Mia was scything through the water without effort, and a part of me wondered whether Peach would be better off on Mia's back.

My thoughts were scattered by the plangent squeal of torn metal and the crunch of shattered glass.

Pierre and his Jeep had crashed. Or been run off the road. Either way…

My heart sank at the screams that issued from behind us. We were toiling through the river, the splashes of our hands audible, but sound had a tendency to carry over water, and Pierre's cries of pain were impossible to ignore.

Damn those monsters, I thought. *Damn them to hell.*

Pierre deserved better.

But somewhere, beneath the anger and the hatred of the Children, there was something else, something paralyzing and insistent and so raw I could barely breathe.

It was my fault. That's what was killing me. Everyone who knew me — from Chris to my mom to Pierre — everyone came to ruin. I glanced at Mia and almost asked her to take Peach from me. I didn't want to hurt anyone else, least of all this amazing little girl I wanted with all my being to protect.

And that was why I *didn't* ask Mia to take over. If I could keep Peach safe, if I could accomplish this one thing, my life might not be a total loss.

Peach patted my shoulder and said, "Keep going, Will. You can do it."

I discovered we were halfway across the river. It galvanized me.

Barley was swimming abreast of us, my friend moving as slowly as we were despite the fact that he had nothing but his clothes encumbering him. Beyond Barley, Haddad was pushing steadily on. He'd shed his military shirt and now wore only a white tank top. I was surprised at the muscle cording his arms. He was in his fifties, but dang, the guy was still in shape. I suspected he was holding back from swimming his hardest in order to remain near us. Mia was treading water, waiting for me and Peach. Beyond her, Anita was moving along steadily, her expression pinched, her eyes moist with more than river water. She'd heard Pierre's last moments, too.

My muscles clenched. I was heartsick and furious, but the full ramifications of Pierre's death had just now slammed home: If he was no longer running interference, there was nothing to prevent the Children from getting to us.

I stroked faster.

Mia sucked in breath. "Oh Jesus," she whispered.

I didn't even turn. I didn't have to.

The Children were closing in.

We were swimming hard, but it didn't feel like enough. Not nearly. Because those creatures, if my suspicions were correct, would slice through the water like catamarans.

My back muscles burned, my legs like blocks of stone, but still I pushed on, stroking and kicking with all I had. I peered toward the shore and beyond, and though I couldn't see the highway beyond the narrow scrim of woods, I thought I could hear the faint *whoosh* of cars whizzing by.

How far was it between the river and the road? Thirty yards? More?

And then what? A crazy memory of a horror film flickered through my head: *The Texas Chainsaw Massacre*. I remembered a survivor fleeing from Leatherface, the woman frantically hailing a driver and struggling to climb inside a truck, all while the psycho's chainsaw buzzed and buzzed.

The images did little to comfort me.

"Faster," Mia said. She took hold of my shirt and began to tug me forward. It didn't help much. If anything, it made the going more awkward.

Barley whimpered, and Haddad urged him to *"Swim! Swim!"*

Impulsively, I shot a look behind us and saw… nothing. No Children, no anything. Was it possible they'd taken another route?

At that moment a pair of Children thundered over the ridge and plunged headlong into the water.

They didn't resurface. Then I understood.

The creatures could not only swim, they could swim underwater for sustained periods. I glimpsed white shapes gliding toward us just under the surface.

Holy shit, I thought. *They move like sharks.*

I lurched forward, my hands scooping frenetically. I've always had a fear of sharks, always been terrified of razor-sharp teeth shredding the flesh of my feet, my ankles.

Every nerve in my lower body became fraught with sensations. Every ripple of water, every gout of fizz, seemed to prickle my skin and send my paranoia into higher gear. Ahead, Anita was nearing the shore, Haddad not far behind. Barley was a little way ahead of me, and Mia was right beside me, still doing what she could to help me and Peach along. I kicked, slapped at the water with what strength I had, but I was weakening, failing, my arms like lead, my reserve energy depleted.

"We can touch," Mia said, and I realized she was right. My foot skimmed the rocky river bottom, and upon contact, my hamstring tightened. I ground my teeth, brought my other foot down, and tried to hop forward until the Charley horse in my leg subsided. Mia was removing Peach from my back and shepherding her closer to shore. The extra weight gone, I was able to stagger on. I saw Anita pushing onto the brown sand. Haddad was trudging forward in ankle-deep water. Mia and Peach were moving ahead of me. So was Barley.

We're going to make it! I thought. *Or at least make it to shore. After that…*

The water lapped at my ribs, but it was getting shallower. The going was slow, so I dove forward, began to swim again.

Something brushed the sole of my foot.

I gasped and kicked out and began to thrash toward shore.

Cold fingers closed over my ankle.

I yelped, glanced back, and beheld the ghostlike fingers grasping me. Beyond that, just beneath the water's surface, lambent green eyes leered at me with ruthless glee. I kicked at the Child with my free leg, but the beast jerked me toward it. I drifted toward its open mouth. The awl-like teeth rippled beneath the water, the creature ready to bite my foot in half. I raised my free foot, kicked out. My heel collided with its bald pate.

It was enough to break its hold. But I knew it would keep coming, and in a panic I plunged sideways. The Child rose up from the water, at least eight feet tall, and snarled at me. Peripherally, I saw Anita disappearing up the bank and into the forest, and I thought, *Go! Stop someone on the highway so we'll have a ride out of here.* Haddad was halfway up the bank, but he'd stopped, probably debating whether to double back and help.

The creature seized my ankle again, and this time it yanked me under it.

In a flash, I knew it was over. I attempted to stand, but it held me in place, right at the water's surface. Leering, it leaned toward me.

Behind it, a shadow swooped toward us.

What the hell?

Then the talons closed on the Child's shoulders, and it was torn from the water, squalling and kicking. I stumbled backward, but I could see well enough the tenebrous wings and the hellish red eyes.

The Night Flyer had saved my life.

Not, I realized, because it wanted me to live, but because these two species despised one another. That had been clear enough back in the shelter. I turned and watched the Child who'd been borne away plummeting toward the beach, the Night Flyer having dropped it from an incredible height. The Child crashed to the sand, the crunching of its bones as clear as my own breathing.

But the Children were still coming. Another was nearing me, and I could see several white shapes gliding just under the water's surface. I pushed forward, but the water was too deep to make good progress. I fancied I could feel frigid fingers whispering over my flesh. Any moment a Child would seize me from behind and tear me apart.

I threw a frenzied glance behind me and spotted several dark shapes swerving toward the river. A Night Flyer plummeted thirty feet, extended its talons, and plucked a shrieking Child from the water. This Night Flyer had less luck. The Child in its grip twisted and managed to scallop the Night Flyer's eyes with its own savage claws, and the Night Flyer spiraled into the river.

Four more Night Flyers swooped down. One plucked a Child from the water as easily as a heron snatching a perch. Another, even larger Night Flyer seized a Child by the head and swerved back the way it had come, the Child grasping the Night Flyer's legs and kicking for dear life. A third Night Flyer attempted to snag a Child, but this time the pale creature was ready for it. It leaped from the river, caught the Night Flyer by the head, and the two of them divebombed the water, where a great tumult erupted, river water and black ichor fountaining into the air like an oil gusher.

I started to smile.

Then I realized one of the Night Flyers was headed straight for me.

Abject terror washed through me, and for a moment, all I could do was stare into its eyes. In daylight, the satanic features were even ghastlier than the ones I'd glimpsed at Sunny Woods. I could see the furrows along its cheeks, and worse, much worse, I could see its lips curling back from its teeth, the lips mottled and writhing in anticipatory delight. The Night Flyer's seething eyes widened. It extended its talons for me.

I dove toward the river bottom, and my muffled underwater hearing told me the Night Flyer had crashed into the water too. A branding iron of pain seared my shoulder. I opened my eyes in the nearly lightless water and made out capering shadows, river fizz, and dredged-up sand. I rolled, thinking only of evading the Night Flyer, and when a scream tore through the tapestry of muffled noises, I pushed to my feet and leapt straight up. When I breached the surface, I was sure I'd find one of my companions in the shallows, clutched by a Child or a Night Flyer and already dead from an attack.

Instead, I discovered a Child atop the Night Flyer who'd gone for me, the Child's teeth sunk all the way to the gums in the back of the Night Flyer's leathery neck.

Voices exhorted me to *Go! Move! Run!* so I splashed forward, thinking, finally, that fate was on my side.

"Look out!" Peach screamed.

I threw a glance behind me in time to see a Child rise from the water, its green irises aglow and its impossibly long arms groping for me.

I dodged it, went under, and scraped the bottom with my side. The water here was shallower; swimming was no longer an option. So I pushed up, began to shamble away.

The Child stalked after me.

I was in waist-high water, backpedaling toward shore at a sharp diagonal. The creature followed, its strides lengthy enough for it to close the distance easily.

With a sidelong glance I saw Peach and Mia and Barley all on the shore, all watching me. I shouted, "Get to the road! I'll be right behind you!"

But they didn't move, didn't even take a step in that direction. I was maybe twenty feet from shore, and beyond the towering creature I spied several more disturbances in the water. Glimmers of alabaster heads. Whorls and eddies where the river churned with the Children's passage. In the distance I spotted winged shapes heading our way. More Night Flyers would be here in moments.

The towering Child snatched at me, and I leaped back with a gasp. My foot landed awkwardly, the rocks on the river bottom large and jagged. I heard a splashing to my left.

Mia.

"Get up the hill!" I shouted, not caring how I sounded, caring only that Mia and Peach and Barley escaped before more of these beasts swarmed. They were coming. Couldn't Mia *see* that?

"Will!" she screamed.

The Child was reaching for me.

I did the only thing I could do. I keeled backward and dropped beneath the water's surface, and as I did, I heard a buzzing voice.

(*no escaping*)

The words scarcely registered. What froze me to the core was the *quality* of the voice. The Children had been in my head before, but this voice was unlike any I'd ever heard. Like the other voices, it had that buzzing, insectile quality. But what distinguished this one from the others was its incalculable *age*. Whatever was speaking had lived for millennia and was certain it would live for millennia more.

I came up spluttering and saw I'd halved the distance to shore simply by digging with my feet and crab-walking backward. My palms were savaged by the rocks, but it was a small price to pay.

(*will suffer a fate worse than death*)

I flinched at the fury in the voice, the outrage of a betrayed king.

(*have disturbed my sleep*)

I shook my head, but the voice buzzed on.

(*harmed my offspring*)

I frowned, almost to the shore now, and tried to make sense of the words. Who was speaking? And how had I disturbed its sleep?

"Look out!"

I jarred to attention at Mia's voice and realized that, incredibly, I'd forgotten about the monster trying to kill me. Its taloned fingers were only a foot away. I scrambled backward. If only I had some means of defending myself, if only—

The knife!

With a groan, I stuffed a hand in my pocket, but the knife was gone. I patted my other pockets, and it wasn't there, and the irony of it made me gnash my teeth. Our passage through the water had been so frantic that I'd somehow lost the knife, and now there was nothing with which to defend myself, nothing but...

I reached down, grabbed the only tool at my disposal.

A rock. Roughly the size of a softball, but comprised of jagged edges and a density that gave it some heft.

The Child darted at me. I got my feet beneath me and swung the rock.

And brained the creature.

The beast must not have been expecting me to fight because it didn't even throw an arm up to defend itself. One moment it was reaching for me, that satanic leer widening, the next its head was whipping sideways, the rock having ripped a trench along its cheekbone. It sank to its knees, and I grasped the rock with both hands, raised it above the beast's head, and smashed downward. I staved in the creature's skull. It flopped forward and didn't move.

Around me, half a dozen white faces emerged from the water.

Oh Jesus, no.

I wheeled around and floundered toward shore. From behind came the splashing of the beasts. Mia and Peach were clambering up the rise. To their right, Barley scaled the hill, my friend moving with more vigor than I'd ever seen.

(*will have you*)

The voice was like icewater dumped on the back of my neck. I didn't need to look behind me to know the creatures were nearing the shore. Our only hope was that Anita and Haddad had managed to corral a passing motorist on the highway. If a car was waiting for us, we might stand a chance. If not, the creatures would surround us and rend us to pieces.

On solid ground, I moved faster despite my bone-deep fatigue. I scampered over the riverbank and charged up the hill. At the crest I was disheartened to discover Peach staring back at me, Mia having to drag her along to keep her moving.

"Run, knucklehead!" I shouted.

Peach got moving again, and I caught up with them by the time we reached the forest's edge. We darted between the first few trees, and as we did, I cast a backward glance.

And immediately regretted it. The moment I looked back, the first creature lurched onto the shore. And now there was no Pierre to aid us, no Jeep to run the Children down. It was us and the monsters and the woods.

No, I thought. We'd come too far and survived too much to die now. I'd murdered one of those bastards with a rock, and I was prepared to fight another.

You got lucky! that mocking voice cried. *That was* one *creature. There's a horde of them approaching, Children and Night Flyers. Do you have enough rocks for all of them?*

"Come here," I said to Peach and gathered her into my arms. She was running just fine but the forest was getting denser, and I didn't want her to trip.

"I can do it," she said into my ear.

I ignored her and sprinted as fast as I could.

From beyond the thicket came the *whish* of cars.

We're so close! I thought.

The bellow of a creature made me gasp. It was that grotesque war cry I'd heard too many times, the communicating shriek that connected these vile beasts and rallied them toward a single goal:

Kill.

Not only were a horde of Children swarming onto the shore — beyond them at least a dozen Night Flyers winged over the river.

I turned and saw Barley stumbling, going down, and then Mia was there beside him, helping him to his feet. They'd been maybe twenty feet ahead of us, but now we drew even, and as Barley and Mia got moving again, we neared the edge of the woods. I spotted the highway up a short rise, and as I clutched my sister to me, a car zipped by. To our right I glimpsed a blue shape, and this one wasn't moving. It was a pickup truck, an older Dodge Ram.

We barreled up the hill.

I glanced back and discovered a Child right behind us. It hissed and groped for my neck.

I lurched forward. Peach and I burst from the forest onto the grassy shoulder, then the road. We veered in the direction of the stopped truck.

"Duck!" Barley shouted.

We dropped, my knees grinding painfully on the asphalt, one hand pushing my sister's head into my shoulder. The Child swooped over us, tumbled end over end, and landed in the ditch on the opposite side of the road. With Peach in my arms, I darted toward the truck and called out, "Start rolling! We'll jump in the back!"

Barley and Mia were dashing that way. Anita was in the truck beside the driver, whoever the saint was. Haddad was jogging along beside the bed of the pickup, evidently to help us climb inside.

Mia went first, leaping onto the bumper and swinging her legs nimbly over the tailgate as though she'd executed the maneuver a hundred times. Barley jumped next. His foot slipped off the bumper, and he went face first into the tailgate. Then he was grasping the bumper, his feet dragging along the asphalt behind him, and I had time to think, *Really, Barley? That's the best you can do?*

Barley apparently realized being towed behind the truck was not going to suffice, because he let go, tumbled, pushed to his feet again, and shambled forward.

From the beach and the woods came the inhuman shrieks of both species, the Children and the Night Flyers, as their battle resumed. That would occupy some of them, I knew, but not all. Both species hated me and the people I loved. Both craved our flesh.

I sprinted harder. Even with Peach in my arms, I moved swiftly enough to draw even with Barley. The truck gathered speed, and I didn't have to look backward to know why. I could imagine the Children streaming from the forest, their toenails clittering on the asphalt.

We were nearly to the truck.

Mia was leaning over the tailgate, arms extended, imploring me to hand Peach up to her. My strength was flagging, but I managed a final burst of energy, lifted Peach, and shoved her toward Mia, who gathered her into her arms and placed her safely beside her in the truck bed. At the same moment, Barley climbed onto the truck's back bumper. He slung an arm over the tailgate, then his upper body. Sprinting behind him, Haddad put a hand on Barley's butt and shoved, and Barley went tumbling into the truck bed.

Haddad and I sprinted side by side. Behind us sounded chuffing breath.

The Children were about to overtake us.

"You first!" Haddad shouted.

I leapt, snagged the tailgate, and with Mia's help climbed over. Haddad grabbed the tailgate and hauled himself up after me.

Halfway over the tailgate, Haddad jolted. His eyes opened wide.

That's when I saw them. Most of the Children were a good twenty or thirty yards behind us, but one had snagged Haddad's foot, was using his body as a ladder to clamber into the truck.

Its jade eyes glowing, the creature hurtled over Haddad, straight at me. It smashed into me and drove me backward. I crashed into the truck bed with the creature on top of me, and we skidded toward the cab. My head smacked the inner wall of the bed, the creature snarling at me and swiping at my face. In the commotion, a tiny foot flashed out and caught the creature in the temple.

Peach!

Growling, the beast swung. Peach ducked, barely avoiding the Child's lethal claws, but without hesitation she kicked the creature again, this time in its ribs.

"Stay away from my brother!" she shouted.

The creature lashed out at Peach, and with a flare of shock and rage I saw her fly toward the tailgate, crash against it shoulder-first, and carom bonelessly onto the steel floor of the bed.

You son of a bitch! I thought, glaring up at the creature.

Mia leapt atop its back, cinched a forearm under its chin. The creature pushed to its feet, thrashed, and though Mia clung tenaciously to its throat, the creature's movements were so wild that Mia repeatedly swung out over the side of the bed.

Haddad had climbed over the tailgate into the truck; he was on his knees, struggling for air. Whether the creature had injured him or he was just winded, I had no idea. But for the time being, he wouldn't be much help.

Movement flashed beside me. Barley crouched near the wheel well, lashing out at the Child with his foot. Though he wasn't inflicting any damage on the creature, he was at least annoying it.

The truck had picked up speed; I estimated we were cruising along at fifty miles per hour. The Children in pursuit were falling behind. The Night Flyers were blitzing the Children in the road and didn't seem interested in pursuing us. Maybe if we could rid ourselves of this last creature, we'd make it out alive, an outcome I wouldn't have believed possible only minutes earlier.

I pushed to my feet, raised a fist to club the creature as hard as I could, but hesitated. What if the Child went flailing backward and took Mia with it? What if Mia landed in the road? She'd be swarmed by monsters, and this bastard would still be in the truck with us. And what about Peach? How badly had this fiend injured her? Her chest still rose and fell, but her eyes were closed, and her limbs didn't stir.

"Hey!" a voice shouted. I turned and gaped at Anita.

Who extended a crowbar through the sliding rear window of the cab. I took it and gripped it like a baseball bat. God, it felt good in my hands.

With all my strength I let loose with a vicious uppercut, the blow so titanic that it spun the creature half around and opened a gash from its mouth to its right ear. Mia dropped safely to the truck bed. The creature staggered, its eyes fogging. Then it faced me, snarled, and began to stalk forward.

Arms closed around the creature from behind.

Haddad! He'd put the creature in a bear hug.

I swung again, this time blasting the creature in the side. I heard a cracking sound and knew I'd shattered at least one rib. It doubled over, which lowered its face to within striking distance. I cut loose and clocked the creature in the jaw. Its teeth clicked together, and I saw a pair of them go twirling out from between its lips.

I flipped the crowbar around, the chisel end facing the creature, and drove it into the monster's abdomen.

The Child roared and crumpled. Haddad leaned on it and rode the son of a bitch down.

"Finish it," Haddad grunted.

I raised the crowbar. The creature swiveled its head up, its eyes slitted. *We'll never stop*, that look said. *We'll destroy you and everyone you love.*

Die, you son a bitch, I thought and plunged the crowbar into its eye.

The chisel sank in. Sclera spurted over my knuckles. The creature's arms brushed feebly at the crowbar. Then its body began to spasm, its death throes frenetic. Ichor sprayed from the wound, coating my fingers, but still I leaned on the crowbar, dug it in, shifting it from side to side to maximize the damage. I remembered how, last summer, Chris's dad had transformed into one of these creatures, how even after he'd been shot nearly a dozen times, he'd somehow sprung up and made off into the forest.

I wasn't going to allow this beast to attack us again.

"Can we get rid of it now?" Barley asked.

"No," Haddad answered. Though he was still gasping for breath and looking like a plague victim, there was something different in Haddad's expression.

I peered over the tailgate and discovered a hellish scene: far back in the road, the Night Flyers and Children were biting and slashing at each other with hideous vigor. And that meant, for now at least, we might escape their wrath.

A gasp from Mia made the thought vanish. She was in the corner of the bed, cradling Peach, whose little head lolled in Mia's arms.

NO! I thought.

I scrambled over and fell to my knees. If Peach was dead, if the creature had killed her, I'd never forgive myself.

"She's breathing," Mia said. "But we need to get her to a hospital."

I tried to process her words. "What do you mean, we—" I broke off and searched my sister's face. Her brow was unfurrowed, her expression seemingly at peace, but far from comforting me, this made my pulse race.

Mia supported Peach's head while I slid underneath my sister and held her in my lap.

Please God, I thought. *If you're out there... please help this amazing little girl. Please help her to be safe and have the life she deserves.*

I put my forehead against Peach's, my tears spilling onto her face. A shadow moved over us. It was Mia, who placed her head against mine. A pair of hands touched my shoulders, squeezed, and I knew Barley was behind me, supporting me. We sat like that for several moments.

Then I heard the voice.

(*Look at me*)

My insides turned to liquid.

(*LOOK AT ME, WILL BURGESS*)

Against my will, I turned back and gazed in the direction from which the voice seemed to echo.

Peaceful Valley.

And there, near the side of the road, above the maples and elms, I saw it, a sight that ruptured the veil of reality and allowed all the shrieking, unspeakable horror of another dimension to spill through.

The towering white creature was at least thirty feet tall. It was like, yet unlike, the Children. It possessed the same pallid flesh, the same lamp-like green eyes — but in addition to its immense size, what set it apart was the depthless evil of its expression, the limitless knowledge in its gaze.

(*You can never escape us*)

I shook my head and tried to suppress a moan. It came out anyway, impotent and afraid, the sound of a little boy unable to escape the monsters under his bed.

The truck motored on, and the giant creature remained where it was, watching us recede. But the eyes glittered with fanatical hatred.

(*All you love will be taken*)

"No," I whispered.

(*And after your loved ones are gone and the worms are feasting on their corpses…*)

I shook my head.

(...*we will have you too*)

I closed my eyes to rid them of the sight, but the gloating expression remained, the ancient madness of those vast emerald eyes.

I jostled as we rounded a curve. I looked at Mia. Her skin had gone a sickly green, her expression haunted. I didn't have to ask why she looked that way.

She'd seen the creature too.

AFTER

The truck driver's name was Jon Speaker. He was a local business owner, and the coach of several high school and youth sports teams. After speeding us to the hospital, he'd been beset by the police and a hundred questions. I felt bad for the guy, who'd after all saved our lives.

But my mind was on my sister.

Her skull wasn't broken, thank God, but she'd sustained a concussion and acute whiplash from the impact of the creature's blow. That word, *whiplash*, made my heart sink every time I heard it. The word brought back the mental images, that brief but horrific film reel of the beast striking out at my sister, of its vengeful hand battering her little face, of her body flying backward and cracking the top of the tailgate. A foot or so higher and she'd have flown over the gate and landed on the road. My head swam with the possibilities, my mind in a constant plummeting spiral as the nightmare of what happened and the even darker nightmare of what *might* have happened vied for supremacy.

It was torture.

I remained by Peach's bedside and ignored the doctors each time they insisted I return to my room. *We've allowed you to visit her*, they argued. *Isn't that enough?*

It's not enough, I told them. *Visiting isn't enough. I belong right the hell* here, *and you can just resign yourselves to that because I'm not moving. Not for you. Not for anyone.*

And I didn't.

—

PEACH AWOKE THAT night just before eleven. Mia and Barley had been in and out all day, but they weren't there when Peach regained consciousness. Part of me felt guilty for not consoling Barley. He'd lost his parents, and I knew a little something about that.

But I couldn't leave my sister, and I hoped he understood. From what I gathered, Mia and Anita were doing all they could to support him. That Anita herself was dealing with trauma just as deep as Barley's occasionally registered in my thoughts, and in those moments, I was amazed at her capacity for selflessness.

Another part of me worried about what Barley had witnessed in the moment I'd stabbed Riggs. Never had I felt less in control of myself, never had I felt more hatred and rage.

Never had I felt more like one of *them*.

Barley had said something about my eyes. Was he about to tell me they were glowing green?

I didn't know. Didn't want to know. And though I tried not to think about it, my mind occasionally drifted to the stark terror in my friend's voice.

But most of my thoughts were on Peach.

I was holding her hand and leaning against her bed rail when I became aware of her eyes on me. I began to smile.

"Can you hear me?" I asked.

She scrunched her nose and answered, "Why wouldn't I hear you?"

I chuckled. "No idea. Forget I said it."

"Did we get away?" she asked.

I judged this question as silly as mine, but then again, she had an excuse. I could see the fog in her eyes.

"We got away," I said.

"Is Barley okay?"

My throat tightened. I tried to swallow the lump there, but it didn't do any good.

"He's sad," I told her. Images of Barley's parents strobed through my mind. His father's broken body. His mom, shot in the chest by Riggs...

"Will?"

I cleared my throat. "I'm here."

"Do you get to stay this time?"

The room seemed to grow quieter, the world to stand still. I'd been thinking about it. Of course I'd been thinking about it. After being incarcerated for more than a year, how could I *not* have thought about it? But hearing Peach verbalize the question rendered it more real. It made me feel like sweeping her into my arms and fleeing from the hospital, it didn't matter to where. The only thing I knew was that we couldn't be separated again. I'd die before they took me away.

"I'm staying with you," I said.

She stared deep into my eyes, wanting to believe it but doubting there could be a happy ending. After all the heartache and disappointment we'd suffered, who could blame her for being cynical?

"Promise?" she asked.

The thickness in my throat again. "I promise."

I had no idea whether or not this was a promise I could keep.

As it turned out, I got my answer early the next morning.

—

I SLEPT NEXT to Peach in her hospital bed. It was crowded, and I struggled to find a comfortable sleeping position. I doubted I'd be able to sleep, given my injuries and all that had happened, but somehow after midnight I must've nodded off. Because the next thing I knew, it was dawn, and there was a hand on my shoulder.

I looked groggily up at Colonel Haddad.

He wasn't smiling. "Come with me."

When I started to shake my head, he added, "We won't be long."

I didn't fully trust him — other than Peach, Mia, and Barley, I didn't trust anybody — but I managed to climb out of the bed without rousing my sister. I glanced back at her on my way out, but then we were through the door and moving down the hall.

It was mostly silent at that early hour, just an occasional nurse shuffling by. A janitor or two. No cops that I could see. No one who looked like he might have worked with Riggs.

Still, my senses were in overdrive. I wasn't going to be taken without a fight.

We stepped into an elevator, and my disquiet deepened. Haddad seemed tense, for one thing. For another, the elevator felt like a cell, and I'd had enough of being locked up. Haddad pressed *B*, and as soon as the doors closed and we began descending, I asked, "Are you the new Riggs?"

He glanced at me. For a fleeting instant I thought I detected hurt in his expression. He had saved my life, after all.

"You can be the judge of that," he answered.

I sighed. "So it's not over."

The elevator stopped, the doors opened, and we stepped out. Into the hospital administrative wing, it appeared.

Being in the basement felt like being entombed. I thought I could be forgiven for feeling that way. My last experience in a facility hadn't ended well.

We made it to the end of the hall and doglegged left. After another short span of hallway, we hooked a right, and there it was, the cedar-red door I was certain would herald my demise. Either they'd kill me, or they'd lock me up forever.

I'd been a fool to go with Haddad.

He seemed to pick up on my anxiety and said, "Whatever happens in there, just remember, it was the best I could do."

If this was meant to alleviate my fears, he accomplished the opposite. Haddad extended an arm, knocked.

In those final moments before the door opened, I came very close to bolting. Where I would have run to, I have no idea. Maybe toward the stairs. More likely to the elevator, where I would have ridden up to Peach's floor. And then? Tear away all the tubes and sensors they'd attached to my sister and make a mad dash with her for the exit.

But the reddish door opened, and I knew there was no turning back.

I walked inside.

And saw Dr. Klinger.

—

I LUNGED FOR him.

Seated as he was across a broad desk, he had time to scramble toward the two government types who populated the back wall.

When they'd finally gotten me under control — Haddad and a pair of guards — they were able to situate me in an uncomfortable plastic chair. One of the government types stepped forward and took a seat. He was roughly Haddad's age, of Asian descent, with raven-black hair that was combed over as if to hide baldness. But upon closer inspection, I didn't think he was balding. Just not very good at styling his hair.

The other man behind the desk appeared to be a well-preserved forty, his hair prematurely silver, his skin pale and wrinkleless. He looked like a guy who'd model clothing in a catalogue. I distrusted him immediately.

Filling out the cramped office were a blond woman who stood beside Klinger, the pair of guards, and someone I hadn't noticed.

Anita.

She sat to my left, hands folded in her lap. I experienced a pang of embarrassment at my hospital gown, which didn't provide enough coverage, but this emotion was fleeting.

The silver-haired clothing model spoke: "Did you kill Riggs?"

I glanced at Haddad, who'd selected a chair beside Anita, but he merely stared back at me.

Had he told them I'd murdered Riggs?

"I tried to," I told the clothing model. "I wanted to. If I had it to do all over again, I'd make sure I killed him."

The clothing model said, "I'm Lee Anderson." A gesture toward the man with the overzealous combover. "This is Fred Park." A nod over his shoulder at the blond woman. "Gladys Foley."

"Are you going to kill me?" I asked.

Lee Anderson's good-humored expression didn't slip, but Fred Park shifted in his seat. Fred said, "We're very sorry about the way you've been treated."

I extended a forefinger at Klinger. "He's not sorry."

Fred cleared his throat. "Things have been handled rather, um, poorly. I think you'll find your new situation better."

"What, I get to read more books now? You'll give me a cell with extra padding?"

Lee Anderson made a negating gesture with both hands. "Those days are ended, Will. As long as you cooperate with us."

"Oh boy," I said, sitting back. "Here we go."

"Listen to them," Haddad said, his voice low but very tense.

"Are you prepared to hear our terms?" Fred Park asked.

I sat forward. "Terms? How about these terms? You let me and my sister go. You let Mia, Barley, and Anita go. Then you never harass any of us again. And if you so much as look at us from this day forward, I'll go straight to the *Indianapolis Star* and tell them everything."

"Told you he was a lost cause," Klinger muttered.

"And Dr. Klinger?" I said.

"Yes, William?"

"Fuck you."

Fred's brow creased, but I thought a grin flickered across Anderson's face.

"This is pointless," Klinger said. "The boy must be remanded to a secure facility. The order for his sister's transfer needs to be—"

"Transfer?" I shouted, pushing to my feet. "She's *seven*. She doesn't need to be transferred anywhere. She needs to be with *me*, you soulless dick."

A hand was on my shoulder, a guard restraining me.

But Anderson said, "Sophia does belong with you."

"Peach," Anita corrected. "She goes by Peach."

"Damn right," I agreed.

Anderson gazed steadily up at me. "Can you please take your seat? I think you'll find our offer better than anything else you'll get."

"I doubt it," I muttered, but sat anyway.

"How would you and your sister like to live in a normal house?" Anderson asked.

"A foster home?"

"*My* home," Anita said.

I'm afraid my mouth fell open. Her eyes were downcast, and I realized she was very nervous, her folded hands lighter at the knuckles.

I glanced at Haddad, who nodded toward Anderson. *Listen to the man*, Haddad's face urged.

I listened to the man.

Anderson said, "You must never tell anyone what happened."

I raised my eyebrows. "You mean the government leading us to a shelter and attempting to machine gun us to death?"

The others looked away, but Anderson's gaze remained steady. "I mean *any* of it," he said.

"It wasn't us who did that," Fred said.

"Then who was it?" I demanded. "The mafia? The Mormon Tabernacle Choir?"

"Clearly," Gladys Foley spoke up from behind Anderson, "there was a failure in oversight. Riggs never should have been given his own department, much less been permitted to act with such impunity."

Klinger shook his head sourly.

"Go on," I said, not yet allowing myself to be hopeful.

"You will be evaluated on a weekly basis by Dr. Klinger," Fred said.

"No deal," I answered immediately.

Anderson frowned. "I don't think you understand. This is the only deal."

"Unless you want things to go back to the way they were at Sunny Woods," Haddad said.

"You agree with this?" I asked.

"I've had to make concessions too," Haddad answered.

"Colonel Haddad will be stationed at Peaceful Valley," Anderson explained, "where we're setting up a permanent installation."

I gaped at him. "Permanent installation?"

"That's correct," Gladys said.

"At Peaceful Valley."

Gladys nodded.

I turned to Anita. "They're batshit crazy."

"Our strategy is none of your concern," Klinger said.

"If it gets more people killed, it sure as hell is my concern."

Anderson and Fred exchanged a glance.

Fred smiled. "Because of your strong character, we feel you could be helpful to our efforts."

"Please don't tell me you want to recruit me."

"We want you to be a high school student," Anderson said.

I stared at him. "Come again?"

"You missed your sophomore year, correct?"

"You know I did."

"Missed getting your driver's license," Gladys put in.

I grunted. "Couldn't have afforded a car anyway."

"Missed taking your girlfriend to the Winter Dance," Fred said.

The thought made my stomach flutter. "I didn't know there was a Winter Dance."

"Missed out on your sophomore season of baseball," Gladys said.

My heart ached at the thought.

Anderson spread his hands. "How would you like to make up for it this year?"

I tried to keep my breathing steady. "Tell me the rest."

"You and Peach would live at the farm with Anita. Peach would go to the elementary school; you'd be at Shadeland High."

For the first time, the ramifications of what Anderson was saying broke through my veil of cynicism. And though playing baseball, dating Mia, and even the stupid Winter Dance sounded amazing, it was the prospect of living together with Peach in an actual home that made my heart soar.

My God, was it possible?

I glanced at Anita, whose eyes glistened. I thought of all she'd lost. Of her husband. Of…

Pierre.

My God, Pierre. I could hardly think of him without crying.

"There would be stipulations," Fred said.

I sank into my chair.

"The weekly sessions, for one thing," Gladys explained.

I supposed I could stomach an hour a week with Klinger if it meant getting my kid sister back. "What else?"

"A non-disclosure agreement," Anderson said.

"My silence, you mean."

Gladys leaned on the table between Anderson and Fred. Apparently, she'd had enough of observing me from afar. "There can be no leeway on this point. If you tell anyone. Peers, teachers… *anyone*… the arrangement is nullified, and you'll be remanded into custody."

I shifted in my seat. "Anything else?"

"You cooperate with us when we need you to," Gladys said.

And there's the catch.

"What does that mean?"

"Precisely what it sounds like," Anderson said. "We're just as disturbed by these creatures as you are."

I highly doubt that, I thought, but opted to let it go.

"Both species," Fred said, "are highly developed."

"And terribly hostile," Gladys put in.

I exchanged a glance with Haddad, whose expression had gone grim.

Fred folded his hands "We need as much intelligence as we can gather. And you," He sat forward, "are the person most intimate—"

"Please don't use that word."

"— most *acquainted*," Fred amended, "with both the Children and the, um…"

"Night Flyers," Anita finished.

"Yes," Fred agreed. "The Night Flyers."

I drummed my fingers on my knees and thought it over. "What about Barley?"

A shadow flitted across Anderson's face. Did he actually feel bad for Barley? I was so used to government employees being devoid of human emotions that the possibility stunned me.

"Dale and his brother will live with their grandparents," Anderson said.

This made sense. Barley's grandma and grandpa were good people who lived less than a mile from Barley's house. That meant he'd be going to Shadeland High with me.

And Mia.

That rush of hope coursed through me again, but I fought it back.

"What kind of cooperation are you demanding?"

"We're not demanding anything," Gladys said. "We're—"

"It comes to the same thing," I interrupted. "Play along, and I get to be with my sister. Break your rules, and I lose everything."

Gladys's lips thinned, but she didn't contradict me.

Anderson appeared to size me up. "We can't tell you what sort of help we'll need because, frankly, we don't know. I can only say that we want to prevent further loss of life."

I nodded. "Then get the hell out of Peaceful Valley."

Anderson glanced at Haddad, who said, "That's not going to work. Since the attack on Sunny Woods, there have been further... incursions."

I cocked an eyebrow. "Incursions?"

"Two instances of people being ambushed by the Night Flyers," Fred explained.

Gladys nodded. "The Peaceful Valley installation is meant to be a containment measure."

"You think you can *contain* those things?"

"We aren't going to hunt the creatures," Haddad said, "but we're creating a perimeter around the park to prevent them from leaving."

"How do you keep the Night Flyers in?"

Haddad looked at Anderson, who said, "That will be difficult. But at least we'll be able to track their movements. Learn their habits, their motivations."

"I can tell you what motivates them," I said. "Just look at the body count."

A morose silence fell over the room.

At length, Anderson asked, "Do we have a deal?"

I glanced at Anita. "Are you sure you want us?"

She watched me for a few seconds, a hint of good humor in her eyes. "Only if you help with the alpacas."

My throat tightened. I wanted to thank her, but at that moment I was incapable of speech.

Finally, I looked at Anderson. "I'd ask for assurances that you guys won't go back on your word, but that would be pointless, huh?"

Anderson only waited for me.

"Okay," I said. "It's a deal."

———

ANITA WAS ASKED to remain in the office with the others. On the walk back to the elevator with Haddad, I hardly dared speak. I was certain this was all a ruse to trick me, and I dreaded the disappointment of having everything ripped away.

In the elevator, I said, "That creature. The one in the truck with us."

Haddad pushed the button for the fourth floor, where Peach's room and my room were located.

"They're going to dissect it, aren't they," I said. "They're going to study it. Like they do in movies."

Haddad stared straight ahead.

I asked, "Did you tell them everything?"

"Almost," he said.

The elevator began to rise.

"You saw it too," I said. "The giant one."

He ran a finger over the reflective steel of the elevator wall. "I saw... something."

I almost pressed him, but I could see even admitting this much had cost him an effort. And though I knew what I'd seen, I wasn't sure I wanted it confirmed. My nightmares were going to be frightening enough as it was.

When we reached the fourth floor, I got out, but instead of following me, Haddad curled an arm around the door to keep it from shutting.

"Take care, Will."

"You trust me not to run?"

"You won't go anywhere without your sister," he said, smiling a little.

He released the door. I was about to tell him how much I appreciated all he'd done for us, but the door slid closed before I could.

I hoped I'd get another chance to thank him.

Feeling like a person in a dream, I headed toward Peach's room. I couldn't wait to tell her the news, couldn't wait to hug her and laugh with her and nag her for not brushing her teeth.

But when I opened her door and peered inside, her bed was empty.

My whole body went numb. Except my heart, which boomed inside my chest. I stepped inside on nerveless feet and glanced about the room. The bathroom was open and dark, the recliner in the corner empty. I jerked my head around, sure the window would be open and the Night Flyer who'd snatched her would be winging away.

The windows were closed.

But Peach was gone.

I stepped into the hallway. Deserted. I took a step to my right, realized the nearest nurse's station was in the other direction, then took off at a sprint, my gown flapping behind me.

The nurse's station was empty too, the whole damned hospital devoid of life. My sense of unreality deepened. Had the Children or the Night Flyers come? Had they taken my sister?

No! I wanted to scream.

I clenched my fists and hurried toward my room, the one I'd refused to sleep in. I was pretty sure that was where they'd stowed my shoes and clothes.

Peach. Sitting cross-legged and chewing on something.

Mia sat on the bed beside her. "I brought her some candy," she explained. "I didn't think you'd mind."

"Nerds!" Peach shouted.

I laughed a breathless laugh and began to smile. Then I was drifting toward them, the tears burning my eyes. Peach and Mia also started to cry, but they were laughing too.

I climbed onto the bed and wrapped my sister up. Peach told me she loved me. Mia hugged us both. We remained that way for a good while, and for the first time in more than a year, monsters were the furthest things from my mind.

CEMETERY DANCE PUBLICATIONS

We hope you enjoyed your
Cemetery Dance Paperback!
Share pictures of them online, and tag us!

Instagram: @cemeterydancepub
Twitter: @CemeteryEbook
TikTok: @cemeterydancepub
www.facebook.com/CDebookpaperbacks

Use the following tags!

#horrorbook #horror #horrorbooks
#bookstagram #horrorbookstagram
#horrorpaperbacks #horrorreads
#bookstagrammer #horrorcommunity
#cemeterydancepublications

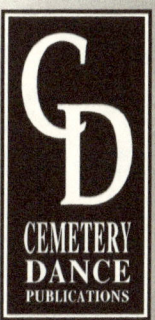

SHARE THE HORROR!

HORROR
DNA
MOVIES
COMIC BOOKS
MUSIC
BOOKS
VIDEO GAMES
IT'S IN
OUR
BLOOD
horrordna.com

www.ingramcontent.com/pod-product-compliance
Lightning Source LLC
Chambersburg PA
CBHW030628020726
47493CB00006B/1615